THE SPAWN OF
LILITH

THE SPAWN OF
LILITH

DANA FREDSTI

TITAN BOOKS

THE SPAWN OF LILITH
Mass market edition ISBN: 9781785656149
Print edition ISBN: 9781785652608
Electronic edition ISBN: 9781785652615

Published by Titan Books
A division of Titan Publishing Group Ltd
144 Southwark St, London SE1 0UP

First mass market edition: April 2018
2 4 6 8 10 9 7 5 3 1

A CIP catalogue record for this title is available from the British Library.

Printed and bound in the United States

Did you enjoy this book?
We love to hear from our readers. Please email us at readerfeedback@titanemail. com or write to us at Reader Feedback at the above address.

To receive advance information, news, competitions, and exclusive offers online, please sign up for the Titan newsletter on our website.

TITANBOOKS.COM

This one's for Mom (aka Dorothy Carol Galante).
I am so proud to have been one of your spawn.
I wish you were here to read this.

THE SPAWN OF
LILITH

PROLOGUE

Yahweh created Adam. When he did so, Adam was lonely, so Yahweh created Lilith from the same dust from which Adam had been molded. But Adam wished to rule over Lilith, and they quarreled.

Lilith was proud and willful, claiming equality with Adam because she was created from the same dust. She left Adam and fled the Garden, finding love with Ashmedai, a handsome demigod. Yahweh sent three angels in pursuit of Lilith. They caught her and ordered her to return to Adam. She refused, saying she would kill children, infants, and babes if forced to return.

The angels overpowered her, and she promised that if any mother hung an amulet over the baby bearing the names of the three angels, she would stay away from that home. So they let her go, but Yahweh, still angry at her disobedience, turned most of Lilith's children into demons, which multiplied and plagued mankind.

Yahweh then imprisoned Lilith. She would remain imprisoned until such time as her human descendants could destroy all of her demon offspring.

Or so the legend goes...

"It does not pay a prophet to be too specific."

—L. Sprague de Camp

"Danger is a very rare commodity in these times, monopolized by intelligence agencies and stuntmen."

—William S. Burroughs

CHAPTER ONE

VAMPSHEE: THE NETHERWORLD CHRONICLES, PART I

EXT – NIGHT – ROOFTOP

CONNOR, handsome half-werewolf, half-selkie, stands on a rooftop as LELA, half-vampire, half-banshee, balances precariously on the edge of the roof.

CUT TO:

CU – THE UNFORGIVING CEMENT BELOW

> CONNOR
> Lela! Don't do it!

Lela looks at her lover, sadness and resignation in her eyes.

> LELA
> I have to, Connor. There's no place for me in this world. I bring nothing but death, either by the taking of blood or the heralding of impending death.

Death. Nothing but death!

She moves even closer to the edge, teetering precariously in her stiletto-heeled boots, despite her supernatural vampiric grace.

CONNOR

No! Before you, my life WAS death! A slow living death as I tried to find my place in this world. As my two sides, werewolf and selkie, warred against each other. You bring both of my halves peace. A contentment and peace neither half has known before.

ANGLE ON LELA

...as she stares at Connor with deep sadness in her eyes.

LELA

I thought our love would be enough to quell my vampiric thirst for blood, and stop the banshee in me from its lethal wail. But it's not. I can't bear living by causing death.

CONNOR

Lela, I'm begging you...

LELA (interrupting him)

I'll always love you, Connor. I'm sorry.

Lela steps off the edge, vanishing from sight.

Connor falls to his knees and raises his hands skyward, shaking his fists.

CONNOR

NO!!!!

†

That's where I stepped in.

Dressed in Lela's skintight pants, billowing trench coat, tank top, and thigh-high boots—all made of black leather except the tank top, which was a blood-red satin—I took my place at the edge of the roof, staring down three stories to where my best friend the airbag waited for me, just out of sight and situated far enough away from the building wall to compensate for the distance my body would push outward before dropping.

Pesky physics.

The street had been cleared of cars, garbage bins, and people. The stunt coordinator and three spotters waited below. Three different cameras waited to catch the fall from three different angles.

This film had a big budget for a piece of shit.

I was doubling for English film star Kaley Avondale. My landing in the airbag would be replaced in the editing bay with a shot of Lela's leather-clad corpse. Never mind that she'd be back for *Rise of the Vampshees: The Netherworld Chronicles II.*

"Ready, Lee?"

I gave the director a thumbs-up, then stared down into the void. My airbag awaited me, some forty feet down.

I'd checked the placement with the stunt coordinator. Cleared the area of anything extraneous that might interfere with my trajectory. I'd run the stunt over and over, visualizing the perfect fall and landing. A basic deadfall.

Nothing fancy or complicated, and nothing I hadn't done a gazillion times before.

And yet...

See, with every stunt—but especially high falls—there's a moment when it's all up to you. You make the decision. Once you push off with your back foot, that's it. There's no turning back.

That moment is special. It dictates that you still have so much respect for the business that it's more important to dive into the unknown and risk injury, possibly death, than to say, "I'm sorry, I'm scared. I can't do it."

It's the moment when everyone is waiting for you to go.

So I went.

†

When I opened my eyes, the first thing I noticed was how much my head hurt.

We're not talking your basic headache here, or even a bad migraine. No, this felt like my skull was stuck between two wrecking balls—one in back and one in front—both smashing into it at regular pulsing intervals.

The second thing I noticed was the smell of antiseptic and bleach.

A hospital?

I heard the sound of beeping and the gentle pulsing of what was either a mellow Darth Vader or an oxygen machine. I tried to move my arms, but they wouldn't cooperate.

"I think she's awake!"

A familiar voice, but one I couldn't place because of whatever was trying to crack open my skull. I tried turning toward the sound, but my head remained stubbornly where it was. When I tried to lift my right hand, something jerked it back into place. Even that minimal effort, however, was enough to drive one last spike of pain straight through my eye.

I slid back into blissful unconsciousness.

†

Next time I woke up, the two wrecking balls attacking my head had evidently been replaced by someone gently pounding nails into my skull.

"Lee? You awake?"

That same familiar voice.

I opened my eyes and found myself nose to nose with a man. I yelped in surprise—although the yelp was more of a croak, as if I hadn't used my voice in a while. The man jerked his head back slightly, then leaned forward eagerly.

"Lee, honey. Do you know me?"

I stared at the face hovering above mine. Shaggy blond hair, sky-blue eyes, handsome, slightly weathered man in his fifties or thereabouts. I recognized him, I knew I did, but the name swirled around in a cloud of pain and fog.

Uncle Sean. The answer appeared in my head as if someone had flicked on a convenient neon sign. *But I usually just call him Sean. And he's not really…*

The thought unraveled before it could finish forming.

"Sean?" My voice barely reached a whisper. My throat hurt.

His face broke into a relieved smile.

"Oh, thank God."

The sound of Sean's voice—warm, concerned, and familiar—sent slow tears trickling down my face. The feel of liquid on my skin made me aware of how thirsty I was.

"Water?" I croaked.

"Sure. Sure, hon."

He vanished from sight, then reappeared with a plastic cup, complete with sippy straw. He carefully put the tip of the straw between my lips.

I took a sip, the cool water like ambrosia to my parched throat.

"Where—" I started to cough. It hurt like hell.

"Don't try and talk, hon," Sean said. "You're in the hospital and your neck is in a brace, understand? You took a bad fall and... broke a few things."

A few things? What few things?

My back?

My neck?

My eyes must have mirrored my fears because he patted me clumsily on one leg. I couldn't see the movement, but I could feel it, which reassured me that I wouldn't be paralyzed.

"Why can't I move?" The words were weak, but clear.

"You're wrapped in a shit ton of plaster and what not to keep you still so all the sprains, strains, and fractures can start healing up. Your neck and back were wrenched pretty badly." He shook his head. "You took quite a pounding, but you'll be okay. It'll just take some time."

"How long—"

Another coughing fit. He brought the straw back up to my lips. I sipped gratefully, the cool water soothing the burning ache in my throat. As I drank, Sean answered my last question.

"You've been out of it for over a week." He paused, swallowing heavily. "We thought we'd lost you, Lee."

"What happened?"

"The airbag. Some damn fool overfilled it and it got shifted a few feet sometime between your last rehearsal and the actual take. Marty—"

Marty, I thought. *Stunt coordinator.*

"—is still out for blood. No one's manned up yet, though. At any rate, your mark was off, you landed in the wrong place, bounced off into the building and then hit the sidewalk. Even you couldn't handle it."

I vaguely remembered the wind rushing up to greet me as I fell, but the memories thankfully ended with the moment I hit the canvas, and not when my entire body smashed into the cement.

"Musta looked like Wile E. Coyote, huh?"

Sean gave a surprised snort of laughter.

"Yeah, kinda." He patted me again, just as awkwardly the second time around.

"That close, huh?"

"Yeah."

Both of us ignored the way his voice choked up on that one word. Neither of us had ever been much for overt displays of emotion. Then he leaned forward, pressing something into my hand. It was cool and metallic. I couldn't see it and I couldn't close my fingers around it either.

"It's your necklace," he said. "The one your mom gave you. I found it with your clothes and bag in your dressing room."

I struggled to remember what he was talking about. An image flashed in my mind, another one of those little neon bursts. An amulet on a leather cord.

"Can you keep it somewhere safe for me until…" I trailed off, unsure how to end that sentence. Until I could walk? Stand? Get the brace off my neck?

"Sure."

Sean removed the necklace again, putting it in his pocket.

"It'll be waiting for you, don't you worry."

After a few seconds I said, "Gotta ask you another question."

Sean nodded. "Shoot."

"Am I gonna get out of here soon?"

Sean knew me well enough to realize what I was really asking. He hesitated.

"It's gonna be a while before you can get back to work, Lee. Maybe a few months. You're gonna have to take small steps."

A few months. I could live with that.

"Maybe even a year."

Now that might be a problem.

†

"I'm hungry."

"It's too soon."

"I don't care."

"Shhhh... You don't mean that."

"You haven't always been this selfish." Sala looked at her brother, visible in the mirror above the bar. He gazed back at her sadly.

"But you have. I just never noticed."

She ignored that, instead pointing across the dimly lit club, where dozens of toned bodies clad in the latest expensive or knock-off fashions writhed to a repetitive techno-beat. An auditory tranquilizer.

"Look. That one," she said.

He followed Sala's gaze, honing in on her choice. A young ripe brunette, lushly figured, thick mane swinging in time to the beat like something out of a shampoo commercial. All impossibly glossy and perfect.

He grabbed her arm. "Sala, no."

Sala's stomach growled.

He heard it. And let her go.

She made her way across the dance floor, gliding between the dancers like smoke through cracks in a wall. Within seconds she stood in front of her target. The girl's beauty rivaled Aphrodite.

Like any rival for a goddess, her fate was inevitable.

Sala waited until the girl paused in her gyrations, giving her time to notice who stood before her. Brown eyes widened and a small pink tongue darted out to lick naturally full lips. Even in her current fragile state, Sala still commanded worship.

"Hello," Sala said.

"Hi." Voice breathless.

"Would you like to dance?"

"Oh, yes."

They linked hands, fingers entwined. The music slowed as if in sympathy with Sala's intent. Their two bodies swayed together in sensual rhythm, hands caressing up and down. Sala so very slender, even sinuous in contrast to the other's full figure.

Slowly, she subtly maneuvered her partner across the room. The crowd seemed to part ahead of them, yet no one seemed to actually see them. Invisible, yet making their presence known.

The two left the dance floor and headed toward the hallway leading to the bathrooms and the back exit. Once outside in the alley, they began kissing, the girl's hands buried deep in Sala's hair, while Sala cupped her partner's rounded ass in both hands.

Soft velvety kisses, tasting of mint and tequila. Under the lone light shining above the back door, the girl's pink and fuchsia silk dress seemed spattered with clots of blood, instead of flowers.

They broke apart briefly, the girl panting with equal parts exertion and lust. Her breasts heaved in the low-cut halter top of her dress. She stared at Sala, eyes glazed with desire.

"I'm Mindy," she breathed. "Why haven't I noticed you before?"

"I don't often come to this place."

"This club?" Mindy reached out and touched the fine lines of Sala's face. Sala caught her hand, her own slender fingers stronger than they looked.

"No," she whispered, leaning forward to gently lick the soft curve of Mindy's ear.

"Where, then?" Her question was lost against Sala's lips as the two kissed again, tongues twining together.

"This world."

Sala breathed the words into Mindy's mouth. She reached one hand inside the girl's top, hand cupping the full breast inside. The other hand curved around Mindy's neck, pulling her even closer into a deepening kiss.

At first it felt like little tingles of electricity, tiny sparks going off in Mindy's mouth wherever Sala's tongue touched her. The frisson shot through her body straight to her groin, a pulsing energy that had her shuddering to orgasm in seconds. Even as those waves started to subside, more jolts of electricity rippled through her, just skating the line between pleasure and pain.

Then it began.

Small thread-like filaments emerged from Sala's tongue, penetrating Mindy's flesh and burrowing deep into the soft skin inside her mouth, then down her throat. More filaments emerged from Sala's fingertips and the palms of her hands, like the tendrils of a jellyfish. Each one finding its own path into Mindy's skin.

Each one sending its own increasingly painful current into Mindy's nervous system. Pleasure became pain and she jerked backward, trying to tear herself away from Sala's embrace. When she did, it felt as though she were ripping her own flesh out.

Sala looked even more skeletal than she had inside—parchment pale, fragile, almost childlike. But her grip around the back of Mindy's neck was inescapable even without the spider web of threads now spilling out of every pore, binding the woman to her in a deadly cocoon.

Mindy would have screamed, but her mouth was full of what looked like spun sugar, the white threads turning a pale pink, then giving way to a crimson red as her life drained away, penetrated by thousands of electric needles. The pain finally stopped when Mindy's heart collapsed in on itself, her other organs quickly following suit. Her body hidden underneath a seething mass of crimson red strands.

Minutes passed and the strands drooped from Mindy's desiccated flesh. Sala's skin was flushed with nourishment, pale skin rosy, cheeks fleshed out. The strands retracted, leaving her holding what looked like a life-sized paper doll, the face drawn in a rictus of pain and terror.

With a sad smile, Sala let Mindy's corpse slide to the ground.

"Better now?"

Sala didn't bother looking at her brother.

"For now, but it won't last. It never lasts."

He wanted to argue with her, but couldn't. He just knew he had to fix this. If he didn't, she would die.

And without her, he would die, too.

CHAPTER TWO

I was totally going to die if I didn't get a job soon. Because if I didn't get a job, I couldn't afford my own place. And if I didn't get my own place, I was gonna kill someone, and then I'd go to prison. Which meant I might as well be dead.

I love Sean. I really do. Most of the time. But I'd moved out two years ago for a reason. The same reason I currently considered uncle-cide as a viable life choice.

Okay, faux uncle-cide. When my parents died in an untimely accident, I'd been left without any real relatives. Sean had been the next best thing, being both my godfather and my dad's best friend. I guess I'd been more or less bequeathed to him in the will.

"Just think," I liked to remind him. *"They could have left you their car, but instead you got me."*

So instead of growing up in a bungalow in Venice Beach where my moderately successful screenwriter parents had lived, I'd spent my formative years on a ranch in the heart of the San Fernando Valley, hanging out with an ever-shifting pack of stuntmen and wannabe stunt-puppies.

That's what I call the newbies.

"You gonna jump any time today, Lee?"

Speaking of newbies…

"Bite me, Randy," I growled, glaring down from my perch on the high fall practice tower.

"Any time, babe," Randy said.

The yard took up most of the acreage and included a barn-turned-equipment-storage, the high fall tower with an airbag, a Russian swing, several trampolines, a butt-load of crash mats, and plenty of space for basic fight training—both armed and unarmed. On any given day you'd find at least a dozen people, both professional and wannabes, training here.

Unfortunately, today one of them happened to be Randy. He had the sort of generic good looks that enabled him to double for any number of equally generically good-looking actors. He also had talent, which should have endeared him to me. It didn't.

Down below, he gave me a mocking grin.

Asshat.

A gust of wind whipped a stray strand of dark hair into my mouth. I tucked it back into the thick, waist-length braid meant to keep the whole shebang out of my way, and concentrated on the task at hand.

The tower—kind of like a metal ladder with additional structural support for stability—had platforms at ten-foot intervals, the highest point being sixty feet above the ground. I'd made it to the twenty-foot platform before my stomach dropped and the backs of my legs started tingling.

Fucking acrophobia.

I'd jumped off cliffs, buildings, and this stupid tower countless times. While most girls my age had been shopping at the Galleria, I'd been practicing my high falls. So to suddenly have lost my nerve after all these years? Well, it just sucked.

If you're involved in the film industry and know anything about stunts, you've probably heard of the Katz family. They're practically Hollywood royalty, at least in the stunt biz. Known for aerial gags and high falls taken from heights considered insane to attempt. I might not be a Katz by blood, but I was part of the Katz Stunt Crew. And the KSC didn't do fear of heights, even if the acronym sounded like a cross between the Russian secret police and a fried chicken franchise.

Problem was, I still bore scars—physical and emotional— from my close encounter with the sidewalk. It'd been six months, and even though I knew the airbag below was inflated correctly and *exactly* where it should be, my gut clenched at the thought of flinging myself off into the void again, even from a measly twenty feet.

God, this pisses me off.

"You got this, Lee."

Joe "Drift" McKenzie, a thirty-something stunt driver, gave me a thumbs up from the sidelines where he watched with his friend Jim "Tater" Tott, a former Army Ranger turned stuntman. They were tall and broad, and both sported mustaches and short cropped beards, making the two of them look as if they should be related. They weren't, but both were long-time members of Sean's inner cadre.

I gave Drift and Tater a bright smile, trying to hide what I felt. Because if they thought I was afraid or in pain, it would mess with how they viewed me professionally. Problem was, I'd been training with some of these guys for years. We all knew one another's weaknesses and strengths.

It's not easy to hide fear from family.

"What the hell, Lee?"

Speaking of family…

I looked down to the base of the tower. Sean's son Seth Katz was eyeing me without love. My stress level immediately shot up a few more notches.

See, I've spent a lot of time practicing Zen and the Art of Asshole Maintenance over the years—more even than learning how to drift cars and crash through plate glass windows. We're talking a *bunch* of hours here.

If looking into Sean's eyes immediately calmed me down, Seth's cold stare generally signaled stormy weather ahead. A disapproving look from him always made my stomach churn, like I'd eaten too much candy and washed it down with a pitcher of cheap margaritas.

Eyes the dark brown of bittersweet chocolate. Tousled black hair. Finely drawn features. Perfect build. All in all, like someone out of Greek mythology. My vote would be Narcissus because, as far as I could tell, Seth didn't love anyone but himself. And even that was up for debate.

"Hey, Seth," I said mildly. "Isn't there a pool with your reflection somewhere, calling your name?"

He looked at me without blinking. Kind of like a shark.

"You're doing 'Blue Steel,' right? Or wait, is that 'La Tigre'?"

Not a muscle twitched. Either he'd never seen *Zoolander*, or didn't think it was funny. Proof that there are some personalities that can't be saved by being really really really good looking.

"Stop wasting everyone's time," he snapped. "Either shit or get off the pot."

"Nice, Seth," Drift muttered. "Real nice."

"Why?" I smiled sweetly at Seth from my perch above. "You so full of shit you can't wait your turn?"

A muscle twitched in his jaw.

"Sometime this century, Lee."

I couldn't call Seth's methods "tough love" because I'm pretty sure he hates me. He didn't used to be such a total dick. For the last six months, though, he'd treated me like something unpleasant he'd found on the bottom of his shoe. I responded by trying to gain his approval. At most it got me the occasional grudging "that didn't suck." You'd have thought I'd have learned better by now, but it's hard to break the habits of a lifetime.

Taking a deep breath, I jumped before I could change my mind.

Whump.

Dead center of the airbag for a perfect deadfall.

Woo-hoo! Satisfied, I grinned up at Seth, who turned his back on me without a word and walked away. I deflated like a cheap air mattress.

A hand shoved itself in front of me.

"Good job, Lee."

I looked up to see Drift giving me a sympathetic grin. Part of me wanted to slap his hand away, prove I didn't need anyone's approval, but it would have been a total bitch move—not to mention a lie of the devil.

I hated the fact that one accident, *one*, could smash my self-confidence, but there it was. And if I wanted to get back to work, out from under Sean's roof and away from Seth's ever-present disapproval, I needed to accept that fact—along with whatever positive reinforcement was offered.

So I grabbed Drift's hand, practically flying off the airbag when he gave a sharp tug. The dude had biceps the size of Africa.

"Thanks."

"Thank you for not biting my head off," Drift grinned.

"Gotta say, bouncing off buildings and sidewalks mellowed you out a little."

"Cheepcheepcheep!"

Stunt-puppy Randy popped up behind me, flapping his arms in what was supposed to be an impression of a chicken, but only if the chicken had epilepsy. I gave him an elbow to the solar plexus without even thinking. He doubled over with a satisfying grunt.

"Or not," Drift said without missing a beat.

I shrugged. "My near death experience just taught me to differentiate between people like you and Tater—" I gave them both a nod. "—and assholes."

Randy looked hurt and angry at the same time.

"What's your damage, Lee? Can't you take a joke?"

I sighed. "Y'know, Squid, you don't get to play that 'get out of jail free' card with me. The whole 'can't you take a joke' defense doesn't play here when you're being a total douche."

Randy's sullen pout would have done justice to any five-year-old with low blood sugar.

"Jeez," he muttered. "That time of the month, or what?"

Really?

You didn't get into the Katz Ranch without an invitation, or a recommendation from someone who was already part of the inner circle, so Randy had to have *something* going for him. Apparently that didn't include a good survival instinct. Before I could rip him a new one, though, Tater cleared his throat, Drift by his side.

"May we?"

I nodded and gave a little one-handed wave. "Please do."

Drift walked up to Randy until they stood nose to nose. More like Randy's nose to Drift's chest, with Tater looming behind. Randy isn't that short, but both Tater and Drift are tall. Drift is *very* tall. He smiled pleasantly.

"You ever been injured doing a gag?"

Randy's gaze shifted uneasily. "Uh, I took a fall off a dirt bike doubling Paul Loggia in *Gila Monster Island*. That banged up my knee pretty good."

"So how long did it take you to get back in the saddle?" This was Tater.

"Uh, I iced my knee and we did another take a couple hours later."

"Right."

That one neutral syllable made Randy flinch. He didn't, however, turn and run. Points at least for a small helping of *cajones*.

"So," Tater continued, "Lee took a four-story high fall and, because someone didn't do his or her job, she nearly died. Now she has a little bit of an issue with the high falls, and *you* think it's okay to make fun of her, even though you've been in the business for, oh, two years now, and she's been doing stunts since she was twelve?" His voice never changed from that pleasant, even tone, yet Randy started cringing like a whipped dog.

"Um—"

Drift tapped Randy gently on the forehead with his index finger.

"Exactly," he said. "Now next time you open your yap to mouth off, Tater and I are gonna rip your head off and shit down your neck. That's a *lot* of shit. Got it?"

Randy gulped and nodded, his face an interesting shade of green not normally found on humans.

"Good." Tater slapped Randy on the back and then gave me a smile. "You gonna teach these jerks how to fight?"

I grinned at him. "Oh, yeah."

I felt my confidence returning. Honestly, I can do just about anything that's tossed my way, but my real specialty is working with weapons. According to Sean, I'd taken to it "like a duckling to water."

Sean does love his clichés.

In this case, though, the cliché was accurate. I loved swords, sticks, quarterstaffs, and axes. Anything with an edge. Anything that can be used in a close-up fight, one on one or in a melee. If it involves chopping, cutting, thrusting, parrying, whacking, you name it, I'm all over it and I'm *damned* good at it.

Stunts aren't just about the mechanics of the moves, although you have to get those down first. Whether you're doubling someone, or doing a background fight, you also need to be able to sell the fight as real. Not everyone can do that, but I can.

I love teaching it, as well. So I turned to Randy.

This was gonna be *really* fun.

"You ready to learn how to swing something other than your dick?" He nodded uncertainly. "Then grab a broadsword and get your ass over behind the barn."

†

Ever wonder what a half-dozen grown men would do if you handed them broadswords?

What they *don't* do is wait for instructions.

One or two start tossing the swords from hand to hand, doing fancy figure eights and posturing because they've seen *Conan* too many times. Others chase each other around doing "up downs," thwacking away and reciting movie lines.

"*I* am the master now."

"Welcome to Sherwood."

Or my personal fave—especially when coupled with a

friggin' broadsword, which is *totally* the wrong weapon—

"I am Inigo Montoya. You killed my father. Prepare to die."

Call me sexist, but women are generally more focused on training than showboating, and so much easier to deal with when I haven't had enough coffee. Although honestly, some days there's not enough caffeine in the world.

"You will drown in lakes of blood!" Randy intoned, striking what I'm sure he thought was a fearsome pose. I hid a smile.

It's fun time, crew.

I executed a diving forward roll on the dusty ground, snatched up my broadsword and sprung to my feet all in one smooth movement. This, at least, I could do without fear or hesitation—not that Seth would give me any credit. If it wasn't from an altitude of twenty feet or more, it didn't count.

It did, however, get the attention of my students. My tank top must've given a flash of my bra. Randy looked like the Tex Avery cartoon wolf, with his eyes popping out of their sockets.

Squid.

"Okay, kids, pair up and let's get going!" I nodded to Tater. "If you'd be so kind?"

He grinned. "My pleasure."

Tater always helped me demonstrate the basics. Some of the newbies assumed that meant he was the real instructor, and I was just his demo dummy. There's something about the stunt field that attracts a higher level of testosterone. But that assumption rarely made it past the first session.

This round, however, my only problem child was Randy, and even he was on his best behavior after his Come-to-Jesus talk with Drift and Tater. To give him credit, when he wasn't being a jerk he was eager to learn, quick to pick things up, and even a little cute in a puppy-wants-approval kind of way.

Is it wrong that I still wanted to smack his nose with a rolled up newspaper?

We launched into a basic cut-and-parry drill, and he actually managed to hold his own. I was just beginning to be impressed when he stopped, mid-cut, forcing me to bring myself up short or do some damage. He stared over my shoulder, and I turned to see what had him gaping.

Oh, for crying out loud… Seth was ascending the ladder, headed to the top platform, gaining sixty feet in the time it took most people to climb twenty.

"How does he do that?" Randy stared with admiration bordering on hero worship.

I shrugged. "Eh, he's part monkey." Hell, even I couldn't blame Randy for being star struck—it was impossible to remain unimpressed. But I knew full well Seth was doing it to show me up.

Well done, asshole.

When he reached the top, he threw a quick glance in my direction. Making sure I saw him. I rolled my eyes and looked away, but only for a moment. Because no matter how much he irritated me, I still loved watching him do what he did best.

Without hesitation Seth launched himself from the platform, arms outstretched like a high diver, flipping his body midair. It looked as though the air itself thickened to slow his descent as he fell—

—and nearly collided with Sean, who soared down in front of him out of nowhere, arms outstretched to either side slightly behind him, a huge grin on his face. He saw me, waved, then twisted in mid-air and swooped back out of sight as Seth's fall accelerated to normal speed. He hit the airbag without his usual grace.

Everyone burst into laughter as Seth launched himself after his father, a vague blur visible around his shoulders. I turned away to hide my own amusement, knowing this would end with the two of them wrestling mid-air until one of them knocked the other out of the sky.

See, there's a reason training at the Ranch is strictly by invitation only. This world is filled with supernatural beings, and very few people know about them. I know, but I'm not one of them.

Sean and Seth, on the other hand, totally are.

CHAPTER THREE

"The Katz family has conquered gravity."

—The Charleston Post Herald

"Angels couldn't fly through the air with the ease and grace of the Katz boys."

—The San Luis Chronicle

The Katz heritage goes back to the Big Tent. Flying-trapeze artists known for their daring, effortless aerial stunts.

"The Katz family takes aerial acrobatics to new heights, seemingly transcending the laws of physics with their show. It's difficult to tell if they're brave, or simply insane."

—Melbourne Journal

Sean and Seth aren't insane. They are, however, part nephilim, which means they've got enough angel in their DNA to allow for things like—well, not flying, exactly, at least not like Superman, but they can manipulate air currents. They ride them, like surfers ride waves.

It's amazing to watch, and if ever there were times I regretted not being a Katz by blood, it was when I watched any of them ride the wind, catching one current after the other, performing acrobatics I could only dream of doing. When I was little—okay, in my teens—I used to play with the lyrics to "The Man on the Flying Trapeze."

> *They fly through the air with the greatest of ease*
> *Those hunky stunt men on—*
> *Hey, where's their trapeze?*

It never failed to crack Sean up, or piss Seth off. I still couldn't decide which reaction pleased me more. Back then, though, even if I knew I couldn't keep up with them—or with any of the more advanced stunt players—I'd enjoyed trying. It was a challenge, and I'd constantly try to up my game and see how close I could get without killing myself.

Now I'd figured out the answer, thanks to whoever screwed up my airbag.

Fuck it. Time to get back to work, running herd on my swashbucklers in training. Just as I turned, though, Seth and Sean plummeted from the sky in a tangle of arms and legs, hitting the ground with an impact I could feel even from that distance. I winced involuntarily, but Sean immediately clambered to his feet and tapped his watch.

"Time, folks!" he shouted so all could hear. Morning playtime was over. The guys grumbled in disappointment, but began filing toward the big canvas bag where they'd dump their swords.

"Make sure you clean off the blades, kids!" I grabbed a rag, sprayed it with WD-40, wiped my sword, and put it in the bag.

"Hey, Lee?"

I looked up to see Randy, broadsword still clutched in both hands as he shuffled his feet in the dirt. He tried to keep his gaze on my face, but kept drifting almost involuntarily back to my boobs.

"Yeah?" I said brusquely.

"I, uh, I'm really sorry for being such an asshole before."

I stared at him for a few seconds, still wanting to smack him.

"Seriously," he continued. "And not just because Drift and Tater threatened to shit down my neck. You're a kick-ass stuntwoman, and you rock with the sword stuff."

Well, hell.

I mentally tossed away my rolled-up newspaper.

"So, are we okay?" He shifted his sword to one hand and held out the other. I gave a mental sigh and shook it. He didn't even try and do the hand-crush that a lot of macho guys do.

Dammit, more points in his favor. Even if he still had trouble keeping his gaze north of the border.

"Yeah," I said, "we're okay."

"Great!" Randy beamed at me, still holding my hand. "That's just great."

"Okay then."

I waited for him to let go. He didn't.

"You should clean off your sword now," I said gently.

"Oh! Yeah." Randy gave an embarrassed laugh, released my hand, and grabbed the WD-40.

I left him to it and went inside to take a much-needed bathroom break.

†

When I finished with the necessaries, I took a few moments

to splash some cold water on my cheeks and wipe off some of the accumulated dust and sweat streaking my face, arms, and chest. Only then did I risk peering into the mirror.

False modesty aside, I have a nice face. Strong cheekbones, full lips, straight nose, and big eyes so dark a blue they almost look black in certain light. Long, thick mane of naturally wavy hair, a shade somewhere between bittersweet cocoa and mahogany. The kind of looks that made it difficult to pin me down to any particular ethnicity. I've stunt doubled everything from Native American to Middle Eastern to Indian to Caucasian.

What wasn't so nice, though, was the scar creeping out from the hairline on my right temple, so I daubed a little bit of coconut oil on it. It had faded some since the accident, but I wanted it gone. I had a few others, as well, on my arms and legs for instance, and a real whopper on the back of my neck consisting of squiggles of raised skin that looked like I'd been branded. None of those bothered me, though—I didn't mind a few souvenirs of my chosen profession.

But not on the face.

At least not yet. Maybe when I was sixty, didn't care so much what I looked like, and could sit around bragging about all the close calls.

I took a quick look at my backside and sighed. Since the accident I'd dropped about ten pounds, but I still had more curves than your average Hollywood actress. I'd never been a size two or even a four. Hell, I hadn't been a size six since seventh grade, but before that damn fall, I'd been *really* fit. I wanted to get back into shape.

Shrugging, I unstrapped a neoprene pouch from around my wrist. It was a variation on the waterproof key pouches available at surf shops, the type with Velcro fasteners. Some fastened around the ankle or wrist, some around the waist. I had several with different strap lengths and switched them out depending on the circumstances and my wardrobe.

Opening the pouch, I pulled out a round gold amulet on a leather cord and slipped it around my neck. It had belonged to my mother and had survived the car crash when she hadn't. I'd worn it every day since Sean had given it to me on my eighth birthday. I wore it when I showered and when I slept. If I couldn't wear it when I was working, it went into a pocket or pouch strapped somewhere on my body.

As a kid I'd believed that her spirit or essence—or whatever you want to call the soul—went into that amulet. Sean had encouraged that belief to help me deal with not only the death of my parents, but with life as I'd known it.

Did I still believe that?

Yeah, maybe.

The gold disc bore an engraved design of what looked like three crosses joined at their base, two of them horizontal with the third rising vertically. From that extended a curved line like half of the infinity symbol, or maybe a lowercase letter "h." The outer ends of the crosses each flared like three quarters of the classic German iron cross.

I didn't know if the material was gold, bronze, or brass. I also had no idea what the design was supposed to represent. For all I knew it said "cheap shit" in Mandarin, or something equally silly. I didn't really care, though I liked to think it brought me luck. Kind of a stretch, considering Mom had died while wearing it.

On the other hand, I'd left it in my dressing room the day I took the nearly fatal fall. So who the hell knew?

Loud male voices and footsteps coming up the hall announced that my quiet time was at an end, even before the doorknob started turning back and forth.

I knew better and should have gone into the private bathroom off of my room, but I'd been in too much of a hurry.

The door rattled in its frame.

Good thing I'd locked it.

"Anyone in there?"

"No," I called back. "The door always locks itself. This is the towel rack speaking."

"Lee?"

I opened the door to reveal a very antsy Drift, shifting from one foot to the other.

"Ever heard of knocking?" I said loudly as he pushed past me into the bathroom. The door shut in my face. "Just remember to light a match this time," I shouted at the closed door.

With a grimace I headed toward the kitchen for a much-needed shot of something caffeinated. I hadn't been sleeping well lately, so maybe the lack of coffee in my system explained why I was so damned cranky. You'd think I'd be used to the whole lack-of-privacy thing by now.

I'd tried keeping a diary, one of those fancy ones with a little padlock. Seth had just picked it with a paperclip, carved a little hollow in the pages, and left a tarantula inside for me to find. A live one. I'd named the furry little guy Klendathu and kept him as a pet until he died a few years later. I'd insisted on holding a funeral service complete with eulogy for the little dude. At least this is what Sean tells me.

See, my memory's been kind of wonky since the accident. I think of it as selectively weird. Some of the strangest things come back to me, but wide swaths of my past have been virtually washed from my brain.

Things I remember?

I remember some of the stunt work I've done over the years. Sean and I went over my resume after the accident, talking about each one, bringing up anecdotes that helped bring back the experiences. Drift and Tater would also chime in on past jobs, as would Seth. According to Drift and Tater, I was awesome. According to Seth, it had only been a matter of time before I bounced off the side of a building. I could have done without Seth's commentary.

Another weirdly clear memory?

Sean throwing epic birthday parties for Seth and me at the Ranch. Themed parties, like superheroes, X-Men, and *Star Wars*. At eight I'd made a mean little Princess Leia, cinnamon-bun hairstyle and all, and Seth had made a respectable Han Solo for a ten-year-old. He'd still bossed me around, even back then.

I also had no trouble remembering random scenes and lines from movies and television shows, including ones that were way before my time. That made more sense, considering I'd spent a large portion of the last six months doing nothing but watching movies and shows from Sean's huge collection of DVDs, or on the multitude of streaming channels available. We had a huge plasma screen TV in the living room and a very comfy couch.

What didn't make any sense at all, however, is why any of these seemingly unimportant things got crystal-clear status in my poor damaged brain, when I couldn't even remember the sound of my mother's voice.

I don't remember missing my parents. In fact, I barely remember them at all. Their faces remain anonymous blurs. Now and then I'd look at the photo album Sean snagged after they'd died—one of those print-your-own deals Mom and Dad had done—and it was like looking at strangers.

Kinda sucks, but the doctors swore it would all come back to me... eventually.

Maybe.

Every now and then, though, something jiggled a neuron or synapse or whatever they're called. Sean and I would be talking, or a random sound or smell triggered something in my brain, and images appeared. With each image usually came a snippet of memory, playing out like a movie reel. Sometimes full-on color with sound, other times like an old silent film in black and white.

At first I tried to write down the details. I carried a notebook with me and kept one by my bed so I could record any dreams that seemed relevant. My handwriting, however, looked like ancient hieroglyphics, so my iPhone's Notes function became my new best friend.

Although I still don't know what the hell "alpha new wave porker" is supposed to mean. One of the risks of using voice-recognition software at 3 A.M. Siri's ways could be mysterious.

†

The kitchen gleamed, all cream-colored cabinets and walls, polished faux light hardwood floors, and amber-flecked recycled glass countertops. Seth took cleanliness very seriously, so despite the near constant stream of sweaty stunt players, the counters always sparkled and the floors shone. Sometimes the shine came from stacks of beer bottles and cans waiting to be recycled, but still, the overall clean factor was impressive.

Copper pots and utensils hung from hooks on the center block, and high-tech coffee machines took up the counter along one long wall. We're talking a Keurig, a Nespresso, and a scary-looking espresso maker that really belonged in an Italian café. There was also a Mister Coffee, and I'm pretty sure at least two French presses were squirreled away in a cupboard.

If I ever fail as a stuntwoman, I could nail a career as a barista. Then I frowned, pushed the thought from my mind, and made myself a quick double cappuccino with the Nespresso machine.

Grabbing an apple and a few packets of string cheese, I went out onto the porch, which ran all the way around the Craftsman-style ranch house. Footsteps loud on the floorboards, I went directly to the west-facing side of the house with its view of the Santa Monica mountains, and where my favorite creaky wooden rocking chair lived. The overstuffed cushions had a permanent Lee-shaped indent in them.

I sat down, my contented sigh echoed by the creak of the chair. Rocking back and forth, I balanced the apple and cheese on my lap while sipping the hot cappuccino, its rich fragrance mingling with the scent of eucalyptus. It tasted great despite the heat of the day. It had to be in the upper 80s, but a slight breeze blew down from the mountains, just enough to cool things off a bit.

From where I sat, there was a clear view of the dirt road below and the long, tree-lined drive curving up before vanishing around the side of the house. I could see everyone coming and going, and for some reason, that made me feel secure. Maybe I'd seen too many spy movies.

Randy left in his spiffy red Dodge Challenger, doing its best imitation of a '70s Mustang, tires kicking up dust as he hit the accelerator, taking the turn onto the paved road way too fast and nearly spinning out. He reminded me of all the obnoxious boys I'd known in school—the type who showed their interest by acting like assholes.

It hadn't worked on me back in the day, either.

I let my gaze wander up to the DuShane mansion, a sprawling Gothic horror at the peak of the nearest mountain. It was one of those weird, secluded places with a Hollywood history. It'd been built by an eccentric 1920s film producer who'd thrown wild debaucheries during his heyday, then spent his last years hiding behind locked gates before dying under questionable circumstances.

Subsequent owners had come and gone. Supposedly more than one had met his or her untimely end there. The deaths weren't as numerous or horrific as, say, the ones in *House on Haunted Hill* or *The Grudge*, but its reputation persisted. The house fascinated me, and I'd sworn to explore it someday, but that day had yet to come.

"How you holding up, kiddo?"

I jumped, sloshing hot cappuccino onto one leg.

"Motherfu—"

I stopped myself when I saw who'd snuck up on me. Sean didn't deal well with the whole swearing thing. So I did my best to ignore the heat soaking into my skin and smiled, albeit through gritted teeth.

"Jeez, Sean, some warning would be nice."

Sean looked sheepish. "Sorry, kid."

He sat down in the chair across from me. Looked down at his knees, then out across the land spotted with scrub brush and sage, stretching back toward the base of the mountains. I watched him, my shoulders tightening.

"What's up?"

"What do you mean?"

I sighed. "Sean, how many years have I known you? You're not telling me something. What is it? Like, did the doctors only give me a year to live?"

Sean laughed at that. Full, uninhibited, and genuine laughter, and the tension in my shoulders drained away.

"You're fine, baby girl."

"Seriously?"

"Seriously."

We creaked back and forth in companionable silence for a few minutes, watching cars leave the Ranch as other vehicles arrived. I munched on my apple and string cheese.

"So," I finally said after swallowing the last bite of cheese. "Are you ever gonna put me on a film again?"

Sean rocked for a few more beats, then looked at me.

"Yeah."

"So… when?"

"As soon as you're okay on the falls again."

I nodded. I'd known this was the case, but I'd needed to hear Sean say so before really believing it.

"What if—" I took a deep breath. "What if I can't get over it?"

There. I'd said it.

What if I *couldn't* get over it? What if my accident had permanently screwed with my ability to take a fall, whether it was six feet or sixty? I'd spent most of my life jumping off of buildings and things like that. It's not like I never thought about the danger when I did it, but the danger never stopped me. Now I couldn't see past it. Suddenly I had this big hole in my life, and I didn't know what to fill it with.

Sean stopped rocking, leaned forward, and took one of my hands, looking at me with those sky-blue eyes.

"Lee, we're the Katz Stunt Crew. We're known for our high falls and aerial work. When people hire us, there are certain expectations that come with the package. You know that, right?"

"Right. So if I can't do falls, I'm no good to you?"

Sean looked uncomfortable. "I wouldn't exactly say it like that."

I had to ask. "Is it Seth? Because I'd think he'd be glad to have me working, and out of the house again."

Sean stopped rocking and looked at me.

"Lee, when you got hurt, Seth nearly lost his mind, he was so worried about you. If he's hard on you now, it's because he doesn't want you to get hurt again. He wants to make sure you can handle whatever comes your way."

Oh, how I wished I could believe him. It would've made me a lot happier if I thought Seth actually cared about me. As far as I could tell, however, he'd have been content if I'd just died on *Vampshee*.

My doubt must have shown on my face.

"Honestly, Lee," Sean said, shaking his head, "both Seth and I would rather have you at home anyway. Give you a break from those guys you kept hooking up with." He gave a little laugh. "That last one was nothing but trouble, am I right?"

I just looked at him.

"I don't know," I said. "I don't remember a lot of stuff. Y'know?"

Sean had the good grace to look embarrassed.

"Sorry," he said. "I keep forgetting."

Oh, the irony.

"Look," I said, leaning forward to give him a good hard stare. "There have to be jobs that don't include leaping out of buildings or diving from helicopters."

"True," Sean said, "but you know how stuff comes up day to day. And we've never made a production wait on anyone or anything to date."

I couldn't argue with that. The Katz motto is "Stay on

Target," which is *Star Wars* for "stay on schedule, stay on budget, and stay employed." If Sean was on a shoot with only a couple of his team, and the director decided he wanted to film an underwater fight instead of a car crash, Sean needed to know that they could handle it.

Drift, for instance, was one of the top stunt drivers in the business, but he could fight, do a fire gag, and throw himself off anything at any height without hesitation. Tater had the same kind of pedigree, as did all of Sean's core team. I'd had it too, before I'd gone all splat on the pavement and lost my mojo.

Still, I pushed a little harder.

"So what if there's a female part that needs doubling, but doesn't include high falls?"

"Lee, hon, if one of those jobs comes along, you'll be there, I swear it." Sean sounded sincere, but his eyes flickered in a way I didn't quite trust. "I can't lie to you, though. I'd feel much better if I knew you were okay with taking some falls, too. You know directors."

I did, and it didn't make me feel any better about my future. I heaved a sigh.

"You know I can't possibly live up to you and Seth, right?"

"Don't expect you to." Sean reached out and patted me on one knee. "I just need you to live up to yourself."

"That makes little or no sense."

"Just get over it. I'll put you on a job soon, Lee. Just give it a little more time, okay? Remember. Small steps." He rocked forward one more time and then stood up in an easy motion. "Guess I should go start the afternoon session."

"Yeah, you should."

"Give it time," he said again. "I swear, Lee, as soon as there's a job where I can, I'll put you on it."

I made myself smile and nodded yet again. I was beginning to feel like a bobble-head.

"You gonna join us?" Sean looked at me with so much love and understanding that I wanted to punch him.

"Later," I said as neutrally as possible. "Tater and I are gonna do some rapier and dagger, and I want to do some wirework. But I think I'll just hang here for a little bit longer, okay?"

Sean nodded. "Sounds good, hon." I tried not to read any disappointment into his tone because I didn't know if it was real, or if I was putting it there.

†

I stayed in the rocking chair a few minutes more. Finished my cappuccino. Tossed the apple core out into the yard where it would be devoured either by grateful insects or whatever other scavengers showed up. A big raven swooped down almost immediately.

Sorry, ants.

The raven picked up the core in its beak, looked at me, hopped away a foot or so, and then settled in to enjoy its snack.

As I watched it, I slowly became conscious of an uncomfortable sensation, that *I* was the one being watched. Normally it wouldn't have bothered me. My job, after all, put me in front of people and cameras focusing on my every move. There was a difference, however, between that and the feeling that someone was stalking you.

Looking past the raven, out toward the mountains rising behind the Ranch, I could swear someone stood there on a jutting slab of rock above the DuShane mansion, a dark silhouette of a man, watching me. Face in shadows, but his eyes flashing with a red glow, as if fires burned inside.

I blinked, shook my head, and looked again.

Nothing.

The figure was gone from its perch on the outcropping.

The back of my neck itched. The raven stopped its pursuit of the apple core, swiveling its head in the same direction, toward the mountains. It froze, one foot in midair.

The air turned thick and heavy. Even though the sun burned down in its early afternoon glory... I would swear the sky darkened. Sound faded out, as if my ears slowly filled with soft wax. Birds, buzzing insects, the sound of voices from the back. All dampened to barely discernable white noise... and then?

Nothing.

I shivered, goose bumps rising on my bare arms.

What the hell?

The gentle breeze rose into a strong wind that gusted through the side yard, rattling the eucalyptus branches and kicking up little whirlwinds of dirt that rapidly grew into serious dust devils. I shut my eyes, shielding my face with both hands as particles of dirt and debris hit my face. A sharp pebble hit my bare arm, the impact drawing a hiss of pain. My hair, still bound tightly in its braid, whipped around my face like a rope.

The raven didn't move, not a feather ruffled.

The wind stopped as suddenly as it had started, dropping to nothing within the space of a second. I slowly lowered my hands, carefully brushing debris away from my eyes before opening them.

When I did, someone—something—stood directly in front of me. The same dark figure, larger than life and smelling like death. I couldn't see his face, even though he stood just a couple of feet away. Eyes glowing red, lit with a fire burning with hate and lust.

I stumbled back, a scream rising in my throat as the back of my knees hit the rocking chair. I collapsed back into the chair, the jolt cutting the scream off before it escaped. My eyes shut involuntarily.

When I opened them again, the figure was gone.

My breath expelled in one long, shaky exhale.

"Holy shit."

Was I really that tired from a few nights of lousy sleep and the morning's workout? Were the injuries I'd sustained causing hallucinations? Or was this something else?

I heard the reassuring chatter of voices around the corner, the eerie quiet broken. The raven took a few more pecks at the core, gave a cursory flap of its wings, and took into the air. I watched it fly out of sight, taking deep breaths until my heart rate finally slowed to its normal pace.

CHAPTER FOUR

Once I thought I could stand without my knees wobbling, I put on a pair of metaphorical big girl panties and rounded the porch to see who had shown up for Saturday afternoon training.

It was a smallish group. Tater, Drift, Sean, Seth, Tobias, Moria, and Jada. Tobias, our wirework expert, was the only full-blooded human there besides me, but just as fearless and almost as graceful as the nephs, and *definitely* more graceful than Drift. Most of us are more graceful than Drift, though. He has cave troll in his family woodshed.

The lack of grace gave Drift a quality of realism, though, and maybe an edge of danger. He could take falls without much padding, and take them hard. Sometimes so hard he left Drift-shaped impressions in the ground. First time I'd seen him "miss" the airbag, I'd freaked and had my cell out to dial 9-1-1, only to have Seth snatch it from me.

"You're too damned easy," he'd said. A quick nod and Drift was sitting up, wiping dust off his pants and wearing a self-satisfied grin. I'd burst into tears of mortification. Hey, I was thirteen and hormonal.

Drift had been mortified, too. I'd gotten over it, but it had taken me a few years before I'd learn to appreciate the macabre humor of this bunch.

†

Moria—one of the few women who'd made it to the inner circle—was halfway up the high fall ladder. I liked Moria. We'd worked on one or two projects together without any friction, possibly because we looked nothing alike. That means we generally aren't up for the same jobs.

Curly blond hair cropped short for practicality, a long thin nose, wide grin and short, compact build, Moria had some harpy blood, which not only helped with the aerial stunts but also made it easy for her to hold her own amidst all the obnoxious male bonding. Not that she's mean. Honestly, Moria was one of the sweetest people I'd met... unless you pissed her off.

Only idiots piss off a harpy.

Forty feet above the ground, Moria saw me watching the action from the porch and waved enthusiastically, using both arms. I waved back, swallowing a bitter pill of envy.

I was less thrilled to see Jada. The tension used to really bother me—the whole females in competition cliché. Then I realized it had less to do with our gender and everything to do with her personality.

She was mostly human, with just a smattering of air elemental in her DNA, and worked hard, although she definitely wasn't as good as Moria or me. At least, not as good as I *used* to be. These days Jada had it all over me when the stunt involved anything above ground. She also looked kind of like me, except two sizes smaller, and we'd been up for some of the same jobs.

Jada pitched a minor fit when I'd gotten the *Vampshee* gig. Accused Sean of nepotism. That had almost gotten her tossed out on her ass. If she hadn't been fairly toasted on piña coladas when she'd done it, she'd have been history. She'd apologized to him the next day, but hadn't said a word to me.

Her hangover was still legend.

I'm not sure which bothered me more—her bad judgment in attacking Sean and me, or getting shitfaced drunk on piña coladas. Who does that? *Get a real drink.*

At any rate, while I'm not saying Jada had a big happy when I got injured, she hasn't shed any tears over the extra work being farmed her way. She found every opportunity to cozy up to Seth, who gave the appearance of enjoying the attention. Not that it mattered to me who he did in his spare time. Hell, they could get married and spawn a squadron of flying babies for all I cared.

I just wanted to be back at the top of my game. Until then, I hoped Jada liked getting the stunt work equivalent of a pity fuck.

Meow.

Just then Moria hollered, "Geronimo!" and threw herself from the sixty-foot platform like a kid doing a cannonball into a pool. Midway down, she twisted in the air, and landed on her back. No fear. Just pure joy.

I sighed. Was it possible to love and hate something at the same time? Because that was how I felt, watching everyone as they took turns practicing falls that should have been impossible or, at the very least, ended in big splats on the ground. Before my accident I'd loved this part of training, but right now it was just a reminder that I couldn't keep up with the supernatural crowd. I wasn't part nephilim or djinn. My great aunt wasn't a harpy or an air elemental. I'd always been limited to what I could do, even after years of practice.

This just sucked.

I sighed yet again and went over to see if Tobias would work with me on the Russian swing.

†

The sound of drums and bass penetrated the walls. Devon, their neighbor's son two doors down, had been working at putting a band together for the last year. They practiced every evening from six to nine, except for weekends. Then the lucky neighbors were guaranteed an afternoon serenade. Sometimes just bass and Devon's unfortunate vocals. Other times drums and guitar were added to the mix.

Sound pollution by way of aspiring musicians.

Oh well, nothing to be done about it other than stuff a towel in the gap between door and floor.

In daylight the room was nothing out of the ordinary. Not even a real basement, just a small windowless annex to the garage transformed into a tacky man-cave. The olive shag rug, fake wood paneling on the walls, and overstuffed plaid lounger screamed "sixties."

Six black candles cast flickering, unstable light as a false promise of protection against the dark, turning the room into something sinister. Five of them marked each point of the pentagram drawn within the borders of a large red chalked circle, at least five feet in diameter. Sigils and symbols, also rendered in red chalk, bordered every inch of the circle.

The sixth candle rested on a wrought iron holder in front of a hooded figure seated in the middle of a smaller circle, also bordered with protective glyphs. A small cast-iron cauldron sat on the floor next to the candle, several jars and vials scattered within arm's reach of the room's lone occupant.

The hooded figure held a piece of paper under the candle, mouthing the words to get a feel for them but taking care not to say them out loud.

Not yet.

Sure, this whole thing might just be a crock of shit—but if it wasn't, the spell made it very clear what would happen if the right ingredients weren't cast at the right time with the right words. Real bad juju. Eyeballs bleeding, guts spilling out onto the floor.

Why take chances?

Taking a deep breath, the figure carefully lit a tea light seated under the base of the cauldron. Spoke slowly and clearly, making sure to enunciate the arcane invocations correctly while dropping each item into the murky liquid. When the last ingredient vanished into the pot, things changed.

The air became thick, almost viscous. Electricity crackled throughout the room, transforming it into something dark and terrible. The temperature dropped, ice crystals forming on the walls. The smell of ozone, rotted flesh, and much worse rose from the cauldron. Writhing shadows appeared in the center of the pentacle, taking shape only to dissolve when they touched the borders of the chalked circle.

The conjuror smiled, despite the shivers that wracked every limb to the point it felt like something might break.

Hot damn.

It had worked.

†

Frowning petulantly, Devon stopped in the middle of "Mango Nation." He'd been rocking it, pretending that his parents' garage was a filled-to-capacity audience at the Troubadour, all of them there to hear him.

"Look, Rick," he said with exaggerated patience, giving a toss of his head and displacing the hank of purple hair that usually rested deliberately over one eye. "We've talked about it, okay? You need to slow it the fuck down, okay? I know the rest of the band's not here, but that's no excuse, right?"

†

Rick just looked at his best friend.

Devon always had to prove something, even when he didn't have the skills to follow through. He wanted to be the next Bono, to stand in front of thousands, raise his hands and be worshipped. He also wanted to wow the crowds with his guitar riffs, though, and he wasn't willing to give up one for the other. He'd missed the last few chord changes while trying to sing the lead on the chorus. It was easier to blame the tempo—and his friend—than admit he wasn't good enough.

"I mean, you rushed the transition to the bridge. You felt it, right?"

The two had played variations on the theme "it's always Rick's fault" many times over the course of their ten-year friendship. Up to this point, Rick had always played along without trying to change the tune. He'd always been easy going, so he'd just kept trying to make the band work. They had something really good, if he could just get Devon to drop the ego.

He'd turned into a decent guitarist after a lot of practice, but still couldn't deal with the complexities of playing and singing at the same time. Plus, his singing voice—nasal with an unfortunate and affected vibrato—was more suited to a mediocre folk band than rock and roll.

Rick just wanted to share the stage with talented musicians who would help create a unique sound. But how was he supposed to tell his best friend that he totally sucked at the one thing he'd always wanted to do?

They'd already been through two bass players—both who'd been really hot on the original songs, but they couldn't deal with Devon. Bam, the current guy, had this awesome gravely baritone voice perfect for the material. He and Rick rocked the rhythm section. They were tight and had the same vision.

Bam also had connections.

"Dude…" Rick took a deep breath and continued, knowing if he didn't get this out now, he never would. "Got a call from Bam this morning."

"Yeah? Did he mention he was gonna be late?" Devon threw an angry look at the wall clock. "Shit, it's already seven."

"No, he didn't. What he said is he's out if you don't change your mind about singing lead vocals."

"Fuck."

Quietly uttered.

"Fuck!"

Louder, as Rick's words sunk in.

"FUCK!"

Devon kicked the speaker closest to him, pulling the force behind the kick just in time to avoid punching a hole in the mesh with the pointy metal toe of his trendy leather boots.

Rick stayed still behind his drum set. He'd known his friend would go off when he heard Bam's news. Couldn't exactly blame him, but he also couldn't summon up any sympathy either. They could either have a successful band, or a vanity project for Devon. They couldn't have both.

Devon unhooked his guitar strap, placing his beloved Charvel So Cal gently in its stand before striding back and forth across the garage.

"Fuck it. Fuck Bam. We'll put an ad in the Recycler and Craigslist, find someone else. Shouldn't be too hard. I mean, bass players are a dime a dozen, right?"

Another familiar refrain, and so not true.

Rick stayed silent.

"We still need to find a good rhythm guitarist, so we can do a two-for-one ad. Maybe we should go for a percussionist too. I mean, we want to round out the sound, right?"

"No."

Devon either didn't hear him, or paid no attention, and continued pacing back and forth in the garage.

"We can try Nextdoor.com too, maybe find someone in the neighborhood to make rehearsing easier."

Rick stood up. Took another deep breath.

"No," he repeated. "Not this time, Dev."

"What?"

Devon stopped and stared at his friend.

"We've done this three times. Had three good bass players. Lost them because you can't admit you shouldn't be on lead vocals." Rick carefully placed his sticks down and stood up behind his kit. "I'm done with this."

"Come on, man." Devon gave a little laugh. "We've been through this before. We can do it again."

"That's the point. I don't want to do it again. Why can't you see that? Bam is the best bass player we've ever had and he's got a great voice. He's exactly what this band needs. I'm sick of losing talented people because you can't step away from your fucking ego."

Dev started to speak, but Rick held up a hand. He'd kept quiet for years. He'd had enough.

"Bam and I work really well together. We've practiced a few times on our own. I would've loved to have seen this band go somewhere. We've been friends for years and you write great lyrics. But you can't sing them. You're not a good enough guitarist and your voice…"

Rick trailed off and shook his head, hoping against hope that Dev would listen to reason.

"Your voice just doesn't work for the material."

"It's my *material."*

And there it was. Dev's refusal to let go of control, uttered in the voice of a petulant kid holding onto his toys. He'd never really grown past that stage.

"You can keep all of it," Rick said quietly. "I'm sure you'll be

able to find another drummer without a problem." Without another word, he slowly and methodically started breaking down his drum kit.

Devon stared at him.

"You can't mean it, man. This is our dream. You can't just walk away from that."

"Actually, Dev, you've turned it into your dream and everything always has to be done your way, and it's never going to work."

"Oh yeah? Well, fuck you!" Devon flung his arm out in a wide sweeping gesture, knocking the ride cymbal and its stand to the ground with a metallic clatter. Then he kicked the bass drum, not bothering to pull the momentum, punching a hole through the head.

Rick stared at his friend in disbelief, then looked at the hole in his drum. There was no coming back from this, and both of them knew it.

"That's it," Rick said softly. He quickly packed up the rest of his kit, loading everything onto his cheap solid-top dolly.

†

Devon watched, trying to think of something he could say that would turn back time, but nothing came to mind except for the words "I'm sorry," and he couldn't bring himself to say them. So he kept silent, letting his best friend walk away from the band and their friendship.

He listened as Rick started up his 1999 Nissan pickup, the idle rough. He continued listening as Rick pulled away from the curb and drove off. He listened until the only sound left was that of his own angry heartbeat, the sound thrumming in his ears, rattling his rib cage. It hurt to breathe.

He couldn't believe he'd kicked Rick's drum. Such an asshole move. Sure, he'd been angry, but how would he feel if someone smashed his guitar? Not like it was expensive to replace, but Rick didn't have the money for any extras right now.

He ignored the sullen, nasty part of him that was more than okay with that.

He can replace it, *he thought. My parents will help. They loved Rick. Hell, they'd pay for it all. He'd just tell them he'd tripped, fallen into it. That would fix everything. Rick would forgive him for being an asshole. He always did. They'd find a replacement for Bam and things would be the way they'd always been.*

Him and Rick against the world.

The way Devon liked it.

The temperature dropped just as the smell hit him. Like stepping into a freezer with a vent blowing in the odor from the back of a one-star restaurant with a month's worth of garbage piled up. Except someone had taken a dump in the garbage after a few small animals had crawled in there and died.

Devon gagged, holding one hand up over his nose while breathing shallowly through his mouth.

"What the fuck?"

The lightbulb that hung in the middle of the garage ceiling flickered. It dimmed as if the seventy-watt lightbulb had been replaced with a forty. Shadows lengthened. Stretching. Elongating as if with a life of their own. They weren't black. That didn't begin to describe the darkness, as if the shadows led to a place where light had never existed.

For the first time in years, Devon wished his parents were home.

Whispers filled the room, coming from the corners. The shadows continued to twist and morph, like taffy in one of those machines at the fair. Devon moved slowly toward the door leading into the house. A shadow stretched out from behind an amp and blocked his way. He stopped short, lifting up a foot and stepping backward when a black ribbon seemed to reach for him. Somehow he knew he couldn't let it touch him.

Another tendril snaked out from under the amp, merging with the first one, widening and spreading across the floor like an oil slick. Dev backed away from it to the center of the room, under the *ever-decreasing circle of light provided by the bulb overhead.*

"This shit is not happening," he said, his voice rising in a whine of fear.

The light flickered again. Shadows spread up the walls onto the ceiling. Blackness oozed down the walls, creeping across the floor toward him. The stench increased, as foul and thick as syrup in the air.

Something brushed against his face. He shrieked, looking up to see inky strands dripping down from the ceiling, impossibly darker than the shadows. Then something brushed against his ankle. He imagined a cat without fur, its skin rotting off the bones and dipped in slime. The freezing cold burned like dry ice where it touched him.

The lightbulb went out.

Devon wanted to scream to call for help, but he was afraid if he opened his mouth that the smell, that taste would get inside of him. Something that foul had to be poison. It would kill him, he knew it.

He was wrong. When he finally did open his mouth to scream, the horrible smell didn't kill him. Instead, razor-sharp talons hooked into his tongue, pulling it out before he could make a sound, and then proceeded to slowly rip the flesh from his bones.

CHAPTER FIVE

"Well, damn."

Drift stuck his head out of the kitchen doorway and peered sadly into the living room.

"The kitchen is officially a beer free zone," he said.

A chorus of groans rose from the couch and chairs scattered around the coffee table.

Seriously?

We'd made a Costco run a few days earlier, and I would swear Sean and I had walked out with at least three cases of craft beer and a metric shit-ton of Stella Artois. How could it all be gone?

"Did you check the fridge in the garage?" I asked.

Drift nodded sadly. "Empty."

I looked at the coffee table and floor, both littered with empty cans, bottles, and several empty pizza cartons. I heaved a huge sigh, reminding myself that I was dealing with a mix of stuntmen and supernatural metabolisms—sometimes in the same package.

"Whose turn is it?" Tater asked, tilting his head to one side. He wasn't exactly drunk yet, but definitely on the road to it, with Tobias doing his best to catch up. I suspected we'd have a couple of couch crashers tonight.

Drift gave a huge belch. Tobias actually *giggled*.

I rolled my eyes and stood up.

"I'll do this run."

"You're the best, Lee." Drift smiled up at me, all happy, lazy, and pretty tipsy.

"Yeah, you're right about that."

I didn't want to say it to Drift, but the thought of even a short trip by myself was my idea of heaven just about now. Moria had already left, and I was stuck with Jada and her increasingly drunken attempts to flirt with Seth—who seemed indifferent to everything except his beer.

At least he wasn't being a prick to me. Even so, I'd had enough of stunt men, nephilim, family, testosterone, and bitches for the day. Besides, I was the only sober one in the bunch.

"You sure you're okay going out, hon?" Sean looked at me through slightly bleary eyes. I counted four empties and one partial on the coffee table in front of him.

"Totally," I assured him truthfully.

I'd only had one beer, and it took a lot to get me tipsy, let alone drunk. Nevertheless, I took my driving seriously. If I got caught, I'd have to blow into a Breathalyzer, and that'd be all she wrote. Most of the guys? Hell, they could be weaving all over the road and still blow at zero. It wasn't fair, and *really* wouldn't be fair to anyone else on the road.

I glanced at the clock. Half past eight. I probably wouldn't make BevMo without breaking the speed limits, but I had other options.

"Arlo's is still open for another hour," I said. "But I'm totally taking the Xterra. My car still hasn't recovered from the last beer run."

Drift ducked his head. He knew what I was talking about.

"Keys are…" Sean paused, brow furrowed. "They're wherever the keys are."

I grinned. "Yeah, I know. I'll find 'em."

†

The keys were indeed where keys were supposed to be, on a hook in the entryway. Maybe not the smartest place if an enterprising thief ever broke in, but it worked for us.

"You sure you're okay to drive?" Sean asked for the fifth time in as many minutes.

"One beer, Sean. I've had one beer. I'm fine—and you're not allowed to ask me again," I added as he opened his mouth. I handed him his half-drunk bottle of Stone Delicious IPA.

"Sure you don't want me to drive you?" Drift offered.

I gave him a look.

Last time I'd made the mistake of letting him drive my car on a beer run, he'd decided to see how fast he could barrel down the drive back to the ranch, make a 180-degree turn, and park in between two other vehicles. He'd actually pulled it off. The cars were fine, but we lost half a case of beer when he hit the brakes. The inside of my poor ancient, battered Saturn still smelled like a cheap-ass brewery.

"No." I shook my head.

"Oh, come on." Drift managed to look innocent and hurt at the same time. "It was only Coors."

"Lucky for you," I tossed back over my shoulder as I opened the front door. "If you'd trashed Tater's fancy IPAs, you'd *still* be hurting."

Tater let loose a giant belch of agreement. I shut the door behind me, shutting out the sounds of more burps, farts, and raucous laughter. Boys would be boys no matter what the species.

The Xterra was unlocked. I slid in behind the wheel, slid the seat forward six inches so I could actually touch the gas and brake pedals, and adjusted the mirrors accordingly. At five foot, nine inches, I wasn't exactly short, but both Seth and Sean topped out at six and a half feet, at least half of that being legs. Sitting behind either of them in a car was an exercise in yoga, knees crunched up to my chin. I quickly learned to call "shotgun" while still in my teens.

Weaving my way between all the vehicles parked haphazardly in the carport and along the driveway, I drove carefully down the long, winding dirt road, heaving a sigh of relief once I slipped through the open gates at the bottom of the hill and turned onto the paved access road. I'd driven this route so many times I barely needed the headlights to navigate. Every pothole was familiar territory and I swerved around them with ease, enjoying the power and easy handling of Sean's all-terrain muscle mobile.

Gotta love four-wheel drive.

The car smelled of sweat and several-day-old chalupas, thanks to a pile of unwashed workout gear and Taco Bell wrappers. I made a mental note to grab a trash bag and clean out all the crap before the odors became a permanent part of the upholstery, then rolled down the front windows to let in the more pleasing scents of sage, eucalyptus, and anise. All three grew in abundance in the hills, and the warm, late-summer breeze carried their fragrance.

By the time I reached Arlo's, our local mom-'n'-pop market and my go-to destination for impromptu beer runs, my mood had improved. Sometimes a gal just needs her own space. There were no other cars in the parking lot, so I pulled into the spot under the lone light, not bothering to lock the Xterra when I got out.

Arlo's is pretty much like any other market you'll find off the beaten path in California, with that faux old-timey western feel to it. Wraparound porch, wooden railing. Lots of vintage-style signs advertising Coke, Shasta Tiki Punch, Eskimo Pies. None of their signs showed products newer than the seventies.

One of my favorite things about Arlo's was the old-fashioned soda machine on the porch, the kind that only carried bottles. You could get ice-cold Mexican cokes, the kind made with sugar instead of high fructose corn syrup. The sign on the machine said a dime. The sodas were actually a buck, but the owners were too lazy to change the sign. When I pointed out that someone could—and in Los Angeles, probably would—sue for false advertising, they put a post-it note on the machine with the correct price.

The wooden stairs creaked when I stepped on them. So did the porch. So, for that matter, did my muscles and joints. I pushed open the door. A little bell jingled merrily and Marge, one of the owners, waved from behind the counter.

Short hair the real blue-black of a raven's wing. Olive complexion. Native American or some other indigenous people, mixed with something reptilian, maybe a Naga. I couldn't quite place it and it seemed rude to ask. Let's just say it involved the ability to unhinge her jaw, and an extra row of upper and lower teeth that were really only noticeable when she'd waited too long to eat or smiled too widely.

Marge only did that with regulars that she trusted.

"Hey, Lee. Beer run?"

I rolled my eyes. "How'd you guess?"

Marge grinned widely, briefly showing off those extra-sharp teeth. "Hon, times you come in here and don't buy beer? Um, let's see. That would be zero."

"Fine," I grumbled. "So shoot me—I'm predictable."

Marge gave a guffaw. "I set my clock on your beer runs, sweetie."

I laughed. "Good to know I have a purpose in life."

The microwave behind her beeped.

"Oh, good." She beamed. "Snack time!" She opened the microwave door, pulling out a couple mugs filled with what might have been very dark coffee. "Hal! Soup's on!" she called.

Hal shambled out from a back room, a tall, lanky man in jeans and a black thermal top, dark hair every which way but neat. The same could be said for his teeth. He and Marge looked like they'd been hatched out of the same clutch of eggs. One of those couples that looks more like siblings than spouses.

He scooped one of the mugs up and took a big sip, sighing happily. The extra teeth retracted.

"Hey, Lee."

"Hey, Hal." I gave a little wave and wandered down the aisle to the cooler on the opposite wall. I had a job to do, and it involved choices.

Important choices.

Stella, Stone, or PBR?

I'd get twice as much for the price if I went for PBR, but I swear the guys drank it twice as fast as any other beer. So really, was it worth it in the long run? I thought not, and grabbed two twelve-packs of Stella, a six-pack of Stone Delicious IPA, and, because Sean was footing the bill, two four-packs of Dogfish Head 90 Minutes.

One of those packs was mine, all mine.

I did this in two trips between fridge and counter, Marge watching me with amusement. "Sure you don't wanna toss in a PBR, just in case?"

She knew us well. I rolled my eyes.

"I'm trying to wean them off of it. Upgrade their taste a little bit. Get you more money every time I have to make a beer run."

"And I appreciate that, Lee. Can't say we don't need the income." Marge shook her head. "Molly's getting huge and, I swear, she eats more than Hal." Molly was Hal and Marge's extremely toothy two-year-old daughter. Definitely what you'd call a "little nipper."

I eyed the rack next to the counter. Marge rang up my purchases slowly, giving me time to toss in a few bags of Sun Chips, taco chips, and Cheetos.

"Am I really that obvious?" I grumbled, grabbing a jar of mild salsa to go with the taco chips.

"Pretty much, yeah. You sure that's it?"

I hesitated. "I'll just go grab that PBR."

Marge grinned.

I headed back to the cooler, pausing when the back of my neck suddenly itched, prickling like something was crawling there. I scratched the offending area, hoping an opportunistic spider or other creepy-crawly hadn't hitched a ride.

The front door bell jingled as someone entered the store and came down the aisle in my direction. Distracted by the damn itching, I didn't pay much attention until a familiar and unwelcome voice spoke.

"Catch yourself some fleas, Lee?" My hand froze mid-scratch.

Speaking of creepy-crawlies…

Skeet Silva. Aspiring stuntman and *Caminhante de Aranha*—Spider Walker to you and me. One of the more obscure shifter breeds around. He lived a few miles from the

Ranch, so this wasn't the first time I'd run into him at Arlo's.

Skeet's family hails from Brazil, and at face value he looks like he could star in *telenovelas*. Medium height, muscular. Dark intense eyes over a straight, longish nose and full lips. On second glance, his lips are a little too wet and red. His limbs are slightly too long for his torso. Add a small head and short neck planted in between broad, sloping shoulders, and it was easy to see the arachnid under the human skin.

Skeet had tried to insinuate himself at the Ranch a year or so back. His ability to spin small but very sticky webs from palms and soles enabling him to navigate walls and ceilings like sidewalks should have guaranteed him a place in the KSC. His inability to take direction due to an excess of ego saw his invitation revoked in record time. There is no love lost between him and any of our crew.

"I said, you have fleas, Lee?"

As if I hadn't heard him the first time.

"Only pest in here is you, Skeet," I said, just so he wouldn't repeat himself again.

He gave a hiss of laughter, misting the air with a fine spray of spit. I took a small step backward to avoid it. He, in turn, moved in just enough to make me uncomfortable. "You're a funny one, you are, Lee. How 'bout you and I go get a drink?"

Uh-huh. This was not the first time he'd hit on me, but no matter how Sean and Seth rag on me for my taste in bad boys, I was *so* not tempted.

"No thanks, Skeet. Got plans already." *No sense being rude, right?*

I turned back to the beer cooler, trying to ignore the renewed itching on the back of my neck as I reached for the door handle. Before I could pull it open, a large hand slapped down next to mine.

Wrong.

"Still too good for me?"

"You really want me to answer that?"

Skeet laughed again, the sound sibilant and menacing. Then he leaned in close, not quite pressing up against me. "Here's what I'm gonna do," he said softly. Sticky threads, like white cotton candy, oozed out from his palm towards my hand. "Wrap you up nice and tight so you can't move. Do what I want. You'll love it."

I jerked my hand away from the encroaching strands and faced him. "You touch me and I'll strangle you with your own webbing. Got it?"

"You having trouble finding something, Skeet?" Hal suddenly appeared at the mouth of the aisle, tone and expression deceptively friendly.

"No." Skeet reached past me and opened the cooler, grabbing a six-pack of Coors. "Just catching up with Lee."

"Well, okay then." Hal stayed where he was as Skeet reluctantly took his beer up to the register, where Marge rang him up without a word. I gave my neck one last scratch as the itching faded away, waiting until Skeet was gone before heading back to the counter.

"Asshole spider," Marge muttered.

I pulled the wad of cash out of my bag and plopped it down in front of her.

Marge shook her head. "You ever hear of using a credit card?"

I shrugged. "I could use mine, but it wouldn't do either of us any good."

Between us, Marge and I packed the chips, salsa, and the two four-packs into a couple of double-bags.

"I'll give you a hand out," Hal said, scooping up the

Stella, PBR, and the IPA. He handled the burden with ease. I waved at Marge, grabbed the two bags, and followed Hal outside to the parking lot and the Xterra.

"It's unlocked," I said.

Hal shifted the beer to one arm and popped open the back hatch.

"How you doin', Lee?" Hal looked at me as he set the twelve-packs inside.

"I'm good," I said, making sure the Dogfish Head and Stone were nestled safely between the two packs of Stella. "I'd be better if I didn't have to go out every night for beer, but I swear, the boys just suck it down faster than—"

"Well, I meant more than the beer runs."

I shrugged. "Need a job. Other than that, just fine."

"You telling me there isn't any work coming down the pipe?"

I slammed the back hatch shut and turned to face him.

"Oh, there's plenty of work, but Sean isn't going to put me on a job until I can get back to doing the high falls. And that…" I trailed off, looking down at the dirt parking lot. "I just don't know if that's gonna happen any time soon."

Hal nodded thoughtfully.

"You ever think he's just afraid of you getting hurt again?"

I snorted. "Hell, people get hurt all the damn time. Sean's used to it."

"He's not used to it being you."

I opened my mouth to argue, and then shut it.

Hal looked at me. "Maybe you should look for work outside the family."

"You mean away from the Katz name?"

Hal nodded. "Yeah. Get a job on something small maybe. You've got enough experience, I bet someone'll hire you."

He yawned again, inadvertently showing off the teeth again. Ragged, sharp little buggers.

"You'd better eat some more," I cautioned.

Hal chuckled, and looked like a friendly piranha.

"Yeah, don't wanna scare the straights, right?"

I couldn't help but feel touched that I wasn't considered one of the straights.

"I'd better get going," I said, opening the driver's door. "Gonna have a riot on my hands if I don't get back soon."

Hal laughed. "You know they're settled down watching *Hooper* for the umpteenth time."

"True, but they'll still want their beer. Especially during the bar brawl scene."

Hal nodded. "Give my best to the crew. And don't worry. You'll be working soon enough." Turning, he went back inside the store, leaving me to wonder at the oddly prophetic tone of his last words.

I hoped he was right.

†

When the conjuror came back later that evening the circle remained, although the candles had melted most of the way down, the wax solidified on the floor. A thin ribbon of it had cut through the chalk lines in one place. Nothing remained of the creatures he'd summoned, however, other than a faint whiff of sewage and sulfur.

But they'd left behind something else from their visit. A partially chewed arm and hand, stuck out of what had been the center of the circle like a hastily planted flower. The petals were fingers, splayed and bloody.

Oh, shit.

Closer examination showed the arm, cut off at the elbow. It appeared to be melded with the cement, as if the ground had been liquid and then solidified around the mutilated flesh.

This couldn't be allowed to happen again. Something had to be done differently. One unexpected body could be hidden.

More than that?

Not good.

Maybe something had been missed in the incantation, some key ingredient that would keep them from leaving the confines of the circle. Perhaps somet0hing more potent than a cow's blood from the butcher's. Too old, perhaps?

Or just too dead.

No energy, no life.

More research was in order. This had to work. Too many things depended on it.

CHAPTER SIX

I stood at the edge of the building, waiting for my cue to step off and take my fall. Wind blew around me, whipping my hair up and around my face, into my mouth and eyes, stinging my flesh like the thongs of a cat-o'-nine-tails.

The cement beneath my feet crumbled and transformed into dirt and shale—a cliff towering above the sea. Foam-tipped waves crashed against rocks, each one cresting higher.

If I stepped off, I'd die. I knew that.

"Lee…"

A masculine voice.

Soft.

Sibilant.

I shuddered with dread. Even worse, the dread was shot through with longing. The two feelings intertwined until I couldn't separate one from the other.

"Lee."

I shuddered as strong hands curved around my bare shoulders, the touch of those fingers and palms burning me with icy cold, as if my flesh had been frozen and then the skin torn away.

The cold fire spread from my shoulders down along my arms, hands, and fingers. The hands shifted to cradle my breasts. I gasped as the icy-cold, tingling fire spread from my nipples down into my groin. My legs threatened to collapse beneath me as a wave of freezing heat coiled in my stomach and spread through my limbs.

I turned to face him.

Eyes glowing red in a dark silhouette outlined against roiling clouds all silver, black, and red, and shot through with jagged bolts of lightning. No features visible except for those eyes, everything else shrouded in stygian darkness. If I stayed here I'd die. But I'd scream with pleasure even as the life ran out of my body.

No.

"LEE!"

I stepped off the crumbling edge of the cliff even as the voice roared my name, nails scratching lines in my flesh as I tore away from the hands that tried to restrain me. I tumbled toward the water and unforgiving rocks below.

I—

†

I woke up, sweat plastering my hair and nightshirt to my skin. My heart drummed in my chest, a rapid-fire rhythm that took a good twenty minutes to slow into normal breathing patterns.

Ever since it happened I'd had some really shitty dreams about the fall. Dreams in which I relived the whole thing, including bouncing off the airbag and smashing into brick and concrete. This dream, however, was the first one that changed the setting and added… a second person.

It's one thing to have sexy dreams. I've had a few in the past, even some that had an element of scary to them. That element of uncertainty that can make bad boys initially attractive. Generally, though, they're not bad enough to make me jump off cliffs.

Or use the word "stygian."

I blamed the high-octane double IPAs I'd consumed the night before. My mouth felt like I'd swallowed a wad of cotton balls, which also pointed an accusing finger at the beer. I groped for the glass of water on my nightstand, still as full as it was when I'd filled it. Which would account for my dry mouth and fuzzy head.

The water was warm and stale, and tasted wonderful.

Setting the glass back on the nightstand, I snuggled back under the down comforter and did some deep breathing, trying to get my heart rate down to its normal pace. I looked around the room of my childhood, smiling at the movie posters for *Hooper* and *The Stunt Man*. Pictures of Zoe Bell doubling Lucy Lawless as Xena and Uma Thurman in *Kill Bill*. All of them autographed, too.

I totally have a girl crush on Zoe Bell.

It was both comforting and kind of scary that Sean hadn't redecorated my room during the two years I lived on my own. I was grateful that I've never gone in for Barbies, pop stars or an abundance of pink. If I had to be immersed back in my childhood and teen years, at least the posters and artwork decorating the walls weren't, say, Justin Bieber.

I picked up my iPhone and glanced at the time. It was 9:30. *Really?*

I wasn't a morning person, but I'd been trying to get up by seven ever since I'd healed. Most call times, after all, were early in the day and I wanted to make sure I could get back in that habit, once I started working again.

Sean didn't usually let me sleep in this late either, which meant he wasn't home. *That* meant he was either out on a job, or talking to someone about a job. One that probably wouldn't include me.

Before I could get a big old "feeling sorry for myself" going, my phone began vibrating and the theme from *Flash Gordon* started playing loudly.

"Flash… ah-ahhhh… he'll save every one of us…" I looked at the caller ID and didn't recognize the number. It was an 818 area code.

"Ah, what the hell," I muttered and answered it.

Not like I had anything better to do.

"Hello." I tried to sound chipper, but only succeeded in sounding kind of stoned.

"Uh, hey. Is this Lee?"

I gave an inward groan.

Randy.

How the hell did he get my number?

"How the hell did you get my number?"

Randy gave a nervous laugh. "It's on the roster."

"Ah." The roster listed all of Sean's regulars. If Randy had access to it, it meant he'd already been added or he'd probably be on it in the near future. "Okay. Why are you *calling* my number?"

"Uh, I was wondering if you'd be able to meet me for coffee later."

"Why?"

Normally I'm not such a bitch on the phone, but honestly, it's a fifty-fifty shot any time before noon unless I'm working. Plus the sleepy bunny stupids made me kinda blunt.

"I wanted to talk to you about something."

"You're not asking me out on a date, right?"

Really blunt.

Another uncomfortable laugh.

"No!" His voice shot up an octave, then came back

down. "No, I mean, I totally would, but this isn't about that. I mean…"

I yawned involuntarily and turned my head away from the receiver, tuning Randy out while he babbled on. Looked at my reflection in the dresser mirror, grimacing at the hollows under my eyes. I really needed to get better sleep, and without any fucked-up dreams.

"…so I was wondering if you'd be interested in working the film."

Huh?

That brought my attention back sharply.

"Did you say work?"

†

An hour and a half later I stood in line at Grindhouse on Rose Avenue in Venice Beach, waiting for Randy to meet me after his workout at the nearby Gold's Gym. I'd scored an excellent unmetered spot around the block on Seventh Avenue, muttered a hasty thanks to the parking gods, and gotten to the destination a good fifteen minutes before the appointed time.

Grindhouse is a local coffee house manned by grouchy hipsters with ironic facial hair. The building used to be a stable back in the day and the place has a sort of grunge vibe, as if it wants to be in Seattle back in the heyday of Nirvana. The coffee and food are both excellent, though, which goes a long way toward making up for the attitudes of the staff.

I eyeballed the selection of baked goodies in the glassed-in display racks as I waited my turn, trying to make up my mind between a scone or cinnamon streusel coffee cake. I had plenty of time to decide because the solitary person ahead of me in line—a skinny, brittle blonde in size zero jeans and a bandana top that didn't have much work to do—couldn't make up her mind either.

"Are the bagels fresh?"

"They were made this morning."

"What kind do you have?"

Instead of pointing out the names on the platters in front of her, the counter dude listed off the various bagels in tones that implied this was a matter of great importance.

"Are your coffee beans degassed before you use them?"

Degassed? Did coffee beans fart?

"They certainly are," Counter Dude beamed, pleased as punch that she'd asked.

Really? So this is what it took to get a smile out of these guys?

"Is the banana bread made with sugar or organic fruit juice for sweetener?"

"It's made with Splenda, actually."

This prompted a discussion that went on for what felt like five minutes. I might as well have not existed. My temper rising and my blood sugar dropping, I wondered if giving the woman a degassed kick to her skinny, organic butt would be worth the lawsuit. Just then she decided on a cup of black coffee and called it a day.

Counter Dude's smile disappeared when I ordered, but I didn't care. Soon I sat at a corner table and sipped an excellent mocha java, munching on a warm, freshly baked wholewheat mixed berry scone. It tasted great despite its healthful pretensions.

"Hey, Lee!"

I looked up to see Randy, freshly showered by the look and smell of things, wearing dark jeans and a tight blue T-shirt, showing off well-muscled arms and his six-pack abs. I'd worn semi-nice yoga pants and a violet tank top. In other words, pretty much what I wore when we trained, except cleaner.

Maybe I needed to try a little harder when I was out in public.

Randy didn't seem to mind. He flashed a wide smile, looking pleased to see me.

"Hey, Randy." I gave a little wave.

"I'm gonna grab a chai tea latte." He plunked his gym bag down on the seat next to me. "You want anything?"

"I'm good. Thanks, though."

He bounded off to the front counter, all eager and bouncy, catching the attention of more than one actress-slash-model. He even got half a smile from the cranky hipster barista who'd barely looked at me when I'd ordered and paid. I wondered if there was a hint of incubus in Randy's family tree. I'd always been relatively immune to that type of supernatural influence, and it would make sense, seeing all the attention he got.

Objectively, Randy was pretty cute. Just not my type. Which made it kind of fun to watch the envious looks I got when he came back to the table. We made small talk for a few minutes, most of it Randy talking about what B-list actors had been at Gold's. Typical Hollywood "who cares" bullshit, but it was less him trying to impress and more a nervous need to fill the conversational void. I waited for him to get to the point, but he didn't seem to be going there.

"So," I cut in. "Tell me about this job."

"Oh! Oh, yeah!" Randy knocked back half of his latte in one gulp and leaned forward. "So here's the deal. I got a job as stunt coordinator on a really small film. Non-union, which is kind of a bummer. Means I'll have to use an alias." He paused, looking first left and then right, as if expecting a union rep to jump out and yell *"J'accuse!"*

"A lot of union actors work non-union shows," I said. "Have you mentioned it to Sean at all?"

Randy gave an uncomfortable shrug. "I just got the job today. I'm totally gonna tell him though." He looked at me, all worried. "Do you think he'll mind?"

I shook my head. "Nah. You're just training with him at this point. You're not officially part of the KSC team yet, and it's not like you snaked a job from him."

"Cool." He let out a deep breath and took another swig of his chai latte. I could feel almost palpable waves of relief wafting off of him.

"So it sounds like this could be a good thing for you," I said in an attempt to move the conversation along.

"Yeah!" Randy brightened again. "My agent isn't totally thrilled, but she gets that this is the first chance I've had to run my own crew, even if it's a small one. A *really* small one. There are a lot of fights in the script, lots of swords. I think I can handle it. Mostly."

He paused again. I resisted the urge to grab him by the shoulders and shake, instead waiting with unusual patience while he summoned the nerve.

"I was thinking maybe you might wanna work on it, too." The words came out in a rush.

There it is.

"You want me to help train the actors, or actually choreograph the fights?"

Randy's face flushed red and I had a feeling his reply was going to piss me off.

"Could you maybe pretend to be my assistant?"

I'd been right. I almost walked out. Almost threw the rest of my mocha java in his face and told him to fuck off. But something about his embarrassed expression stopped me. He looked like a puppy that'd peed on the floor and knew it was going to get yelled at, but still hoped it'd be forgiven. Maybe even get a treat.

I clenched my jaw, gave an inward sigh. Took a long sip of my drink before answering.

"Let me get this straight," I said. "You want me to pretend I'm your assistant, and that I didn't teach you everything you know about sword fighting."

"Um… yeah."

"That it?"

"Um…"

I'd have to teach Randy to stop with the "ums" if we were going to work together.

"Spill it, Randy."

He took a deep breath and plunged ahead. "Okay. There are some female roles that'll need stunt doubling, and the budget only allows for one stuntwoman." He gave a sheepish smile. "Actually the budget only allows for me and one other stunt person. The director's already hired a bunch of actors who say they can fight."

Better and better.

"So you want me to choreograph the fights, help train these actors who may or may not know a hilt from a blade, and double an as-yet-unknown number of actresses for—" I raised an eyebrow. "How much are they paying?"

Randy mumbled something, his gaze flickering off to some point beyond my left ear. I waited until he finally looked straight at me, focusing on my eyes instead of my boobs for once. Then I leaned forward.

"Come on, Randy. How much?"

He gave a heavy sigh and ripped off the Band-Aid. "A

hundred bucks a day. Flat rate. No adjustments for stunts."

Six months ago I would have either laughed in his face or punched him for what, under normal circumstances, was an insulting offer. A hundred a day was, plainly speaking, shit for pay. Hell, SAG minimum daily rate was around nine-hundred dollars, last time I checked, and something like thirty-five hundred a week. Those numbers didn't even include the adjustments for individual stunts, which varied by the complexity and the risk involved.

Now? A hundred bucks a day was more than I'd seen since the accident. Three weeks to shoot meant at least fifteen hundred bucks, maybe more if it was six days per week instead of five. So instead of laughing, punching, walking out, or any combination of the three, I asked another question.

"What are you getting for the job?"

"I'm getting three hundred a day," Randy confessed.

Which was shit for pay, as well, especially for a stunt coordinator, and made me slightly less outraged over the amount I'd make if I took the job.

"I can totally slide you an extra fifty for any stunts you do that involve more than fight choreography. I know you're worth a lot more." He hesitated and then plunged ahead. "I just figured… I mean, I heard you wanted to work and… well, I could really use the help. Bottom line."

If anyone had told me a week ago that I'd be grateful to Randy for anything, I'd have laughed in his or her face. But unless he was lying about his own pay—and it would be easy enough for me to check—he was playing straight with me. And dammit, I really did want to work.

"I appreciate that," I said. "Anything else?"

He brightened. "I think they're paying twenty-five a day

for extras to fill out some of the scenes, like the audience watching the gladiatorial games. Stuff like that."

I shuddered and shook my head. "No thanks. Twenty-five bucks a day isn't worth the boredom. Are there any female fighting roles?"

Randy's face scrunched up in thought. It looked like it hurt. Then he shook his head.

"I don't think any of the gladiators are women. There are lots of female concubines, though."

"Swell."

Not.

"But I can talk to Rocky—that's the director—and see if he'd be open to having a girl fighter. Seems stupid not to when we're gonna have the best of the best on set, y'know?"

Irritation at the word "girl" warred with gratification at "the best of the best." I decided to take the ego boost for the moment, and worry about educating Randy at a later date. His intentions were good, and I could work with that.

"So, what do you think?" Randy eyed me hopefully.

"Three weeks, huh?"

"Well, more or less. Shooting starts a week from tomorrow, and they'll pay for a few days of training so we can work with the actors, choreograph the fights and stuff."

I blinked in surprise.

"Not a lot of pre-production time."

"Low budget," he said, shrugging as if that explained everything.

Not all films with shoestring budgets did things in a slipshod way. Some student filmmakers, for instance, spent *months* doing storyboards—planning out every move, every angle, every shot before shooting one frame of film or minute of video. The rush here didn't bode well for the finished product.

Still… it was work.

"So, you in?"

I nodded before I could change my mind. "I'm in."

Randy's face lit up, his enthusiasm lending some genuine personality and charm to those generic good looks. "Great! I'll tell Sean about it tomorrow morning."

"If he's in a good mood, he may even give you some tips."

"You think he'll mind you doing non-union work?"

I shrugged. "I doubt it, but he won't hold it against you no matter what. Sean's fair."

I spoke with an assurance I didn't actually feel. I had no idea how Sean would feel about me taking a job outside of the family. Frankly, though, I didn't care. If Sean wouldn't put me to work, I had every right to find it on my own. And I'd make sure he didn't hold anything against Randy, no matter how he felt.

"Cool," Randy said. "I'll let you know as soon as I lock down rehearsal space and a time."

Neither of us suggested the Ranch. My guess was Randy didn't want anyone around to spill the beans about which one of us was actually the expert. I didn't mind. I wanted to work and money was money, so eating a little humble pie would be worth it. Besides, last thing I needed was Seth trying to make me look bad in front of the actors.

Hell, getting paid for time away from Seth?

Priceless.

"What's the name of the movie?"

"Uh, *Steel Legions*."

I snickered. I couldn't help it.

Randy gave a sheepish grin. "Yeah, I know. Cheesy, huh?"

I downed the last of my mocha java and pushed my chair back. "I'd better get going. Let me know when we start rehearsals."

"Will do!"

I stood up, retrieving my oversized hobo bag off the back of my chair, and turned to leave.

"Hey, Lee?"

I turned back warily, really hoping he wasn't going to ask me out.

"Yeah?" I asked.

"Thanks."

Oh.

"You're welcome."

I started to leave again, then stopped. *Time to act like a gracious adult, instead of a bitchy teen.*

"Thanks for asking me."

There. That didn't hurt, did it?

Randy beamed. "This is gonna be great!"

†

Sean was more than gracious to Randy, full of advice and encouragement. I got a different response.

"So," Seth sneered at me from across the kitchen table. "You're doubling a bunch of eye-candy, choreographing the fights, and letting someone else take the credit for the work."

Sean gave him a warning glance. Seth ignored him.

"Seriously, Lee?" he persisted. "You're getting paid a hundred bucks a day for shit."

I shrugged. "It might be fun—and it's *paid*. Which is more than I can say for anything else I've done since the accident."

Sean winced. So did I when I realized how tactless I'd just been.

"Sean, I'm sorry." I reached out and put my hand on top of his. "But you know I need to *do* something, right?"

"I know, hon."

Seth gave a disgusted snort, pushed away from the table

and left the room. Sean and I both ignored him.

"And honestly," I added, "Randy really needs the help. So it's good for both of us, y'know?"

Sean nodded, but still looked unhappy. "I just hate to see you waste your talents on something this low budget. You won't even get a chance to show what you can do."

I shrugged, unwilling to argue with him.

"Small steps, right?"

CHAPTER SEVEN

When I agreed to work on *Steel Legions*, the title screamed bad eighties exploitation and the budget didn't add any confidence. What I didn't realize was the degree to which I underestimated the level of craptitude.

We're talking a depth of suck that, with a bigger budget, would be a contender for a Razzie award. *MST3K* terrible. The type of awful that requires drinking games in order to make it bearable. Except when you ended up with alcohol poisoning, it still wasn't worth it.

Where to start?

Randy and I held four training sessions the week before the shoot officially began. For lack of better location, we held them at Griffith Park. The production company—Chieftain Productions, henceforth known as Cheapo Productions—wouldn't pay for rehearsal space, so our options were limited.

Those actors who said they "knew how to fight"?

They didn't.

"I wouldn't bet on these guys in a slap fight against a five-year-old," I'd muttered to Randy as we'd watched them go through basic sword drills. He'd nodded glumly.

"If we can't whip them into shape, we're gonna end up beating out *Deathstalker III* for worst sword fight."

I just stared at him. "Not on my watch, Squid."

I'm not sure when it happened, but "Squid" had become my affectionate nickname for Randy, who no longer minded the term—as long as it came from me.

"I'm gonna try and bring in another stuntman," he said. "At least then we'll have one more who won't totally suck."

"Or you could talk the director into having one of the gladiators be a woman," I suggested sweetly. "Unless you've already done that." He got that "don't beat me, I'm just a puppy" look again, which meant he hadn't yet broached the subject.

Nevertheless, Randy and I had ironed out a decent working relationship. I did my best to pretend to defer to him in front of people, and he did his best to pretend to be in charge. In reality I handled most of the drills and gave most of the directions. I was mostly okay with it and Randy—to give him credit—treated me like a partner instead of an assistant.

By the end of the third day, the actors had actually improved to the point where maybe—just *maybe*—they'd be able to convince audiences they were gladiators. It would help if the audience was on something, mind you, but at least we could see progress.

Then primary shooting began in a now defunct YMCA gym in the industrial part of Santa Monica. The gym had closed in the late nineties and had since been used as a location for a number of film and television productions. Bits and pieces of old sets still littered the place—some fake rocks here, some scaffolding there, and piles of full trash bags no one had bothered to remove.

The concrete interior was cold, damp, and smelled like a cross between mildew and disinfectant. Didn't matter that the outside temperature was in the mid- to high-seventies. Inside it was sixty degrees, tops. Which was great for the actors doing fight scenes, but I wasn't doing enough actual fighting to keep warm. The poor concubines had to be freezing in their skimpy costumes. After the first day, most of the actors and crew took to wearing warm coats and sweaters.

Then there was the script.

The title *Steel Legions* conjured visions of robot armies, but the movie was about illegal gladiatorial games held in a secret compound, all for the amusement of the decadent rich. The production designer turned an Olympic-sized pool into a gladiatorial arena, with ancient wooden bleachers standing in for VIP seating.

The hero, a budding all American basketball star named Johnny, had been kidnapped along with his girlfriend, Betty, who would be killed if he didn't fight. Johnny juggled a busy schedule of boffing Vixenia—the evil genius behind the games—while fomenting rebellion among the fighters and saving his virginal girlfriend from the sweaty clutches of Axegard, undefeated gladiator and all-around bad guy.

Wacky hijinks ensued.

EXT – DAY – GLADIATORIAL ARENA

JOHNNY

I'll kill you, you scum!

AXEGARD

Hahahahah! You don't have the guts to kill me. But soon I will have your guts skewered on the end of my sword, while your pretty girlfriend watches. And then I will skewer her with my other sword! Hahahahah!

BETTY

Noooooooo!

The actor playing Axegard actually said "Hahahahah" when he was supposed to be laughing. His real name was Axel, and I'm pretty sure he'd insisted that his character's name be changed so he could remember it without writing it on his hand. To say that he wasn't the brightest bulb in the chandelier would be an understatement.

On top of that, he was a sadistic asshole without any concern for his fellow actors—he needed to come with a warning label.

Axel attended only one rehearsal, the last one before filming started. He actually looked pretty good when he fought, probably because his intent was real. See, he had no idea how to make a fake fight safe, nor did he seem to care. This, in turn, improved everyone else's timing—if only in the name of self-preservation.

Meanwhile, I was doubling not only Vixenia and Betty, but the concubines as well. Never mind that I was at least six inches taller than Heather—the actress playing Betty—and twenty pounds heavier than Vixenia. I ended up getting stuffed into facsimiles of their various costumes whenever any of them had to be tossed around, slapped, or punched.

At first I wondered why they even bothered. Reacting to a slap or a punch wasn't exactly rocket science, and honestly, the finished product was going to look goofy as hell with me doubling all the females in the film. Then I did a quick scene with Axel. His job was to grab one of the concubines and throw her to the floor.

Two moves.

Simple, right?

Not so with Axel. When he grabbed me, his fingers dug into my shoulders like pincers. He threw me to the ground hard enough to knock the wind out of me for a few minutes. And that was just rehearsal.

To give Randy his due, he tried to intervene.

"Uh, Axel, you don't need to use that kind of force. Lee's a stuntwoman. She can make it look real."

Axel's reply?

"It will not look good if it is not real." Axel didn't use contractions. Kind of like an alien on *Star Trek*, the original series.

"Uh, yeah, but—"

"Axel is correct," the director chimed in, cutting Randy off. "Lee, you are a professional, yes? You can handle this?" He didn't use contractions either.

I bit my tongue before I answered.

"Sure."

I did my best to ignore Axel's look of triumph. Then, when the next break came, Randy took me aside.

"You don't have to put up with that kind of abuse, Lee." I could tell he was genuinely upset on my behalf. "I mean, look at your arms." There were bruises where Axel's fingers had dug in. I just shrugged.

"These'll fade by tomorrow. I heal quickly. Just ask my doctors."

He cringed at that. "Sean would hand me my ass in a sling if he knew I'd let you get hurt on set."

"Sean would expect me to be responsible for myself in this situation," I said, becoming exasperated. "Now that I know what to expect, I'll be ready for whatever Axel throws at me."

Randy frowned, shaking his head. "It isn't right."

"No, it's not, but it's not your fault. If the director won't back us up, we either make the best of the situation or we walk." I gave him a look. "We both need the work."

Randy muttered something under his breath, but dropped it.

Then the director—a skinny Colombian with the improbable name of Rock Navida—added to the rich broth of bad. "Sweeetie," he said to each girl, in an accent as indefinable as Christopher Lambert's in *Highlander*, "I'll give you an extra twenty-five today if you show your teets in dis scene."

Since all of the concubines placed a higher price tag on their naked breasts than twenty-five bucks, the answer was always no. This didn't stop Navida from making the rounds again the next day, but he never thought to raise the price.

See, Navida was cheap. Take the size of the crew, for instance. Where most films had between five to ten minutes of end credits, *Steel Legions* might end up with thirty seconds to a minute. One production assistant, a director of photography, a first AD who also doubled as second AD, a makeup supervisor with no one to supervise, a wardrobe mistress, a set designer handling the props, as well, two stunt people, and an on-set caterer, Star Catering.

Normally craft service is the social hub on a film in between takes, kind of like the kitchen is the most popular room at most parties. On *Steel Legions*, however, craft service was the equivalent of a hot zone. Gayleen Star, owner of the company and its sole cook, only charged a dollar fifty per head. Considering the quality of the meals, she was overcharging by at least a buck forty-nine.

Rumblings of unrest among cast and crew became louder

with each meal, although some of the noise may have been our digestive tracts. Luckily there was a Taco Bell a block away. The money we spent was more than worth the time we didn't spend in the bathrooms.

†

At the beginning of the third week of shooting, Randy came to me at the end of the day and asked if I'd consider playing one of the concubines.

"You've got to be kidding me." I laughed, setting out broadswords, axes, and a couple of spears and shields in the locker room we used as a staging area, making sure they were cleaned and ready for the next morning's shoot. "I'm already doubling the heroine, the villainess, and a half-dozen slave girls."

"Concubines," Randy corrected me.

"Whatever," I snapped. "The point is, I really don't have time to play an extra on top of everything else. Besides which, I already told you I *hate* doing extra work."

"I know, I know," Randy said, his hands out in a "please don't punch me" gesture. "But it's not really extra work. You'll get a credit."

"Be still my heart," I muttered.

"Rock says if you'll be one of the concubines, he'll give you a fight in the arena."

I set the halberd down with a thump and turned to face him.

"Seriously?"

Randy nodded. "You'd be fighting Axel." He scratched his head, an embarrassed look on his face. "Rock thinks it would be good if one of the concubines refuses to have sex with him and has to fight him instead."

I gave a snort of laughter. "Finally, a note of realism in this piece of shit." I thought about it for a minute. "Sure, I'll do it if it means I get some screen time doing an actual fight."

"You sure? I mean, that guy's out of control. Look what he did to Jermaine. Dislocated his shoulder during their fight."

Jermaine had been one of our gladiators, now permanently out of the arena and relegated to guard duty. I think he was secretly relieved—no more fights with Axel, no more injuries. I hoped he had health insurance.

"I'll be fine," I said. Then I gave Randy a sideways glance. "I don't have to have sex with him first, though, right?"

"Jeez, no!"

"Are you blushing, Squid?"

"No!"

He totally was. It was so cute I almost forgave him. Almost.

CHAPTER EIGHT

Early the next morning I went to see the costume supervisor, an understandably grouchy woman named Cora. I say "understandably grouchy" because she was the entire costume department. She did the shopping, the fitting, and helped actors dress when needed. If that meant having to touch Axel…

Well, I sympathized.

My sympathy ran out quickly, however, when she pulled out my concubine costume. I stared at the scrap of leather in the woman's hands.

"I am not wearing this."

"It's a corset," she said with a sniff. "And it's the only thing I've got that's actually a size eight, so you're going to have to live with it."

"I've seen strippers wear bigger pasties," I retorted. Okay, maybe I was exaggerating just a little, but seriously, eight wasn't exactly the gargantuan size she was implying.

Cora gave me a flat look. "You're playing a concubine. You think you're gonna wear jeans and a T-shirt?" She thrust the corset out and I reluctantly took it from her, holding it up for a better look.

It actually wasn't too bad. Dark-brown leather with brass

buckles and straps hither and yon, little brass findings in the front for closures. An overbust style, with enough length to cover the hips midway. It looked like something a steampunk dominatrix would wear.

"Here."

Cora tossed me a pair of fishnets, a G-string, and a pair of high heels, one after the other. I caught the stockings and G-string, but let the heels tumble to the ground.

"I am *not* wearing those," I growled. "I'm supposed to do a sword fight in this costume, and I'm not being nearly paid enough to cater to some adolescent wet dream fantasy, and maybe break an ankle in the process."

Cora shot me a look, but reached back into a pile of shoes and pulled out a pair of ankle boots that looked like they'd escaped from the same Jules Verne fantasy as my corset. Lots of buckles and straps and such. The heels, however, were thick, stacked, and only two inches high. There was also decent traction on the sole.

I could fight in those.

"Okay," I said grudgingly. "These'll do."

"Great," she said. "So glad you approve of them."

I took the hint and left.

†

Later that morning I had to do a scene with the gladiators and other concubines. It took place in the gladiators' quarters after combat, a sort of après bloodshed celebration involving wine and women. Navida was determined to make the most of what he saw as an orgy scene, even without bare breasts.

The other concubines were already paired with their gladiator dates by the time I got on set, and I thought I'd lucked out when I was paired with Chas, a ruggedly handsome blond actor in his twenties with an easy-going attitude. One of the ones who'd been fun to work with during the training sessions.

The makeup gal wandered around and indiscriminately spritzed fake sweat on gladiators and concubines alike. Lights and camera angles were set. Then Navida arrived on set and took one look at the various pairings.

"No, no. Dis is no good."

All of the girls were shuffled around until he was satisfied. To my quiet horror, I was paired with Axel right off the bat.

"See, this one," Navida explained, "she wears black leather. She is dangerous. This will be a contrast when Axel takes Johnny's virginal girlfriend, see?"

All I saw was that I had to spend the next few hours cuddling up to a man who didn't need to be spritzed with fake sweat. He generated his own supply and evidently didn't believe in deodorant. Chas ended up with a blonde concubine in a pink teddy because Navida thought he would choose another blonde.

"And they are both tall, too," Navida added. "Their children will be superior specimens."

Okay, he didn't actually say that last part, but he was thinking it.

The blonde gave me a sympathetic look when she took my place. I tried not to hate her even though she was slender, busty, gorgeous, and obviously not a bitch. Then when I took my place next to Axel, he jerked me down onto his lap.

"Leather makes me hard," he said, and he shoved his hand down the front of my corset. In keeping with my dangerous image, I drove my elbow back into his solar plexus.

It went downhill from there.

†

By the time noon rolled around my blood sugar was

dangerously low. If I had to stand one more minute of Axel groping my butt and adlibbing lines like "Your ass is like a ripe peach, hahahah!", something was gonna snap. Possibly Axel's wandering hand.

When we filmed the scene where my character refuses to cooperate, my acting was probably the most realistic in the film so far.

"If you don't want to fuck, then you want to die," Axegard growled. Given the choice in real life, I would totally take my chances in the arena, so it was a snap to deliver the response.

"I would rather die than let you touch me again." I had to stop myself from adding, "But odds are good that I'll kick your ass, douchebag."

Then we broke for lunch.

I hurried to the catering area, a mirrored room formerly used for classes. Gayleen stood on the other side of the table, serving spoon in hand and a glower on her face.

I watched in cautious anticipation as she lifted the lid to reveal the day's lunch offering—stuffed cabbage.

Little white globules of fat clung to shiny purple cabbage leaves that held what looked—and smelled —like dog food. They were lined up neatly in the heated metal catering trays, surrounded by a reddish swamp of tomato sauce and grease. Steam rose up, pooling across the top of the dishes like an alien fog.

"And you let it on the ship," I muttered under my breath.

Someone behind me gave an indelicate snort of laughter. I turned to find the pink lace blonde next to me in line. She grinned at me and mouthed, "Good one." Gayleen plopped one of the fledgling aliens on my plate before I had a chance to do more than smile in response.

I did my best to keep from breathing until I'd left the room and dumped the plate into the nearest trash can. I

found Randy and made him go—gladiatorial garb and all—
to the Taco Bell. After lunch we were supposed to film the
fight between me and Axel, and I was determined to do it
with stable blood sugar levels.

Randy returned with our lunch and I fell on the bag
with a heartfelt thanks. While I dug into the first of four
crunchy tacos, leaning against a bag of weapons, he chowed
down on his own monster of a burrito, all the while casting
surreptitious glances at my fishnet-clad legs.

I just ignored it. After dealing with Axel, Randy's inability
to stop checking me out seemed harmless, especially since I
knew he had a genuine crush on me. I tried to discourage it
as gently as possible, but at least it wasn't offensive.

"Concubine in black leather! On set, please!" It was Aaron,
the AD, and his voice echoed through the building, finding
its way through the halls to our room. I scarfed the remaining
tacos in record time, gritted my teeth, shot an admittedly
undeserved glare in poor Randy's direction, and stalked out
down a dank hallway.

Making my way down a flight of crumbling cement stairs,
I entered what used to be the pool, now a gloriously tacky
gladiatorial arena. The production designer had made the
most of a roll of cut-rate gold lame, by way of set dressing.
Navida, dressed in tight black pants and a form-fitting,
V-neck T-shirt, stood in the empty shallow end of the pool.
Don't get me started on cheap symbolism.

"Ah, there you are!" he exclaimed when he saw me. "My
leather girl!"

Leather girl?

That was just so wrong on *so* many levels. If he hadn't
been the man more or less in charge of my paycheck, I
would have killed him by now.

"You are ready for your fight, yes?"

"That's what you're paying me for, yes." I tried to smile, but my face didn't want to cooperate. Navida didn't notice.

"This is good!" He put an arm around my shoulders, long fingers casually draping over my collarbone, fingertips grazing the top of my right breast. "I see this as a short fight. A woman who is willing to risk her life to win her freedom. She wins? She goes free. If she loses—"

"She doesn't have to sleep with Axegard," I said sweetly. "How short a fight are we talking?"

"It depends." His fingers snaked down a little further. My eyes narrowed. I knew what he was doing, the weasel.

"You see, she is only a concubine. She is not a fighter. Axegard, he is a gladiator. His pride, it is wounded. He will show her no mercy. She is terrified. The fight, it would not last long. Maybe two or three moves at most."

Oh, hell no, I thought. I wasn't going to have worn this stupid costume and put up with Axel pawing me, just to end up with "two cuts and I'm dead" on screen.

"Yes, but she's desperate," I challenged him. "And who's to say what this woman did before becoming a concubine. Maybe she was a martial artist."

Navida nodded thoughtfully—or at least with a good facsimile of it. "This might be so," he said, like someone attempting a half-assed Dothraki imitation.

"Besides," I pressed, "don't you think his anger and wounded pride would make him want to draw the fight out? Female viewers would appreciate seeing a woman hold her own before watching her die." Okay, most female viewers would actually prefer to see my character kill Axegard, but I didn't think Navida would be open to a rewrite.

Besides, Johnny had to kill Axegard because of the male ego cliché that ruled this movie. I wasn't quite sure where sleeping with the villainess Vixenia fit into the whole thing, though.

Navida nodded again, his brow furrowed and mouth pursed as if thinking really, really hard. His index and middle fingers were about two inches from nipple territory. He had about a half inch to go before I snapped those fingers and slapped his face.

Luckily for Navida's fingers—and my continued employment—Randy showed up on set at that moment. He had a bunch of weapons in his arms, including a couple of aluminum broadswords that I'd borrowed from Katz's stash the night before. I'd sneak them back into the stash when the shoot was over.

"Need a hand?" I asked brightly, sliding out from under Navida's questing arm to help Randy.

Deprived of his prize, Navida scowled at me and asked, "How will you have time to choreograph a fight between you and Axel? I have seen the troubles our experienced actors have with these fights."

I raised an eyebrow, but kept my tone level.

"I'm an experienced fighter. Besides, Randy and I choreographed all the fights, so I already know it." It was bullshit, but it sounded good.

"Yes, but does Axel have time to learn a new fight? He is good, yes. Very good, but he is only human."

I didn't bother arguing either of those points.

"He doesn't have to learn a new one. We'll do the one he was supposed to do with Jermaine."

Navida considered my logic. "I think the concubine would be scared and maybe not fight so well."

"I think she'd be scared and pissed off and fighting for

dear life," I replied with what I thought was admirable calm. What I really wanted to do was pick the idiot up by his collar and shake his skinny ass until he stopped being such a sexist asshole, but I wasn't willing to make that kind of time commitment.

If only he'd make up his goddamned mind.

"As stunt coordinator, I'd like to see this fight in the finished movie," Randy said unexpectedly. "It'd be a shame to waste the choreography." I shot him a look of surprised gratitude. While I knew he wouldn't stand in my way, I hadn't expected him to actually back me up.

Navida pursed his lips again and made a little scoffing noise that sounded like a half-hearted fart.

Randy narrowed his eyes, looking less like a puppy and more like a wolf for the first time since I'd met him. His corneas went from green to gold in a flash, and then back again in the space of seconds.

Lycanthrope, I thought. How did I not notice this before?

There was more to Randy than met the eye.

"Yes, then," Navida said, taking a small, almost unconscious step away from his stunt coordinator. "We will try this—but if you are hurt when you fight with Axel, I cannot be responsible."

"She won't get hurt," Randy said. "And I guarantee you'll get one hell of a fight on film, too. Probably the best one you'll have."

"I think this will be a good fight, too."

The voice came from the entrance, and we turned to see Axel standing there, all oiled up and ready to gladiate. He could move quietly for someone his size.

"You think you can handle the heat, little girl?" he added. He looked me up and down in a way that would have gotten him kicked out of the Ranch so quickly he never would have known whose boot did the kicking.

"You ready to rehearse?" I kept my tone neutral.

"I am ready for more than that, little girl."

I rolled my eyes. "Let's see if you can keep up with the choreography first."

†

Axel did his best to beat me into the ground with his muscles, but I'd learned long ago how to deflect someone trying to overpower me using strength alone, by using their own momentum against them. Sean had put me in judo and aikido classes, along with several different karate styles and even krav maga.

I resisted the temptation to use one of the more aggressive disciplines on the jerk, instead either slipping to the side or underneath his reach when he tried to grapple, without letting him establish a solid grip on me.

Jermaine had a year or so of aikido under his belt, so we'd put those moves in the original choreography. Seeing how that had ended for Jermaine, however, I stayed on my toes. I knew Axel would do his best to hurt me—and probably feel me up—just to prove that he could.

By the end of the hour-long rehearsal, I was tired but unhurt. Axel was winded and more than a little pissed off.

"She fights too hard," he said, sounding like a sulky Germanic five-year-old.

"But this looks good," Navida declared with genuine enthusiasm. "My leather girl, she can fight! It will make her defeat even more tragic, yes?"

Randy and I exchanged quietly triumphant looks.

"Sure," I said.

†

"You sure you're okay for this fight?"

Randy paced back and forth like a caged wolf. Funny, but now that I'd noticed the fluctuation in his eye color, other subtle signs suddenly became obvious. He was either a beta wolf or something not quite as fierce, like a fox. I'd ask him later, if and when he ended up in the Katz inner circle.

"I'll be fine," I reassured him. "Just like you told Navida, okay?"

I was all dolled up in my corset, fishnets, and boots, hair pulled back into a tight braid. I had my amulet safely tucked away in a pouch around my ankle and was ready to kick some Axel ass. Even if I had to die—on film—to do it.

"Let's just get this damned fight on film," I said.

"Digital video," Randy replied.

"It's a figure of speech, Squid."

"Sorry." He grabbed me by the arm as I headed toward the door. "Just be careful, okay?"

I stopped, looking at him.

"You know I can handle this, right?"

"I know," Randy said, "but I don't trust him. He wants to hurt you. And Rock's too stupid to do anything about it."

"Rock has a testosterone crush on Axel."

"I don't think that's actually a thing," Randy said doubtfully.

I patted him on one cheek. "You're cute, but kinda naive." He blushed. I shook my head and gave him a one-armed hug. "Seriously, I'll be fine, okay?"

"Yeah. Okay." Randy hugged me back, using both arms.

"C'mon," I said, stepping away. "Let's shoot this puppy."

CHAPTER NINE

"Cut!" Navida yelled.

He glared at Randy, who'd shouted for him to pause after Axel slammed his blade into my forearm hard enough to make me drop my sword. Then he looked at me and shook his head sadly.

"My leather girl, you must get this correct on the next take. We are running out of time. Maybe this fight, it is too much for you after all."

I picked myself up off the ground where I'd landed for the third time in as many takes, bent the arm, and flexed my hand a couple of times to make sure nothing was broken, then glared up at Axel with narrowed eyes.

"You missed your parry, little girl," he said with a nasty grin.

"You cut instead of parrying," I said between gritted teeth. "Try sticking to the choreography."

Axel laughed, not bothering to deny it. I knew he'd done it on purpose, and that was that.

He was *so* going down.

"Lee, you okay?"

Axel strode over to the sidelines to get a bottle of water as Randy hurried over to my side.

"I'll live," I said, watching Axel's retreating form. "He might not."

"Look," Randy said. "He's fucked up on purpose three times. If we'd gone for steel instead of aluminum blades for this fight, or if you hadn't dropped your arm so quickly when you saw he was going for a cut there..." He trailed off and shook his head. "Hell, you'd be heading for the ER about now."

I looked at him suspiciously. "You're not thinking of calling it off, are you?"

He didn't answer.

"Randy, you can't!"

"I'm not gonna risk your health, or my reputation," he growled. "This piece of shit film isn't worth it, okay?"

Did he really have to find his inner alpha now, fer crissake?

I grabbed his arm before he could walk away.

"Randy, listen to me." I lowered my voice, but not the intensity. "I've worked my ass off on this film, doubling everyone with boobs, for less than minimal pay. Rock calls me his 'leather girl.' You have no idea how that makes my skin crawl. In order to get him to even agree to let me do an actual fight, I had to spend *hours* getting groped by Axel. I want this fight. I *need* this fight. If you call it off, I'll have to kill you."

"Lee, I—"

I held up a hand.

"That asshole wants nothing more than to prove I can't handle it because his ego is involved, and I'll be damned if I give him the satisfaction."

Randy looked at me. His eyes shifted colors again. I stared him down until they returned to their normal shade and we'd established who was boss.

"Are you sure?"

"Oh, yes. Quite sure." I straightened the bodice of my corset and gave my sword a fancy flourish just because I could.

He gave a deep sigh and then nodded. "Okay. But let's get it in the can this next take."

I grinned at him. "It's digital video, Squid."

He grinned back. "Figure of speech."

We exchanged a fist bump and waited for Axel to finish his water break. Most of the cast had been assembled because Rock thought Vixenia would want to make an example of my character, for daring to defy her will. It was kind of awesome because I'm pretty sure that all the actors *and* their characters were rooting for the concubine in leather, and not Axegard.

The cameras were ready to roll, or whatever the video equivalent would be.

"You ready to lose again, little girl?"

I looked up to see Axel, all six foot whatever of him, standing in front of me, leering at my cleavage. I just smiled and nodded, having left my list of pithy one-liners at home.

Everyone got into place. Megan, the makeup gal, came trotting out to blot the shine off my face. I smiled ruefully.

"You know I'll start sweating as soon as the fight starts."

"You'll look great when you start, though."

She went over to needlessly spritz Axel with fake sweat. The production assistant-slash-script supervisor held the clapperboard in front of the main camera.

"You are ready?" Navida called to me and Axel.

We both nodded.

"Axel and concubine fight, take four!"

"You ready to die, bitch?"

"I'd rather die than have you touch me again."

Axel charged, swinging his broadsword down toward my head without controlling the momentum or using safe distance. I parried, knowing it was coming and bracing for the impact, which I felt all the way to my toes. I swept his blade to the side, slicing toward his midsection with a speed he didn't expect. He barely evaded the cut, even though it was choreographed, stumbling backward with a surprised grunt.

I took advantage of the moment and attacked with a series of cuts that sent Axel back-peddling, barely making his own parries. He wouldn't have made them at all if he hadn't been so familiar with the choreography. I had to give him points for that.

Axel hit the side of the pool, hard. He rebounded with a flurry of blows that sent me reeling backward, arms flinching under the impact. At least he stuck to the moves, but if he hadn't been pulling any punches in the previous takes, now he was hammering me with all of his strength.

I fell to the ground, parrying yet another blow that came in aimed straight at my head. I mean, straight at my fucking head.

This asshat has a real problem with rejection.

I caught the edge of Axel's broadsword in a clean parry. The next move was supposed to be another blow from him, then my arms giving out all weak and quivering.

Cue one dead concubine.

Axel swung down in another cut to my head, using all of his considerable strength. Instead of my arms going all wimpy, I parried the blow, threw it off to the side and delivered a pommel to his solar plexus. Hard, fast, and without mercy. Then I rolled out of the way and got to my feet as he fell forward onto his knees, gasping for air.

"I will *not* be yours," I said in my best theatrical tones.

A round of applause started. I'm not sure who started it. Maybe the other concubines. Maybe the makeup gal. Whatever, in a short time the entire room echoed with the sound of clapping and cheers. Navida looked like he didn't know whether to be pissed off or pleased.

Either way, it was totally worth it.

I sketched a little bow and walked off set.

Randy caught up with me as I reached our hidey-hole.

"Oh my God, Lee, that was amazing," he enthused as he followed me inside.

I shot him a sideways glance. "So you're not mad at me?"

"Hell, no. If you hadn't taken Axel down, I was gonna have to do something after the way he went after you. You'd have been seriously hurt if you weren't so good at what you do."

I gave a rueful smile. "If I weren't good at the fights, he wouldn't have felt the need to prove something. Of course, it would've helped if I'd slept with him, but then I'd have to kill myself."

I sat down, unzipping my boots and pulling them off.

"Did Rock like the new ending?"

Randy shrugged. "I didn't ask."

"Well, if he wants to reshoot the whole thing he can pay me a shitload more than a hundred bucks a day."

"Yeah, I don't think that'll happen."

I tossed the boots into a corner, loosened the lacings on my corset so I could take a full breath, and retrieved my amulet from its pouch.

"So you think he'll fire me?" I asked, slipping the leather thong around my neck.

"I doubt it." Randy tried manfully not to watch as I pulled an extra-long tank top on over the corset before opening the clasps in front and letting it drop to the floor. "I mean, there are only three days of shooting left, and we, uh…"

He trailed off as I started to pull off my fishnets. I took pity on him and went behind one of the standing lockers before shucking my stockings and shimmying into a pair of jeans.

"You were saying?"

"Oh, yeah. We still need to get the scene where you double Vixenia driving during the chase scene. It's not like there's time to find anyone else."

I gave a non-committal grunt and slipped into purple Converse high-tops.

"But we're done for today, right?"

Randy looked at his iPhone. "Yeah, it's nearly eight. They're getting a couple more bits with Vixenia on her throne, but you're good to go."

Since rush hour was over I could drive up the Pacific Coast Highway and take the back way home. I had great night vision, so the twisty roads leading up and over the Santa Monica Mountains would be a snap.

"Awesome," I sighed. "I am so ready to have a beer and get some sleep."

Then I looked around at the weapons scattered on the floor and benches and heaved another sigh. Randy caught my glance and shook his head.

"Uh-uh. I'll take care of everything."

"Really?"

"Really. Get some sleep, okay? We're off tomorrow, so I'll see you Monday out in Little Rock."

"Promise you'll clean the blades and not just dump 'em in the bags?"

"Promise."

I gave Randy a spontaneous bear hug, surprising us both.

"You're not so bad after all, Squid."

I left before he could embarrass either of us by saying something mushy. But it was nice discovering someone you thought was an immature douche was just immature.

Walking upstairs and through the defunct gym, I headed toward the back exit and the parking lot as the sun's last rays flickered through sealed skylights. The hallway leading out was dim and kinda creepy, especially since everyone else was still downstairs.

I passed by the upstairs restrooms, then retraced my steps to the women's room. After all, I had a long drive ahead of me, even though rush hour traffic had passed.

After I did my business, I splashed cold water on my face, patting it dry with my T-shirt as there were no paper towels in the dispenser. I looked tired and I had a faint red mark on one cheek where Axel had "accidentally" smacked me with his forearm during rehearsal. The bruise on my forearm was now a nice shade of green, blending into purple, with a knot in the center. A nice reminder of what I'd put up with to do my job.

I had to wonder how much of this type of crap I'd avoided being part of Sean's inner circle for all these years, or if I'd just gotten exceptionally unlucky with *Steel Legions* and Axel.

At least Axel has a bruise or two of his own to show off from our last take. The thought made me feel distinctly unprofessional, which pissed me off because it hadn't been my fault. Well, actually it had. I'd changed the choreography and deliberately slammed the jerk, but he'd practically *begged* me to teach him a lesson.

Ah well.

Picking up my bag, I left the bathroom.

And walked straight into Axel.

CHAPTER TEN

For a moment, I assumed that Axel had just needed to use the men's room. So I just said, "Excuse me," and walked past him.

Or tried to.

He grabbed my arm, yanked me back, and leered at me.

"If you don't want to fight fair, then we can do something else."

Fight fair?

"Oh, you have *got* to be kidding." I tried to pull away, and his fingers dug into my bicep like chunks of stone. A brief image of the Thing from *Fantastic Four* flashed into my mind.

"You wanna let go of me now, or I'm gonna kick the shit out of you," I growled.

Where the hell did that *come from?* Definitely not the brightest thing to say, considering the circumstances. And not surprisingly, he didn't let go.

Instead Axel shoved me back against the wall, holding me there with his forearms against my shoulders, his body pressed up against mine. The smell of body odor was inescapable.

The worst part? My struggles were turning him on.

Axel grabbed my jaw, hard, to hold my head in place

while he mashed his mouth against mine in the most un-erotic and painful kiss I could remember. Harder is not better, especially when someone's teeth are grinding into your lips. He finally lifted his head and smirked at me.

"You know you want it."

Being mauled was bad enough. Being forced to listen to bad clichés at the same time?

So not happening.

I should have been scared. Any normal person would have been screaming for help at that point, but my fight-or-flight instinct kicked over into fight without hesitation.

My bag still clutched tightly in my right hand, I swung it up and around, hitting him in the kidneys as hard as I could. He gave a surprised grunt of pain and let go of me. I should have left it at that and hightailed it out of there, but fueled by self-righteous anger, I swung out again with the bag and followed that with a knee aimed at his groin. The bag glanced smartly off his chin, but he easily blocked my knee with one hand and took advantage of the moment to grab both my wrists and slam me back against the wall.

The bag went flying, and the back of my neck started itching.

WTF?

"Stupid bitch!" He punctuated his words by slamming me against the wall again. His skin darkened, a rich crimson suffusing his face, neck, and arms. Not just a flush of anger, but actual crimson, as if Ted Turner decided to colorize him. Veins stood out on his temples, pulsing and undulating like worms crawled under his skin. Blunt points bulged out on either side of his forehead, stretching the skin without quite breaking it.

Navida had been wrong. Axel was definitely *not* human.

He let go of my wrists and grabbed my shoulders, lifting me off the ground so that my feet dangled in the air, and slammed me against the wall yet again, pressing his groin into mine so I could feel his arousal, which was larger than it should have been.

A weird and powerful jolt of energy surged through my body. Like someone had thrust a lightning rod at the base of my skull and lightning had hit with a vengeance. The back of my neck itched so badly it felt like fire ants. Fury swept over me like a vengeful wind and I suddenly knew I could win.

I shoved my hands against Axel's pecs and pushed, treasuring the surprise on his face as he stumbled back a step and released his grip on my shoulders.

"In what country," I demanded, "is this considered *foreplay*?"

I kneed him in his freakishly substantial groin. He didn't expect it this time around. When he doubled over, I slammed my elbow against his temple, hitting that soft sweet spot just right. Axel hit the ground face-first with a satisfying *crunch*, one that hopefully injured his manly bits.

More energy surged through me, the King Kong of adrenaline rushes. I felt invincible. I had to stop myself from kicking him in the face. Part of me, a very dark part, wanted to feel his jaw break, or even better, find a blunt object and smash his skull in.

I could kill him, I thought. *I should kill him. People would thank me.* But I held the impulse back by sheer will and common sense. No way I was gonna let this fucker send me to jail.

So I stood over his prone body, feeling an almost irresistible urge to beat my chest and give a primal yell, like Tarzan or Arnold in *Predator*.

Oh, the hell with it.

I let the yell come roaring out, a sound of ferocious triumph that echoed up and down the hallway. I did not, however, beat my chest.

"Holy shit, are you okay?"

I whirled around to see the blonde in the pink teddy, now dressed in street clothes, hurrying up the hallway toward me. Megan, the makeup gal, was close behind her.

"I'm good," I said.

I took a step or two away from Axel's prone body, then suddenly staggered, clutching the wall for support as the energy surge vanished in as big a hurry as it had arrived.

Megan and the blonde pulled me away from the wall toward the back door, stopping only so Megan could scoop up my bag. My last glimpse of Axel was of him lying on the floor where I'd left him, a confused look on his unconscious face. You could almost see the thought balloon, *"Where girl go?"* along with chirping birds.

"Are you okay?" the blonde said again. She looked me up and down, then glared back at Axel as we went out the door. "Fucking Priaptic demon," she muttered just loudly enough for me to hear.

Priaptic demon?

The door closed behind us with a metallic clunk.

"Check her head for lumps," Megan instructed. "She may have a concussion."

"Seriously, I'm fine," I assured her, even though I still felt kind of dizzy. "My car's the Saturn over there. If we could just—"

"You *cannot* be fine," Megan said with equal parts concern and exasperation. "That jerk was tossing you against the wall like a racquetball! I mean, you're probably experiencing both delayed shock and guilt transference."

What?

"No, really, I'm—"

"That's when the victim of an assault reacts by blaming herself in some way for the attack."

"I'm not—"

"It wasn't your fault. Just cry and let it out. Society's to blame, you know, because—"

I raised a hand. "Okay, *stop*."

Megan did.

"I don't feel guilty," I said earnestly. "In fact, I'd say my only regret is not smashing the asshat's head in."

There was a brief silence as Megan processed this new information.

"Oh." Another pause while she switched lanes in her brain. "Oh. Well… that's a good thing."

"With a tire iron," I added helpfully.

"That's a very healthy reaction."

"With spikes on it."

"That's—"

"Kind of homicidal, if you ask me," the blonde cut in. I smiled and nodded.

"Yup."

"Well, yes," Megan said a little nervously. "Not that there's anything wrong with it, under the circumstances, of course!"

"The only reason I didn't smash his head in," I added, "is because Axel still has scenes to finish. And I doubt Rock would pay for reshoots with a different actor. Gotta be professional, y'know?"

That shut Megan right up. The blonde took pity on her.

"Maybe you could grab Lee some water or a soda?"

Megan nodded eagerly. "Sure! I'll be right back." She set

my bag down by my feet. I reached out and grabbed her by the hand.

"Don't tell anyone what happened, okay?" I said.

"You don't want me to get Randy?"

"No. I don't want Randy to lose his job, which'll happen if he tries to beat the shit out of Axel. Plus I don't know if he'd win or not, so let's just leave him out of it."

"But we have to tell Rock what happened."

I shook my head. "Rock comes out here and sees his star lying on the ground, I'm not gonna get any sympathy. Hopefully Axel's learned his lesson." Megan looked dubious, but nodded and disappeared back into the building.

I picked up my bag and took a step toward my car. Sweat sprung up on my forehead and I knew if I didn't sit down, I'd fall down. As the parking lot and surrounding buildings swayed side to side, I sat down on the asphalt and dropped my head onto my knees.

The blonde sat next to me.

"You okay?"

"Will be."

I waited until things stopped moving, hoping Axel didn't revive and come looking for me in the meantime. Took a few deep breaths, then looked at the blonde.

"I'm kind of embarrassed because you know my name and I don't know yours."

She smiled, a big, genuine smile showing lots of—but not too many—white teeth. "Eden. Eden Carmel." She pronounced "Carmel" with the emphasis on the second syllable, like the town Carmel by the Sea, and not like the confection. "And I just know your first name."

I held out my hand. "Lee Striga. Nice to meet you."

We shook hands.

"You kicked some major ass in there," she said. "On set and just now. Watching Axel get taken down twice, it was all sorts of awesome." She had a great voice. Well-modulated, a little smoky without being rough. She sounded like an adult instead of someone stuck in her pre-teens, a failing for a lot of actresses these days.

"It felt pretty awesome doing it, gotta say," I admitted. "I'm not sure how I managed it the second time around, though."

"Maybe it was, like, when a mom lifts a car to save her kid or something like that," Eden suggested.

"Maybe." It was as good a theory as any.

Another brief pause.

"So," I said. "Priaptic demon, huh?"

Eden shot me a sideways look. "You heard that, huh?"

"Yup."

"You don't seem surprised or anything."

"Nah. I come from a background that's pretty much 'there's more to heaven and earth, Horatio.'"

She nodded. "Me, too."

Another beat of silence before I spoke again.

"So priaptic… is that, like, a demon with a permanent erection?"

Eden laughed. "Something like that. I mean, they don't have erections twenty-four seven, but it takes very little stimulus to get things up and running. Think of them as the frat boys of the netherworld. Axel's one of the worst, even though he's only a half-blood. He's so annoying that the succubae have put out a restraining order against him."

"Seriously?"

Eden nodded.

"Wow, and here I thought he was just a horny creep."

"He totally is," she said, nodding. "He's just a horny creep on demon steroids."

I shook my head in disgust. "Who the hell thought it was a good idea to cast him in the role of a rapist?"

"He probably came cheap."

The double entendre, intentional or not, made me snort.

"Plus," she continued, "I don't think Rock has a clue that any of his actors or crew are anything but human."

"He hasn't... Axel didn't pull this shit on any of you, did he?"

Eden shook her head. "No. He usually behaves himself on set. Just too much rough stuff during the scenes. You have no idea how grateful all of the actresses are that you're on the film."

"That's what Rock's almost paying me for."

She grinned, then suddenly snapped her fingers.

"Hey, I know this little bar on the Venice Beach boardwalk that's open late, plus I know the bartender. He gives me great deals."

She smiled happily without any hint of innuendo and yet still managed to come across as totally sexy, sort of a cross between a naive Disney princess and a succubus. I thought about her offer. We were already in Santa Monica, and it'd be a quick drive. I could chill out and let the adrenaline fade out naturally.

Besides, when was the last time I actually went out with someone for drinks? I really couldn't remember. As far as I knew, if I'd had any female friends before the fall, they'd faded away during my recovery. So this would be a welcome change.

"Sure," I said. "I'd love to."

Eden's smile widened. "Great! I'll text Megan and tell her we're heading out, so she doesn't have to come back upstairs."

"Would she want to go?"

"I doubt it. She's still got at least another couple of hours left, and she's an early bird." She pulled an iPhone in a rose-pink case out of her jeans pocket. "Hey," she said into the phone. "We're heading out now just in case Axel wakes up cranky, so forget the water. Good luck keeping everyone pretty!"

She looked at the screen. "What the fuck, Siri? I said 'pretty,' not 'petty.'"

She fiddled with corrections, hit "send," and then turned her attention back to me with smile worthy of a toothpaste ad. "If you can find parking on Rose or on Main Street thereabouts, that'd be perfect. The bar's called Ocean's End and it's a little hole in the wall between On the Waterfront and the bike rental place. Easy to miss if you don't know it's there, so meet me at On the Waterfront."

"That sounds great," I said, and I meant it.

CHAPTER ELEVEN

I lucked into metered parking on Rose Avenue just east of Main Street itself, the meter thankfully unenforced after 6 P.M. I'd talked nice to the parking gods on my way to Venice, and whichever one was on duty paid attention. I left a Hershey's Kiss on the lip of the parking meter. I had yet to find a deity that didn't like chocolate.

I grabbed my old leather bomber jacket out of the trunk for protection against the cool breeze blowing in off the ocean. Such a change from the warm dusty winds out at the Ranch.

People walked past in small groups, mostly young techies out to spend some of their hefty paychecks on craft beer and good wine on Main Street or Abbott Kinney. There were still some old-school locals living in Venice, but a lot had been forced out by rising rents after Google moved into the neighborhood. I'd so love to live out here, but it was out of my price range. Then again, a cardboard box on the boardwalk was currently more than I could afford.

The back of my neck itched again, and I resisted the urge to scratch back there. Of all the scars I'd gotten in the accident, that one annoyed me the most. The others had finally stopped itching once that part of the healing process finished. Why this one couldn't get with the program, I did not know.

Rose Avenue itself was relatively quiet as I walked toward the boardwalk, with a few rowdy locals drinking out on balconies, but their conversations and other sounds were oddly muffled. The air seemed heavy, as if a storm was building, but no clouds appeared in the night sky. For no particular reason, I felt isolated and yet vulnerable.

Was I being followed?

Red eyes, burning with hate and lust...

Looking around, I drew my bomber jacket closed and zipped it shut. I wasn't normally shy about showing some cleavage, but after my freaky-ass dreams, the incident in the back yard, and half-demon Axel McRapey, I didn't want to call any attention to myself.

A few more steps... then vision suddenly split in two. I stopped and shook my head in confusion, immediately regretting the movement when a wave of gut-churning dizziness hit. Reaching out for a nearby pole, I missed it on the first try, my fingers going through its ghost image. I managed to grab the real thing on my second try and clung to it, waiting for the wave of dizziness to pass and fighting not to throw up then and there.

Roaring filled my ears and I slid down the pole like a really crappy stripper, folding over on myself when I reached bottom. I shut my eyes, willing the world to stop spinning.

So much for staying inconspicuous.

"Miss, are you okay?"

A worried voice spoke next to me. A female voice, older maybe, but I couldn't answer. Couldn't shake my head—if I moved or even opened my mouth, I'd throw up. I just knew it. All I could do was keep my head down on my knees, both hands clutching the metal pole in front of me. I wondered distantly if this was a delayed reaction to my encounter with Axel, or if it had to do with the accident.

It's not a tumor, I thought involuntarily, hearing Arnold's voice in my mind. I giggled, then choked back the bile that rose in my throat. My chest tightened, my throat constricted, and I gasped for air.

A cool hand rested on the back of my neck.

"Just breathe," the voice said gently. Suddenly everything loosened up. The spins and nausea seemed to retreat away from the soothing fingers gently rubbing my neck.

"Breathe," she repeated.

I did, inhaling slowly and deeply, letting the chill ocean air fill my lungs and clear my head.

"Thanks," I said faintly once I knew I could talk.

"You're welcome." Her voice came from a distance. The touch on the back of my neck vanished. Oddly, I also smelled the faintest hint of chocolate.

Huh?

I opened my eyes, relieved to see only one pole in front of me, instead of two. Sounds carried clearly again, a dozen conversations vying for my attention. The aura of menace, that sense of being watched...

Gone.

I looked around for my Good Samaritan, but the only person within ten feet of me was a kid in board shorts and a hoodie, carrying a skateboard under one arm and a six-pack of Coors in the other hand.

Huh.

As I carefully stood up, I noticed a crumpled piece of silver foil by one foot, a little strip of white paper sticking out of one end. I picked it up, then looked down Rose, across Main Street where I'd parked my car. I had a feeling if I went back there, the chocolate would have vanished.

"Thank you," I mouthed.

"*You're welcome…*"

The soft reply might have been a whisper on the breeze.

I'm totally stocking up on Hershey's Kisses, I thought. With that, I resumed my walk toward the beach.

†

There was a time back when Venice wasn't so gentrified. When boardwalk commerce had mainly consisted of local artists, fortune tellers, and the street performers doing their shows and passing the hat. There'd been a few restaurants and permanent storefronts on the east side, but nothing like what it had become.

Mind you, I loved Venice Beach and the boardwalk, even though it could be a total crowded, tourist-filled circus on hot summer days. The west side of the walk was still the territory of street vendors and performers. Mimes, musicians, and jugglers took spots in between tarot card and palm readers. Scattered among those were dozens of arts and crafts booths, and way more temporary tattoo stands than necessary.

The east side was more like a bizarre strip mall, with at least half a dozen T-shirt stores, along with shops selling lots of cool imported stuff like jewelry, clothing, shoes, and more. There were medical marijuana dispensaries, skate and surf shops, restaurants and bars. If henna tats were too tame, there were plenty of actual tattoo parlors.

The stores and vendors had closed up shop around six, but there was still plenty of foot traffic what with the bars and restaurants. A relatively new brew pub sat on the corner of Rose and Ocean Front Walk, crowded inside and out. I couldn't remember what it had replaced. Stores and restaurants came and went from year to year.

On the Waterfront was hopping, most of its outdoor seating taken. The inside looked similarly packed. The beer garden was a sea of tables and bodies, the wait staff moving adroitly through the crowd with platters of food and drink.

Mmmm, beer. But I kept walking, figuring I could find the bar without Eden's help, then just text her once I arrived.

Before I knew it, I was at the next corner, past the bike rental place. I must have walked right past Ocean's End without noticing, no doubt while staring enviously at other people's drinks. So I turned and walked back the way I came, going slowly past the bike place and—suddenly I was right back where I'd started.

How the hell had I missed the bar twice in a row? Maybe I'd gotten the block wrong. No, I distinctly remembered her saying "just north of Rose Avenue."

Okay, color me annoyed.

Could Eden have been jerking me around? Even as the thought flickered across my mind, I dismissed it. I'd just met her. I mean, yeah, I'd worked with her for two weeks without getting to know her name—which was admittedly lazy and a little bit rude on my part—but surely that wasn't reason enough for her to do anything that shitty. Right?

I took a deep breath, determined to try it one more time. "Lee!"

I turned at the sound of my name. Eden waved at me from the other end of On the Waterfront, a wide smile on her face. I waved back, and tension I hadn't realized I'd been carrying slithered off my shoulders.

Hurrying over to where she stood, I noticed a table of twenty-something males checking her out over the partition. Tipsy hipsters sporting ironic facial hair, they all had big glass boots of beer in front them, with several empty pitchers in the middle of the table. Oblivious to the stir she was causing, Eden smiled happily as I reached her.

"You made it!"

"I did?" Looking around, I *still* didn't see Ocean's End. "I figured I was on the wrong block or something."

"Told you it's hard to spot," she said, "That's why I said I'd meet you here." As she spoke, two of the guys at the table whispered to each other, one of them pointing in Eden's direction. They weren't even trying to be subtle.

"You're causing a ruckus." I said, and I gave a small nod toward her admirers. She looked over, and her smile widened.

"*We're* causing a ruckus." She gave the table a little wave. One of the guys clutched his chest, while the other grabbed himself a little lower, and the group cred dove into the gutter. Eden just shook her head and giggled.

"This place is too crowded," she said. "Let's get out of here."

I followed her back toward the bike shop, where she turned into a little alley I would *swear* hadn't been there only a few minutes earlier. I hesitated, looking at the walls on either side of the cobblestone walkway, and wondered how I'd missed it twice in a row.

About ten feet into the alley, the walkway dead-ended into a wooden door, a ship's wheel dead center on the planked wood. A weathered driftwood sign bore the words "Ocean's End" in fading blue paint, and hung above the door. A dimly lit lantern dangled from an iron hook next to the sign.

"Come on!" Eden reached out and grabbed my hand, giving me a little tug. "See, you can only find this place if the owner likes you—and first he has to meet you."

I grinned. "Hipster techies need not apply, eh?"

"Ooh, wait until you see Manny's whiskers. Those guys are amateurs in comparison." She led the way to the door, her face eerily illuminated by the flickering light cast from the lantern. I was pretty sure it held a candle and not a bulb. So far this place took retro to the limits.

I paused, casting a glance back to the entrance of the alley as people strolled past without once looking in our direction. "They don't see it, do they?"

"Nope! And now they don't see us either."

That could come in handy, I thought.

Eden pushed the door open and we walked inside.

CHAPTER TWELVE

Ocean's End was old, with dark wood. A buttload of it. High walls, beamed ceiling, and small tables and booths around the perimeter. Lots of pictures on the dark walls, mostly seascapes, lots of stormy white-capped waves, ships awash in salt water. Not a sunny, happy sailing vessel in sight.

A couple of plank-style tables ran most of the length of the room, which seemed longer than possible. One of those "bigger on the inside" places. About half the tables and booths were full, the customers lit by candles flickering from randomly spaced wall sconces.

There looked to be plenty of lively conversations going on, but the sound level was pleasantly low. Music played quietly yet clearly from all corners of the place. Great acoustics, but when I checked for speakers, I didn't see any. Whoever set up the sound system knew his or her business.

The bar itself was a length of polished redwood at least twenty feet long and a good six inches thick, with another five-foot piece giving it an L shape. Not shiny polished, but smooth nonetheless, as if someone had taken a slab from one of the old-growth trees instead of nailing planks together.

Only a couple of customers were currently seated at the bar. Two older females with waist-length hair and oddly textured skin. Liquid dripped from the sodden hemlines of their skirts. The rest of their clothes, including the skirts above the hems, were bone dry. The vibrant green shade of their hair might have been expensive dye jobs, but somehow I doubted it. If more than one or two of the patrons were actually full-blooded human, I'd eat my bomber jacket.

Behind the bar was the *pièce de résistance*. Lit by fat pillar candles on either side, it depicted a sailing ship being dragged underneath the ocean by what might have been a giant squid, water roiling with tentacles above and below, with at least four wrapped around the hull of the doomed vessel. Sailors dressed in 18th-century garb screamed, the terror on their faces remarkably—and disturbingly—rendered.

I stared at it, simultaneously amused and appalled even as I admired the skill of the artist. I nudged Eden. "I want that one above my bed," I murmured. "I don't have enough nightmares."

The sound of someone clearing his throat rumbled from back behind the bar, bringing to mind the warning growl of a pissed off grizzly or a volcano with pre-eruption indigestion.

"Uh-oh," Eden murmured.

Uh-oh?

A shock of flaming red hair rose into sight, lending support to the volcano analogy. It was followed by a broad, strong forehead, an intimidating red unibrow the same shade as the hair, and slate-gray eyes, the color of angry storm clouds. Next came an aquiline nose and a... well, a mouth. I'm not entirely sure what it looked like because it was mostly hidden by a truly impressive mustache and beard.

Eden was right. Hipsters would weep with envy. Both beard and 'stache had to be at least a foot long, and were thick and wavy, like his hair—which fell well past his shoulders down his back, the front drawn back in narrow braids. Bits of seashells, frosted multicolored glass, and silver beads were woven into his beard at random intervals. The side of the mustache flowed into it, trimmed just enough at the top to leave him a gap for eating. He wore the front of his hair in two braids, similarly twined with shells and silver beads.

The whole effect worked, all organic and wild. I still wasn't a fan, mind you, but at least he didn't come across like a trendy douche. I wasn't sure if I should say "Arr, matey" or request permission to come aboard, and sensibly opted for neither.

He stared at me balefully. "Eden, your friend doesn't like my choice of art." Irish accent, thick and unexpectedly sexy. I'd been expecting Groundskeeper Willy from *The Simpsons*.

"I didn't say I didn't like it," I protested mildly. "It's just kind of... grim. Would it be too much to ask for one or two calm beaches at sunset? Maybe a nice couple in white, walking hand in hand?"

"Do you know what a grim is, young lady?"

Oooh, that accent.

"The spirit of an animal," I answered immediately. "Although they can occasionally be human. Buried alive in a churchyard to protect the grounds. Or, if you're into Harry Potter, a black dog that means death for whoever encounters it."

He glared at me from beneath that bushy unibrow for a good ten seconds. I tried not to look smug. Still, not doing so well at the whole "making him like me" scenario. I might never find this place again.

I peered more closely at the painting. If I looked very carefully, I could see something under the water. Something with tentacles on a face with three dark eyes. "Is that a run-of-the-mill squid, or Cthulhu?"

"Spell it."

"What?"

"Cthulhu. Spell Cthulhu."

"Is this, like, the spelling bee of the damned?"

His eyes narrowed. "Just do it."

I thought about it for a few seconds.

"C-T-H-U-L-H-U. Cthulhu." I gave a little curtsy.

Manny nodded with grudging approval. "You're a smartass, but at least you're an intelligent smartass." Something about the word "smartass" uttered in a thick Irish accent was irresistibly cute. I grinned at him, no longer intimidated by those dark-gray eyes.

No, wait, they're blue.

Or were they green?

Maybe it was the lighting in the bar, but Manny's eyes seemed to be shifting like the colors of the sea. Deep green, slate gray, the turquoise of the Mediterranean, all swirling together before settling momentarily on a particular shade. Kind of like an ocular mood ring.

"Do I have to answer any more questions?"

"Only what you want me to pour you."

Eden nudged me in the ribs. "He likes you."

Manny gave a loud harrumphing snort. "She's earned a drink, that's all. What'll you have?"

I looked behind the bar again, this time at the selection of bottles glittering along the back wall, as well as all the beer taps on display. Manny poured Eden a glass of Sanford chardonnay while I perused the impressive selection, finally settling on a bourbon barrel aged stout called Dragon's Milk. High octane, high calorie. Bliss by any other name. Normally only comes in eight-ounce pours, at most. Manny drew me a full pint without batting an eye. My eyes widened at the sight of it.

"Anything you can't handle?"

"No, sir."

He nodded. "Didn't think so."

I started to pull out my wallet, but Eden put a hand on my arm. "We'll put it on my tab tonight."

I looked at her in surprise. "Are you sure?"

She nodded. "My treat. Heck, it's the least I can do for the woman who kicked Axel in the balls." She turned to Manny. "She really did."

"*Dia uilechumhachtach*." Manny eyed me with renewed respect. "I'll buy you the next round for that alone."

"Yup!" Eden turned back to me. "That's Irish, by the way, for—"

"God Almighty," I said without thinking.

Eden looked at me, surprised. "You speak Irish?"

I thought about it.

"Not really." I shrugged. "I guess I just must have heard that expression before."

"I think there are a great many things you've heard before, lass," Manny said slowly.

"Well, yeah, but…" I trailed off as I caught sight of his expression. Manny was looking at me and *through* me, the irises of his eyes swirling with different colors, each expanding and retracting, blending into the next, like two pinwheels. The pupils seemed to spin in the opposite direction. I thought of dark whirlpools.

"Many are the things you have seen before, as well, and will see and hear again, forgetting each time unless you can break the chains that bind."

Huh?

I found myself transfixed, unable to turn away even as I thought his words sounded like the lyrics of an '80s rock anthem.

"Shadows are coming your way, girl," he continued. "Not of your own making, but still close to your blood. Shadows that kill. Shadows that rend. Two are one, but separate and—"

"Okay, I think that's enough." Eden reached forward and clapped her hands under Manny's nose. His eyes snapped back into focus, irises settling on a deep blue. The chill that crept down my spine stayed where it was, though.

"Oh, feck," he muttered. "Did I go off again?"

Eden nodded.

"You did."

Manny turned to me.

"Sorry, lass," he said ruefully. "That happens at times, and not always when I expect it. I hope I didn't frighten you."

"That's okay," I said, even though it wasn't. "*Sláinte*." I held up my pint glass in a mini-toast, glad that my hand didn't tremble as I did so. Part of me wanted to know what he had meant, and part of me didn't. It really had been that kind of day.

Manny picked up a half-full glass from behind the bar and clinked it against mine.

"*Sláinte*, lass."

"And thank *you* for picking up the tab," I said to Eden by way of clearing the weird from the air.

"Piffle!" Eden waved her free hand dismissively. "My pleasure. You can get it next time."

"Deal."

I started to follow her away from the bar.

"Lass."

I turned back to see Manny studying me, his expression solemn.

"I don't remember what I said to you, but I do know you need to be careful. That much I'm sure of."

"Um… thanks."

Eden led me to a booth across from the far end of the bar. It gave us some privacy with the advantage of proximity if we wanted another drink.

"This is quite the place," I said as we sat down.

"It is, isn't it?" Eden smiled happily. "I tripped over it one day. Walked by the alley at exactly the right moment when someone else was leaving. Luckily Manny was in a good mood that night, or he'd have kicked me right out."

I laughed. "He's like an agent, then. Only takes referrals."

"Something like that."

"Does he always go all Cassandra on his customers?"

Eden stared at me blankly. "Cassandra?"

"Yeah, you know. Or maybe you don't," I added hastily when she raised a quizzical eyebrow. "Cassandra was a Greek princess who was given the gift of prophecy by Apollo, but then he got all butt hurt when she wouldn't sleep with him. He cursed her so no one would believe what she predicted."

"So she could see the future, but couldn't do anything to change it, all because some god didn't get his rocks off?"

I laughed. "Yup, that's about it."

"Well, I don't know if Manny's predictions are always accurate, but according to some of the longtime regulars, he's always had them. I don't think he's ever turned down an offer of sex, though."

Hmm. I might have a hard time getting past all the facial fuzz.

She picked up her chardonnay. "Anyway, cheers!"

"Cheers." I clinked my pint against her wine glass.

We made small talk for a while, slipping comfortably into a good old-fashioned gossip session about the cast and crew of *Steel Legions*. Then Eden told me a little about growing up in Ann Arbor, Michigan. Something about her seemed comfortingly familiar, or familiarly comfortable. Not sure which, or if it even mattered.

After an hour and most of a pint of Dragon's Milk, I found myself opening up to her in a way I didn't do with anyone at the Ranch. I told her about my accident, my memory loss, and even about my fucked-up relationship with Seth.

"You know he likes you," she said.

"No way." I snorted. "How would you know? And that sounds totally high school, anyhow."

"Oh, come on." She smiled over the rim of her glass. "Do we ever really change?"

I considered her words.

"I'd like to think so. I mean, maybe our emotions don't change, but the way we deal with them? Jeez, I *hope* so!" I paused, then added, "Anyway, he totally doesn't. Like me, I mean. Honestly I think he hates me."

"No, I mean he *likes* you likes you. That's his problem. He's probably got some sort of weird guilt trip going on and can't handle his feelings.

I stared at her. "You have *got* to be kidding."

"Totally not kidding," she said. "I've seen this before. It's the adult version of a kid dipping pigtails in the inkwell. You know, being a shit because he can't deal with his emotions."

"Ugh. Let's just drop the subject."

"Why? I mean, it's not like you two are related." She tilted her head to one side and gave me a considering stare. "Are you?"

"Well, no," I said uncomfortably, feeling suddenly awkward. "But we might as well be. I've lived with him and his dad since I was five."

"Hmm." Eden's expression was unreadable in the flickering candlelight.

"What about you?" I asked. "Haven't you ever had a dysfunctional relationship?"

She laughed at that, a totally uninhibited and natural laugh, and things felt right again.

"Oh, yeah, you could definitely say that, but it was a long time ago. I was young, stupid, and didn't know any better." She took a sip. "I'm a lot pickier now."

I heaved a huge sigh. "I need to follow your example. I swear, am I *ever* gonna meet someone who isn't a bad boy?"

Eden cocked her head to one side. "Do you want to?"

I stopped and thought about it. "Yes. Yes, I do."

"Then you will."

We clinked glasses and drank. I finished my stout.

Eden noticed. "You want another one?"

I shook my head. "I'd love one, but no way in hell I'd be in any shape to drive."

"Well…" Eden leaned forward. "I live a couple blocks down the street, and we have a couch, and you *probably* shouldn't drive for a while anyway, so how about you just crash at my place?"

"I couldn't."

"Why not?"

"I—"

"Seriously, why not?"

"Because Sean will worry about me."

"So text him."

Oh.

"I can do that."

"Uh-huh." Eden grinned at me. "So how about I get us a couple more drinks?"

†

A few hours and I'm not sure how many drinks later we waved goodbye to Manny and stumbled out of Ocean's End, giggling like the schoolgirls I'd said we weren't. We leaned on each other for support and headed south on the boardwalk. A few blocks up, we turned left onto one of Venice Beach's walk streets.

I nudged Eden. "So are you showing me the way to Hogwarts now?"

"What is it wizards say when they fly? Aspirate?"

"Expectorate?" I offered.

We both giggled.

"*Any*way," Eden said, "this is just a regular old street walk. I mean, walk street. Something. Anyway, nothing magic about it, except the guy in 101B. He's pretty sweet." We reached a dark wrought iron gate leading to a multi-storied red-brick apartment complex with a central courtyard. Eden fumbled in her knock-off Coach bag for a few minutes, finally pulling out a set of keys. After a few tries she managed to open the gate, stumbling slightly as she navigated a short flight of steps directly to the right.

"I'm down here," she said unnecessarily.

I made my way unsteadily after her into the darkened apartment, banging an arm against the doorframe. I shut the door behind me without further injury, which was pretty damn good considering the at least three pints of Dragon's Milk I'd drunk.

Eden switched on a light, illuminating the room in a soft rosy glow. I looked up at the ceiling where rose-colored silk draped across its length. An antique-looking light fixture hung in the center of the room. It was rose gold and reflected that shade into the room. Very flattering, like being filmed through Vaseline and gauze.

"Nice," I said.

Eden saw me looking at it and giggled. "I call it my Cybill Shepherd lighting." The living room was opulent—all silk or velvet pillows, rich fabric on the couch and two matching chairs, lots of fwoopy drapes and hangings, candles. Like Cost Plus had exploded and all the cool stuff had landed here. Cinnamon and vanilla scented the air. I wanted cookies.

I hiccupped.

Crap.

Eden pointed to a couch the color of good red wine. "Make yourself at home, and I'll get you a glass of water."

She vanished around the corner as I hiccupped again. I plopped down on the couch, immediately sinking into its overstuffed velvet cushions. It was almost like sitting on a cloud. Or at least what I imagined a cloud would feel like.

Another hiccup.

I tried holding my breath. It didn't work.

"Here."

Eden reappeared with a glass of water. I took it gratefully and swallowed it in a series of gulps while holding my breath. Last thing I remember was the glass slipping from my fingers and the feel of something soft and warm draped over my shoulders as I drifted off to sleep.

†

The sound of screaming woke him.

He'd stayed up far too late. Hadn't gone to bed until four in the morning, and finally drifted off with the help of a very strong prescription medicine. The high-pitched shrieks, pulsing with fear and pain, pulled him out of a deep, drugged sleep riddled with dark dreams.

At first he thought they were part of a dream. He and Sala, standing on a dais above their worshippers. The screams of the dying—a mix of ecstasy and unimaginable pain—as their gods drained the spectators of their life essences.

Then he woke in a tangle of sheets, the slippery silk wrapped around his limbs, sweat oozing from his pores in the mother of all night sweats. Realized the screams—now stilled—were part of his waking reality. Sala had been out to play while he'd slept.

He shut his eyes.

A good meal used to keep Sala going for years at a time. Back in the old days, their followers would bring offerings, making the hunt unnecessary. Some were willing, others had to be dragged screaming to their fates. As their worshippers diminished in number, so did their offerings until neither type of nourishment sustained her.

Thus the hunt.

Over time, as her body and mind failed, the feedings increased. They went from once a century to every fifty years. Then every quarter century, speeding up to each decade, then each year. As her symptoms progressed, she needed nourishment every few months.

Now?

In a matter of days her body would use up the nutrition it had just taken. Her cheeks would become sunken hollows, eyes deep in haunted sockets. Her breathing becoming labored, like that of someone lying on a deathbed.

Then the whole cycle would start again.

How soon would it be before she required food every day? He had to be realistic. There might—no, there would come a point when no amount of food would sustain her.

He had to find a cure. Something that would enable her to last longer between feedings, and maintain her sanity. If not, in her hunger and madness, she would drain the world.

Until he did, she would have to be contained. Starting tonight.

He got up slowly, slipped on a pair of dark-blue Derek Rose

pajama bottoms and matching top. His tastes were expensive, and he could afford to indulge them. He could also afford to hire someone very discreet to come in and clean up any mess Sala might have left.

Still, he hoped there wasn't too much.

CHAPTER THIRTEEN

I woke up the next morning to someone shaking me gently by one shoulder. I grumbled and burrowed under an incredibly soft down comforter. No one should have to wake up when they were snuggled under a comforter as comfy as this one.

"Lee," a familiar voice said. "I hate to wake you, but I have a lunch date in two hours."

I reluctantly opened my eyes to see Eden standing over me in a pink cotton sundress, looking as fresh as someone in a commercial for feminine products. You know the ones. She'd be the woman standing on the beach wearing white and looking supremely confident because her tampons would *not* let her down.

"What time is it?" I mumbled.

"Just a little before ten."

I sat up slowly and cautiously.

Hmmm.

Except for my mouth tasting like the contents of a moldy beer keg, I actually felt fine. Considering how much Dragon's Milk I'd had, that was saying something. I hoped my metabolism continued to be this friendly for a few years.

"There's an extra toothbrush and towels in the bathroom,"

Eden said brightly. "But first, I thought you might like this."

She handed me a large white mug that said *Coffee keeps me going until it's acceptable to drink wine.* The smell of dark, rich caffeine wafted up to greet me.

"Oh, I think I love you," I sighed, taking a sip.

"I added a little honey and some cream. You seemed like the honey and cream type. Hope that's okay."

"Okay?" I smiled happily as I had another swallow of what may have been the best coffee I'd had in, like, forever. "It's perfect."

Eden sat down across from me in a chair that matched the couch, cradling a black mug with white lettering that said *I Will Not Keep Calm and You Can Fuck Off.*

"Did you sleep okay?"

I nodded. "Best night's sleep I've had in a while." It had been. No freaky-ass dreams, which was a nice change. "Thanks again for letting me crash here."

"Totally my pleasure," Eden smiled. "No way you were in any shape to drive home last night."

I sat bolt upright, nearly spilling my coffee.

"My car! It's in the metered parking spot!"

"Don't sweat it," Eden laughed. "Today's Sunday."

The adrenaline rush left as abruptly as it had hit, and I sunk back against the couch cushions. "Oh, thank God. I just can't afford the ticket right now."

"I totally feel your pain," Eden said. "I swear, I should build street cleaning tickets into my budget, you know?"

Finishing my coffee, I excused myself, grabbed my bag, and went into the bathroom to get cleaned up so I didn't overstay my welcome. I brushed my teeth and washed my face, digging in my bag for the deodorant I always carried. I found it, along with my iPhone, and pulled them both out.

Oh, crap crap crappity crap.

Not the deodorant. The deodorant was fine.

The phone, on the other hand?

A bunch of missed calls and voicemail notifications from Sean and Seth, one after another, like a tsunami of stress heading my way. And those were only the ones that fit on the screen.

I used the touch ID and went into the list of missed calls and voicemails. Five from Sean, three from Seth. Then I checked the texts and found a series of increasingly worried messages from Sean, plus a bunch of angry ones from Seth.

The gist of them all?

Where was I?

Why hadn't I called?

Where the *hell* was I?

What the fuck? I knew I'd sent a text last night. I mean, yeah, I'd gotten kind of tipsy, but I took Sean's feelings pretty seriously, and would never have wanted him to spend the night worrying about me. Although seriously, I didn't remember checking in with him this much back when I'd had my own place.

Then I looked at the bottom of the thread from Sean. There was my text.

> Sean, staying at a friend's place
> tonight.
> See you in the morning!

Only problem? I'd never hit "send."

I started to listen to one of the messages from Sean and then thought better of it. I deleted them along with the voicemails and texts from Seth, which I didn't need to hear or read, and honestly, hadn't wanted in the first place. He'd never been good at letting Sean and me manage our own relationship.

I went ahead and typed up a quick apology text to Sean and then sent it along with the one that hadn't gone through last night. Then I punched in his number and braced myself for a big fat helping of guilt trip for breakfast.

At least I had good coffee to wash it down.

†

I got home an hour and a half later, taking my time on the drive home. Every now and again my mind played over what Eden had said about Seth. Each time my brain went down that path, though, part of me instantly ran in the opposite direction. Way too Jaime and Circe Lannister for my taste, even if we weren't related by blood.

A small part of me, a *very* small part, wondered if there wasn't at least a drop of truth to it. Seth and I used to get along, even have fun together. Now barely veiled hostility was the norm, and I couldn't pinpoint when it had started.

No sooner had I pulled up into the carport and turned the engine off when the driver's side door was flung open. I looked up to see Seth glaring at me, looking all pissed off and stormily handsome, like the cover model for a gothic novel.

"Hey, there," I said cheerily. "Didn't realize you were offering valet service now." I got out of the car, pushing past him and pulling my stuff from the trunk. Then I went inside, calling Sean's name as I walked into the front hallway.

"He's not here." Seth slammed the front door shut behind him. The house suddenly felt very full of his presence.

"Where is he?"

"Out."

I rolled my eyes. "Real mature, Seth." Tossing my bag on the couch, I went into the kitchen. There would need to be more coffee if I was going to deal with my asshole cousin. So I grabbed a mug and got the Nespresso machine doing its thing, pulling out a can of whipped cream from the fridge. Coffee *mit schlag* would do quite nicely.

Seth followed me in, spoiling for a fight which I had no intention of giving him. I'd used all my extra energy up yesterday with Axel.

"You really are something." Seth looked at me with the same kind of disgust most people reserve for when they find used Band Aids in their food or dog vomit under their pillow. "Couldn't be bothered to call, huh?"

"I texted, okay?" I glared at him as I swirled whipped cream into my coffee mug. "Or at least I typed a text and *thought* I sent it. Look, it was an honest mistake. I talked to Sean this morning. He's already forgiven me. So why the hell can't you just drop it?"

"Do you have any idea how worried he was?" Seth stomped across the kitchen floor and threw the fridge door open, grabbing a beer before slamming the door shut. "Do you even care? Or were you too busy screwing your new friend to think about that?"

Oh, for Christ's sake.

"Not that it's any business of yours," I said carefully, trying very hard to keep my temper in check, "but I spent the night with a girlfriend. An actress from the film. She offered me a place to crash because we went for drinks after wrap last night, and I overdid it."

"Of course you did," he said unfairly, clutching his beer. I felt my temper fraying, which pissed me off even more because I didn't want to give him the satisfaction of seeing me lose it.

"So you'd rather I'd driven home drunk?" I countered.

"Would you prefer that to the thought of me screwing some guy?" I shook my head in disgust. "Jesus Christ, Seth. Your priorities are totally fucked up."

"And yours aren't?"

I added more whipped cream to my mug, slowly and deliberately.

"Here's the thing, Seth. I don't remember what I was like before the accident, but I'd like to think I wouldn't deliberately do something to make Sean lose a night of sleep over me."

"You have no fucking idea what you've put him—put *us*—through over the years."

"You're right, I *don't*." I slammed the whipped cream can down on the table. "But I'm doing my best here, and I'm sick and *tired* of you never giving me a break. You've given me nothing but shit for taking this job."

"You shouldn't have—"

"Let me finish!"

He shut up. I wanted to declare a national holiday.

I took a deep breath before continuing.

"The only reason I took the job, aside from helping Randy out, is so I could start making money so I can get the hell *out* of here so I don't have to deal with *you* anymore. And, hey, if that happens, you won't have to deal with me either, unless we work on the same job. That doesn't look too likely, so you should be pretty much free and clear."

Tears burned behind my eyelids. I hated myself for it. The last thing I wanted was for Seth to see any weakness on my part, because I knew from past experience he'd go in for the kill.

I grabbed the whipped cream and put it back in the fridge without looking. In my haste to get it done and get the hell out of the kitchen, I knocked over a jar of salsa, which tumbled out of the fridge toward the floor. I grabbed for it, but Seth was quicker. He caught it before it smashed on the tiles.

I started to straighten up, but Seth grabbed my wrist with his other hand, pulling my arm up so he could look at it in the light. All of the bruises I'd gotten from my encounters with Axel stood out all ugly and greenish yellow.

"What happened?" Seth's tone didn't exactly soften, but the edge of anger was gone.

I shrugged. "Did a fight yesterday. The guy had something to prove."

"Did he hurt you?"

"Just bruises," I said, trying not to show how glad I was that he'd asked. "Nothing that won't fade in a few days."

"Why didn't Randy stop it?"

"I wouldn't let him. I could handle it."

Seth laughed, a sound devoid of humor.

"Of course you could." It wasn't a compliment.

I sighed and sat down at the kitchen table. "Look. You're not going to get the same type of shit I do on set. Or any other woman, for that matter. You don't have anything to prove, and you're not a target for harassment. I did what I thought was best for the job, and Randy backed me up. He's solid."

"Good. Because if Randy had let something happen to one of his people on the job, we don't want him in the KSC."

I gave a bitter little laugh. "Gee, for a second I thought you might actually care. I should've known better."

"Don't be childish."

"Pot to kettle, anyone?"

He ignored that.

"What's the guy's name? The one who hurt you?"

"Axel…" I paused, realizing I didn't know Axel's last name. "Big Germanic guy. Turns out he's half Priaptic demon, which is a new one on me."

Seth slapped a hand to his forehead and sat down across from me. "They cast a fucking Priaptic demon?"

"Half-breed," I corrected. "I guess that's not a new one for you, and yeah, they did. According to Eden, the director didn't have a clue. He's not the brightest bulb. I don't think anyone knows except the two of us."

"Eden's this friend you had drinks with?"

I nodded cautiously. "She's one of the actresses on the film."

"So the director doesn't know that Randy's—"

"A shifter? Doubtful." I shot Seth a sideways glance. "I didn't know either until he got pissed off at Axel, and his eyes got all wolfy for a minute."

He gave a small smile. "You used to be better at spotting these things."

"I used to be better at high falls, too."

"True."

I drank some of my espresso, enjoying the contrast between the bitter brew and the sweet whipped cream while Seth sucked down half of his beer, a PBR. We sat in almost companionable silence, drinking our respective beverages. It felt like an armed truce. Fragile and precious at the same time.

Seth gestured toward my now empty mug with his equally empty beer bottle.

"You want another one?"

"Nah, but if we have any beer that isn't fucking close to water, I'd take that."

"What?'

"You know. 'Why is PBR like sex in a canoe? Because it's fucking—'"

"'—close to water,'" Seth finished.

We shared a rare smile between us, knowing Sean would have totally frowned on the language. We'd done the same thing in our teens. It had been a hell of a long time since we'd been on the same side of a joke.

"I'll see what we've got," he said. "Gotta say, though, with Drift doing most of the beer runs the last few weeks, it's been lean pickings."

"See? I *am* good for something."

Seth shot me a look before rummaging around in the fridge. He pulled out a couple of Stone Delicious IPAs, tossing me one just as the back door opened and Sean walked in.

He paused warily in the doorway, looking at the two of us with our beers as if he were a member of a bomb squad unsure if he needed to cut the red or the blue wire.

"Hey there," I said, standing so I could greet him. I'd already done a major *mea culpa* over the phone, and Sean had said we were good. Still, a hug seemed like a good thing about now.

"Hey yourself, hon." Sean returned my hug warmly, managing to squeeze all the things that already hurt. I couldn't help the hiss of indrawn breath as his arms pressed into my bruises.

Sean set me back immediately, hands on my shoulders and stared at me with concern.

"You okay?"

"I'm good," I said as Seth growled, "Priaptic demon got frisky with her."

"Half-demon," I corrected, giving him a glare. I really hadn't wanted to go into detail, at least not quite so soon.

Oh, well.

CHAPTER FOURTEEN

When I finished telling Sean about the drama with Axel, I hoped that would be the end of it. However, he wasn't content to leave it at that.

"So he transformed when you were filming the fight and the director didn't freak?"

"Well, no, he just tried to beat the crap out of me when we were filming the fight," I replied. "Rock is a sexist jerk, but I'm pretty sure he doesn't know what Axel is."

"Then how did you know he was a Priaptic demon?"

"He got all red, veiny, and… er… obvious about it later," I said reluctantly. "It got kind of ugly and I—"

I stopped. What *had* I done?

"I guess I had some sort of mega adrenaline rush, 'cause I threw him off and kicked him in the nuts hard enough to knock him out."

"That must have been some kick," Seth said, leaning against the fridge and looking like he belonged in a Hunky Stuntmen calendar. I couldn't tell if he believed me or not.

"He pissed me off," I muttered.

"He must have." Sean sat down next to me, reached out, and covered one of my hands—the one without the beer in it—with his. "What happened after that?"

I shrugged. "Adrenaline rush went bye-bye and I sat down for a few minutes until I felt normal again." I didn't see the point in telling him about my weird episode in Venice Beach.

Seth and Sean exchanged one of their patented father-and-son looks, something they'd perfected over the years. I swear they passed information back and forth through osmosis. They must've come to some conclusion, though. Sean nodded, Seth sat down next to him, and they both looked at me.

"What?" I asked. "You guys are making me nervous."

"Hon, there's something—"

My phone vibrated in my jeans pocket and the *Flash Gordon* theme blared from my backside.

"Hang on," I said, pulling my phone out of my pocket. Neither of them would be offended if I checked to see who was calling. In our business, it could mean a gig.

I recognized the number.

"It's Randy," I said. "Might be about tomorrow's schedule. I should take it."

Sean made a "go ahead" gesture. Seth drank more beer, and I took that as an okay on his part, as well. Pushing away from the table, I hit "answer."

"Hey, Randy." I stepped over by the kitchen door, my back to the table.

"Hey, Lee! I didn't wake you up, did I?"

"Nope! Been up for a while and already had three cups of coffee. You're safe."

"How're you feeling?"

I smiled, touched that he'd thought to check up on me.

"A little stiff and a couple of bruises, but not bad. I'll be ready to go tomorrow, no worries."

"Hell, I'm not worried about that," he said with a laugh. "Smartest thing I did was hire you."

Auww… Randy was earning brownie points all over the place.

"Everything set for tomorrow's car chase?" I asked. "And do I really get to drive a Cayman?"

Seth's eyebrows shot up, and he mouthed, "Lucky bitch."

Randy chuckled. "Yup! One of Rock's pals is into sports cars. Dude must have money coming out of his ass, if he doesn't mind loaning us the Cayman for a shoot. Rock figures Vixenia would have something extra nice."

"So what do *you* get to drive?"

"Vixenia's other car, which just happens to be a NSX."

"Drift is gonna be jealous," I said, impressed. "Too bad we didn't have that kind of budget for the rest of the film."

"No kidding," Randy agreed. "But, hey, I figure we should get something out of this, aside from bruises and a shitty paycheck."

There was a pause. I decided to give Randy a nudge.

"So, anything else before I go?"

"Oh, yeah! This may be good news for you, too, which is really why I called." He paused, probably for effect, then said, "So I got a call from my agent this morning. I signed with her right before getting the job on *Steel Legions*, and she wanted to know if I knew any female stunt players looking for representation. I didn't know if you already have an agent, but you were the first person I thought of. She seemed really interested."

"That's great! Who's your agent?"

"Faustina Corbin," Randy said with a total fail at nonchalance. Not that I could blame him.

Faustina Corbin was *the* top agent for supernaturals in

the industry, one of the very few who handled paranormal clients, which can run the gamut of magical, mystical, ghostly, and otherworldly beings. She'd been after Sean and Seth to sign with her for, like, forever, but the Katz boys preferred to fly solo even if some of their stunt crew took on agency representation.

Faustina also had the reputation among those in the know for *only* representing supernatural talent. Which made me reluctantly conclude that this had to be a mistake.

"Uh, Randy, you know I'm not a supe, right?"

"Sure!" He sounded surprised that I'd even ask.

"Okay. But even more importantly, does Faustina know I'm human?"

Both Sean and Seth shifted in their chairs at my mention of the agent's name.

"Well, she didn't specifically ask for supes, just female stunt players. I think it's fine as long as you know about supes, and don't mind working with them, y'know?"

"Huh."

That one syllable did not do justice to the sudden burst of excitement hammering in my chest.

"Anyway," he continued, "she asked me to ask you to give her a call when you had the chance. She takes calls on weekends, so I thought I'd let you know a-s-a-p, in case you were interested."

"Thanks, Randy. That's really nice of you."

"Aww, you deserve it, Lee. Lemme give you her number."

"Hang on a sec." I grabbed a pen and paper. "Okay, shoot." He rattled off a number in the 310 area code and I scribbled it down.

"Well, thanks," I said again. "Hey, Sean needs to talk to me so I'd better run. See you tomorrow, okay?" I hung up and stared at the number I'd written down.

Huh.

"What's up?" Sean's tone sounded deliberately nonchalant, as if he and Seth hadn't been listening to every word on my end of the conversation, and probably most of Randy's too. They had really good hearing, and Randy wasn't soft-spoken.

"Faustina Corbin's evidently looking for female stunt players," I replied with equal nonchalance. It was probably just as genuine. "Randy recommended me. I thought she only represented supernaturals, though."

"Why the hell do you need representation?" Seth looked offended at the very thought.

"Um… to get more work maybe?" I wanted to say more, but I didn't want to hurt Sean's feelings, especially after last night's text screw up. I also didn't want to ruin the unexpected truce with Seth, although the frown gathering on his brow should have come with a storm warning.

"That's just—"

"That's not a bad idea."

Seth and I both shot startled glances at Sean.

"No, really," he continued, holding up a hand to head off Seth's inevitable argument. "Look, Seth, until Lee gets back up to speed on the falls and aerial work, she needs to be working." He gave me a rueful smile. "I get that now, Lee, and I'm sorry I was so stubborn about it before. And no disrespect to Randy, because I like him and think he's a good kid, but I'd rather see you get paid what you're worth. You should have gotten a big pay bump for working with someone as unstable as a Priaptic. Faustina would have made that happen."

He looked at Seth. "The more Lee works, the more her confidence will build and the sooner she'll be back working with us." He smiled at me. "And then maybe you won't need an agent anymore. So give her a call. Set up a meeting and see if you think it's a good fit."

Nodding, I started to dial Faustina Corbin's number, then stopped. "You wanted to talk to me about something, didn't you?" I said, still holding the phone. "I can call her later, if you want."

"It's okay, hon," Sean said. "I think it can wait."

†

After much reading and online consultation, it was time to try again. It appeared as if everything had been done correctly. The ingredients were right, the incantations as they should be. By all accounts, the creatures summoned, while dangerous, should be easily controlled.

When asked why the demons had taken such a sacrifice, the answers had been unanimous. "We don't know." Maybe there'd been a mistake, so infinitesimal as to not have been caught. Several practitioners opined that the blood sacrifice might indeed have been stale.

It was time to try again. Too much depended on the success of these experiments. Hopefully no one else would die.

But if they did?

It was worth it—as long as things could be brought under control.

†

"Delfino, are you coming in? The tamales are ready!"

Esther looked out the kitchen window of her Echo Park home, to the carport where her son fiddled under the hood of her ancient Toyota Corolla. The late afternoon summer sunlight faded behind the hills to the west, replaced by lengthening shadows.

"In a few, Mama!" he called back. "Just finishing up with the oil change. Gotta make sure you have a smooth ride to work tomorrow."

"Okay. Just don't be too long. Te quiero, mi hijo!"

"Yo tambien, Mama!"

Esther smiled and went into the living room. She was lucky. Del was such a good boy. It could have gone so badly. He had only been ten when his dad died. Instead of running wild, he'd taken the role of what he saw as his mama's protector. He was the man of the house, and men took care of things. They worked. Brought home money and paid for food.

Delfino found his true love early in life, thanks to auto shop in high school. It'd kept him out of trouble, given him something else to do while his former friends got drunk or, worse, shot each other in the streets.

He'd rather fix his mama's car than go out drinking.

At least that's what he told her. She thought it was a mentirijilla—a little white lie—but what was the harm in that?

Yes, she was a lucky woman.

She hoped he'd hurry in before the tamales got cold.

†

Out under the Corolla, Del finished draining the old oil into an aluminum roasting dish that substituted for an oil pan. If any stray drips missed that, the plastic sheeting he'd spread out would catch them, He didn't want any stains in the driveway.

Del had inherited his mama's love of cleanliness and order. Even as a kid he'd kept his room clean, everything in its place. Funny how he'd fallen in love with a profession where it was impossible to avoid getting filthy.

Still, he'd do his best to wash the grease and grime off his hands and face and change clothes before sitting down at the kitchen table. Del's stomach growled at the thought of the homemade tamales waiting for him, his insides clenching with hunger.

Sure, his friends thought he was a mama's boy because he'd stayed home to work on her car instead of going out to whatever local hangout they'd picked for the night. Let them think what they *wanted. He'd stay out of trouble, get his mechanic's license… and in the meantime, enjoy the best damn tamales in the LA basin.*

His stomach growled again, a low liquid sound, almost scary.

Funny, he hadn't felt it that time.

The light under the car flickered, as if telling him to hurry.

Del finished installing the new gasket on the plug, tapping his wrench with a rubber mallet to tighten it in place. He smiled at a job well done, just about to slide out from under the car when the light flickered again.

And went out.

Startled, Del dropped the wrench. It clattered onto the concrete, the resulting echo much louder than it should have been.

That growl again, this time coming from the front of the car. Definitely not his stomach.

Something snuffled at his feet and legs where they stuck out from the undercarriage. Del chuckled, a wave of relief washing over him.

"Milo, you stupid mutt. You scared the shit out of me."

Milo, their asshole neighbor's pit-bull, must have gotten out of his yard again. Scariest looking dog in the complex, but a total pussy. All it took to stop Milo from barking was a stern glance. From a five-year-old.

But man, that smell. Like someone had taken a shit and mixed it with rotten meat.

"Jeez, Milo, what the hell they feeding you?"

Another growl sounded, this time seeming to reverberate all around the car. Both liquid and guttural at the same time. It didn't sound like Milo, or like any dog Del had ever heard before.

His skin crawled.

The temperature dropped abruptly. His shirt, all damp with sweat, suddenly stuck to his flesh in icy pinpricks. Del thought if he tried to pull the fabric away, his skin might rip off with it.

"Madre de Dios," he breathed, switching to Spanish without

conscious thought. Something scraped against the passenger side of the Corolla. Del imagined long steel nails raking dents in the metal, the sound overly loud and painful on his eardrums. His scrotum constricted, as if his entire nutsack was trying to crawl up inside his body and get away from whatever was out there.

Something snuffled his legs again. Del held perfectly still, wanting desperately to curl up into a tiny ball under the car, wait until whatever was out there went away. But if he moved… would it bite him?

He shut his eyes, the words to the Lord's Prayer spilling out of his mouth in Spanish, the way his mom had taught him.

"Padre nuestro que estás en los cielos, Santificado sea tu Nombre. Venga tu reino…"

The reek of dead things filled his nostrils and he tasted rot on his tongue. His stomach heaved involuntarily, bile filing his mouth in a sour rush.

He kept talking.

"Hágase tu voluntad en la tierra como en el cielo… Danos hoy el pan de este día y perdona nuestras deudas como nosotros—"

Jesus, why was it so dark?

"—perdonamos nuestros deudores y no nos dejes caer en al tentación sino que líbranos del malo."

The world went black. It was like someone had thrown a tarp over the car, blocking out all the natural light, leaving him in total darkness. Something brushed up against his side. He screamed and involuntarily sat upright, bashing his head against hard, sharp metal.

Dazed, Del fell backward. He had just enough survival instinct to push away on the dolly, rolling backward out from under the Corolla. He emerged into an unnatural darkness composed of roiling shadows shot through with an unhealthy rainbow shimmer.

They blocked out the sight of his house above.

Del stayed frozen in place, staring up from the dolly. It had to be a concussion—he was seeing things.

"This isn't real. Isn't real. Isn't—"

Claws dug into Del's scalp and neck and pulled him back under the car.

†

Esther glanced up at the clock and shook her head. It'd been ten minutes since she'd called Del in for dinner. He probably lost track of time. He did that when working on cars. Time to give him another shout.

She opened the kitchen door to the outside. "Del, mi hijo, your food is getting cold and—"

The words froze in her throat as she looked down into the carport where her son's legs and feet kicked and twitched against the concrete. Dark liquid pooled out from under the car, followed by something darker and more fluid that settled on Del's legs and... and shredded them.

†

Later, when the police arrived—summoned by a neighbor who heard Esther's screams—all she could tell them was that her boy had been eaten by the shadows.

CHAPTER FIFTEEN

I sat in the small lobby, trying to ignore the smells of ancient cigarettes and desperation. Photos of celebrities and movie posters lined the walls. If Faustina's reputation and Randy's recommendation hadn't preceded her, I would have wondered how many celebs or movies were actually connected with the Mana Talent Agency, and how much of this was just putting on a good face.

Ah, Randy.

He was hoping that if Faustina took me on as a client, it could lead to more jobs together. I liked Randy, would work with him again in a heartbeat, and wouldn't even mind hanging out and drinking beer. I just didn't want to date him. He was a puppy. A cute puppy, but the only things puppies inspired in me was the desire to cuddle them or shoo them out of the way, depending on my mood.

Randy wasn't looking for either.

Still, I couldn't help but smile when I thought of our last day of filming on *Steel Legions*. The car chase was everything we'd hoped it would be—so much fun it nearly made up for the rest of the shoot. I'd never driven a car that handled as well as the Cayman, which lessened the pain of having to do the driving while dressed in Vixenia's ridiculous costume.

Seriously, it was like Frankenfurter's answer to Nascar.

Who thought *that* was a good idea?

I took a surreptitious glance around the lobby. Two other hopefuls waited there, as well. An extremely curvaceous female in pants and a shirt tight enough that they might as well have been skin. Face like a young Angelina Jolie, including lips so full they were almost distracting. Even reading a magazine, she exuded sexual promise.

Definitely a succubus.

I hid a smile, wondering how many succubae and incubi Faustina Corbin saw on a weekly basis. Seriously, I'd bet at least one out of every hundred aspiring actors and actresses have a seductive demon in their bloodline. It's how the talentless become superstars.

Across from the succubus sat a painfully thin male humanoid with a pale-green complexion, so faint it could be dismissed as a trick of the light. His hair was light blond, also subtly tinted green so it looked as if he'd been swimming in chlorinated water for an entire summer. A kelpie, or maybe a dryad. I didn't want to be rude and check for gills, and the difference between earth and water critters could be tricky to spot.

I was the only full-blooded human in the room.

Still, Corbin had agreed to see me. Whether as a favor to Randy, an attempt to get on Sean's good side, or out of genuine interest, it was yet to be determined. Still, I'd make the most of the opportunity. I needed an agent, and I needed work.

"Lee Striga?"

I looked up to find a pleasant-looking woman somewhere in her forties smiling at me. Glossy dark hair drawn back in a bun, a few wrinkles on her forehead and tasteful crow's feet at the corners of both eyes. Just enough to give her character without really making her look old.

The perfect receptionist.

"That's me." I smiled and stood up, making sure my top didn't ride up over the waistband of my low-rise jeans and trying not to be conscious of the fact I wasn't a size two. Or four, or even a six.

The woman smiled again and nodded toward the door.

"This way."

Clutching my resume and headshot, I followed her down a hallway carpeted in plush hunter green, toward a closed door with an embossed FC on frosted glass panel. Much classier than the lobby led one to expect.

The woman opened the door, gesturing for me to go in. I did, noticing and appreciating the immediate aura of "relax" that washed over me when I stepped inside. More plush carpeting, dark leather furniture, armchairs like the ones you'd find in a men's club or a hunting lodge. A large dark-wood desk hunkered down against the far wall, dominating the room. Instead of the walls being wood panels—which would have completed the whole men's club décor—they were cream colored with elegantly framed photos of very high-profile clients. All of them supes, though most people wouldn't know it.

The door shut.

"Have a seat."

I glanced away from an autographed photo of last year's Best Actor winner, the inscription thanking Faustina Corbin for all her hard work, and looked at the woman who was sitting across from me on the far side of the big desk.

"So," I said. "You're not the receptionist."

The dark-haired woman who'd escorted me in gave a low chuckle.

"Well, yes, I am, at least for today." She smiled at me. The smile, while not devoid of warmth, also wasn't quite human. I couldn't quite place my finger on what she was. Yet.

Give me time.

"Tracy is out with the flu. So it's just me." She smiled again. "You want some coffee or water?"

I shook my head. "I'm good, thanks."

Faustina Corbin heaved a sigh of relief. "Thank goodness, because I have no idea how to work the fucking Nespresso machine. Which is actually a real pain in the ass, because I do *not* have time to deal with the lines at Starbucks."

"Nespresso? We have one of those at home." I spoke without thinking. "I can show you how it works, if you want."

She eyed me hopefully. "I'll be honest. I would kill for a latte about now." I almost asked if she'd sign a new client for a cappuccino, but decided against it.

Corbin pointed over to a tiny kitchenette tucked away in an alcove. An older model Nespresso machine sat in glossy red splendor, a selection of cups and saucers piled up around it. There was a mini-fridge on the floor, with an array of sweeteners and those fancy little shakers full of cinnamon, vanilla, and chocolate perched on top.

Setting my purse and resume on my chair, I went over to the alcove and pulled out some non-fat milk from the fridge.

"So you put your milk here," I said, filling the little reservoir in front. "The water goes in the back." I checked and it was already topped off. "Then you pick out which capsule you want—"

"I like the black ones," Faustina cut in. I looked up to see her smiling contentedly at me from behind her big-ass desk. I raised an eyebrow.

"So you don't want to know how to use this?"

"I'm good."

My eyebrow went even higher.

"You're doing *great*," she added with an expansive wave of one hand. "And honestly? I won't remember. Call it laziness, call it a short attention span—"

"Call it convenience," I muttered, hitting the button for two shots and steamed milk. Honestly, a trained monkey could operate one of these things. Which made me wonder if Faustina Corbin only took on clients who'd make her lattes.

"What was that?"

"Did you want any sugar in this?"

She brightened even more.

"How about honey? Is there honey over there?"

I looked. Sure enough, a SueBee honeybear sat in between a jar of Splenda and a box of sugar cubes. Honey had dripped onto the sugar cubes.

I squeezed in a dollop, then added a little more. Then, because I was there, I made myself a quick cappuccino, then started to clean the milk reservoir.

"Don't worry about that. Someone'll deal with it later."

"How'd you know I was going to clean it?" I picked up both our beverages, trying not to slosh on the carpet.

She shrugged. "I've seen Tracy do it."

"Sure you don't know how to use this and weren't just making me jump through hoops?" I set her latte down midway across the desktop, noticing that she was perusing my resume.

Her smile widened.

"You're a Katz, right? There's no need to make you jump through hoops. You kids fly through 'em." She took a sip. "Ooh, this is good!" She gave a happy sigh and drank more latte before turning her attention back to me, or rather, my resume. I took my seat and waited while she looked it over, nodding and muttering to herself.

"Hmmm. Yup. Uh-huh…"

I sipped my cappuccino. Was it my imagination or did it taste better than the ones I made at home?

"So I guess my question is, why do you need an agent at all? If you're one of Sean's protégés, he pretty much books the work without an intermediary. I call him if something comes down the pipe I think might interest him, and he's sent me a few potential clients, but we have a very informal agreement." She looked up. "I'm assuming he's told you this."

I nodded. "He did."

"So? Tell me why you need me."

A weird way to put it, but okay.

I took a sip of my cappuccino. "You know I'm adopted, right? Sort of a faux Katz. I don't fly. At least, not without wires and CGI."

"Yeah, I know, but Sean pretty much raised you, which means you've done more high falls and aerial stunts than a lot of seasoned performers, right?"

I guess I could have—and maybe should have—lied right then. Said I'd be willing to do falls. Then find a way to get out of those jobs. But wouldn't that be worse? I'd get a reputation as being unreliable and lose whatever cred I might still have left.

So I nodded, albeit reluctantly. "Thing is, I'm looking for stunt work without quite so many high falls and aerials for a while. I'd like to stay out of helicopters and avoid jumping across skyscrapers."

Faustina raised an eyebrow and studied me in silence for a few seconds, one of those silences that seemed like an hour. I stirred restlessly in my comfortably plush chair. Maybe I should have lied.

No, I had to be honest, even if it cost me an agent.

"What else can you do?"

"Pretty much any kind of stunt, excluding deep sea diving. Haven't trained too much with scuba equipment, and I'm not really interested."

"Can you swim?"

"Yup. I can surf, water ski, windsurf, and hold my breath for a very long time, but I haven't taken it past that level. Too busy throwing myself off tall buildings, I guess."

Faustina's next question was interrupted by the buzz of an incoming phone call. She had one of those old-fashioned intercom style phones with several lines.

"Sorry, hon. I'll try and make this quick." She punched the lit button. "Mana Talent Agency, this is Tracy speaking." Her voice went up an octave, taking on a perky tone more suited to a cheerleader than an agent.

"Oh, it's you." Her voice dropped to its normal tone. "Yeah, I'm on it. Yeah. I think Langdon would be perfect. No, he hasn't tried to eat anyone else on set." She rolled her eyes at me. "That was a bullshit rumor started by his ex. You know how these things go." She paused and listened. "Yeah. Uh-huh. M-hm. Uh-huh."

After about a minute of this, she finally cut into the seemingly non-stop flow of words coming out of the receiver. "Look, I'm with a client, so how about I call you back in a half hour or so. Uh-huh. Thanks. Bye."

She hung up and shook her head.

"I swear people will believe just about anything about ghouls. Langdon is the sweetest thing and besides, he only eats carrion. Why on earth would he want to eat an extra? Or anyone else, for that matter."

I shook my head, playing dumb and keeping my opinion

to myself. Sure, most ghouls only feed on corpses, but they *will* go after people if they're hungry enough, or if the prey is weak or injured. It'd been hot gossip around the Ranch when a ghoul got tossed off a low-budget horror film after attacking one of the extras who'd passed out from low blood sugar.

Which meant Faustina also played spin doctor for her clients. I wasn't sure if this was a good thing or a bad thing— it might go either way. Then again, she's been in the business for more years than I could count, so she'd been doing *something* right. Even if it meant lying some of the time.

"Normally Tracy deals with this," she explained. "I don't know how to put the damned thing on 'do not disturb,' and I think I accidentally deleted the 'we are out of the office' voicemail this morning. She won't let me do anything for myself, and this is what happens."

"Hasn't she ever been out before?"

Faustina snorted. "Are you kidding? She barely takes time off for Christmas! I have to chase her out of here. She would have dragged herself in this morning if I hadn't threatened to fire her. We only have one bathroom, for chrissake."

"Wow," I said. "That's devotion."

Faustina shrugged. "It happens. The devotion, I mean. Just not as much as there used to be."

I raised an eyebrow.

"You mean you don't know?" Faustina gave a delighted laugh. "I thought Sean would have told you. I used to be a Dacian goddess of harvest, back in the day. Lost most of my followers when the crops failed one year. I didn't feel like trying to drum up new followers, or fight some other local deity for theirs. Then when the Dacians were assimilated into Rome and Greece… well, who wants to take on Jupiter and Zeus, fer chrissake?

"So I came out here. Hung out with some of the Native American pantheon for a while and then... well, this is a great industry for reinvention."

I stared at her, fascinated.

"Sean's told me that a lot of the minor deities—ones people pray to every day—used to be big leaguers until they got shoved out of the limelight."

Faustina nodded. "Very true. When a god or goddess's worshippers stop worshipping, for whatever reason, there are certain choices we face. Some do what I did and make a career change. Others respond to random prayers and create a new niche in the market. And some do their best to stay in the big leagues, taking on new identities. Yahweh did it a few times and hit the big time."

She shook her head in disgust.

"Monotheism really screwed a lot of us. Christianity, Islam, Buddhism..." She finished her latte. "Thank God for Hinduism."

"What about Scientology?" I had to ask.

"Oh, that's just irritating. Seriously, who wants to be a Thetan?"

I laughed even though I was still trying to wrap myself around the fact that this woman was once a goddess. Then again, I'd felt just a wee bit compelled to make her a latte...

"Do you tell everyone this?" I asked.

"Oh, no," she replied with another whimsical smile. "I just have a good feeling about you. And I usually trust my feelings."

"Does that mean you're signing me as a client?"

"Oh, hon, I knew that before you walked in the door."

CHAPTER SIXTEEN

I went directly from my meeting with Faustina to Cedar Sinai Medical Center, a few blocks away on San Vicente.

It was time for my monthly appointment with my neurologist, Dr. Strangelove. Okay, that isn't really his name, but it suits him better than Dr. Jones. Which *is* his name. I mean, seriously, I've seen pictures of female cosplayers who look more like Harrison Ford than my neurologist.

Head shaped like an egg, with a shiny bald pate. Thick tortoiseshell glasses that made Harry Potter's specs look subtle. The Coke-bottle lenses magnified his eyes to the point I felt like I was being stared at by two poached eggs with brown yolks. Combine all this with a nervous tic that takes the form of an inappropriate giggle, and you have a Peter Lorre character in the making.

Still, despite his oddball appearance and mannerisms, he's the best neurologist in the area. I'm just glad he's not my gynecologist.

We went through the usual series of tests to make sure my brain was doing what it should be and not doing anything out of the ordinary. While covering my right eye and following the movements of his finger with the left, I told him about the bizarre episode of vertigo I'd experienced.

"And you say it just hit you out of the blue?" He gave a little giggle without any apparent self-awareness. I ignored it.

"I guess. I mean, I'd had kind of a rough day on the job and gotten tossed around a lot doing a fight. I had a pretty major burst of adrenaline late in the day so maybe it was just the aftermath. I probably didn't eat enough either."

"Has it happened again?"

I started to shake my head, stopping when his finger moved in an inch or so from my nose and doing my best to focus without crossing my eyes.

"No. I've had weirder dreams than usual, but that was pretty much it for vertigo."

"Dreams, huh?" Another giggle. Possibly a titter. "What kind of dreams?"

"Oh, dreams about falling, stuff like that," I answered vaguely. The thought of sharing anything even vaguely sexual with this guy skeeved me out. He nodded, looking disappointed that I had nothing more interesting to offer.

"How is your memory doing?"

I shrugged. "About the same. Still can't remember much of anything about my parents. And yet I can easily summon up irritating commercial jingles and old television theme songs without breaking a sweat."

"Hmm."

See, now why didn't he giggle when I said something that was *supposed* to be funny? It didn't make me like him any better.

"I know it's hard to believe," he said seriously, "but you're luckier than most people who've suffered falls as severe as the one you had. I'd say half of them ended up as vegetables, and those that didn't were lucky if they retained a learning level higher than grade school."

He patted me on the shoulder. I had to restrain myself from smacking his hand.

"I really do think your memories will return," he said. "Possibly when you least expect them. In the meantime, if you have another episode of the vertigo, give me a call. We may want to do a CAT scan and make sure there isn't something else going on inside that noggin of yours."

And there went the giggle.

Ugh.

†

Half an hour later, I breathed a sigh of relief when I emerged into the exhaust-choked air of the parking lot. It was preferable to being inside. I hate the sterile smell overlaid with the inevitable odor of illness and impending death that permeates hospitals and medical centers. Even the nice ones.

I checked my phone. One missed call and a voicemail from the same number. I put on my earbuds and listened to the message.

"Hey, Lee, it's Eden! You know, from Steel Legions? *Megan, you remember Megan, right? Makeup girl? Anyway, she has some free passes to a student film screening at USC tomorrow night. Guess it's time for the latest batch of creative geniuses to strut their stuff. They are geniuses, y'know. Their mommies done told them. Megan says this particular film is supposed to be the best of the batch and that the director is being touted as Tarantino meets Branagh. Hmm, if Tarantino and Branagh were put in the telepod, what movie would they make? Pulp Shakespeare? Anyway, give me a shout and let me know!"*

I grinned and hit the "call back" button.

"This is Eden."

"Hey there, it's Lee calling you back."

"Lee! Guess what? I just got an audition for tomorrow!"

"That's awesome!" I said with genuine enthusiasm. "Guess what? I just signed with an agent."

"That's double awesome! Which one?"

"Faustina Corbin."

She gave a low whistle.

"Nice! I'm with Wolf Lupin and he's good, but he's *totally* not Faustina Corbin. Omigod, I'm so happy for you! We need to celebrate!"

The nicest thing? I sensed no sour grapes.

"I'm in," I said. "We need to celebrate your audition tomorrow, too 'cause you're totally gonna kill it."

"So you wanna go to this screening? Free wine and free food after the film. Megan's going with her girlfriend, who did the costumes, and I *so* don't wanna go by myself. Not in the mood to deal with some guy who thinks he's gonna get some, either. You wanna be my date?"

I laughed. "Sure. What's the film?"

I could almost hear her shrug. "I don't remember, but given the hype and Megan's taste in movies, I'd say we're looking at pretty high levels of pretentious crap."

"And yet she worked on *Steel Legions*?"

"I know, right? Anyway, free wine?" She sounded hopeful.

"I'm there."

"Awesome. Meet me at my place at five, and we can drive over together?"

I glanced at the time. Four o'clock. That gave me more than enough time to get to Venice Beach.

"You got it."

†

A few hours later I sat in a darkened theater with Eden, Megan, her girlfriend Tandi, and about fifty other people. Hyper aware of Tandi's involvement in the film, Eden and I tried desperately not to giggle as we watched *Dark Magistrate*, which told the story of a corrupt female judge who takes justice into her own well-manicured hands for reasons that remained unclear even as the end credits scrolled down the screen.

According to the one-sheet we were handed upon our arrival, *Dark Magistrate* was directed by Derek Conalt as "a sonnet to film noir, brilliantly realized and directed with bold originality."

Missing was the more accurate description of "annoyingly artsy and derivative." Eden and I got the giggles thirty seconds into the opening credits, during which a montage of delicate lacy underwear wafted lazily to the ground. The capper was a revolver, spinning in slow-motion, falling into the middle of the pile of lingerie and discharging a bullet.

"I love my phallic symbolism subtle, don't you?" Eden whispered.

The film—and our behavior—went downhill from there. It was full of slo-mo, and more shaky cam than a Bourne flick. Dutch angles popped up frequently. At least half of the movie revolved around men trying to discover what lingerie the judge was wearing under her judicial robes. The other half involved her killing anyone who got a peek at her panties.

It should have been called *Deadly Drawers*.

We tried to rein it in for Megan and Tandi's sake, but it was a struggle, especially at the end when the judge smashed her last enemy's head in with a gavel, shrieking, "Objection overruled!"

Finally, the lights rose in the house, and the cast and crew were called down front to take a quick bow before heading up to the lobby for the reception. As soon as Tandi headed down the aisle, Megan turned to us with an expectant look.

"Well? What did you think?" Before we could say anything, she continued, "Wasn't it just amazing?"

Really?

"Well, I was certainly amazed by the size of her lingerie collection," Eden said with an admirably straight face. It didn't work. Megan shot her a look.

I turned my laugh into a coughing fit as seamlessly as possible.

"Seriously, though," she said to me. "I mean, how often do you see a movie written and directed by a man with such a strong female lead? Most men would have made the judge a man."

I couldn't stop myself. "Wouldn't that have undercut the entire subplot about her underwear?"

"It's not about the lingerie," Megan shot back. "You saw what it said on the one-sheet. This movie is a deft blow for feminism."

I couldn't help it. I snorted. "Oh, come on."

Megan answered with a withering glare. "Well, I'm going to meet Derek at the reception." With that, she swept past us and joined the stream of people heading up the aisle. Eden looked at me.

"You wanna meet the director?"

"I'd rather meet the free drinks."

†

They'd set up tables with refreshments in the lobby, reminiscent of intermissions at high school plays. Instead of punch and homemade cookies, however, there was sushi, bread, crackers, several different kinds of cheese, pates, and meats. Plenty of red and white wine, along with sparkling water.

"Someone dropped some serious cash for this," Eden whispered.

"Is this normal?" I asked.

"I'm guessing that the Boy Wunderkind comes from money."

Eden began filling her plate with reckless abandon. I followed her example. Plates filled and cabernet in hand, we looked around for Megan. She and Tandi were on the fringes of a group of people gathered around a skinny, intense guy who I assumed was Derek Conalt.

"You wanna meet him?" Eden asked doubtfully.

"Hell, no," I said. "When the nicest thing you can say to someone is 'it was very interesting,' it's better to abstain. And somehow I think Megan will appreciate our discretion."

Eden and I perched on a square planter outside of the theater, plates balanced on our knees as we ate. Her plate teetered back and forth every time she took a bite. I marveled that she could remain so slender while eating like a stevedore.

"Do you really think Megan believes the whole feminist thing about the movie?"

Eden shrugged. "Hard to say, although I think if Tandi wasn't involved she'd be a little less strident about it. But this is Tandi's first real break, so I'm sure Megan wants to be as supportive as possible."

"That makes sense," I allowed. "But what doesn't make sense is all those funky Dutch angles and the pseudo-realistic shaky cam. Was it supposed to be artsy or do you think there was actually a reason for it?"

"It's actually supposed to represent the protagonist's disconnection with reality, and her increasing disorientation as her sense of moral and ethical values gets lost in her homicidal dementia."

Huh?

Eden and I looked up to find a tall, lanky guy in khakis and a crisp white shirt standing there, staring at a point somewhere between us. Average looking, with craggy features. Not ugly, mind you, just nothing special, except for a pair of intense hazel eyes that appeared to focus on a trash can a few feet away.

He had a glass of white wine—a real glass, not a plastic cup, mind you—and a superior expression as he continued in a distinctly British accent, "At least that's what Derek will tell you."

"And you are…?"

The superior expression ratcheted up just a notch. "I'm Connor Hayden, the DP."

Perhaps I would have stated my thoughts more tactfully if I'd known the director of photography was within earshot. I mean, normally I'd have been mortified at putting my foot in my mouth, but somehow his smirk irritated me. So I decided to go for broke.

"Aside from all that psychobabble," I asked sweetly, "is there any point to shooting a film that way? Camera work for those discerning viewers who want to come up with their own interpretation? Or do the makers of motion-sickness drugs fund the films to drum up more business?"

"Me-*ow*," Eden said, not quite under her breath.

Hayden looked directly at both of us for the first time, one eyebrow raised. His gaze skimmed Eden, gave me a cursory once over, went back to Eden and then finally settled on me. He really did have exceptionally nice eyes.

"So. You didn't like the film, then?" It could have been a question or a statement, given British speech patterns. Either way, it sounded condescending.

"It was funny," I offered.

"It wasn't supposed to be funny."

"Neither was *Showgirls*. And yet…" I let my words trail off, finished my wine, and looked sadly at my empty plastic cup.

Eden immediately stood up. "I'll get us some more." She winked at me and went inside.

I munched on some brie on top of a rosemary crisp and waited.

Hayden cracked first.

"So, what do you consider good cinematography? I mean, since you're clearly an expert, you must have an opinion on the subject."

I considered the question. "A lot of old film noir. *Blade Runner. The Duelists.*"

He nodded approvingly.

"Classic *Star Trek*," I continued.

His nodding stopped.

"The *Lord of the Rings* movies. *Tron: Legacy. Dawn of the Dead.*" I couldn't resist adding the last one just to see the expression on his face, which was that of a man who'd bitten into a lemon dipped in vinegar.

"Interesting choices," he finally replied.

"I'm not all that picky." I shrugged. "I just don't like it when the camera work ends up being so clever-clever that it gets in the way of telling the story." I picked up a celery stick dipped in some sort of sundried tomato humus dip and took a bite, not caring if he answered me or not.

He nodded as if he'd come to a decision.

"It's been interesting talking to you."

"Likewise," I said. I suspect we had the same definition of "interesting."

He turned and walked back inside. I continued to eat,

wondering why I was so unperturbed by the fact that I'd just been rude to a complete stranger. Probably because my opinion had bounced off his armor without leaving so much as a scratch. Connor Hayden *clearly* didn't give a shit what I thought.

Eden returned with more wine.

"What happened to your new friend?" she asked, handing me a cup filled to the brim.

"He moved on to more complimentary pastures."

"Or greener fans?"

We both giggled.

"Any sign of Megan?"

Eden rolled her eyes. "She's in earnest conversation with little Kenny Shakespeare."

"Do you think he's as pompous as his DP?"

"Worse!"

"I don't know," I said doubtfully. "It's hard to top a guy who's too proud to drink wine out of a plastic cup."

"Hey, we need to toast your good news!" She raised her cup. "Here's to your new agent!"

"And your audition tomorrow!"

"To the future," we said at the same time.

We *thunked* our cups together and drank.

†

"Please… Let me out. I'm hungry. So hungry."

He shook his head.

"I can't. You know I can't."

She started sobbing. He knew she would. He hated it. It was so hard to resist her tears. Even though some of it was pure manipulation, he knew she suffered.

"Please! I hurt. I'm going to split open from the hunger."

"I'll fix it," he said softly, as much to himself as to her. "But I

can't let you out yet. You know I can't. I can't hide it anymore. You have to trust me."

"Please..."

Somehow he shut the sound of her sobs away from his consciousness.

CHAPTER SEVENTEEN

Flash! Ahh-ahhh…

I thought it might be time to change my ringtone.

I hadn't drunk even close to the amount Eden and I had consumed at Ocean's End and I'd gotten to bed at the respectable hour of eleven, but it still seemed awfully early for my phone to be ringing. Or singing, as the case may be.

Why *was* my phone under my pillow?

I groped around and pulled it out, glancing at the number. *Faustina.*

I immediately sat up and hit "answer."

"This is Lee," I said, doing my best to sound like I'd been up for several hours, worked out, showered, and had five cups of coffee.

"This is Faustina," she said brightly. "Sorry I woke you."

So much for my acting abilities. Then again, she didn't sound sorry at all. I flumped back down in the nest of pillows and blankets.

"No worries. What's up?"

"Can you be in Culver City by nine thirty?"

"A.M. or P.M.?"

She chuckled. "Ooh, you're a funny girl; A.M., of course."

I glanced at the time. Seven. If I got up and got out in a

half hour, I'd have a hope in hell of making my way through rush hour traffic.

"I can make it."

"Excellent! You have an interview. It's a moderate-budget horror film. Small cast, small crew. The stunt double for the female lead recently left the project, and they need a replacement yesterday. Pay's SAG minimum, weekly rate. You'll be seeing the producer, Herman Dobell. I've emailed him your resume and headshot, but you might take a copy just to be on the safe side. Never hurts, right? Got a pen?"

All of this was rattled off without so much as a hint of breath in between words or sentences. Maybe she didn't need to breathe.

I grabbed a pen and notebook off the bedside table.

"I'm ready."

"It's on Jefferson Boulevard, south of the ten, off of Robertson. Stephen J. Cannell used to have some of his studio operations there. Now there are a bunch of creative think tanks and shared work spaces where everyone sits on pillows. Still a couple of production facilities, though."

I nodded, even though she couldn't see me.

"Any suggestions on wardrobe?"

"Something tight but not too tight, and give the impression you can handle whatever comes your way. Your resume pretty much speaks for itself. Good luck!"

With that, she hung up.

I immediately stumbled out of bed, making a beeline for the shower. I stayed in there for five minutes, during four of which I ran the water steaming hot. The last minute I ran it cold enough to wake me up. I didn't have time to dry my hair so I just pulled it back into a tight braid coiled at the nape of my neck.

Then I pulled on a pair of snug jeans with some Lycra in the fabric in case I needed to demonstrate any martial arts or gymnastics. Plus they were comfy. How did women live before the invention of stretch fabric? I paired those with a tastefully tight cherry-red V-neck T-shirt and a pair of black faux motorcycle boots. The boots looked tough, but were supple enough to allow for plenty of movement.

I looked curvy, but all the hard work I'd done on *Steel Legions* had definitely paid off. I was back to fighting trim, even if my trim was a size or four larger than the Hollywood standard. A quick smudge of a smoky eyeliner, some mascara, and Burt's Bees Black Dahlia lip stain, and I was good to go. The only jewelry I wore was my mother's amulet.

Sean and Seth were already out, working on *Twitch*, a big-budget action flick with plenty of stunts involving helicopters, tall buildings, and wire work. A film adaptation of the latest hot YA dystopian series with lots of angsty teens, a repressive authoritarian government, and a heroine named Justice. Who, by the way, was blind.

I was pretty sure Jada was one of the stunt players on this one. I hadn't asked Sean a lot of questions about the project, but she'd dropped some pretty heavy-handed hints when I was around. Like "Gee, Sean, thanks so much for hiring me on *Twitch*!"

Try as I might not to think nasty thoughts about her, it wouldn't break my heart to hear that she'd accidentally done a face plant that wasn't in the script. Say, in a big old mud puddle. No bodily injury. Just a little… humility.

My ill-temper faded a bit when I saw that one of the guys, most likely Sean, had brewed a pot of coffee before they'd left, and there was still more than enough left to fill one of our many travel mugs. I threw in a splash of cream and sugar, and dashed out the door.

Rush hour at either end of the work day is brutal pretty much all over the LA Basin, but the 101 is its own special piece of hell heading south in the morning. I could take the 101 to the 405, head over the dreaded Sepulveda Pass, and connect to the 10, or I could drive over the Santa Monica Mountains to Pacific Coast Highway—a suckfest all on its own—and take surface streets once I hit Venice Beach. According to my GPS, both routes were moving at the speed of a very unambitious glacier.

I decided to suck it up and take the 101.

†

It took a full hour to get to Sunset Boulevard and then another forty-five minutes to reach Culver City. By the time I turned onto Jefferson Boulevard, I had a full bladder and approximately five minutes to make my appointment on time.

One thing Sean hammered into my head once I started working for him was never be late for a meeting or a call time. If I was going to be late, I better be either dead or in traction. I couldn't use either as an excuse today, so I drove a little faster than the speed limit advised while looking for the address.

There were several rows of converted warehouses behind iron fences on the south side of Jefferson, running the length of several blocks. They looked kind of like airplane hangars, all rounded tops and metal exteriors. Every two buildings shared a gated entryway, with the addresses posted clearly next to the gates.

Third one down I found the match for the address Faustina had given me. I swerved across the street, barely missing a gardening truck barreling down Jefferson. Ignoring their justifiably outraged honking, I pulled into the first available parking spot and hustled up to my destination.

The building had big double elephant doors, currently closed. There was a much smaller glass door that had the address plastered in larger letters right above it, as well as a sign that said *Dobell Studios*. I didn't see anyone inside and expected the door to be locked, but it opened easily.

In the lobby the walls were free of art or posters. To the right of a single desk, a hallway vanished off into the distance, with several closed doors leading off of it. I hoped one of them was the bathroom.

The rest of the lobby consisted of a couple of blandly upholstered chairs, a water cooler, and a little table with a few magazines—mostly *People*, *Entertainment Weekly*, and my favorite junk magazine, *US*. I mean, gotta love the Fashion Police, right? And it always comforts me to know that "Stars Are Just Like Us."

A bell sat on the front edge of the desk, like the sort you'd ring at a hotel to get someone's attention. I rang it once and then hastily sat down, crossing and re-crossing my legs while I tried to lose myself in an article.

"Hi there." A male voice, soft-spoken and soothing, like auditory honey. The word that came to mind was "mellifluous."

When I looked up, the man standing in front of me gave the impression of a human praying mantis. Tall and thin, almost ascetic at first glance. Prematurely graying blond hair, ice-blue eyes that would look at home on a husky, and a thin face with high cheekbones so sharp they looked as though they might cut you if you touched them.

He wore what looked like an expensive suit that fit just a little too loosely, as if it'd been tailored when he was ten pounds heavier. The overall impression was that a harsh word or a strong wind would blow him away. I found myself wanting to speak very quietly and gently, and offer him soup.

"Herman Dobell." He held out his hand with a smile that transformed his rather ordinary face into something special. "I'm the producer."

"Hi." I smiled at him with my best friendly-yet-professional smile. "I'm Lee. Lee Striga." Taking his outstretched hand, I shook it. A nice grip, firm but not trying to prove anything. I tried to ignore the little frisson of electricity I felt when our palms touched.

"Sorry you had to wait," he said, letting go of my hand almost reluctantly. "When I can, I like to greet people myself. See what they're like right off the bat."

"So no receptionist?"

He shook his head. "Not for interviews. You can tell a lot about someone when they think they're waiting for an assistant, instead of someone in charge."

I thought I might like this guy.

"Did you learn anything about me?"

"Well, I know that you're punctual, and you're polite. Not a bad start." Dobell smiled again, showing off those cheekbones to advantage. My eyes flickered involuntarily—and briefly—to his left hand.

No ring.

Of course, that didn't mean anything in this town where women wore wedding rings to avoid unwanted attention and men hid them to keep their options wide open.

Not that I'm cynical or anything.

"Let's go back to my office," he said.

I nodded, putting the *US* down as I stood up.

"Will I be meeting with the director and the stunt coordinator, as well?"

"Well, Miss Striga," he said gently, "I'm not just a producer on this film. I'm also the executive producer, and I believe in a very hands-on approach. When I back a production, I meet everyone who's hired and make sure that they'll bring the qualities and talent that I demand."

"I see," I said.

"I've given a lot of people their first chances in the industry. The director is one of them. He's talented and creative, but sometimes his criteria are very different from mine. Perhaps it's my ego talking, but when it comes to certain judgment calls, my experience speaks for itself."

It sounded like Herman Dobell had some control issues. Then again, if he was putting out the money, who was I to give a shit?

"Would you like some coffee?"

"I'm good, thank you."

"Are you sure? I'm going to have some. I kind of hate drinking alone, even if it's just coffee."

I hesitated.

"Don't worry," he added quickly. "I make good coffee. None of that instant crap."

Well, okay then.

"In that case, I'd love some. If you don't mind, though, I'd love to make a pit stop first. It was a long drive here."

"Of course. Right this way." Dobell led me down the hall and pointed the way to the ladies' room. "Here you go. My office is two doors down on the left. Meet me there when you're done."

I thanked him and was halfway through the bathroom door when he said, "How do you take your coffee? And is Americano okay?"

"Cream and sugar, please, and absolutely!"

He gave me another one of those heart-stopping quicksilver smiles, and headed off down the hall.

I did my business, took a quick glance at my face in the bathroom mirror to make sure my makeup was still doing its job, and hurried back out. I was anxious to continue with this meeting. Herman Dobell intrigued me on a number of levels, and not just because he'd promised me coffee.

Although that didn't hurt.

†

A few minutes later I sat across from him in front of a utilitarian desk in a small, windowless office. A big mug of extremely good coffee rested in front of me. A table in the corner housed an expensive Breville espresso maker and the aroma of freshly ground coffee beans floated in the air.

The office, while relatively small, held a remarkable jumble of books, scripts, head shots, and resumes in semi-organized fashion. At least a hundred scripts were stacked on top of one another in a couple of white Ikea bookcases, while the head shots and resumes took up most of a utilitarian desk, separated into six piles. Dozens of books seemed to hang suspended midair thanks to some free-standing metal shelves scattered around the room. One was only partially filled and kind of reminded me of a human spine.

"Those are cool," I said.

He grinned. "Aren't they? They're called spine towers, and they're great when you've run out of wall space for bookshelves."

He had my resume on the desk directly in front of him, all by its lonesome. I recognized the head shot, one I'd had taken a month before the accident. He tapped the picture with an index finger.

"Great shot. You have amazing eyes. They show well, even in black-and-white."

"Thanks," I said, having learned long ago to accept a compliment without trying to persuade the giver they were wrong. "Although, honestly, it doesn't matter all that much when you're doing stunts. My eyes have yet to be featured in a close-up."

"Ah, but I imagine this—" He tapped the picture again. "—has gotten you through a few doors, if only because the producer or director wanted to meet you."

I barely stopped myself from rolling those amazing eyes. "Well, hopefully it's my resume that got me through *this* door." I gave him what I hoped was a friendly yet neutral smile. I didn't want to alienate a possible employer, but if he'd called me for an interview to ask me on a date—well, he'd picked the wrong head shot.

"I'm sorry," he said, shaking his head. "That came out rather badly."

I took pity on him. "No worries."

"Seriously, your resume is really impressive. When Faustina tossed your name into the ring, I didn't realize you'd worked with Sean Katz." The phone rang. Dobell glanced at the screen, then looked at me apologetically. "Can you excuse me for just a minute? I need to answer this."

"No problem."

He stuck on a Bluetooth headset, swiveling his chair to face the other direction. I turned my attention to the books on the free-standing shelves and did my best not to eavesdrop.

A lot of *New York Times* bestsellers, genre fiction and literary, as well. One shelf was devoted to nonfiction, with a lot of books on religion, myths, and magic. Another held history books covering a wide range of subjects—everything from wars to weapons, clothing and architecture to diseases. I pulled out a book on the outbreak of Spanish influenza and flipped through it.

"Sorry about that."

Startled, I swiveled my chair back around to face him.

"No worries." I hastily put the book back in its place.

Dobell glanced down at my resume again. "*Vampshee*. Wasn't there a stuntwoman injured on that show?"

I heaved an involuntary sigh.

"I'm sorry, is there a problem?" He didn't say it as if he expected there to be one, though. It sounded like he was concerned that he had offended me. Of course, he *was* the producer. It was his job to be diplomatic.

"It's just that there are certain expectations that come as part of the Katz Stunt Crew," I said slowly. "When I got injured on *Vampshee*, it made it difficult for me to live up to those expectations. Since most of the jobs they're offered include lots of high falls and challenging aerial work, I'm trying to take a step back and build up my resume in other areas."

"I see."

"So if you're thinking this would be a great excuse to add a three-story jump by one of your characters, that probably won't work for me—not at this time. A few months from now? Maybe. But not quite yet."

He laughed. "There's none in the script, and none are planned. Most of the stunts involved in *Pale Dreamer* take place in close-quarters. Our leading lady can't do a realistic punch to save her life, and we have a pretty intense knife fight. She also happens to be violently afraid of heights, and doesn't even like to stand near the edge of a ten-foot drop. So even if we did decide to add any such stunt, we'd most likely use a green screen and CGI."

That was a double-edged sword, so to speak. On one hand, special effects have the potential of putting a lot of stunt players out of business. After all, why pay union wages when you can fake it with CGI?

On the other hand, there are certain stunts that are just crazy-ass dangerous, and it would be better to do them in the FX department, than see someone lose their life trying to do the impossible. There's always someone crazy enough to try, though, and they're not always supes.

"So," he said. "Do you have any questions you'd like to ask?"

Speaking of which…

"This is a little awkward, but I guess I'd like to know if you're looking for a supe for this job. I realize it's a little unusual, since I'm with MTA, but I'm actually a hundred percent human."

"Miss Striga," he replied seriously, "if I hire you, it'll be for the same reason I've hired everyone else on any of my productions, and that's for the skills and talent you'll bring— not for your genetic heritage. As it happens, most of the cast and crew on *Pale Dreamer* aren't supernatural. Not by intent— it's just how it played out this time. I've got no prejudices one way or the other, and hope you don't have any either."

I let out a sigh of relief.

"Awesome."

He smiled. "So… any other questions?"

"Who would I be doubling? Faustina didn't have time to tell me much."

"Fair enough," he said, wrapping both hands around his coffee cup, a heavy white ceramic mug that reminded me of old-time diners. He inhaled the steam rising from the dark brew before continuing.

"First of all, let me apologize for the short notice. This was a last-minute thing. We've had the cast and crew filled out for the last couple months while the set was being built.

When I realized we had to replace Gracie, I didn't want to waste any time."

"If I can ask, was it an issue with her work?"

"More like an issue with our lead," Dobell said. "She can be a bit temperamental."

"I see," I said.

Oh, shit, I thought. "Rather temperamental" is generally a polite way of saying "total bitch."

"You might've heard of her," Herman continued. "Portia Lambert."

Oh, crap. I'd heard of Portia Lambert. Most people involved in show business had heard of her. Hell, anyone who read the tabloids was familiar with her. Portia was a former child star who'd made it big in the nineties in *Brentwood High*, one of those shows about the oh-so-dramatic problems of privileged teenagers living in an expensive ZIP code.

Ms. Lambert had started with the reputation of a diva, and when she'd hit eighteen she'd taken the attitude to new heights. She'd been canned from *Brentwood High* after three seasons because of her inability to get along with any of her costars, even though her character Molly was one of the most popular with viewers.

Supposedly she'd mellowed out after a few years of little or no work and had landed *Enchanted Pages*, a series about a bookstore owner who's an amateur sleuth and a witch. The series ran for a few seasons, but Portia was released from her contract after season two because of rumored substance abuse. The writers brought in her character's cousin to take over the bookstore, the sleuthing, and the witchy business.

"Let me ask you this." I set my mug down and leaned forward. "Did Gracie quit or was she fired? Because if I have to worry about walking on eggshells around Portia, I'm not interested."

Did I just say that?

Lord, don't let Faustina find out I just said that.

Herman Dobell looked at me. I couldn't read his expression so I plunged ahead.

"I'm all about playing nice," I continued, "and I don't mind catering to fragile egos, because that's part of the game and I don't have an ego stake in my work, other than doing a good job. But getting fired on a whim doesn't appeal. On the other hand, if my predecessor quit because she couldn't deal with a little heat, that's her problem, not mine."

"You don't pull punches, do you?"

Maybe I should apologize, I thought. Instead I said, "I don't see the point. You said yourself you don't have a lot of time to find a replacement. The quicker we figure out if this is a good fit for both of us, the better for your production and the faster I can look for another job, if I need to."

I didn't seem to have any control over what came out of my mouth.

Dobell steepled his fingers and stared at me thoughtfully, as if coming to a decision. This was it. He was going to say "thanks but no thanks." Faustina would never send me out on another audition. I'd live at the Ranch until I died, reduced to doing beer runs for all the cool kids.

"Okay, fair enough," he said.

I let out a breath I hadn't realized I'd been holding.

"Gracie quit," he continued. "She and Portia were at odds pretty much from day one. Physically Gracie was a decent match for Portia." He paused, then added, "Back when she was in her teens."

"Ah. I think I see where this is heading."

"Yeah, I'm sure you do. Gracie is nineteen. She's gorgeous, talented, but not that mature."

I hadn't been that mature at nineteen either. Hell, I wasn't all that sure I was particularly mature at twenty-seven.

"Needless to say, that didn't help the situation. She knew she was younger and better-looking than Portia, and there was definitely some flaunting going on."

Oh man, I hoped he wasn't going to dump all the blame on Gracie. If so, that would tell me everything I needed to know about the guy.

"That being said," he continued, "Portia piled on the attitude pretty thick as soon as she saw what was essentially a younger, fitter version of herself, standing there in front of her."

"Like seeing herself in a mirror," I said, "but knowing she'd never look like that again."

"Exactly that." He stared at me intently. "I'll tell you something, Ms. Striga. You're still younger than she is by at least a decade, probably a little more. Overall you're a better match for Portia physically. Even more important, you're more emotionally mature than Gracie. I think Portia might be more comfortable with you and therefore less likely to act out. If she does, though, can you deal with it?"

I nodded. "I've worked with a lot of difficult people over the years—including my cousin, who's one of the most temperamental people you'd ever hope not to meet. We haven't killed each other yet, so yeah, I can put up with a little bit of attitude."

"Good." He sounded pleased.

"Now that we've got that out of the way," I said, "maybe you could tell me a little about the production."

His eyes lit up. "Indeed. We've got a small crew. I find that fewer people actually do a more efficient job on a smaller-budget film, and we stand a chance of the audience actually sitting through the credits."

I smiled at that, and he continued.

"The shooting schedule is tight but manageable. It's a small cast, as well. Six main characters, a couple of extras in a flashback scene. Small, contained sets. Most of the story takes place on a small spacecraft."

"Faustina said it was a horror film?"

"Horror with some sci-fi elements. Some humor, too."

Humor is good, I thought. *As long as it's intentional.*

"It's about a deep space satellite repair crew who run into a derelict ship, and bad things happen."

"Tell me nothing bursts out of someone's chest."

Dobell laughed. "Nope. No exploding eggs, either, and no humans used as incubation chambers. The writers are a husband-and-wife team. Dan and Breanna Tymon. They've done a few low-budget films and the scripts are always good. The dialogue crackles, and they've always delivered something unique, even when they've had to recycle derivative crap."

Sounded good to me. "Where are you filming?"

"Here."

"In Los Angeles?"

He waved a hand in the air.

"I mean here. A lot of the buildings on this stretch of Jefferson are converted warehouses, many of which used to be small soundstages. This one still is. I lucked out and snapped it up when it came on the market." He smiled at me. "Next question?"

"Who else is in the cast?"

"Our lead actor is Ben Farrell. He did some low-budget

horror films in the late eighties and then got out of the business."

"I've seen *Dead Maze* a few times," I said.

Dead Maze was one of the first zombie movies to catch on with George Romero fans. Low budget, nihilistic, and gory, it had rapidly achieved cult status. Farrell enjoyed the same kind of low-grade stardom that Bruce Campbell achieved after the *Evil Dead* movies. I'd watched it at least twice during my convalescence. Sean and I were both suckers for horror movies.

Dobell nodded approvingly. "Farrell started hitting the convention circuit a few years ago, and now he's looking to get back into film. The writers pretty much wrote this part with him in mind."

Nice for him.

"And our two villains are played by Joe Scout and Angel Cortez."

I recognized those names as well. Both had been working steadily for the last twenty years and—like Farrell—had achieved a degree of low-budget cult stardom. Angel was a well-known B-movie scream queen, past her prime only in the eyes of Hollywood ageism. Still beautiful and—unlike some of the other scream queens—a damn fine actress.

Joe Scout, a character actor, was likewise very good at his craft. Notorious for taking a script and running off the reservation with improvised dialogue. Since his improv tended to be better than a lot of the scripts, he continued to get work.

"We were about to sign Imogene Lee as the ingénue," Dobell continued, "but she got a better offer."

"Ah."

Imogene's reputation was about as bad as Portia's. She was touted as the next Megan Fox, but without the brains.

"We pay SAG minimum," he said. "Is that going to be a problem for you?"

"Totally fine." There was no need to reveal the sad state of my bank account, or my last pathetic paycheck.

"Excellent." He steepled his fingers and looked at me. "So… any more questions?"

I thought about it. "Not that I can think of at the moment."

"I asked our stunt coordinator to meet with us here at ten thirty." He glanced at his expensive watch. "That gives us a half hour, so how about I show you around the set? I'd like you to see the layout so you'll have an idea of the kind of space you'll be working in."

CHAPTER EIGHTEEN

I followed Herman Dobell out of his office to closed double doors at the furthest end of the hallway, ones with push handles. He pushed one side open and gestured gallantly with his free hand.

"After you."

The doorway led into another hallway, this one substantially wider. There were a couple of closed doors to the left.

"Costumes and Makeup departments," he said.

"Nice."

There was another set of double doors at the other end. Above those doors was a carefully hand-lettered sign.

RED LIGHT MEANS WE'RE FILMING. YOU SHOULD KNOW WHAT THAT MEANS IF YOU'RE WORKING HERE.

I laughed. "Does anyone make that rookie mistake anymore?"

"Oh, sure. You'd be surprised—even when the light's lit. Usually a PA, someone new to the business. I cut them some slack… the first time."

Grinning, I shook my head.

"Oh, man. When I was six, Sean was working on some new pilot on the Warner Bros.' lot. They were filming inside one of the soundstages. The gal looking after me, some poor production assistant, kept trying to tell me I had to wait until they were finished filming before I could go see him." I gave a rueful laugh. "You try telling any six-year-old that she has to wait."

"I see where this is going."

"Oh, yeah. I ignored my handler and ran into the middle of what was evidently a *very* expensive scene to shoot. Let's just say the director didn't give me a pass for my age *or* the first time mistake."

"Ouch."

"Ouch indeed. On the upside, I haven't made that particular mistake again." The sounds of hammering and power tools filtered faintly through the door. The red light was currently off. "Still working on the sets?"

"Just some last-minute touchups and adjustments. We're pretty much on schedule to start filming next week." He pushed the doors open and we walked onto the soundstage, dimly lit with overhead bulbs so high up that they barely cut through the shadows. The space stretched back at least a hundred yards, and about half that in width—about the size of a football field. The ceilings had to be at least forty feet high, maybe more. The word "cavernous" came to mind. A few bats would have fit right in.

"Any reason it's so dark in here?" I asked.

"You asked about supernaturals? Rafaella—the production designer—and her crew are light sensitive."

"Ah." I didn't ask what they were, but gnomes or dwarves seemed a fair guess. I heard hammering, sawing, power tools, but didn't see anyone beyond a glimpse or two of dim figures moving in and out of the shadows.

The closest third of the soundstage belonged to part of a spacecraft. A large portion of the hull had been built, looking as though it floated in the shadows. There were ladders and stairs leading up to interior platforms. The exterior appeared to have lived a hard, rough life.

"This looks great."

Dobell looked pleased. "Well, the set for the hero ship was actually constructed over fifteen years ago for another film. The building's former owner kept it in decent condition and rented it out to low-budget and student projects. When I bought the soundstage and facilities, it was still here. We put some work into it over the last month or so, updated it so now it doesn't look quite so much like it belongs in a Crazy Casa production."

I snickered. Movies involving mutant mash-ups of various reptiles, sea creatures, insects, and mammals were Crazy Casa's stock-in-trade. Lots of bad CGI and a high body count for countless bikini-clad starlets and their hunky male counterparts.

It's been speculated that their development team had a big hat filled with pieces of paper, each one bearing the name of some critter. Whenever they needed a new movie idea, someone pulled two slips out of the hat and they ended up with classics like *Crocsnake*, *Arachnogator*, and *Spider Chimp*.

The exterior of the spacecraft was painted a medium gray. About ten feet above our heads there were letters stenciled along the side in white. *Bootes*.

"Boots?"

"According to the writers, it's pronounced 'booties.' Or 'bootey,' depending on which character is speaking."

"Okay, that'll probably make sense once I read the script."

"Well, it's an inside joke between the writers, so maybe not. But it's a good script. Funny, creepy, scary. Trust me, it hits all the right notes."

We walked around the curved front of the spacecraft. The other side exposed the interior sets, all cross-sections like one of those books about how things work. Some of the sections had partial ceilings, while in others the walls stretched up, merging into the shadows of the open soundstage.

A ship's ladder led up to the interiors. "Mind if I take a look?"

"Not at all. Do you need a hand up?"

"Is that a trick question?" I flashed a smile over one shoulder. Scrambling up the ladder, I found myself on what looked like the bridge of the *Bootes*. Simple, but realistic. Two swivel chairs with instrument panels directly in front, sitting below the forward windows. More screens and panels covered the walls on either side. A lot of care had been put into the details. Closer examination revealed things like old car window cranks and a coffee grinder, built in and made to look like something that belonged here.

"Very creative," I commented to Dobell as he joined me up on the set.

"Rafaella is amazing," he agreed. "So is her crew. I don't think I've ever met anyone who can do so much with so little and consistently stay under budget."

We did a walk-through of the rest of the interiors. There was a cabin with an Israeli flag plastered to the wall, a Blu-ray player, and DVDs of movies like *Alien* and *Terminator*.

"No Netflix, huh?"

He laughed. "No. We're aiming for low-tech here. Most horror, fantasy, or science fiction requires some sort of suspension of disbelief. Hopefully the audience won't overthink it too much."

We walked down a long stretch of corridor, about twenty feet of it, to another half-open room with a bunch of random parts lying on the floor and a table, as well as stacked on shelving units.

"This is the repair bay," he explained, then he pointed across the way and down. "And that is the cargo area. The original set designer installed heavy steel racks used for storing auto salvage parts," Dobell continued, pointing out some examples. "Great idea, so we built on it. A lot of the sets are modular, too, so we can expand the shooting space a little bit and create new rooms as we need them, with minimal time and effort."

"We'll be filming fights on the actual sets, right?"

"That's right. Very little green screen, I think. Do you see any problem with that?"

"Not really. No doubt your stunt coordinator will tailor the choreography to the sets. I don't have any issue with the space."

He gave me an approving nod. "Darius is going to love you. Gracie was a little rattled by the close quarters."

"Darius?"

"Darius Ciobanescu, the stunt coordinator."

"I don't think I know the name."

"Oh, I did a couple of films with him in Romania. Darius wanted to do some work over here, so I pulled him in for this project. You'll love him!"

Sam Raimi, Quentin Tarantino, James Cameron, all of them had a reputation for hiring friends and sometimes family. There's nothing wrong with nepotism, as long as the job gets done. I hoped Dobell was as careful in his choices.

We reached the end of the *Bootes* set and climbed a ladder back down to the ground. I was pleased to note that the ten-foot drop to the cement floor didn't bother me at all.

The rest of the soundstage was shrouded in darkness, so even I couldn't see more than a few feet in front of me. Dobell gave a call out in a language I didn't recognize, although it sounded vaguely Nordic. Lights flickered on further into the soundstage, casting just enough of a glow further back in the cavernous space to show the exterior of another spaceship, all jagged edges.

The surface was... disturbing. Seriously, whatever the set designer used to paint the exterior succeeded in creating a dark, oily sheen that screamed "bad guys in here!"

It looked alien, hostile.

"That," Dobell said, "is the Morganti vessel."

"The Morganti being the bad guys, right?"

"What was your first clue?"

He gave me a quick, boyish grin and then led the way over to the Morganti ship, which was even creepier upon closer inspection. I stared up at it, impressed and repulsed at the same time.

"What kind of paint did they use?"

He shrugged. "I'm not really sure. I just know Rafaella showed me the concept drawings and then a sample of the paint that totally blew me away. Come on. If you think the exterior is creepy, wait till you see the inside."

I followed him almost reluctantly to a dark indentation in the middle of the ship's hull. And oh, wow, he wasn't kidding. The interior was borderline nightmarish. The set designer utilized shapes and curves not normally found in modern-day architecture and gave the impression of something not of this world.

"Damn."

Dobell nodded, satisfied with my reaction.

"I know. It's good, isn't it?"

"It's…" *Fucked up.* "…disturbing."

"Perfect!"

I sniffed. "It smells like fresh paint in here."

"Well, fresh as of last night, but close enough."

More of the dark, oily-textured paint covered the interior walls, with splashes of a lighter shade reminiscent of the inside of oyster shells. But unlike mother-of-pearl, the colors used here were almost sickly. A pallid gray tinted with bilious green, mixed with a weird shade of purple that just seemed wrong. The overall results made me feel borderline nauseous. I blamed it on paint fumes in an enclosed space and kept walking. The floors were slotted metal, like the floors in a livestock feeding pen.

Not a very comforting image.

We stopped after a few feet, in a stretch of corridor with alcoves set into the walls, each one bearing a different item. Almost like trophy displays.

One item in particular, a mask with two faces, caught my attention. Very similar to the classic drama mask for comedy and tragedy, but depicting a man and a woman instead. Neither side of the equation looked happy. It looked like a real artifact, something that would be found at an archaeological dig. I felt drawn to it, something familiar sparking memories I couldn't quite grasp.

I turned to ask Dobell if he knew its origins and found him studying me intently, his expression strange. I must have turned my head too suddenly, because suddenly a blinding pain struck me between my eyes. The back of my neck itched as if a family of fleas had just taken up residence.

I gasped and reached out blindly, grabbing the railing in front of me as I was hit by an all-too-familiar dizziness.

Oh no, I thought. *I will* not *have the shit hit me now.* All I needed was for Dobell to think I was Miss Fragile. I'd never get the job.

I will not faint, I will not faint, I WILL NOT FAINT.

I didn't. The worst of it passed, leaving me shaken but not stirred. When I knew I wasn't going to pass out, I looked at Herman Dobell again, only to find him gripping the railing too, sweat dripping down his brow.

"Are you okay?" My voice sounded weak to my own ears, but he didn't seem to notice. He started to nod, then stopped, holding a hand up. The knuckles were still white from clenching the railing.

"Just dizzy. I'll be okay. Just…" His voice trailed off.

I waited, noticing how thin his features looked in the eerie lighting. I wondered if he was on the tail end of something like mono or Lyme's Disease.

"Okay. Better now." He took in a deep breath, steadying himself. "Wow. That was not good."

"I think we should get out of here and let the paint dry," I said. "And maybe open the elephant doors, get some fresh air in here if it won't upset the design crew too much."

"Yeah. I think you're right. I could use some more coffee, too."

"Sounds good to me."

He took his other hand off the railing, gave a little shake of his head, and led the way out of the set. We emerged at the far end of the soundstage, where another set of elephant doors was partially obscured by flats of wood and pieces of metal, all painted in the same disturbing shade as the rest of the ship. It smelled fresh, as well. I averted my eyes. Silly, I know, but just looking at it made my stomach give a final queasy flip.

The further away we got from the Morganti ship, the better I felt.

There were a couple of doors off to the side. Dobell saw me looking.

"FX, set design, and props department."

"This is a seriously great facility," I said, meaning it.

"It really is. I was lucky to get first crack at it when it came up on the market. There's not a lot of storage space for, say, multiple sets and wardrobes. But I'm not too worried. The property next door may come on the market, as well, and that would pretty much solve all my problems." He paused, expression rueful, adding, "Well, not all of them, but at least the ones that are film related."

The shadow that passed over his face came and went so quickly that most people probably wouldn't have noticed it.

Dobell's jacket pocket chirped. He took out his phone and glanced at the screen.

"Jack is running late today. He's not going to be here until noon."

"And Jack is…?"

He smacked himself on the forehead. "I am so sorry. I don't know where my head is at today. Jack Garvey. He's the director. I thought I'd mentioned that earlier."

"You may have," I said diplomatically, even though he hadn't. "At any rate, I don't mind waiting, if you think it would seal the deal."

He smiled at me. "Don't worry, you've got the job. Meeting with Jack would just be a formality at this point, anyway."

"If you're sure." I gave an uncomfortable shrug. "It's just, some people get kind of twitchy if they're left out of the process."

Dobell waved a hand dismissively. "He's got plenty of other things on his mind about now. It's much more important for you to meet Darius." We reached his office. The door was ajar, and he glanced at his watch.

"Ah, good! He's here."

Darius Ciobanescu stood up when we walked in. Dark hair, dark eyes. Short and stocky, with a lot of compact muscles under jeans and a light-weight long-sleeved cotton shirt. We took each other's measure quietly and thoroughly.

He emanated a quiet competence and a strength that didn't need any advertising. We sat down, he looked at my resume, and asked me a few questions in a thick but understandable Romanian accent. Looked at my resume some more, nodded with a satisfied grunt, and then shook my hand.

"Welcome to the team."

CHAPTER NINETEEN

Anyone who's ever tried to make it in show business will tell you that the best thing to do after an audition or meeting is to not think about it. Some people—usually ones who spend lots of money on New Age self-help books—will tell you to visualize the preferred outcome and then send it out of your mind.

"Envision yourself putting your outcome in a little boat and then send it sailing down a river. If you let it go, like the baby Moses, it will find a nurturing environment and achieve great potential."

Or it could end up wandering around in a desert for forty or so years with a bunch of disgruntled Israelites.

None of the articles or books tell you what to do when you actually get the job. I decided to give Eden a call and see if she was finished with her audition. Sadly, her phone went straight to voicemail.

Rats.

I left a quick message explaining I'd scored a stunt job, ending with, "I hope you rock your audition today. Talk to you later maybe?" I wanted to celebrate, dammit!

Deciding to head home, I stopped at BevMo and picked up a bunch of good beer, raiding the craft brew section with the enthusiasm of someone who would soon have a decent paycheck.

When I arrived at the Ranch, Sean and Seth were still out on set for the YA dystopian flick. The back yard was totally deserted. So I put the beer in the fridge, keeping out a Modern Times Monsters' Park stout, which I carefully poured into a large snifter. I took a sip and sighed in contentment. If I ever stopped exercising, I'd need to develop a taste for less fattening beverages.

Then I texted Sean.

> Got good news. Ready
> to celebrate. What's your
> ETA?

A few minutes later a text came back.

> Not sure what time we're getting out
> of here. May have to celebrate later.
> Can't wait to hear your news.

Well, hell.

I thought briefly about calling Randy. He was fun company and I knew he'd be happy for me, and totally into celebrating if he wasn't busy. But somehow that didn't seem fair to him.

I really liked the guy and wanted to stay friends with him. Doing anything that might lead him on, even inadvertently, wasn't the way to go about it. So I reluctantly shelved the idea. Instead I pulled out my copy of the *Pale Dreamer* script, taking it, my phone, and my glass of stout outside to the porch.

There I glanced up at the rock outcropping, a little

nervous, but there were no dark intruders in sight. Relaxing, I read and drank, enjoying the breeze wafting down from the mountains.

†

I finished the script and the beer at about the same time, equally satisfied with both of them. Herman was right about the writing. It *was* good. Both funny and creepy, with humor in just the right amount alongside the action and the scary stuff. Thrilling, fast-paced, and yeah, original and kind of edgy.

The two main characters, Jeanette and Jake, were, respectively, an Israeli soldier and a born-again Muslim. Piloting a deep space repair ship, they find a derelict craft that's reminiscent of a horror fun house, filled with corpses and an out-of-commission female android named Zoe.

Jake and Jeanette cart Zoe back to the *Bootes* and bring her back on line. Zoe tells them about the Morganti, decadent thrill seekers searching for new forms of destructive and sadistic pleasure. They played dead while Jake and Jeanette explored their ship, but now they're awake and eager for more fun.

Jeanette had most of the action, including a truly kick-ass knife fight against Shaad, the male Morganti played by Joe Scout. Darius was doubling Joe, which meant this could be an awesome piece for my demo reel. It was one thing to work opposite an actor in a fight, but getting to work with someone who really knew what they were doing?

That was the best.

I put the script down, excited and frustrated at the same time. *Dammit, I wish I had someone to celebrate with*. This was *so* totally unfair.

My phone beeped next to me. I looked down to find a text message from Randy.

Hey Lee! Got another job, some
motorcycle stunts for a Vin Diesel
flick! You wanna have a beer and help
me celebrate?

Okay then… That officially took the onus off me. I grinned and hit the call back for Randy's number. As soon as I got off the phone with him, I called in a couple of pizzas for delivery.

Randy pulled up at the Ranch about an hour later. I went out to meet him, pleased to see bags full of yet more craft beer and munchies in the back seat. He saw me, jumped out of the car, and I blurted out my news.

"You got the job!"

He grabbed me in a big bear hug, picking me up and spinning me around. I let him do it without argument. It felt good to have someone happy for me.

"And I wouldn't have gotten it without Faustina," I said after he'd set me back down on my feet. "Which means I wouldn't have gotten it without you."

"That's just kind of awesome."

"Congrats to you, too," I said, not wanting to hog all the attention. "Vin Diesel, huh? That is so cool!"

"I know, right?"

I gave him a spontaneous hug of my own—not quite picking him off the ground, but close. We grinned at each other, happy energy sparking between us.

The kiss that followed seemed a perfectly natural extension of the happiness, hitching a ride on the high of all the good news.

Hmmm, I thought. He tasted good. Like chai tea.

He didn't kiss like a puppy either. No sloppy tongues or more enthusiasm than technique. I mean, there was plenty of enthusiasm on both sides, but Randy could kiss and he knew just where to press on the back of my neck and scalp, thumbs tracing my jawline.

Within what seemed like seconds, our clothes were flying off onto the carport floor. He somehow managed to free my hair from its pins and braid, running his fingers through its length as we continued to kiss. We ended up in the back seat of Randy's Challenger, bags of beer and food shoved to the floor. A tiny voice at the back of my head kept saying "Wait." I promised the voice I'd deal with it later.

†

A very short but very entertaining time later, Randy and I started pulling our clothes back on, sweaty but satisfied. I didn't ask him why he had condoms in his glove compartment, and he didn't answer. It was enough that they were there when we needed them. I was *so* not ready for kids.

I'd just pulled my jeans up when another car roared up the road below, going much faster than common sense dictated.

"Oh, shit, is that Drift?"

Randy and I looked at each other, then scrambled for the rest of our clothing. By the time the car—still breaking speed records—sped up the drive, we were both dressed and pulling out bags from the back floor of the Challenger.

Nothing to see here, right?

We watched the car, a red Camaro that had put in some time, screech to a stop a few feet away. A skinny Hispanic kid in board shorts and an aloha shirt jumped out of the car.

"You ordered pizza?"

"That would be me," I said. "Hang on a sec, I'll get my wallet."

Randy reached out and put a hand on my shoulder.

"Let me get this."

"You sure?"

He cocked his head to one side and smiled.

"Yeah. You can get the next one."

I let him pay. Partly because I got the whole male ego trip, but also because I really couldn't afford it. So I carried the beer and snacks inside while Randy dealt with our Nascar pizza delivery kid. The bags held a cornucopia of yumminess from Trader Joe's. Dips, chips, snacks like bacon-wrapped scallops and tempura shrimp, and enough beer to satisfy the after-party for any of our Saturday training sessions.

As the Camaro sped off down the drive, the front door opened and closed, and Randy joined me in the kitchen with two large pizzas.

"Hungry?"

"Hell, yeah."

"If I say something about celebrating with a bang, will you hit me?"

I gave him a sideways look. "Bad, Squid. *Very* bad."

"I thought it was pretty good, myself."

And there it was. The suddenly uncomfortable squiggly feeling in my stomach that told me I might have made a bad decision.

"Look—"

"Wait." Randy put the pizza boxes on the counter. "I know what you're gonna say, and you don't have to say it, okay?"

"I don't?"

He shook his head. "Nah. Look. What happened was great. More than great. More than I ever expected. And while it would be great if it happened again, I'm okay if it doesn't."

"You are?"

Did I sound a little insulted there?

"Yeah. I mean, no, but yeah." He shook his head. "I like you, Lee. A lot. You're kind of amazing all the way around. But if I have to choose between sex and losing your friendship, it's an easy choice. It would be nice if I didn't have to choose, but I'm not stupid."

I looked at him for a moment. Really looked at him, past those generically handsome features.

"No," I replied. "No, you're not."

Pulling out a couple of plates for the pizza and another snifter, I opened two more Monster's Park stouts, poured them out, and handed him one. I tilted my head to one side and smiled at him.

"Did you know your eyes go all gold when you're turned on?"

We settled on the couch with our pizza, beer, and snacks, and binge-watched *Kolchack: The Night Stalker*, a series made in the early seventies about an intrepid and kinda ghoulish reporter with a sixth sense for supernatural stories. We made it to the middle of Episode Five—the one that featured a werewolf on a cruise ship—before I fell sound asleep, head resting on Randy's shoulder.

†

I woke up the next morning in my bed, a full glass of water on the bedside table and a note that said *Thanks for sharing the celebration.*

Sean and Seth had come and gone since I'd fallen asleep, and someone had put away the leftover beer, pizza, and food.

I smiled.

Every now and then, not only do life and people not disappoint you, they exceed your expectations. Next time I had a crappy day, I'd do my best to remember this.

Then I saw another note, attached to a lavender bra.

My bra.

The one I'd been wearing when Randy arrived.

Oh, shit.

This note read, *Found this in the carport. If you can't keep your clothes on, at least try and pick them up when you're done.*

No signature, but I recognized the handwriting.

"Fuck you very much, Seth," I said softly.

CHAPTER TWENTY

Coffee. Coffee now.

It was five thirty in the morning on the first day of the shoot. My call time was eight. I'd wanted to beat the traffic so I'd gotten up extra early and driven the scenic route down PCH. Not sure why I bothered since my sleep-fogged brain barely registered anything beyond the other cars.

My usual mega-sized travel mug of java wasn't doing its job. I think there was something in its contract about not being effective before 6 A.M. At least I had more than enough time to find a Starbucks and get more caffeine into my system.

It seemed strange that I even had a call time today. The shooting schedule showed a couple of scenes with Jeanette by herself and one with Jake, with some dialogue between the two over the ship's intercom system. Sure, I'd be working with Darius on the fight choreography, but there didn't seem to be anything that would require stunt doubling or an actual call time.

Oh, well—I got paid, regardless. I'd feast from the craft service table and enjoy being away from the Ranch, earning a decent wage.

Despite the godawful hour—or maybe because of it—the

Starbucks parking lot in Malibu was nearly full. There was a tiny little spot at the far end, just big enough for the Saturn. About a quarter of it was taken up by an inconsiderately parked Miata with the cryptic vanity plate DIROFOT. I managed to squeeze out of the driver's side door without injury to either car, although my back didn't think much of the early-morning contortions.

Inside there were only two people in line ahead of me. One, a painfully skinny brunette in black slacks and a button-up-the-front, long-sleeved, fitted broadcloth shirt was all hyper awake and talking rapidly on her Bluetooth while the cashier tried to take her order. The other, a tall blond guy who looked vaguely familiar, read a copy of *The Hollywood Reporter* while waiting his turn. The tables were filled with earnest-looking people working on their laptops, earbuds firmly in place to cocoon them against the outside world.

I yawned and tried to ignore everything except for the aroma of coffee and baked goods.

The blond guy gave me a cursory glance as he left, but found nothing interesting about my black yoga pants, oversized green hoodie and face free of makeup. He walked out without a backward glance. Something about that nagged at my memory, but I had more important things to think about, like whether or not I wanted "a pastry with your drink, miss?"

I didn't, but I *did* want a turkey bacon breakfast sandwich.

Five minutes later I walked out with a triple cappuccino and my sandwich. The red Miata was thankfully gone and whoever had pulled their Mercedes into that spot was better at parking between the lines, allowing me to get into my car without feeling like I was auditioning for Cirque de Soleil.

By the time I reached Dobell Studios, the sun had risen, my

brain was almost firing on all cylinders, and my enthusiasm for the day ahead had washed away the last of my internal whininess. There were already several other cars parked in the lot, along with a big-ass Star Waggon taking up the entire back row of spaces along an expanse of grass and trees. Next to that a red Miata.

DIROFOT.

Finally, it hit me.

DIR… director.

"Director of Fot."

Fot… foto… *photo.*

"Director of photography."

Oh, shit.

The blond was Connor Hayden. And his presence here at this ungodly hour could only mean one thing. Of all the films on all the soundstages in all of Los Angeles County, he had to DP on mine.

Some people would have made a big deal out of this, called it a "synchronistic life event" and insisted that there was a cosmic reason Connor and I had crossed paths again. For me, it foreshadowed lots of shaky cam and weird angles. Fight scenes filmed in extreme close-up. *Ugh.*

Climbing out of my car, I retrieved my tote bag from the trunk and reluctantly followed the sound of voices emanating from the elephant doors in the side of the huge, corrugated soundstage. Draining the last of my cappuccino, I steeled myself and went inside.

The soundstage was dark, with only three lightbulbs above the elephant doors. Several long metal tables were set up on either side, and everybody who'd already arrived was congregating at the tables, hovering like moths around a bug lamp. As I drew closer, I saw why.

Bagels, pastries, coffee, juice, fruit, cereal. A very respectable craft service, with a table for food and a table for beverages. A comfortably plump blonde woman somewhere between thirty and fifty sat behind the food table, eyes at half-mast as she sipped a cup of coffee.

Herman Dobell stood next to one table, mug of coffee in one hand, talking to his DP. Meanwhile, a short, pudgy guy in khaki pants and a navy-blue polo shirt carried on an animated conversation with a man and a woman, both dressed in black jeans and T-shirts. Both tall and slender, the woman with auburn hair worn long and straight. The man clean-shaven, dirty blond hair cut short. All three looked somewhere in their thirties.

No one noticed my entrance. I took advantage of this, moving close enough to eavesdrop. Hayden appeared to be holding forth on the virtues of Steadicam versus handheld while Herman nodded, either genuinely interested or faking it.

"—while the Steadicam allows you freedom of movement without taking the time to lay track, and it does a good job of following unpredictable action, handheld gives a more visceral, *genuine* feel, but it's an acquired taste. Both can move over varied terrain with much greater ease. This is a positive, given the set configuration and—"

Boring, I thought. I turned my attention to the pudgy guy instead.

"—last scene to reflect a change of heart for Jake. The bright star I'm talking about? It's actually the Star of Bethlehem, and it makes Jake realize that he needs to follow Jesus now!"

"That's not why Jake's a born-again Muslim, Jack," the woman said with forced patience. "He switches religions the way some people redecorate their houses. It's his quirk."

Ah, Jack. Must be the director. And I'd bet the couple was Dan and Breanna Tymon, the screenwriters. It was odd, though, to have the writers on set at this point in the production. Their job was pretty much done, and a lot of producers preferred to have the writers as far away from set as possible. But, as in so many other areas, Herman didn't play to type.

"Yes, but wouldn't it be great if Jake has followed all of these other religions over his life *except* for Christianity?" Jack countered with painfully earnest enthusiasm. "See, this way it becomes *more* than a quirk, and when he finally figures it out, he realizes that this is what he's been waiting for!"

The Tymons exchanged a quick look.

"Don't you think that's kind of insulting to the people out there who might not feel the same way?"

"I don't see why," Jack said indignantly.

"Look," Dan said with a lot less patience than his wife. "That's not the point. It's a character quirk. A lighthearted take on religion, not a heavy-handed message of any sort."

"But—"

"No buts. We've been over this before. This isn't up for negotiation. Right, Herman?" Dan raised his voice to catch the producer's attention.

It worked. Dobell turned toward the writer, shaking his head when he saw who was involved in the conversation. "Tell me you're not trying to talk them into the Star of Bethlehem again, Jack."

Then he saw me lurking in the background and smiled.

"Lee! Let me introduce you to everyone. Everyone, this is Lee Striga, Portia's stunt double. Lee, Jack Garvey, the director."

The pudgy guy stepped forward and shook my hand with three enthusiastic pumps before releasing it. "A pleasure, Lee."

"Breanna and Dan Tymon, the writers."

I beamed at them. "Love the script!"

They beamed right back.

"Kat's the magic worker behind craft service."

The sleepy-eyed blonde smiled at me. I smiled back.

"And this," Herman continued, "is Connor Hayden, our Director of Photography. He's fresh out of the USC graduate program, and we're lucky to get him."

Connor didn't bother with the usual polite disclaimer. It was clear he agreed we were blessed by his presence.

I nodded coolly. "Hi, there."

Connor held out his hand. "A pleasure to meet you," he said with just enough inflection to avoid being rude. He didn't look any more impressed with me now than he had at Starbucks, if I'd even registered on his radar. I shook the proffered hand, judging his grip.

Definitely *meh*. Not clammy or wimpy. Just… lazy. As if he couldn't be bothered to put any real effort into it.

"We hope to get some exciting stuff from Connor on this film," Herman said.

Connor looked at me and said, "Well, I'm sure it won't meet Classic *Star Trek*'s standards of excellence, but I'll do my best."

Shit.

I was trying to think of an acceptable response when I was saved by the sound of footsteps heading our way from the dark corners to the right. Considering how loud they were, I expected someone about Drift's size. Instead, a tiny sylph of a girl—her frame swimming in a dark-blue hoodie at least two sizes too large—stomped her way into the circle of light.

Short spiky hair dyed a vibrant blue. Small, pointed nose

topped by a pair of large brown eyes that seemed too big for her face, like an anime character come to life. She headed straight for Herman and Jack, fairly bristling with irritation.

"Okay, guys," she said in a voice surprisingly big for her size. "One of you needs to tell Portia that we are *not* doing glamour makeup for this film. We've been over this several times, and she's still insisting. I've told her this isn't a Sy-Fy original."

"I'll go have a word with her." Herman put a reassuring hand on the girl's shoulder. "Just remember, you're dealing with an actor's insecurity."

"Or insanity," she muttered.

I snickered at that. Herman noticed and introduced us. "Lee, this is Kyra Gilbert, our makeup supervisor, and first runner up on the last season of *Face Off*. Kyra, Lee is Portia's stunt double."

"Nice to meet you," I said. "And I'll wear any lipstick, without complaint."

She gave a wry smile. "Well, it's going to have to match Portia's, but I can promise you that it won't be Scarlet Harlot Sin."

"That's actually a shade?"

She nodded. "Sadly, yes."

"Well, it *is* a step above Slutty Sangria."

Her smile widened. "Or Prostitute Pomegranate."

"Or—"

Jack stepped in. "Is Portia almost finished in Makeup?" Even in the dim light I could see he was blushing.

What the hell is this guy doing in the film industry?

"Pretty much," Kyra said. "Although she was threatening to wipe it all off and make me start again."

Herman gave an almost imperceptible sigh.

"I'll talk to her."

"While you're at it, can you tell her it's not my job to get her coffee? I don't even know what constitutes a 'skinny mocha.'"

This time the sigh was clearly audible.

"I'll send Pete out on a Starbucks run. Tell Portia I'll be there in a minute."

Kyra nodded, satisfied, and headed toward the double doors. Herman started to follow and then stopped.

"Lee, why don't you come with me, and I'll introduce you to Portia. You might as well get into makeup and wardrobe early, since you're here."

"Sure thing."

"That's a great idea," Jack said enthusiastically.

Connor nodded. "It would be useful to have a stand-in for lighting."

I glanced sharply at Connor. "No offense," I said, "but a stunt double and a stand-in are two entirely different people."

"Why would I be offended?"

His superior little smile made my knuckles itch. I wanted to smack the annoying smug off his face. Instead I turned to Herman and Jack.

"I'm assuming Portia has a stand-in?"

Because if she has a friggin' Star Waggon, you sure as hell should be able to afford one.

Jack looked sheepish. "Portia fired her."

Of course she did.

I stopped myself from rolling my eyes.

Herman nodded. "Normally we use extras for stand-ins, give them a bump in pay. But, as you know, the script is short on extras. I'd ask a PA, but both of them are male this time around."

"Totally wrong for the play of light and shadow on her face," Connor interjected.

I kept my mouth shut, but no one gave me a medal for self-restraint.

"I know it's a lot to ask," Herman continued, "but I would personally appreciate it very much if you could help us out today. I'll get someone else in for the rest of the shoot, I promise." He gave me a hopeful smile, all boyish and charming. It may have been totally calculated, but it still had the desired effect.

Dammit.

"Sure," I said, folding like a shitty poker hand.

Problem solved, Connor turned to Jack and began discussing the day's shooting schedule. Thus dismissed, I followed Herman to Makeup.

CHAPTER TWENTY-ONE

As we walked back through the double doors, I nearly collided with a man coming through from the other side. He stopped his momentum just in time to avoid knocking me over, grabbing my shoulders to steady me.

Herman shook his head. "Jaden, one of these days you're going to kill someone, the way you barrel through those doors."

"Oh. Yeah. Sorry."

Late twenties, dark-brown skin, olive-colored eyes. Short black curly hair sticking straight up as if he'd run his hands through it repeatedly. Wiry muscles and a lean build. Blue jeans and an *Avengers* T-shirt in need of some serious time in a washing machine. Totally cute in a mad scientist kind of way, including an air of twitchy distraction that made my skin itch and wonder if he owned a DeLorean.

"Lee, this is Jaden, our special-effects coordinator. Lee is Portia's new stunt double."

"Hey," he mumbled, gazing off toward the back of the soundstage.

"Hi there," I said, offering him my hand.

He took it and we shared a brief handshake. Jaden's palm and fingers were crusted with dried paint and old glue, and reminded me of lizard skin.

"I can't wait to see how you handle the effects," I continued. "I'm really looking forward to the Morganti shadow tricks."

Jaden's body jerked back, almost as if I'd hit him with a mild Taser jolt. Herman put a steading hand on his shoulder, his expression concerned.

"You okay, Jaden?"

Jaden shook his head, almost like a dog shaking off water. He looked me in the eyes for the first time and smiled. "I'm sorry," he said. "Just really preoccupied. Lots to do still."

Herman clapped him on the back. "Jaden's worked his ass off on the Morganti sequences," he said warmly. "They're going to be great."

"You going for CGI?"

Jaden's smile grew secretive. "Now that would be telling. Let's just say I'm still playing around with possibilities. We'll probably use some green screen in places, especially for parts of the knife fight, but I guarantee no one's going to be disappointed with the final results."

Someone hollered his name down at the far end of the soundstage, past the Morganti ship.

"Gotta go," he said. "Hey, Lee, looking forward to working with you." He took off at a fast clip, vanishing back into the shadowed reaches of the building.

"He's always in a hurry," Herman commented. "I've been trying to teach him to slow down. Talented as hell, though. This is his first full-length feature."

Of course it is. I got the feeling if Herman could go back in time, hang out at Schwab's Drugstore, and discover Lana Turner, he'd totally do it.

We continued through the door into the middle hallway, then reached the open door to the makeup room just in time to hear a clattering sound as several somethings hit the floor, followed by a female voice.

"I *told* you I don't like any of those colors!" someone shouted, and I had a feeling I knew who it was. "Are you deaf or just *stupid*?" Herman and I exchanged looks. He took a long, deep breath and went inside. I followed, staying behind him and—hopefully—out of the line of fire.

Four swivel chairs lined up in front of a long mirror hanging above a countertop running the length of the far wall. There was plenty of adjustable lighting, and a truly impressive makeup kit—one of those things that seems small and then unfolds into multiple sections. This one looked like it might grow up to be a Transformer. Tubes of lipstick were strewn across the countertop in front of the one occupied chair. A half-dozen or so lay scattered on the floor.

Portia Lambert, already in costume, sat in one of the chairs. She wore khakis tucked into flat-heeled ankle boots and an olive-drab tank top. A nice enough figure, definitely rounder than the current craze for stick insects with boobs. Long dark hair, straight with bangs, the color a little too uniform to look natural. Big brown eyes with long lashes, frown lines in the forehead. A small straight nose. Thin lips. They might not be so thin, though, if they weren't always clenched in an expression of perpetual dissatisfaction.

Veruca Salt all grown up.

Somebody didn't get her an Oompa Loompa.

Kyra picked the lipsticks off the floor, her own lips pressed into a thin line of displeasure.

"Portia," Herman said, "I'd like you to meet Lee, your new stunt double."

Swallowing, I said, "Looking forward to working with you." I smiled politely, not wanting to seem over-enthusiastic.

She looked me up and down dismissively. "You're working *for* me, not with me. Don't forget it."

Okay, then. A number of replies sprung to mind. Instead I kept it simple. "Nice to meet you, too."

The frown lines deepened.

Herman stepped forward.

"Portia, may I have a word with you?"

She rolled her eyes. "I suppose so. You *are* the producer."

"Why yes, yes I am, nice of you to remember." Except Herman didn't say that. Instead he smiled graciously.

"Thank you. Let's go to my office." He turned. "Kyra, if you can get Lee into makeup, we can start lighting the first scene."

Portia pushed herself out of the makeup chair and sauntered out of the room without a second glance at either me or Kyra. Herman flashed us an apologetic smile and followed her.

We waited a few beats, listening to their footsteps move down the hall and through the door that led to the front offices. Then we looked at each other and started laughing.

"Okay, then," I finally said.

"Have a seat." Kyra gestured expansively toward the row of chairs. I sat down in one well away from the chair previously occupied by Portia. Heaven forfend I be in her seat when she came back.

Kyra did a quick and efficient job on me, while telling me about her stint as a contestant on *Face-Off*, a popular reality show featuring makeup artists.

"I totally should have won," she said, "but I swear there's a gender bias with some of the judges." A moment's silence while she carefully applied eyeshadow to my lids with feather-soft strokes. She stood back, took a critical look at her work and nodded. I took advantage of the pause to ask a question.

"So, aside from Portia, how's the rest of the cast to work with?"

Kyra shrugged. "I've only met them briefly," she said. "So far everyone seems nice." She smiled. "Ben Farrell is great. A real sweetheart."

Good to know.

"What about the crew?"

"Well, I can't say enough good things about Herman. But then you've probably figured that out on your own."

I nodded. "Yeah, he seems almost too good to be true, especially in this business. Really invested in giving people a shot."

"He saw me on *Face-Off.*" Kyra smiled wistfully. "Luckily he was more interested in working with me than the guy who took first place."

"Is this Jaden's first gig, too?"

Kyra frowned. "I think so, but I'm not sure. He's a real pain in the ass."

"Herman and I ran into him just a few minutes ago. He seems kind of twitchy."

Kyra rolled her eyes. "That's one word for it. You'd think special effects is the only important thing on this film, the way he goes on about it."

Everyone always thinks their department is the most important. It's the nature of the beast. I kept the thought to myself, though, and said, "Really? That's a shame. He seemed nice enough."

"Oh, he can be charming, don't get me wrong." A bitter tone crept into her voice that seemed strangely out of place. "But honestly, he's a snake. You can't trust him. He's already tried to tell Herman and Jack that I'm not good enough. He's got ideas that don't match mine, and he doesn't understand that FX and makeup should work together. Jaden's not interested in collaboration, though. He just wants to tell me how to do my job."

I stayed quiet as she applied a neutral-colored lipstick and then spun the chair around so I faced the mirror.

"There. What do you think?"

I looked at my reflection. "Wow. Can I take you home with me?" Kyra had managed to make me look attractive and awake without making me look particularly made up. When men said, "Oh honey, you look great without makeup!" this was totally what they were talking about.

She did my hair in a quick sloppy French braid. Her fingers brushed the scar on the back of my neck. I winced reflexively.

"I'm sorry, did I hurt you?"

"It's okay," I said. "Just an old injury that's still a little sensitive."

She nodded sympathetically, and even better, didn't ask any questions. "I'll be more careful next time."

We heard distant footsteps, coming from the front hallway.

"We finished?"

Kyra nodded. "Wardrobe's next door. Joan's in charge. You'll love her."

I was up and out of the room just as the doorway to the front offices started to open. I knocked on the door of the costume department, then ducked inside without waiting for an answer.

The room, relatively small, was divided up into sections by the clothing racks, with men and women's clothes further sectioned off by character name. There was no sign of the wardrobe supervisor.

The back of the room was partitioned off by a tall painted silk screen, all done in designs of Chinese-style dragons with vivid golds, deep reds, and black lacquer. I heard a rustling noise back there.

"Hello?" I called out. "Anyone here?"

No answer.

I poked around further back, checking out the rack that had Jeanette's wardrobe on it since that was what I'd be wearing. Nothing fancy or sexy. Just khakis and tank tops, along with a couple of olive-green jumpsuits that looked like they'd escaped from the first *Alien* movie. Stuff I could move in. Fight in.

Best of all? No leather corsets.

"Hey there," a deep voice said from behind me. I jumped like a startled cat, turning to see a very tall, broad-shouldered man in his late fifties grinning down at me. I instantly recognized him as Ben Farrell. He matched Drift and Tater for height. Wide shoulders, too. A mix of Asian and African-American, he reminded me of an older version of the singer from Fine Young Cannibals. Ben was in great shape, especially for someone creeping up on sixty.

It just wasn't fair. Guys could play romantic leads until they died, but unless you were, say, Helen Mirren, a woman over forty just wasn't considered sexy—at least not by the majority of those who did the casting. It sucked.

"I didn't think anyone was in here," I said weakly. "Sorry if I startled you."

"Now, you kind of *look* like Portia," he said, "but there's no way in hell she'd ever say sorry for anything, and you're at least ten years younger than she is. So I'm thinking maybe you're her stand-in."

"Actually, her stunt double," I corrected him, "although they talked me into doing some stand-in work today, for lighting purposes. Evidently Portia canned her *actual* stand-in yesterday."

He laughed, a deep rich chuckle, and then shook his head.

"On a movie with this budget, she should be standing in for her own damn self, like the rest of us are doing."

"Have you worked with Portia before?"

"I have not." He shook his head. "This is the first and the last time I hope to have the privilege of working with Miss Lambert. I'm Ben, by the way."

I shook the hand he held out. My fingers vanished in his grip.

"I know. I've seen *Dead Maze* more than once. I'm Lee Striga."

His eyes narrowed. "Your name sounds familiar."

I didn't bother suggesting a reason why. "I've done a lot of stunt work," I said and then neatly changed the subject. "Is anyone from Wardrobe here? I'm supposed to get in costume ASAP, so they can light the first scene."

"Joanie was here a minute ago. I think she just went to, uh, powder her nose."

I grinned at his euphemism. "I'll wait for her."

"Well, I guess I'll see you on set." He gave a little salute and turned to leave. "I'm standing in for myself, don't you know."

Working with Ben Farrell just might make up for working with Portia.

†

I spent an hour and a half acting as Portia's stand-in so Connor and his gaffer could get the lights set for the first scene—Jeanette's cabin, one of the early ones in the script. She wakes up to find out there's a satellite nearby that needs repair, and the *Bootes* is about to enter an asteroid field.

Meanwhile Jake, her shipmate, has turned the ship around to face Mecca. This segues directly into a scene where Jeanette stalks down the corridor to the bridge, yelling at Jake via an audio link.

Connor and Paul—the gaffer—spent a lot of time muttering about key and fill lights, blue tones versus red, and a bunch of other technical terms that meant nothing to me as they tried different placements to see what worked best.

I kept a cup of coffee close by and did my best to pretend that I was a posable Barbie doll instead of a person, because that's pretty much how Connor seemed to view me. Nevertheless, I did my best to cooperate and follow instructions, including hitting my mark.

I was good at that. No false modesty. When your life sometimes depends on your ability to stop your body—or a car, motorcycle, or weapon—within a matter of precise inches, you learn to be really good at finding and hitting that mark.

Connor actually seemed a little impressed. He gave what *might* have been a nod of approval when I jumped off the bunk bed and landed exactly where he wanted me for the fifth time in a row.

He and Paul then nattered in a corner for a few minutes, more things about 1Ks versus 2Ks and "I need a bloody 5K, dammit!" C-stands, fill spots, and other stuff. They seemed to be trying to figure out if they had enough lights to set up for the next scene.

As much as I hated to say anything nice about him, I admired Connor's proactivity. Setting a scene's lighting could be one of the most tedious time-sucks in the industry, depending on the DP and his crew.

Jack stuck his head around the corner of the cabin.

"How's it going? We gonna be on schedule?"

"Of course," Connor said, as if surprised he would even ask. "I think we may even have time to light the corridor for the next scene, although we really could use a 5K. Do you know if Herman's ordered it yet?"

"Uh, not sure," Jack replied. "I'll check with him."

"Good. We're pretty much done here." Connor glanced at his wristwatch. "We can get started lighting the corridor. We have, what, half an hour before we start shooting?"

Jack clapped his hands together. "That would be great!"

I sighed. I couldn't help it. It would be nice if someone asked me if *I* minded. Darius and I were supposed to start working on the choreography for the knife fight. We were going to block out the basics in a small clearing of trees at the edge of the parking lot fence and then move inside later when the soundstage was available.

Jack must have felt my irritation, because he looked at me anxiously and said, "Lee, that's okay with you, right?"

"Sure."

I mean, what else was I going to say?

At least he'd asked.

"That's great!"

Oh well, at least there were no hygiene-challenged Priaptic demons on set.

CHAPTER TWENTY-TWO

Connor and Paul finished up with most of the corridor lighting about the time Portia deigned to show for her first scene of the day. She brushed past without a word, looking totally put out. Not a clue as to how many people would kill for the chance to be where she was now.

Or did she just not care?

If I ever make it big, I told myself, *and become that much of a jerk, I hope someone just shoots me and puts me out of everyone's misery.*

I hightailed it out of there before Connor decided he needed me for anything else. I hunted down Darius, who was happily camped out at the craft service table, doing his best to drain the coffee urn. He nodded when he saw me approach.

"You are ready?"

"You have no idea."

He smiled at that. Just enough to show me that he had a sense of humor lurking behind his dour Eastern European façade. First we headed over to the props department to get weapons and meet Michael, the department head. A lot of films have actual weapons handlers, but *Pale Dreamer* didn't have enough weapons or a big enough budget to warrant it.

Props was located at the back of the soundstage, behind

the Morganti spacecraft. It was housed in one of the larger rooms, next to the Lighting Department, Set Design, and FX. I tried to ignore the skin-crawling sensation I got walking past the Morganti set, that sense that something was *off*. I'd have to film at least one scene there, when Jeanette was chased by the ambulatory corpses of the Morganti's previous victims. So I had to get used to the creepy-crawly sensation.

The props room was dimly lit and looked like a well-organized junkshop. Heavy metal shelves lined the walls and held pieces of unidentifiable machinery, bits I recognized from radios and video machines, auto parts, and tools. One shelf held weird *objects d'art*, ancient-looking weaponry, the kind of stuff I'd seen as set dressing on the Morganti ship.

Sitting in an incongruously comfy upholstered rocking chair, behind a small table and among all of the organized clutter, was Michael, an attractive older man somewhere in his fifties. Short, impeccably styled brown hair shot through with silver. Designer "skinny" jeans and a tight Lacoste polo shirt in a deep wine shade. He gave me a nice professional smile when I walked in.

The smile increased in wattage and switched from professional to personal when Darius came in behind me. Michael looked me over with more interest, giving me a quick up and down.

"You must be Portia's new stunt double."

"Guilty," I said.

"Oh, no, hon, *she's* the guilty one."

Does anyone on this film like Portia?

"We need the knives," Darius said.

"Rubber or steel?"

"Rubber to take with, steel to show."

Michael stood up from his chair and reached into a plastic

organizer with multiple drawers, each neatly labeled as to the contents. He rustled around for a moment, then pulled out two sets of identical knives, slapping them down on the table.

One pair consisted of basic combat knives, with seven-inch blades and black woven nylon sheaths. The other pair looked suitably alien, the blades jagged and painted with the same sickly iridescence as the Morganti craft. One blade from each pair did indeed prove to be rubber.

"Wow," I said, impressed. "These are amazing."

"Yeah, Jaden did a good job with the replicas," Michael said. "Not my area of expertise."

"Not your usual type of job?"

He gave an aggrieved sigh. "I'm used to picking out the perfect tea cup for River Byers on shows like *Model Women*. Now?" He shook his head. "Knives, swords, skulls, auto parts…"

"How did you happen to take this job?" I asked curiously.

An embarrassed expression flashed over his face. "I had a couple of slow years after a family illness. My partner Duane…" He paused, smiling sadly. "Well, Duane was diagnosed with stage four lung cancer. I stayed home to take care of him. By the time I was ready to go back to work, it seemed like it had pretty much dried up. Hollywood has a short memory and not a lot of gratitude."

Amen to that.

"Well, a friend of a friend introduced me to Herman. He was willing to give me a chance to prove I could do something different."

Of course, I thought, wondering briefly how Herman had managed to make it in Hollywood, given his propensity for hiring lame ducks and has-beens.

Do I qualify as a lame duck?

I decided not to pursue that line of thought.

Darius and I went outside and got to work on the choreography. It was exactly what I needed after dealing with Portia's attitude and the tedium of stand-in work. We worked up a good sweat and even better choreography. The knife fight was *so* gonna kick ass.

That satisfaction almost made up for my irritation I felt when Jack approached me during lunch, at one of the picnic tables set up outside the elephant doors. He had an unctuous smile on his face.

"Lee, I know you're busy working on fights with Darius," he said, "but we could really use you again tomorrow morning, just for an hour or so—maybe get here early again? We have a couple of shots in the corridor where you could really help." He wasn't quite smart enough to sound apologetic.

"Tomorrow morning?" I looked at him over my plate. "I thought that was on the call sheet for today."

He scratched his head, looking a little sheepish. "I was hoping to get to it today, but the first scene's taking a little longer than planned. It's okay, though," he added brightly. "We budgeted in a few extra days, just in case."

Just in case Portia acted up, I surmised.

"The corridor scene's already lit though, right?"

He nodded vigorously. "Yup, all finished. There still just *might* be some places where we need your help." He seemed reluctant to get any more specific than that.

Oh well, I thought. *I'll just beat the early-morning traffic again*.

†

"Okay, then," Jack said, rubbing his hands together. "Portia, Jeanette is *really* pissed off at Jake because he's turned the ship around to face Mecca. So let's *really* see the irritation in your body language as you walk down the corridor."

"Are you shooting this from the front or the back?" Portia folded her arms across her chest, giving Jack a preview of her ability to show irritation.

"Well," Jack replied less enthusiastically, "we're going to do one take from the front, getting all the dialogue, and then another take from the back with the same dialogue. We're lit for both, right Connor?"

Connor nodded from behind his camera, which was set up at the far end of the corridor. Effie, the boom operator, lay on her stomach on a sturdy metal railing overhead so she could follow Portia's movements with the microphone while staying out of the shot.

"You get to film me doing my lines from the front," Portia said coldly. "Beyond that, my stunt double can have *her* ass shot."

Great. Now I'm a butt double.

Jack looked a little sucker-punched, but rallied admirably. "Well, okay. Sure. Whatever you want. Lee, you okay with that?"

I gave a little wave from the sidelines. "Whatever you want, Jack." He already had enough shit from Portia. He didn't need any more from me. Besides, I had a feeling he'd been expecting this. Why else was I here?

"Okay, then," he said, animated again. "We'll film the front angle first. Lee, take a break and we'll film it from the back in about an hour."

Coffee, I thought. Because it was too early for beer. I hurried away from the set and toward the craft service table.

"She's a charmer, ain't she?"

I jumped at the sound of the deep voice next me, then grinned when Ben fell into step beside me with a big smile of his own.

"Hey there," I said, happy to see an actor with a good attitude. Too bad I couldn't double him, instead. "I didn't think your call time was until two."

"I'm here to feed Portia lines."

"The script supervisor can't do that?"

"Portia doesn't do lines with someone who's not playing the actual part."

"Can I assume she's gonna stick around and do the same for you, when she's not actually onscreen?"

He laughed then, a big bark of genuine amusement. "Assume that and it'll make an ass out of you and me."

"That's a 'no', then."

"Big damn 'no'."

"Well, if I'm not working on fight choreography with Darius, I'd be happy to read lines with you."

Ben cocked his head to one side and nodded slowly. "That would be greatly appreciated, and I'd be happy to take you up on it."

"What's your first scene today?"

"First scene with Jake and Jeanette on the bridge."

"Ooh," I said, "if memory serves me, it's one where Portia has lines, and her face will be on camera. I might actually get to work on the fight scenes."

"Oh, I wouldn't count on it." Ben shot me a wry grin. "You never know when they're gonna wanna film Portia from the back. And if that's the case, it's going to be your ass on screen. Not hers."

I groaned. "I swear, she's one butt-cheek short of half-assed."

Ben's laugh was more of a roar that time around.

CHAPTER TWENTY-THREE

I got used to the early-morning wake up, painful as it was, and driving over the mountains. The breakfast spread and coffee waiting for me on set made the pain a little more bearable.

My job as Portia's stand-in didn't look to end any time soon. Either they couldn't find anyone willing to put up with her abuse, or I was just so good at the job and immune to her bitchiness that they didn't want to replace me.

I found it oddly easy to let Portia's verbal jabs bounce off my thick skin. There was something pathetic about her. Sad and worn out, as if she wasn't only over the hill, but had fallen down the slope and rolled a few times on her way to the bottom. It wasn't her age either, although I'm sure she felt the pressure of being a woman nearing forty in such an unforgiving industry.

Maybe *Pale Dreamer* was her last gasp, a swan song of sorts, or she had some hope that it would rekindle her career. She may not have known herself. Either way, there was something desperate about the woman.

Connor Hayden and I achieved an uneasy truce. I continued to make his job easier and he continued to treat me like a piece of lighting equipment. I suspected he treated his lights better than most people, so that was fine by me.

Herman split his time between the set and his office. It might have been my imagination, but it seemed as if with each passing day he got a little skinnier, his face just a little more drawn. As if something was dining on his insides. Yet he continued to be gracious and even tempered, even when dealing with Portia. I wanted to ask him if he was okay, but didn't want to cross some invisible line with concern that might not be welcome.

When I wasn't butt-doubling Portia, Darius and I worked outdoors on the choreography. We needed to run it on the actual set, but that would have to wait until the day before we were scheduled to start filming the fight.

I also helped Ben run lines. We usually sat in the lobby, enjoying the air-conditioning and comfy chairs. I liked getting away from the soundstage and the mini-dramas going on between Jack and the Tymons, Jack and Portia, Portia and—

Well, Portia and *everyone*.

Joe and Angel finally arrived on set, and Portia had walked past them without a word, setting a new standard for rudeness that flummoxed us all.

Angel was absolutely gorgeous, approaching her fifties with the kind of beauty and dignity I'd always associated with actresses from the thirties and forties. Cascades of dark hair shimmering with highlights. Golden-brown eyes with long lashes. It was ironic, really, since she was known for movies like *Space Planet Slave Girls*, *Ghosts of Bikini Island*, and *Call of the Sex Vampires*.

Joe Scout was a quirky character actor in his fifties with mobile features, equally adept at playing the amiable sidekick, uptight cop, or psychotic villain. I could see why Portia would see Angel as a threat, but Joe? Go figure.

As soon as Portia was out of earshot, Ben quickly introduced me to them as "Portia's non-evil twin." When they found out I was willing to run lines with them, I became their new best friend—and very busy.

†

Given my newfound popularity, free time became a rare commodity. So when it appeared as if I wasn't needed, I decided to stretch and get in a little workout before anyone noticed I was gone.

Slipping outside helped alleviate the slight nausea I felt whenever I got too close to the Morganti ship. The paint used on that part of the set had dried, but the smell still lingered. I'd definitely be taking Dramamine when we were shooting on that set.

I grabbed my TRX and went to find a good place to sling it. There were some trees at the back of the parking lot, on the other side of Portia's trailer—a couple of big oaks with sturdy branches poking over a chain-link fence. I picked one at just the right height and attached the suspension trainer. Then I unzipped my jumpsuit, shrugged out of the arms, and rolled it down around my waist. My exercise bra covered more territory than most bikini tops.

The temperature was nice, in the low eighties with a light breeze blowing. Definitely summer, but a real contrast to the eyeball-boiling temperatures we got in the San Fernando Valley.

I started with some basic rows. Doing the reps nice and slowly to get the maximum results for the effort. Got to love the TRX—it looks like it'd be so easy, but it was a kick-ass workout if done right. The first time I'd used it, I thought it was going to kill me.

I went from the rows to leg lifts, then triceps extensions.

I put down a small foam pad under my knees and tortured myself with some fallouts, a particularly grueling exercise that targeted the arms, shoulders, back, and, oh yes, the core.

"That looks like fun."

Startled, I nearly finished by falling on my face, catching myself with a jolt that wrenched my arms. Pulling myself back to an upright position, I looked over to see Portia leaning against the backside of her trailer, watching me while smoking a cigarette. Her expression, while not what I'd call friendly, lacked its usual hostility.

It was weird.

"Hi," I said warily.

She took another drag off her cigarette. "Do you do this kind of thing all the time?"

"The TRX? Or exercise in general?"

"Exercise in general, I guess."

"Well, yeah, it's pretty much part of the job description."

She nodded, moving her hand so the ash spilled onto the asphalt instead of the grass. I liked her just a little bit more because of it.

"I hate exercise," she said conversationally. "Always have, except walking and horseback riding. Going to the gym? Forget it."

"I like horseback riding, too," I agreed, "but I don't get a lot of chances to do it, and I can't pack up a horse and take it with me on set."

That actually got a smile out of her. "I guess not." She took one last puff and then stubbed her cigarette out on the pavement.

"Show me how to do that."

I raised an eyebrow.

"Which part of 'that' do you want to learn?" I asked after a cautious moment.

"Whatever you were doing last." She shrugged. "I figure it's all pretty much the same."

I laughed, I couldn't help it.

"What?" Portia frowned. "What's so funny?"

"Hey, sorry," I said quickly, not wanting to jinx the moment. "It's just that, it's *not* all the same. This thing may look easy, but it's not and I wouldn't be doing you any favors if I tossed you into it right off the bat."

Even if some people might pay me to do it.

Portia looked at me suspiciously, almost as if she could read my mind.

"Fine," she said. "Whatever you think I should start with."

I nodded. "Okay, let's start you off with some rows."

"This hurts," she said after two repetitions.

"That's because you've never done it before," I replied with what I thought was admirable patience. "Try a couple more."

She did and then glared at me. "It's too hot."

"Unzip the top of your jumpsuit, roll it down, and you'll be fine."

I gestured to myself as an example.

"Not going to happen." Portia glared at me, as if offended I would even suggest such a thing. I rolled my eyes—couldn't help it.

"Fine. Then don't. If you want to do this, great. If you don't, then whatever. I'm not a fucking personal trainer."

"Well, you're my stunt double."

I stepped back from the TRX and looked at her.

"Yes, and this means that when you do stunts, I will double you. This does not mean that I'm required to put up with your shit the rest of the time." I was careful to keep my tone even. "If you want your very own personal trainer to abuse, then you're going to have to pay an hourly wage for that, and you'll be paying someone who has a lot more patience than I do."

Her glare intensified, as if she thought it could get me to do what she wanted. Except I don't think she had any clue what she wanted me to do. Kind of like a cranky toddler who needs a nap.

I matched her glare with a calm look of my own. It would've been far too easy to lose my temper and yell, but it wouldn't have helped, nor would it have made me feel better. So I waited.

Portia let go of the TRX handles.

Time to storm off in a huff, I thought.

To my surprise she heaved an aggrieved sigh, unzipped the top of her jumpsuit, and pulled it off of her arms, tying it off below her chest.

Okay, so Portia wasn't in the best of shape. Not a lot of muscle definition and maybe slightly thicker through the middle than Hollywood likes, but she had nothing to be ashamed of either.

Sometimes I really hate this business.

"Okay, give me a set of ten."

She actually got back on the TRX, doing some rows. It was hard for her—a lot harder than it should have been—but I doubt Portia had done anything by way of strength training in years, if at all.

I also got the feeling she didn't have a lot of friends. That she was so used to either rejection or disappointment that she used insults and a shitty attitude to deal with it. Her constant demands were the equivalent of a little kid throwing a tantrum in order to test boundaries.

Or maybe I was full of shit, and Portia was just a bitch.

Fifteen minutes later I'd led her through the rows, some triceps extensions, and a couple of standing fall outs. There was some swearing involved on her part, but overall she didn't do badly.

Cracking open a bottle of water, I took a swig, then offered it to her. There was hesitation, as if she was tempted to demand that I fetch her her *own* water, but she must've thought better of it. She did, however, drain the rest of my bottle, and she didn't bother to say thank you.

I hid a grin.

"You're probably going to be kind of sore tomorrow."

She waved a hand dismissively. "Okay, it wasn't *that* hard."

"Uh-huh. Who's done this before? Not you. Just remember the first time you went horseback riding, and how you felt the day *after* the day after."

A reluctant grin flickered across her face.

"So if I'm too sore to do any of my scenes, you'll be working double-time."

I almost said something snarky, but then I realized Portia was trying to make a joke. Not something that came easily to her.

So instead I said, "I don't know about you, but I could use some more water. How about I go grab us a couple of bottles?"

She smiled, and I swear it was the first genuine smile I'd seen on her face since I met her.

"I've got some in my trailer," she said. "If you want, you can—"

"Lee!"

I looked up to see Eden, of all people, waving at me from the other side of the parking lot. All blonde and pretty in sandals and a rose-colored dress circa the '60s, looking fresher than anyone had the right to look. Then again, she hadn't been working out.

"Eden!" I waved back, surprised and delighted to see her. She hurried across the asphalt and gave me a big hug.

"What are you doing here?"

"I was going to ask you the same thing," she laughed. "I'm working on a film on the soundstage over there." She pointed at Dobell Productions.

"Oh my God, I don't believe it. You're our Zoe?"

"How did you know…" She stopped, her smile growing wider with delight. "Oh my God, don't tell me *this* is the stunt gig!"

"It is! I'm doubling Portia Lambert and… Well, hey, let me just introduce you." I turned to Portia. "This is—"

"Yeah, whatever." Back was the uptight, bitchy façade. "You two go and have your slumber party or whatever the hell. I have work to do." She stalked back around to the front door of her trailer and vanished inside.

I just stared after her.

"What the hell just happened?"

"How about I get my stuff from the car," Eden said, "and you can show me around set?" I shot her a puzzled glance. She flickered her gaze up at one of the trailer's windows, definitely open. I saw the curtains inside flutter as if someone had pulled them aside and then let them fall back.

Still confused, I unslung my TRX from the tree, tucked it into its bag, and walked with Eden back to her car where she retrieved her purse and a large tote. Then we went through the front office door and were safely out of earshot of Portia's trailer.

"Okay, so tell me what that was all about," I demanded.

"Well, it's easy to see that she doesn't like to share, and that includes friends. Things blew up big time during the third season of *Brentwood High*, because she thought the actress playing Angie got too chummy with one of the extras.

Same thing with *Enchanted Pages*. Portia Lambert doesn't make friends easily and when she does, I guess she's a cross between *Single White Female* and a very clingy limpet."

"That's sad," I said, and I meant it.

"That's one word for it," Eden said. "Rumor has it she's so possessive of the people in her life that she's actually had restraining orders filed against her by former assistants, when she wouldn't stop calling to demand intimate details of what they were doing and with who. That woman is in dire need of therapy."

Damn. Imagine having to *hire* friends.

As badly as I felt for Portia, I couldn't get involved in neuroses at that level of fucked-up-ness. There were enough issues of my own to contend with. I smacked Eden lightly on one arm as we went past the reception desk.

"You already knew I was working on *Pale Dreamer*, didn't you?"

"Oh, yes," Eden said serenely. "I thought it would be more fun to surprise you once I realized we were on the same movie. Was I right?"

"You were."

"So I need to get into costume and makeup, and I'm just dying for some coffee." We went through the first set of double doors.

"Wardrobe there and Makeup there," I said, pointing. "The coffee at craft service is good, but the producer makes some kick-ass brew of his own."

"A very interesting man, our producer," Eden commented. "And not bad looking either, although he needs to eat a few decent meals."

I shrugged, feeling oddly protective of Herman. So I changed the subject.

"You'll never guess who the DP is."

Eden raised an eyebrow.

"Do tell."

"Remember *Dark Magistrate*...?"

"No." Her eyebrows shot even higher.

"Oh, yes."

"Has his personality improved at all?"

"Sadly, no." I heaved a sigh. "Why are the cute guys such assholes?"

"Ah, you think he's cute?"

"I didn't think so when I first saw him, but his looks have grown on me. Kinda like mold."

"It's the accent," Eden said with utter confidence.

"Must be," I agreed glumly. "But he's still a jerk."

CHAPTER TWENTY-FOUR

Portia's attitude, already crappy, took on new depths of suck after Eden joined the cast. The brief flicker of friendliness she'd shown as we bonded over the TRX had vanished, and she was worse than ever.

It had to be difficult for her. I mean, men practically dislocated their necks checking out Eden as she walked past. Even Michael gave her an approving once over. I don't know that Portia had ever commanded that sort of attention, even in her Hollywood prime.

Portia sat in a pilot's chair on the bridge of the *Bootes*, one foot tapping on the floor in what sounded like ill-tempered Morse code. All of the shots in the scene showed Portia's face either full-on, in profile, or reflected in the bridge viewport, so no stand-in was needed.

As a result, I'd been free to work on fight choreography with Darius for three hours in eighty-degree weather. We decided to take a much-needed break in the cool air-conditioned set and hear what Jeanette's lines sounded like coming out of Portia. The Tymons and Eden stood down on the sidelines next to me, Eden still in her Zoe costume, all sexy silver jumpsuit and makeup heightened to give her a perfect but not quite human appearance as befitted a good "entertainment model" android.

Joe stood off to the side of the camera, reading his lines. His character Shaad was still on the Morganti ship at this point, talking to Jeanette from his bridge. The scene on that set would be filmed another day.

"Oh my God," Portia exclaimed in between takes. "If this jackass can't stick to the script, why the hell did I bother memorizing *my* lines?"

Joe—the jackass in question—didn't seem offended by Portia's outburst. If anything, he seemed amused by it. But we'd done an earlier read-through of the script, so he *knew* the lines. Why was he changing them now?

"He's doing it on purpose," Eden whispered as if reading my mind.

Breanna and Dan exchanged a few muttered words.

"Joe," Breanna said in a conciliatory tone. "Portia has a point. These lines, this dialogue is supposed to play off each line before it. Your improv is great—you always add a lot—but we really need you to stick to what's written in this scene."

"You got it," Joe said amiably. "Just thought I'd try a few things, but you're right. This is one script that doesn't need my help."

"Your help," Portia said with a sneer. "I suppose that the other films you've worked on would've been shit without you."

Joe shrugged, not bothering to answer. The next take, however?

Word perfect. Though Portia still found it in her to complain.

"Now that you've managed to remember your lines," she said with withering contempt, "would you mind picking up the pace? If you keep chewing up the scenery, the audience will forget my character completely."

Joe cocked his head to one side.

"I don't think you need my help with that," he said.

Oh, boy.

Portia took off her character's headset and threw it on the console in front of her.

"That's it!" she bellowed. "I have had it!" Lurching up, she shoved away from her console chair. Since it wasn't secured to the floor, the chair flew backward and collided with Effie. Only Gaffer Paul's quick reflexes saved her from crashing to the floor, mic and all.

Portia just shoved her way past, stormed down the ladder, and off the set. I melted back into the shadows, staying out of her way until she'd slammed through the double doors, likely on her way to Herman's office.

"This is just great!" Jack exclaimed. "We budgeted in extra days for shooting, but at this rate it'll never be enough." He stood and headed for the ladder. "I've got to talk to Herman."

"You'll probably run into Madame Diva," Joe observed. "You know she's gonna be raising hell. And whose idea was it to hire her again?"

Jack flushed bright red, but still descended the ladder and hurried off. Everyone left on the set looked at one another.

"Right. Looks like we have a break," Connor said, putting aside the camera. "Lee, why don't you and Darius show me the knife fight, so I can start working out angles and lighting? Anything to keep moving forward."

Joe nodded. "I'd like to see it, too."

Nodding, I trotted away to grab Darius from his usual perch by the coffee urn, then we hustled back to take advantage of the rare opportunity when the set was free and clear.

Most of the centerpiece fight took place on the *Bootes* bridge, but parts of it moved to different areas of the ship, with Shaad blending in and out of the shadows, rendering Jeanette unable to anticipate his movements. Darius and I had done our best to stick to the appropriate dimensions when we'd blocked out the fight, but even with the close-quarters choreography we'd developed, putting it into action on the set was a game changer.

A lot of the time you can cheat the angles, make something look dangerous, up close, and personal, when you're really working at a safe distance. In close quarters like these though, it would be harder to cheat. Luckily we were both adherents to what I called "precision choreography."

If Darius said he was going to stab an inch to the right of my torso, I knew that's where the tip of the blade would be— one inch away from the right side of my torso. And I didn't have to worry about him randomly deciding to change the choreography. Shit like that was how people got hurt.

Like moving an airbag sometime between rehearsal and the take, I thought wryly. No, working with Darius was like finding the perfect dance partner. *Fencing with the Stars*.

We ran the fight sequence on the bridge. Connor and Joe stood out of the way and watched, Joe whistling in appreciation at some of the moves, especially when we got up to speed.

"Now," Joe said when we took a breather, "I'm, uh, not really going to have to do any of those moves, right? Because I'm thinking that would end up with someone in the hospital."

"No." Darius folded his arms. "Close-ups only. Nothing else."

"And we're using rubber knives for most of the fighting,"

I added. "It would take some work to punch a hole in someone with one of those."

Joe shook his head. "Trust me, kiddo, if anyone could do it, I could. I'm good at many things, but all this fighting stuff? I'm one actor who doesn't want to do his own damn stunts."

"Can I have everyone's attention?"

We all turned. Herman stood at the edge of the set, coffee cup in one hand. He looked tense, and his other hand rested on the back of a chair. I suspected he was using it for support. Jack stood at Herman's shoulder.

Portia?

Nowhere in sight.

"Okay," Herman said, "I'm going to apologize in advance for this, because I know some of you may have already made plans based on the original shooting schedule. Unfortunately, Portia has experienced a couple of health issues—"

"Mental health issues," Joe muttered.

"—and we feel it would be better for her to take a day or two off to recuperate. In the meantime, we'd like to move up the scenes involving Shaad and Rheyza on the Morganti ship, as well as film the fight between Jeanette and Shaad. In fact, maybe we should do that tomorrow. We can get the close-ups when Portia's back. This way we'll be able to make some headway on the shooting schedule and hopefully stay on track. Lee, Joe, Darius… How do you all feel about this?"

"Works for me," Joe said.

Darius grunted and nodded.

"Me, too," I said.

The tension on Herman's face dissolved.

"Thank you," he said quietly. "You have no idea how much I appreciate this."

"Aw, shucks," Joe said with exaggerated humbleness.

Herman smiled. "Connor, Paul? Let's sit down and figure out the new shooting schedule for the next few days. I also want to check with Jaden, and how soon he'll be ready with the FX for the ritual scene."

The Tymons exchanged concerned looks.

"I thought we agreed to save that scene for the last day of the shoot," Breanna said with a frown.

"That was the plan," Herman agreed, "but sooner would be preferable. We'll need to let Jaden be the final judge."

"Did I hear my name?"

Jaden appeared behind him as if summoned, a plate of raw veggies, hummus, and Cheetos in one hand and a can of Coke in the other. Herman quickly filled him in on Portia's mini-hiatus and the proposed changes in the shooting schedule.

"How soon do you think you'll be ready for the ritual scene?"

Jaden frowned. "I'm thinking I need another few days before I'll have the effects under control. I'd like to try another test run or two first, but I'll do my best to get the fine-tuning hammered out in about a week."

"That long?" Herman didn't look happy. "Any way you can speed it up?"

"I'll do my best," Jaden said. "But this isn't something you want me to rush. Trust me."

†

Darius and I ran the knife fight for the rest of the afternoon, under the watchful eyes of Connor and Paul, who took notes on angles and lighting. We wore full costumes for the rehearsals, to make sure we'd accounted for them properly.

The fight incorporated a lot of hand-to-hand, as well, with Jeanette getting thrown against various hard surfaces. By the time we'd finished for the day, I sported an impressive collection of bruises, despite strategic padding.

Totally worth it. It felt so good to be doing what I did best.

Even Connor looked at me with something like respect. "That is going to be fun to film," he said without any of his usual supercilious snark. I flashed him a quick smile before heading toward the restroom to freshen up a bit.

I'd stayed at Eden's apartment the last few nights, leaving my Saturn parked in the Dobell Studios lot. It made the early-morning call time a lot easier to face. Since she, Kyra, and I had plans to go out to Ocean's End for drinks tonight, it also meant I could indulge in a drink or two without worrying about the long drive home.

Even better, I could pretend I had my own place again. I'd missed that.

On the way to the restroom, I went to craft services for another bottle of water. The elephant doors were open, letting in the last hour or so of light before the sun set around eight. The sun's fading rays only penetrated ten feet or so into the soundstage. The gloom seemed to swallow the light before it could reach any further.

I found Eden at the table, chatting with Ben, Joe, and Angel and helping Kat clean up the food and get things ready for the next morning.

"Ready to go?" Eden smiled brightly, face scrubbed clean except for a little bit of lipstick.

"Give me about fifteen minutes to get changed and I'll meet you in the lobby, 'kay?" I grabbed a bottle of water, turning to head back to Wardrobe when I noticed Portia walking across the soundstage toward a side door that led out to the back of the lot. She looked tired and miserable.

I knew I'd regret it, but I couldn't stop myself.

"Portia!" I called.

If she heard my voice, she ignored it.

"Portia, wait a sec!" I turned up the volume and hurried across the cement floor, catching her just as she reached the door. She stopped, one hand on the door handle.

"Portia—" I started.

"What?" She cut me off, her voice a whip crack of impatience.

"Look," I said awkwardly. "I know you're not feeling great, but a few of us are going out for drinks and... I thought maybe you'd like to join us."

She stood there for a moment, considering my words. I thought she might actually say yes. That she just needed someone to reach out to her, make her feel welcome.

Stupid me.

Portia slowly turned and looked me up and down with a sneer. "You have *got* to be kidding," she said without bothering to hide her contempt. "I don't waste my time with the help."

My face flushed with anger and I held up my hands in a gesture of defeat.

"Fine," I snapped. "I give up. Go do whatever it is you do. See you in a few days." With that I turned and stomped away, trying to ignore how long the pause was before she opened the door and left the building.

By the time I'd reached wardrobe, the flush of anger had faded away, leaving me with a mixture of frustration and pity. That woman was her own worst enemy.

"Hey, hon," our wardrobe supervisor said. A woman of few words, Joan was comfortably round, with the kind of breasts described as "pillowy." She favored vaguely anachronistic rayon dresses in rich, jewel tones. Kind of Guinevere meets Arwen.

I shimmied out of my costume, handing it over with an apologetic smile.

"This is gonna need to be washed," I said. "Fight rehearsal."

"Compared to Darius's wardrobe, yours smells like roses," she assured me.

I grinned. "Good to know."

I threw on jeans, a violet T-shirt, and purple Converse high-tops, retrieved my bag from my little locker, and went next door to see if Kyra was ready to go.

"Give me five minutes and I'll be ready," she said as she gathered a couple of stray lipsticks off the counter and put them in her makeup kit.

"Cool. I need to put my knife back in the props room, so how 'bout I meet you and Eden out front?"

Kyra nodded and continued cleaning up.

Having said that, I realized I'd forgotten to pull the knife and sheath off the belt of Jeanette's costume. Back to Wardrobe I went, where Joan was just about finished putting everything away for the night.

"You need something else, Lee?"

"Just checking to see if I left the knife in my costume."

Joan flashed me a friendly smile and continued with her work. I located Jeanette's wardrobe rack and rummaged through it. The belt was there, as was the sheath, but no knife.

Shit.

I must have left it on set.

I hurried back into the soundstage. Most of the lights were already off. Even craft service was shut down, the elephant doors now closed. Three of the ceiling bulbs were lit—two on either end of the soundstage, and one shining some light in between the two ships. Not a lot of illumination to work with. Part of me was tempted to wait and just retrieve the knife the following day, but Mike wouldn't leave until all the props were returned. So I got my ass in gear and climbed up onto the *Bootes*.

Moving slowly, I made my way to the bridge, letting my eyes adjust to the very dim light and wishing all the way I'd thought to grab a flashlight. Reaching the console, I ran my hand over its surface in case my eyes missed what I was looking for.

Nothing.

I did the same with the chairs and came away equally empty-handed, heaving a frustrated sigh. Mike wasn't gonna like it if I lost one of his props.

This was the only part of the set where I'd had my knife out of its sheath. It had to be here. Frustrated, I tried my luck again on the console, this time searching more slowly and thoroughly.

My patience was rewarded when I felt the familiar shape of the rubber handle under the top ledge of the console. When I tried to grab it, however, I knocked it forward an inch or so—enough to send it tipping off behind the console, where it hit the ground with a muffled clatter.

"Shit," I muttered, dropping to my knees and crawling under the console to see if I could retrieve it relatively easily. No dice, of course. I had to wriggle around to the side of the console and reach between it and the wall, the space just wide enough for my arm to fit back there. I tried not to think of spiders or other creepy-crawlies.

Ah hah, I thought as my fingertips grazed something solid. I couldn't quite get a grip on it, though, and I didn't want to push the knife further in, to where I'd need a broom handle or something to get the damn thing out.

I turned my body a little more sideways, allowing me to

slip my arm in another half an inch or so, just enough to grasp the tip of the handle with my thumb and forefinger. I tried to pull my arm out and it wouldn't budge, the meat of my shoulder wedged in between the wall and the back of the console.

Great, I thought. All I needed was Connor to come along and find me stuck there, my butt being the first thing he'd see. The thought of my humiliation was enough to motivate me to give a single hard tug backward, successfully extracting myself and the knife—although I did leave some skin off the back of my hand.

"Ouch," I said, untwisting myself from behind the console.

A sudden noise made me freeze, halfway to my feet. A low rasping noise. The sound a snake makes when its scales slither across the desert sands.

Slowly, quietly, I straightened up to a standing position and listened. Even with my eyes adjusted to the dimness, when I looked past the bridge, I still couldn't see anything but dark on dark. My noise wrinkled as I caught a faint whiff of what smelled like sulfur. Not just sulfur, though, but also something similar to the paint used on the Morganti set.

Then there was the smell of rotting garbage, and the very air felt heavy, thicker than it should be. The hairs on the back of my neck stood on end even as the skin beneath them itched.

The noise came again, from somewhere back in the *Bootes* set, this time followed by sibilant whispers.

Something was back there.

Screw this.

I had no intention of finding out what. Scrambling down the ladder to the cement floor, I skipped a step or two in my haste. When I reached the bottom, I paused briefly to listen.

Nothing.

The sounds—if there'd been any in the first place—seemed to have stopped. I still smelled a weird ozone-like tang in the air, though, which grew stronger as I hurried past the Morganti ship. As I neared the back of the soundstage, it became apparent that the smell originated from behind the closed door of the FX department.

No light penetrated the crack under the door.

I thought briefly of knocking, checking to see if everything was okay and that Jaden hadn't knocked himself out with some weird mix of chemicals. I even took a step toward the door. A dry, rustling noise behind a stack of wooden pallets stopped me in my tracks.

Screw it.

Sure he'd gone home, I practically ran back to the props department, startling Michael when I burst through the door, all out of breath.

"Here you go," I said, slapping the knife on his desk.

He raised an eyebrow. "You okay?"

"I didn't want you waiting on me."

Not really a lie. More like a half truth.

"Well, I *am* ready to get out of here, so thank you." Michael put the knife in its drawer behind the desk and stood up. "Give me half a sec and I'll walk out with you."

I was more than happy to wait, even though part of me wondered when, exactly, I'd become afraid of the dark.

†

Portia walked out to the Star Waggon. Her driver wasn't due for another few hours, but she sure as hell didn't want to go out for drinks with her stunt double or any of those other losers—especially the bimbo playing Zoe.

A very small part of her, stuffed far back in a rarely used dusty cupboard of her brain, wanted very much to go out with Lee and the others. That small voice had protested when she'd shot Lee's suggestion down. Portia had told it to fuck off.

She heaved a martyred sigh. Why had she agreed to do this stupid film?

She knew the answer to that.

Money.

Of which she had very little. Why else would she be staying in a trailer—even a nice one—if she had a place to live?

She'd managed to keep secret the fact that she could no longer afford her Hollywood bungalow by renting it out to Frank, an aspiring actor who also worked for a small limo company. Frank was happy to be discreet in exchange for cheap rent, a good address, and the occasional photo op together.

Extremely hunky and very gay, Frank was interested in playing romantic leads and not quite willing to come of the closet. Being seen with Portia did them both some good.

Maybe he'd even let her live in her old house for a month or so when Pale Dreamer wrapped and her Star Waggon went away.

In the meantime, her driver would continue to pick her up, take her to one of several restaurants that still treated her like a star, and then bring her back to her trailer after everyone else had left for the night.

Another small part of her realized that no one really noticed, or cared one way or the other.

Portia made her way to the trailer's well-appointed kitchen and pulled a bottle of red wine down from one of the cupboards. She didn't bother looking at the label and didn't really care what the varietal was, or the vintage. She didn't care how much it cost. She just wanted something to drink.

This particular bottle had a screw top, which made it even more appealing. No fucking corkscrew needed. Opening it with a quick twist of her wrist, she poured about a third into a generously sized wine glass and took a sip. Not great, but it was drinkable. Got even better after she'd drunk half of the glass in one hefty swallow.

Better top it off, Portia thought, and she did so.

Then she sat and thought about the movie. As much as she hated to admit it, she liked the script. It was okay. Maybe even better than okay... and Dobell seemed to have his shit together.

But Jack Garvey? What a joke.

Why the hell he'd wanted to shoot a scene of her walking away from the camera was beyond her. Could he waste any more of her time, or the audience's? They paid to see her face.

Okay, maybe they paid to see her ass, too—or used to—but ever since a particularly unkind review of her last picture had included a remark about her expanding backside, Portia refused to be photographed from that particular angle.

No, her stunt double would actually have to earn her salary. Not like there was anything difficult about the stunts Lee had to do in the movie. A knife fight? Anyone could do that.

The only thing that mattered was the power to call the shots in life. To snap your fingers and have your wishes granted. Anything else was unacceptable. She'd learned that from her asshole parents.

Still, she knew on some level she was being unreasonable. Knew every time she behaved like a spoiled bitch she risked never getting hired again. And yet she just couldn't seem to stop. Always pushing boundaries, but when someone tried to set any of their own, she dug in her heels.

Topping off her glass again, she stretched out on the small but comfy couch near the trailer door, made sure the blackout curtains blocked the parking lot lights, and did her best to relax. She wondered what it would be like to be satisfied with her life for once. Wondered what it would take to make her happy.

She took another sip.

The temperature in the trailer suddenly dropped.

"What the fuck?"

She looked up at the thermostat above her head. She specifically requested that the temperature stay at a steady 75°. Even as she watched the gauge, it dropped from seventy to sixty to fifty degrees. The descent slowed at that point, but still crept, finally stopping at the forty-degree mark. Not exactly cold enough for ice to form on the walls, but it sure felt that way.

Portia sat upright, spilling wine on her designer sweatpants and the couch.

"Dammit!"

This was the last time she'd work on anything with a "moderate" budget. If they couldn't afford to get her a decent trailer, then they couldn't afford to have her on their project. She stalked back to the bedroom, grabbed a sweater from the pile of clothes on the bed, and pulled it on over her T-shirt.

The lights in the trailer flickered. The overhead light in the living room went out.

Then the smell hit. Nothing could have prepared her for the stench that suddenly filled the trailer. If someone had taken dead animals, shit, spoiled food, and every other foul thing she could think of, dumped them in a metal pot and left it out in the sun for a few hours, it couldn't have smelled that bad.

Portia gagged, the wine she'd drunk bubbling up like acid in her throat. She threw up before she could stop herself, vomit splashing on the couch.

Stumbling to her feet, she groped for the handle of the door, fingers numbed by the increasingly frigid air, wanting nothing more than to get outside and away from the horrible smell.

Yellowish-red lights blinked on in the hallway. They went out. Then came on again. Almost like—

Like eyes opening and closing.

A low liquid noise—a cross between a purr and a growl—came from that direction. Portia backed away, the back of her knees hitting the couch. She sat down involuntarily, vaguely aware she'd landed directly in her own puke.

Another sound emanated from the shadows under the dining room table. It sounded like water trying to find its way down a clogged drain.

Maybe that's all it is, *she thought.* The drains. A faulty septic tank. *She'd fire the shit out of someone for not taking care of that. They knew better. They—*

One of the shadows reached out and swiped her across one forearm. Pain flared instantly. Four cuts opened up as if by magic, blood flowing freely and dripping down onto the carpeted floor.

Outrage overrode the pain.

Who the fuck let an animal into the trailer?

Another set of claws raked across her right calf, the pain so intense she thought she might puke again. She looked down to see the fabric of her sweats shredded, blood oozing out of each tear.

Portia had never been a coward. She didn't have the time or patience for fear. Even now, as the shadows around her took on a life of their own, her overriding emotion was rage.

How could this be happening? Things like this weren't supposed to happen. She hurt other people before they had the chance to hurt her.

The lights went out.

†

Ocean's End was hopping when Kyra, Eden, and I arrived—standing room only, with customers lined up two and three deep the length of the bar. A lot of the patrons had taken off their day faces and were letting their true natures show. Kind of like taking off a tight business suit and slipping into sweats and a T-shirt.

We got lucky and scored a booth tucked against the wall across from the bar just as a group of tipsy sea nymphs got up to leave, their hems dripping water in their wake. I thought I recognized one of them from my first visit to the bar.

"I'll get the drinks," I offered as Kyra and Eden grabbed some napkins to soak up the puddles under the table. I squeezed my way through the crowd until I found myself at the bar in front of Manny.

He had some help tonight, a tall, slender girl who looked like she'd taken a wrong turn on her way to Rivendell. Large lavender eyes and a silken mane of silvery blonde hair that fell below the small of her back. She made jeans and a tank top look like formal wear, her movements quick and graceful. She projected an aura of calm, and Manny's eye color, currently a vibrant turquoise, held steady despite the hectic pace.

He gave a nod when he saw me. "Dragon's Milk, then." It wasn't a question.

I grinned. "That'll do me. I also need a Butter chardonnay and a mojito."

"I'll put this on Eden's tab, then."

I shook my head and slapped my now balance-free credit card on the bar. "This round's on me." Manny gave a satisfied nod, as if he'd asked a question and liked the answer. I felt like I'd passed some test I hadn't known I was taking.

Somehow I made it back to our booth without spilling the drinks. Kyra's eyes widened when I set her birdbath of a mojito in front of her.

"Holy shit," she said.

"Manny *does* do generous pours," Eden agreed.

I raised my beer. "Here's to two stress-free and *Portia*-free days." We clinked glasses carefully and drank.

"Omigod, this is the best mojito I've ever had," Kyra moaned with the kind of ecstasy normally reserved for an orgasm or chocolate.

"Is this your first time here?" I asked.

"Second. I went on a date with one of the other contestants from *Face-Off* a few months ago, and he brought me here."

"I take it that it didn't work out," Eden speculated.

Kyra snorted. "Not even. His mom was a shifter. Hyena. He *totally* inherited her laugh. And the shit he thought was funny?" She gave a little shudder. "One date was more than enough. There aren't enough mojitos in the world, y'know?"

"Eden? Eden Carmel?"

The three of us looked up to find a male humanoid standing in front of the table. Like a lot of the other customers, he'd chosen to show his true nature. Dark-gold skin, blood-red corneas, the "whites" of his eyes ebony. Nose so short it would have to grow an inch or so to earn the title of "snub." Thinning gray hair pulled back in a man-bun. Short, slump-shouldered, pot-bellied, and bandy-legged. His suit looked expensive, probably tailored to make the best of a bad deal. He leaned over close to Eden, showing sharp yellow teeth in a smile that managed to be creepy and smarmy at the same time.

"When are you going to give that has-been Lupin the boot and let me give you the representation you deserve?"

Eden gave a coquettish laugh. "You're such a tease, Marty."

Marty reached out and draped his fingers over her shoulder, where they sat like pudgy gold worms.

"Just say the word, Eden, and I'll do more than tease."

Ugh. My skin crawled as if it was trying to leave without me.

Somehow Eden kept her smile in place, possibly because she opted to drink some chardonnay in lieu of another response. So Marty gave Kyra a dismissive once-over and then turned his attention to me. I didn't like the speculative expression as he looked me up and down. Like I was for sale and he was considering the purchase.

"Who's this?" he purred. His voice, no doubt meant to seduce, grated on my nerves, the auditory equivalent of biting on tinfoil. Looking into his eyes was like looking at burning coals in little black caves. The scar on my neck twitched.

"This is Lee Striga," Eden replied when it became obvious I wasn't going to answer. "She's a stuntwoman."

He nodded, eyes narrowing in recognition.

"All healed up, are we?" The words, meant to sound solicitous, came across as vaguely menacing.

"Yup," I said, offering the barest of nods.

"She's with MTA," Eden added with a certain amount of pleasure.

He scowled. "Faustina Corbin. Well, when you get tired of her games, you think about giving me a call."

I took another sip of beer by way of response. I didn't have Eden's patience for Hollywood politics. Marty's scowl deepened. Before he could say anything else, however, someone called his name from the front door of the bar. He looked up, his expression brightening.

"Gotta run, kids. Seriously, Eden, think about ditching Lupin."

"Uh-huh!" Eden gave a little wave as Marty hurried off to greet the newcomer, his feet making sharp *clip-clop* noises on the wooden flooring. I snuck a peek. Yup, hooves.

"An agent, huh?"

"A real bottom feeder," Eden replied, shaking her head.

281

"You'd think a Scaenicus demon would be a little more savvy and a *lot* less pushy."

"A Hollywood agent who's actually a demon?" Kyra shook her head. "What are the odds of *that*?"

"Fifty–fifty," Eden and I said at the same time.

The three of us cracked up.

CHAPTER TWENTY-FIVE

No Portia meant relatively little drama on the set.

Jack still argued with Dan and Breanna over the satanic associations of the Morganti race and pushed for a clear-cut God-versus-Lucifer resolution. Kyra and Jaden got into a couple of spats over the Morganti—they fell into a gray area between FX and makeup. *Sans* diva, however, it was the difference between a category five hurricane and a quick and sudden storm.

The first day we succeeded in filming the entire knife fight minus the close-ups. Connor and Paul transitioned smoothly from shot to shot with an ease that showed how efficient they could be when not hampered at every turn.

Day two we shot some scenes that included Jake and Zoe. I did my butt-doubling schtick when needed. Things moved over to the Morganti bridge for the second half of the shooting schedule, and I got to watch Joe and Angel try to out-evil each other while still succeeding at being creepy-ass villains. It made me appreciate the script all over again, and Jack actually got to direct with assurance and some skill.

It was therefore with a distinct lack of enthusiasm that Eden and I went to set the day Portia was due back. When we arrived, there was a funereal air hanging over the craft service tables, indicating that everyone else much felt the same way. She was still nowhere to be seen, however, so I grabbed some coffee and headed over to Makeup.

†

"Where the hell is Portia? She's more than an hour late!"

Jack looked at his watch and then around the set as if expecting his missing star to suddenly appear.

She didn't.

We were filming a scene where Jake and Jeanette first enter the Morganti ship through the connected airlocks. Ben was there, already in costume and makeup. In my stand-in role, I was helping Connor and Paul set up the lights for the shot. Peter and Brad—our production assistants—stood by waiting for tasks to be assigned.

"Have you seen her?" Jack glared at me as if somehow I was responsible for Portia's absence.

"Uh, *no*."

"Well, you're her stunt double."

Seriously?

"And your point?" I glared back at him, annoyed. "Last time I checked, my job description didn't include playing nanny." It was a little bitchy, but I was already going far beyond the call of duty—and my contract.

"It's fine, Jack. She'll be here." As if by magic, Herman— the talent whisperer himself—appeared from the shadows, all smiles and reassurances. He patted Jack on one shoulder, as if soothing a high-strung horse.

"Well, someone needs to go haul Portia out of her trailer," Jack insisted.

Peter and Brad looked at each another, their lack of enthusiasm painfully obvious via their lack of volunteering.

Herman sighed, and I knew he was about to go do the dirty work himself.

He looked tired, and frail, as if something was eating him from the inside out. It worried me. Could it be cancer? Surely he was undergoing treatment. Part of me wanted to ask him, but I knew it was none of my business.

What I could do, though, was shoulder this particular burden.

"I'll go check on her," I said.

Herman gave me a grateful smile. I, in turn, shot Peter and Jake a disgusted look.

"You guys are *so* getting white feathers."

They just stared at me blankly. Ben, on the other hand, was old enough to get the reference and chuckled.

Good enough for me.

Passing through the elephant doors, I went to beard Portia in her overpriced den. Her chauffeur's town car was parked next to it, and I peeked inside.

Empty.

Most likely they were both inside the trailer. *Oh, man...* I had enough problems already, and I *so* didn't want to be the person who interrupted her while she was boinking her driver.

Taking a deep breath, I climbed the steps and rapped sharply on the trailer door. It opened on its own, moving an inch or two away from my knuckles, and instantly I felt like I wanted to vomit as a rancid smell floated out through the crack.

Ugh.

It had to be the trailer's septic tank. Maybe that's why the driver was inside—to check whatever was broken. It also might explain why Portia was late. So I pushed the door open a little bit more.

"Hello?"

No answer.

"Portia? You there?"

I rapped again, just to be polite. The door opened further and I stuck my head inside, instantly regretting it as the stench grew more powerful—raw sewage and something else I couldn't quite identify.

"Portia?"

My voice sounded flat in the thick air. I waited a few seconds for a response. The only sound was an insistent buzzing.

Flies?

Very reluctantly, I took a couple of steps inside. The blackout curtains were closed and the lights were on, even though it was daytime. The soles of my shoes stuck to the carpeted floor, lifting away with a slight ripping sound, like pieces of Velcro being pulled apart.

Weird.

I took a few more tentative steps, wincing as the carpet suddenly squished beneath my feet. I glanced down… and froze in place.

Reddish-brown stains spattered the neutral-beige carpet, dried in some places and still wet in others. Blood oozed out from beneath my feet. My horrified gaze traveled up to the walls and ceiling, which looked as though someone put carmine paint in a blender without a lid and turned it on "high."

Even worse were the chunks of partially clothed meat scattered across the floor, couch, and other surfaces. There was a small, feminine hand lying on the kitchenette counter top, and I recognized the sapphire ring it wore.

My stomach began to churn.

Mixed up with the smaller, more feminine pieces were

some bits I could tell came from Portia's driver. A leg in the tattered remnants of black slacks. A partial hand, thumb, and fingers, thick and large-knuckled.

The lower half of a masculine face, mouth opened in a perpetual scream.

The buzzing in my ears might have been flies, or a warning sign that I was about to faint. I saw two torsos— one male, one female. Both had gaping holes under the left breast, where the heart should be. The rib cages were splayed open as though something very strong had grabbed each set of bones and pulled them apart, scrambling the insides beyond recognition.

Flies continued to swarm, some of them lighting on the piles of meat, no doubt laying eggs. The thought made me gag. I shoved a hand over my mouth in a vain attempt to keep my breakfast inside. I did, however, manage to stumble out of the trailer before losing it.

Once I'd finished voiding my stomach, I made my way on unsteady legs back to the soundstage to break the news that Portia actually had a good excuse for missing her call time.

†

Several hours later the police and people in white protective suits swarmed the parking lot in back of the studio. Yellow tape went up around the town car and Star Waggon, as well as a swatch of the trees and grass to prevent anyone from entering and contaminating the crime scene.

Reporters and photographers hung back reluctantly on the other side of the barricade, shouting out questions to whoever was close enough to ignore them.

"So you said when you came out here, the trailer door was open?" Detective Maggie Fitzgerald stared down at me where I sat on the passenger seat of her car, as far away from the trailer as possible. Fitzgerald was known among the supernatural community, and headed up the quaintly named "Kolchak Division," a special unit of the LAPD that handled "weird" cases. She had a commanding voice, smooth and rich, with an edge that dared you to not take her seriously.

I took her very seriously indeed.

Tall and broad shouldered, she looked about as black Irish as they came. Dark hair pulled back into an impeccably executed French braid, not one strand out of place. Dark-blue eyes showing some sympathy, while withholding judgment.

"It wasn't exactly open," I answered. "When I knocked, it opened a little bit. I don't think it was latched."

She nodded, scribbling in a small black notebook.

This was our second time around—third, if you counted the responding officer who'd first questioned me. Detective Fitzgerald had explained that sometimes more details came out with the second or third interview, and they didn't want to miss anything that might help them figure out who— or what—had done this. What she *didn't* mention was that repetition also helped trip people up when they were lying.

"So what happened next?"

"Like I said, it smelled disgusting. I thought maybe the septic tank had broken, and that her driver was inside trying to fix it."

"Do you think it's reasonable that Miss Lambert would've expected a limo driver to fix the septic tank in her trailer?"

I shrugged. "Portia wasn't known for being reasonable."

A small smile played across her mouth.

"So why did you go inside without waiting for her to answer? Seems as if she would've been unhappy at that kind of intrusion."

"She was an hour late for call time, and we had a crew

and other actors waiting on her. Frankly, she doesn't"—I stopped, gave a little shake of my head—"*didn't* pay my salary," I corrected myself. "So if she got pissed off, I could live with it. It wouldn't have been anything new."

"Did you happen to see anyone come out to Ms. Lambert's trailer before you left—when was it—" She looked at her notes. "Two nights ago. Wednesday night?"

"No. She made it very clear she didn't want anyone coming out here. If Portia could've posted a security guard to keep people away, she would've done it."

"So you and Ms. Carmel and Ms. Gilbert left at what time?"

"It was about nine o'clock."

"And you didn't come back here after you went to…" Her pause was deliberate.

"Ocean's End." I supplied the name yet again. "And no, Kyra went back to her place and I crashed at Eden's. It's just a couple of blocks from the bar."

"You didn't notice the town car parked out here for two days?"

I shook my head. "The last two days I've gotten here at the butt-crack of dawn, stumbled straight from my car to craft services for coffee, and spent pretty much the entire time inside either rehearsing or shooting. Most people park over at the front of the lot, not around back."

Her next question deviated from the script.

"Ms. Striga, were you aware that Portia Lambert was actually living in the trailer?"

Huh? That was out of left field.

"You mean staying here, instead of going home at night?"

"I mean *living* there. Ms. Lambert was renting out her home because she couldn't afford the mortgage payments.

We believe her driver, Frank Gough, was the tenant."

My mouth dropped open, and it took an effort to shut it.

"That's... that's sad," I finally said, and I meant it.

"Had you met Mr. Gough over the last few weeks?"

I shook my head. "No, not really. We may have waved at each other once or twice, but I don't think I could pick his face out of a batch of head shots."

She nodded, her expression neutral, then had me *again* describe what I'd found inside. I did so, doing my best to keep my stomach from flipping pancakes. Then a man in protective overalls poked his head out of the front door and called to the detective. She excused herself and joined him. They talked in undertones, but I still managed to pick up a couple of words here and there.

The man vanished back inside the trailer and Detective Fitzgerald rejoined me at the town car.

"They're bringing out the bodies now," she warned me gently.

There was barely enough inside the bags to give the impression of two people. They looked more like laundry bags than body bags. I shut my eyes after the first glimpse, putting my head back down between my knees until the urge to throw up again receded.

"Okay, I think we got everything for now," the detective said. "Thank you for your cooperation. I may need to talk to you again down the line." She shook her head. "Whoever or whatever did this was pretty brutal."

"That's an understatement," I muttered.

"Yeah, it is. All I can say for now is just keep an eye on the phases of the moon."

I looked up at her. "Uh... what?"

"It was nearly full when this happened, and it's full now.

We've got two more nights of it."

"You think it was a werewolf?"

She shrugged. "We've had a couple other unsolved murders similar to these. They took place over the last full moon. It's not a perfect fit, but might explain the condition of the victims' bodies and the timing of their deaths."

I almost asked, *"Since when do werewolves take the hearts?"* but decided to keep the thought to myself in case it might lead to another round of questions.

A sudden ruckus at the perimeter of the crime scene caught her attention. Reporters trying to get the lowdown on what happened, rapid-firing questions hurled at a hapless police officer. Some of them even pushed at the tape barricade.

"Excuse me, Ms. Striga."

Detective Fitzgerald lowered her brows and raised her voice, opening her mouth to emit a high-pitched wail that probably had dogs howling within a square-mile radius. The sound filled the air, seeming to come from all directions. The reporters winced, some clapping hands over their ears.

Fitzgerald closed her mouth. The sound stopped. The officer looked relieved, though the reporters looked as though they'd had a close brush with death. Yet none of them seemed aware of where the sound had come from.

Weird.

Detective Fitzgerald turned back. "Can you please send Mr. Dobell out?"

I nodded and opened my mouth to say, *"Banshee, right?"* But I decided against it because I really needed another cup of coffee. All I said was, "Absolutely."

Then I made my escape.

CHAPTER TWENTY-SIX

Cast and crew huddled around the craft service table, talking in low voices. I found Herman and passed along Detective Fitzgerald's request. He hurried outside. Then I grabbed a cup of coffee, liberally dosing it with cream and sugar before sinking into a chair and trying to get my thoughts straight.

Since the studio itself wasn't a crime scene, it might be possible to keep filming. But what the hell were we going to do without a lead actress? Turned out I wasn't the only one thinking along these lines.

"—have to find someone else pronto," Joe was saying. "We're only a few days into production. It's a damn shame what happened to her, but it's no reason to stop filming."

Angel frowned. "That just seems cold," she said. "We should give it a few days before even talking about this."

"Look." Ben stepped in at this point. "The hard reality is that there's already been a lot of money put into this film. I'm guessing most of us need the work, am I right?" Several people nodded their assent. "And you think about it, in any other industry, do offices shut down when someone dies?"

Okay, he has a point. I also agreed with Angel that it seemed a little premature to be having this discussion.

"What do *you* think, Lee?"

I looked over to see Eden sitting in a chair pushed back away from the table. She cradled a mug of hot tea in her hands.

"Well," I said slowly, "when Jack Tyree died doing an eighty-foot fall on *Sword and the Sorcerer*, they not only finished the movie, but used his final take in the film."

"Now *that* seems cold," Joe commented.

"Hell, no," I said. "Jack was a stuntman. He died doing what he loved, and the greatest insult would've been *not* using his last work in the film. I felt the same way when I got hurt on *Vampshee*. I could've died in that fall, but I got lucky. I'll tell you, though, if I'd woken up and found out they hadn't used that take? I'd have been pissed-off as hell.

"What's different here," I continued, "is that we're talking about replacing Portia. There's no real way to give her that last moment on screen, and that sucks for her." I was surprised to feel tears burning under my eyelids. I hadn't liked the woman. She'd made it impossible. But I still felt for her. She'd had an unhappy life and died a horrible death.

Everyone was quiet for a few minutes.

Connor looked at me with a speculative expression.

"The closest thing we can get to giving Portia her last shot on screen," he said, "is to replace her with you."

What the fuck, dude? I stared at him.

"Um, actually I think she'd be spitting *furious* at the thought."

"Think about it," Connor pressed, locking eyes. "Better someone like you, who comes close to her physical type. Do you really think she'd thank us for replacing her with a twenty-something starlet?"

"I'm only twenty-seven," I muttered.

He rolled his eyes. "You know what I mean."

"Besides," I objected, "I'm not an actress. I'm a

stuntwoman. I'm trained in fights and falls. I've crashed the occasional car and been set on fire a couple of times, but I've never taken an acting class in my life."

Connor stared at me challengingly. "You seemed perfectly comfortable with the lines when you were running them with Ben, Joe, and Angel."

Dan and Breanna both nodded in agreement.

"Absolutely," Breanna said. "You and Ben actually sound like a more believable team than he and Portia ever did."

"Honestly," Dan added, "the way she read her lines, no one would believe they'd have survived together for so long out in deep space."

Ben chuckled. "I can't disagree with that."

Herman came in through the elephant doors, his forehead crisscrossed with worry lines. He looked tired and drawn, as if he'd lost another five pounds overnight. Jack immediately turned to him, seemingly oblivious to his producer's exhaustion.

"They gonna let us keep shooting?"

"Yes." Herman dropped down in one of the folding chairs as if someone had cut his legs out from underneath him.

"Are you okay?" I moved next to him and knelt.

He smiled wanly. "Nothing a cup of coffee wouldn't help."

Production Assistant Peter immediately hurried over to the beverage table and poured coffee into one of the heavy-duty paper cups, adding a liberal amount of cream and sugar. Herman took it gratefully. After a sip or two, a bit of color came back into his face.

"The police have given us permission to continue filming starting tomorrow," he said. "There are no real leads as to what happened to Portia, but because it happened outside of the studio itself, and in her trailer, they're assuming she was the specific target. Most likely her driver walked in at the wrong time.

"Nevertheless, they'll have a couple of police officers patrolling the parking lot for the next few days. Just in case." He drank some more coffee. "The trailer and the surrounding area will remain taped off, including the back of the parking lot and a section of the park. They'll be going over the area with a fine-toothed comb, to see if any trace evidence shows up. Detective Fitzgerald also suggests that if we have to go to the parking lot after sunset, we go in pairs.

"In the meantime, we have an obvious problem to solve. Portia needs to be replaced, and from what I overheard, it sounds like I'm not the only one who's reached the obvious solution."

He looked up at me.

Oh, crap.

"Lee, I'd like to have a word with you in private."

"Sure," I replied even as my heart sank. I knew what he was going to ask and I didn't want to hear it.

†

Once inside his office, Herman sat down heavily behind his desk. I perched gingerly on one of the chairs.

"I take it you're not sold on the idea."

I didn't even try feigning ignorance.

"No, I'm really not," I said. "I'm not an actress. I mean, I've always done my best to convey the emotions of whatever part I'm supposed to be doubling, but I've never worried about lines."

"You know you're a natural, don't you?"

I shrugged, totally uncomfortable at this point.

"Seriously." Herman leaned forward. "Your line readings with Ben were better than Portia's. The two of you have a natural camaraderie that works for the story. The writers agree, your fellow actors agree—and even though I know Jack had his heart set on Portia, I know he's relieved. Not that she's dead," he added hastily as my eyebrows shot up, "but working with her was a lot more difficult than he'd bargained for."

"Look," I sighed. "I don't want to let anyone down. I also don't want the police looking at me cross-eyed because I've suddenly and conveniently taken over a dead woman's role."

"I understand that, and we will make it very clear, should the subject come up, that this was *not* your idea. From a purely financial perspective, this is the logical thing for the production. It'll save us time, and saving time will save us money." He leaned back and added, "We'll definitely adjust your salary." Then he quoted an amount that made my eyes widen.

"So think about it," he concluded. "But not for too long."

I thought about it.

If I took the job, Herman wouldn't lose money putting the production on hold, while he and Jack found another actress to play Jeanette. And honestly, I had a blast running lines with Ben. It would look nice on my resume… and then there was the money.

"Will you do it?" Herman looked at me hopefully.

I couldn't say no to him.

"I'm in."

The smile that brightened his haggard face was worth all the insecurity and guilt that were turning my stomach into an acidic butter churn.

"I'm assuming you won't mind doing your own stunts."

That made me smile.

"I'll consider it."

CHAPTER TWENTY-SEVEN

INT – BOOTES BRIDGE

JEANETTE
You just love the sound of your voice, don't you?

SHAAD
Not as much as I'm going to love the sound of your screams.

†

"And… cut!" Jack gave a thumbs up, beaming like he'd just won an Oscar for Best Picture. "That was great, you guys! That's a wrap for the day, and for the *Bootes*."

Joe and I high-fived each other. This scene, where Shaad appears behind Jeanette on the bridge of the *Bootes*, led straight into the first part of the knife fight. We were shooting the close-ups of the fight with Joe today. Some of the takes we'd shot during the actual fight had shown my face, and they could be used now that I was playing Jeanette.

I was almost sorry we'd already filmed the fight. I loved doing what I'd trained to do, and that choreography had been particularly awesome. Not that I wasn't having fun with the acting.

I'd spent so much time as Portia's stand-in, I pretty much had all of Jeanette's lines memorized. Playing off Ben seemed like an extension of our off-camera camaraderie. Working with Eden, Joe, and Angel was just as much fun.

We were into the fourth week of shooting, with two weeks to go. Most of the scenes on board the *Bootes* were in the figurative can, and we were running ahead of schedule, instead of behind. If not exactly a well-oiled machine, the cast and crew got their shit together in way that hadn't been possible with Portia on board.

Part of me still felt guilty, though. Portia had died horribly. But her death hadn't been my fault, so I tried my best to let go of any residual angst I felt taking over her part.

Wherever she was, I *really* hoped she wasn't pissed off at me. The last thing I needed was for her to come crawling out of my TV like one of those nasty Japanese ghosts. They can be mean assholes.

As well as things were going, Herman's physical condition continued to deteriorate. If his weight loss continued at this pace, he'd soon resemble a mummy with parchment for skin. The initial attraction I'd felt for him had been replaced by pity and concern. I don't know how he managed to do his job each day, yet he kept going, like a desiccated Energizer bunny.

Next up on the shooting schedule, Jake and Jeanette would explore the Morganti ship, finding Zoe and a bunch of creepy-ass shit including ambulatory corpses, body parts, and torture devices. I *really* wasn't looking forward to spending a lot of time on that set, but hey, I didn't have much choice—especially now that I was the star, stand-in, and stunt double.

On the plus side, it wouldn't be much of a stretch for me to act paranoid.

Peter trotted up with a sheaf of papers in one hand. "Shooting schedule for tomorrow and Tuesday," he announced, handing them out. I took mine, glancing at my call time and scenes.

INTERIOR – MORGANTI SHIP

Jake/Jeanette find Zoe.
Jake/Jeanette/Zoe Airlock
Ritual Shaad/Rheyza
Ritual FX Darius/Lee

I frowned.

"Huh. What's up with the ritual scene?"

Peter shrugged. "Don't know."

"That was a rhetorical question, Peter."

"A what?"

Before I'd decided if I had the patience to explain the meaning of "rhetorical," Jack joined us.

"Everything okay, Lee?"

"Just wondering what's up with the ritual scene. It's been moved up to tomorrow. Last I heard, Jaden wasn't satisfied with the effects yet."

Jack looked unhappy. "He's not, but Herman's insisting. He says he wants to see the finished results before—" He stopped abruptly.

I lowered my voice. "Herman's sick, isn't he?"

Jack's eyes flickered to the left, looking over my shoulder. "Well, I'm not sure, but—"

"Jack, it's painfully obvious." I gave him a look. "Please don't bother lying, okay?"

He sighed. "Yeah, okay. He's sick. He won't say what's

wrong, but the way he's been talking, I'm guessing some sort of fast-moving cancer. He doesn't want people to know. I don't... I hate thinking about it. He's been really good to me. I just hate to think of him dying without being saved."

Jack looked so genuinely distressed that I could almost forgive him for that—the assumption that their way is the *only* way. There's definitely more to heaven and earth, Horatio, but not the limited version so many people think there is.

I quickly changed the subject. "Do you know why Darius and I are listed on the call sheet for the ritual scene?"

"We're only going to have one take to get this particular shot, and there're some pyrotechnics involved that could make Joe and Angel uncomfortable. So both Jaden and Herman want to do the money shot with you and Darius. I know it means doubling someone other than yourself—"

I will not laugh. I will not laugh.

"—but we'd appreciate, *Herman* would appreciate it, if you'd sit in for Angel. I'm sure he meant to ask you himself, but he's been—"

Distracted, I thought.

"Distracted," Jack said. "So—"

I held up a hand. "Stop drilling, Jack. You struck oil."

He looked blank.

"I'll do it," I said.

†

The ritual scene took place in an octagonal-shaped chamber on the Morganti ship. The walls were about eight feet in height, and each section of the octagon held a glass trophy case containing a severed head. Some of the heads were human and others distinctly alien. All looked as though they'd died in agony.

Kudos to Jaden for some truly gruesome work.

Side-by-side, Darius and I sat cross-legged on black cushions that blended in with the floor. Every surface of the alien craft's interior was a variant of the shade used on the exterior. For the set-up, the set was lit with a 2K bulb, unfiltered.

I looked at myself in the reflection of a glass trophy case on the other side of the circle. Kyra had done an awesome job—deathly pale skin, hair so dark it seemed to eat the shadows. We wouldn't be filmed from the front, but the reflections of our faces would be seen in the glass of the cases, so we needed to match Joe and Angel.

We sat in a chalk circle just outside of a larger one with an inner and outer border. A pentagram was drawn in the larger circle so its points touched the edges of the inner border. A variety of esoteric ingredients—red powder in a small glass vial; two shallow bowls, one holding dirt, the other mixed herbs; a small bone; a polished ebony stone; a glossy blue-black feather; and what looked like the dripping, bloody heart of a large animal—lay spread out in front of Darius.

A cast iron cauldron sat in the center, balancing on three stumpy legs, an unlit tea candle beneath it. In between the borders were sigils interspersed with black candles. The sigils and borders were drawn in an unpleasant glow-in-the-dark yellowish-green reminiscent of drying algae, unnatural sea creatures, and bile. It made me twitchy and slightly nauseous, like everything else on the Morganti set.

Connor stood behind the camera, which was set up to the right and in back of us. Herman stood a few feet behind him, Jack next to Herman. Gathered in a group and well out of the way behind them were Ben, Joe, Angel, and Eden, with Michael, Kyra, Joan, and Effie close by.

Peter stood by with the clapperboard. He was kind of like me—standing in for positions that hadn't made the budget cut. Brad, the other PA, had gone home sick.

Paul did a final check on the four lights set up on C-stands around the outside of the octagon, all bearing filters to create an unhealthy green glow that shimmered around the edges. A soft spotlight, nestled in a short, fat candle holder, created classic under-lighting on our faces.

"Now remember," Jaden said, hunkering down next to us. "It's going to get kind of crazy, but you're going to want to stay right where you are when the effects really start popping. They're not exactly pyrotechnics, but we don't want you and Darius getting any of the splashback from the materials. If you stay in your little circle here, you'll be just fine."

I wondered what he meant by "materials," but kept my mouth shut. If Darius was cool with this, then so was I.

"I gotta say," Jaden continued, "I am *so* glad we're using the two of you for the money shot, instead of the actors. You're both used to this stuff, so some smoke and mirrors won't be enough to make you jump. We need to get this in one take."

He pointed to the cauldron. "When everything's a go and the effects are activated, you'll see stuff come out of there. It's kinda like a high-tech fog machine. Then it'll move to the outer rim of the circle. Got it?"

I nodded. Darius grunted.

"Just remember," Jaden said again, "you two don't have to say anything. We're not rolling sound on this take. We got the actual dialogue in the close-ups so I'll read the lines to make sure everything is synced with the effects. Darius, you'll put the ingredients in the cauldron. Do you remember the order?"

Darius grunted again by way of reply.

One grunt for yes, two grunts for no. Kind of like a Neanderthal Ouija Board.

Herman stepped out from behind the camera. He smiled, the expression a little ghastly with his skeletal face and the stark lighting of the 2K.

"Folks," he said, "I want to thank you for all of your hard work. For the flexibility you've shown. I'd also like to extend my appreciation to those who are done filming for the day and who've stayed to watch this. I'm so proud of Jaden for what he's done and it means the world to me that you're all here to witness it." Then he looked at me, ice-blue eyes almost luminescent.

"Lee, you've been a bulwark of strength and tolerance. I cannot thank you enough for all you've done." He paused, then added, "And all you've yet to do." With that he went back behind the camera, sparing me the need to respond.

"Okay. Everyone ready?" Jaden lit the candle under the cauldron, rubbed his hands together, and went over in front of the camera. Picking up a control box of some sort, he knelt on the floor as close as he could get to us without being in the shot.

"Remember, I've done this before, so don't worry."

Paul turned off the 2K. Immediately the octagon was awash in a blend of muted, unearthly colors not found in nature, and my stomach gave an uneasy turn. *Maybe I should have taken two Dramamines.*

"Ritual FX, Take One," Peter said, holding the clapperboard in front of the camera and bringing it together with a sharp crack. He immediately dropped out of the way.

The camera rolled. Jaden spoke.

"*Amelatu Abanaskuppatu Tiamatu, ati me peta babka!*"

His voice rose, uttering the word at the end of the phrase

in a harsh staccato as Darius tossed the open vial of red powder into the cauldron.

My skin crawled for no discernable reason.

"*Annitu, dalkhu sa ina etuti asbu!*"

In went the bone.

"*Bu'idu salmu la minam Kurnugi, Erset la tari, La'atzu!*"

Next, the ebony stone.

"*Nisme annu nusku! Nisme annu sisitu! Elu ma semu annu kishpu!*"

Darius tossed in the feather, a pinch of dirt, and a sprinkling of the herbs.

The incantation was in a language I didn't recognize, even though it seemed oddly familiar. Jaden showed a surprising level of commitment to the lines. I didn't expect that from an FX guy.

As each ingredient entered the cauldron, the crawling of my skin increased. Was it my imagination or was the temperature dropping? Shivers rippled through my body and the crawling of my skin increased until I was fighting the urge to jump up and get the hell out of there.

"*Uzna sakanu. Pana sakanu. Kima parsi labiruti.*"

I forced myself to remain in place.

"*Lequ annu libbu!*"

As Jaden uttered the final word of the incantation, Darius dropped in the gory heart. When it hit the cauldron, three things happened simultaneously.

The temperature plummeted until what looked like ice crystals formed on the surface of the trophy cases. A rank odor rose from the cauldron in a rush, as if something inside had exhaled, its breath foul. And oily-sheened black shadows followed the smell, rising up into the air, writhing and shifting in front of us.

The roiling blackness was reflected in the trophy case

across from us, undulating, tendrils swallowing each other like a misshapen Ouroboros.

There were a few sharp intakes of breath.

"Jesus Christ," Jack said under his breath.

I did my best to breathe through my mouth in shallow gulps of air to keep as much of the stench out as possible. I doubted Morgantis barfed. I wondered if the powder that had gone in first had possessed some sort of hallucinatory properties. Whatever, however, it was spectacularly creepy.

The shadows continued their macabre ballet, twisting and turning, then swarming around the edge of the chalk circle as if testing the boundaries. The air in front of one of the things seemed to *bulge* as if the shadow pressed against it. Things shimmered, vibrated, and it looked as if the shadow was tearing a gash in the air so it could squeeze through past the barrier and—

"Cut!" Jaden yelled.

Someone, probably Paul, turned the 2K back on. Light flooded the chamber, a bright glare that cut through the darkness and sent up tendrils of steam. The shadows evaporated and the air began to warm again, although the smell remained.

Someone started clapping somewhere in back of the camera set up. I shielded my eyes with one hand and saw that it was Herman. He stepped out onto the set, followed by the Tymons.

"Brilliant," Herman said. "Absolutely brilliant."

Breanna nodded. "That was truly spectacular."

Everyone on set joined in the applause—even Jack joined, although he looked as though he could use the services of an old priest and a young priest about now.

Then someone screamed.

CHAPTER TWENTY-EIGHT

The scream sounded again, filled with pain and fear, the intensity hurting my ears. Underneath the high-pitched cries came another sound—a rending noise as if heavy fabric was being ripped apart.

It cut off with a wet gurgle.

Without even thinking I leapt to my feet, stumbling over Darius, and pushed my way through the rest of the cast and crew to reach the darkened corridor. My eyes couldn't adjust to the gloom fast enough to prevent me from tripping over something beneath. I went sprawling, catching myself on both hands before bashing my chin on the slotted floor.

My hands slid on a surface that was unexpectedly warm, liquid, and slick, stopping against a yielding softness. A gassy, coppery smell assaulted my nostrils.

"Get some light in here," I yelled even as I tried to backpedal.

"Here!" Connor called as a strong beam of light penetrated the gloom, illuminating what lay on the floor. There was Effie's face, mouth open in a now silent scream.

I pushed away from the all-too-familiar bloody mess that had been our boom operator, her ribcage decimated, a hole in the cavity where her heart should be. Other organs had been torn apart, left to ooze out onto the slotted floor. I could hear liquid dripping to the ground below.

"Lee, what's happening?"

I turned. Angel stood behind me, partially blocking the beam of light from the 2K. Her eyes widened in horror as she took in the scene before her. Even as I opened my mouth to warn her away, something reached out of the shadows and snatched her up by her arms and head. Blood splattered me in the face, neck, and chest as she vanished back into the set.

"Angel!"

I jumped to my feet and swiped at the viscous liquid in my eyes, fully intending to go after her. Then her screams cut off with a horrible rattling sound, and there wasn't any point. I heard the rasping slithering noise. Something hissed and chuckled. The sounds came from nowhere and everywhere.

"Lee!"

"Ben, get everyone out of here!" I yelled back. "I'm right behind you!"

Chaos ensued. People screamed and shouted, scrambling to get out of the enclosed space and back to the soundstage. I stumbled backward into the ritual chamber, afraid to take my eyes away from the darkness where Effie's corpse sprawled. Only Connor remained in the chamber. He ripped the colored gel off one of the other lights and used the beam to illuminate the way off the Morganti ship.

"Are you hurt?" he asked.

I shook my head. "It's… it's not my blood."

He nodded grimly. "We have to get out of here."

The hissing, slithering, and chuckling sounds got louder.

"No shit." We spun and made our way down the corridor. "Did anyone else get hurt?" I almost said "killed" but couldn't bring myself to do it. The reality of what I'd just seen would set in soon enough. It was a miracle that I wasn't already gibbering in shock.

"I don't think so. Jaden got everyone moving as soon as Effie—" He shook his head and swallowed hard. "As soon as she screamed."

Jaden. Whatever had just been unleashed, it was his doing. *Special effects my ass.* He had a lot to answer for.

The temperature dropped again. I stopped short and my arm shot up to prevent Connor from going any further. Sniffing the air, I smelled sulfur. Underneath that were less pleasant odors—garbage left out too long. A dead rat left in the walls of a house in the summer. An overflowing septic tank baking in the summer heat. All of it combined to create a stench fouler then any of its parts.

I gagged, sounding like a cat with a hairball. Connor manfully tried to pretend he wasn't affected, but green was not his natural color.

"It's here," I said in a low voice.

"*What's* here?"

"Hell if I know," I snapped back.

The light behind us flickered on and off. The temperature dropped further. It felt like I'd crawled into a freezer. I thought I saw ice forming on the walls next to us. Then a liquid growl came from the dark doorway next to us.

This is so *not good.* I pulled the Morganti prop knife out of its sheath. A seven-inch blade didn't seem like much in the face of that menacing, visceral sound, but it was better than nothing. At least that's what I told myself.

Something leapt at me. I felt the wind of its passage and heard claws swiping through the air. I ducked to one side, but wasn't quite fast enough. Razor-sharp tips grazed my arm. *Son of a bitch!* Giving an indrawn hiss of pain, I lashed out with the knife. Something in the shadows gave an unearthly squeal.

Yes! I'd tagged it. Whatever *it* was.

Out of the corner of my eye I saw the shadow in the corner of the corridor. It expanded, taking on a different shape, like the silhouette of some large predator—a cross between a dire wolf and a jaguar, maybe. Where was a cryptozoologist when you needed one?

Whatever it was, it lunged for me again, aiming for my head. The smell, already throat-clenchingly noxious, grew even stronger as the thing detached from the other shadows, like an amoeba splitting off and giving birth to more of its kind. It revealed an open mouth filled with jagged ebony teeth, backlit by an otherworldly glow from its throat.

Reacting purely on instinct, I dropped down, stabbing upward with the knife at the same time, letting the creature's momentum drag the edge of the blade through its underbelly as it passed overhead. If the noise it made before had been a shriek, this time it was a wail of anguish. Foul-smelling black goo spattered down on the floor and on my head.

The thing hit the wall and fell to the ground, thrashing in agony as it gave howl after ungodly howl. Still crouching, I turned to face the fallen predator to see if it would attack again.

Connor stayed where he was, frozen in place.

The shadow creature gave one last shudder and lay still. I got to my feet, approaching it with caution in case this was a demonic fake-out. As I watched, however, another gush of viscous black fluid ejected from the wound I'd inflicted, along with a gout of the same stuff from its mouth.

The thing was actually darker than the shadows that gave birth to it. The initial impression wasn't a bad one, of a dire wolf combined with some sort of prehistoric feline. Only instead of fur, its skin was slick, covered with an oily sheen that reminded me of all things Morganti.

I knelt by its side, doing my best to breathe shallowly through my mouth and trying to forget that smell was particulate. I wanted to get as close a look as I dared to see what, exactly, we were up against. As I leaned down, however, the oily texture of its skin began blistering, bubbles rising and popping like the surface of a tar pit, the flesh dissolving before my eyes.

Within seconds, the whole mess had vanished, the liquefied critter absorbed into the flooring. The smell, unfortunately, lingered on.

"Wow," I said. "That is truly disgusting."

"Yes," Connor said, sounding shell-shocked. "That was…" He trailed off, shook his head and then said simply. "You were amazing. Thank you."

Ah, for a tape recorder. Still, I found myself oddly embarrassed by the praise. "I'm just glad I had this," I said, holding up the prop knife.

"The black gunk didn't stick to it, either."

I glanced down at the blade, which was totally clean. I rubbed my finger along its length and realized it was the one made of rubber.

Not steel.

"Holy crap," I whispered. My knees went wobbly and I started to shake as the realization truly sunk in.

"A rubber knife," I said weakly.

Connor held onto me, keeping me steady until the shaking and the wobbling stopped. Even then, he kept his arm around me until we could start moving.

Down in the soundstage, someone had turned on the main

bank of lights. It helped, but not enough—my vision was blurred. There were people crowded back toward craft service. For some reason the elephant doors weren't open. I scanned the group and didn't see any sign of Jaden. When I blinked, or tried to, Angel's blood made my eyelashes stick together.

"Lee!" Kyra ran up to us, Eden close on her heels. "Oh my God, I'm so glad you're okay!"

"When Angel went back there, and we heard the screams—" Eden looked ashamed. "We shouldn't have left until we found out if you were okay or not."

"You both did the right thing," I assured her. "We need to call the police, get ahold of Detective Fitzgerald. I think we found Portia's killers, and they sure as hell aren't werewolves. Did either of you see where Jaden went?"

Eden shook her head but Kyra nodded.

"I saw him head back to his hole in the ground," she said without love.

I narrowed my eyes.

"Okay, you three get out of the building. I'm going to go find Jaden and make him tell me what the hell he's done, and how we make it stop." I started to move, but Connor grabbed my arm.

"You're not going back there," he said. "It's not your job."

"That asshole turned something loose with his so-called effects," I growled. "Something that kills. Four people have already died, maybe more. I want to know what he did and why."

"Don't be an idiot," he persisted. "*You* said we needed to call the police. Well, that's what we're going to do, because it *is* their job. Now come on." He grabbed my arm again and we followed Eden and Kyra back toward the exit.

CHAPTER TWENTY-NINE

I'd expected to see the elephant doors wide open, everyone out of the building. Instead the remaining cast and crew—all in the midst of varying degrees of panic—clustered tightly around the exit.

"Get those damn doors open!" Jack yelped, a note of hysteria raising his voice by half an octave. His panic level was creeping into the red, unlike the Tymons, who seemed to be handling things relatively calmly. Ben and Peter pulled with their combined strength, but the doors refused to budge.

"They must be locked from the outside," Peter said, panting from the exertion.

"There *are* no locks on the outside," Connor said. He pushed through, grasped a thin metal bar at floor level, and pulled it up out of a hole. Then he did the same thing with the other door, sliding first one, then the other open and letting in a breeze from outside. Our relief was short-lived.

There was no light out in the parking lot.

Sure, the sun had set, but this was a well-lit lot, and there should have been an ambient glow coming in from the streets and surrounding buildings. There was nothing.

Just a sea of darkness.

Jack pushed his way to the front, shoving a weeping Joan out of the way.

"Wait," I said. "Something's wrong. You can't see the cars."

"I'm not waiting for anything," he said, his voice tremulous. "I knew the devil was in the script. I *knew* it. Satan's loose, and he'll kill us all if we stay!"

"Jack—"

Smacking my hands away as I reached for him, he practically threw himself into the black hole of a parking lot.

Seconds later he fell to the asphalt, body sliced apart like a Thanksgiving turkey. He'd died without uttering a sound.

Joan was right on his heels, and stopped short, face ashen. Her eyes turned up in her head and she collapsed face-down across the threshold, with only her head and neck outside the building.

"Get her inside!" I yelled. Ben and Joe immediately grabbed Joan's legs and dragged her back inside.

Her head was already gone.

Someone screamed. Maybe Kat.

Grabbing the door nearest me, I slid it closed again. Connor did the same with the other one, shoving the metal bars back in place.

"Kyra, see if you can get a hold of the police," I said.

She nodded.

"I'm not getting any bars," she said.

No cell phone signal? We were in Culver City, for chrissake. There were satellite towers everywhere. They even outnumbered the Starbucks.

"I'll be right back."

Before Connor or anyone else could protest, I took off at a sprint toward the inner doors, pulling them open and dashing down the hall. The fluorescent lighting still cast its harsh glare on the linoleum. I tried not to think of poor Joan as I hurried into Wardrobe, reached under the counter, and pulled out my tote.

Grabbing my iPhone, I punched in the passcode. One bar, which was more than we had in the soundstage. I pulled up my list of favorites and hit Sean's name without a second thought.

It rang once.

Twice.

I braced myself for his voicemail message.

Three.

"Lee? What's up, baby girl?"

I nearly collapsed with relief. That voice, so full of comforting warmth.

"Sean?" My voice cracked.

"Lee?" Sean's tone sharpened. "What's wrong?"

I told him in as few words as possible. He listened without interrupting, which made me love him more than ever. When I'd finished, there was a brief pause as he assimilated all the information.

"You killed it with a rubber knife?" I don't know what I'd expected him to say, but that wasn't it.

"Yeah, I know. Weird, huh? I—"

"Lee, listen to me. Are you wearing your amulet?"

"Huh?"

"Your mother's necklace. Are you wearing it?"

"I don't… Sean, why are you—"

"Lee, please. Just trust me. *Are you wearing the amulet?*"

"I…" I put my hand up to my neck. No necklace. "No, I don't—"

"Are you sure?"

"It's not around my neck, but—" I stopped and patted

around my waist, feeling the almost indiscernible bulge of the neoprene pouch.

"I've got it."

Sean's sigh of relief was audible.

"Okay, good. Now—"

Whatever he said was obscured by static.

"Sean?"

More static. Then the line went dead. I checked the readout. No bars.

The battery went dead, too.

"Shit!"

At least Sean knew something was wrong and would call the police. All we had to do was wait it out. I pulled off my Morganti costume, grateful to shed the blood-encrusted leather and wig. I put on my jeans, tank top, and boots, tucking my phone into a back pocket. There was a box of baby wipes on a table. I did my best to clean the blood out of my eyelashes and off my face.

Starting out of the wardrobe room, I paused by the rack holding Jeanette's costumes. I'd left the knife in its sheath on the belt yet again, intending to take my props back to Michael at the end of the day's shoot. Pulling out the belt, I strapped it around my waist and unsnapped the fastener on the sheath. If I'd killed one of those things with a rubber knife, it seemed likely that stainless steel would be even more effective.

Suddenly I froze in place.

There was a furtive sound near the door, like someone trying to sneak quietly down the hallway. Creeping over, I peered out just in time to see Jaden headed in my direction, toward the front offices. He glanced back over his shoulder to make sure he was free and clear.

I smiled grimly.

He wasn't.

Waiting until he'd passed Makeup, I stepped out in front of him.

"Got a minute?"

Jaden gave a startled shriek and jumped back. I don't know if he was trying to make a run for it, but I didn't wait to find out. Grabbing him by the shirt and one arm, I swung him around and pitched him through the doorway into Makeup. He landed hard on his hands and knees. Before he could scrabble to his feet, I seized the back of his collar, muscling him into one of the chairs.

It wasn't hard to do. Jaden didn't have a lot of muscle going on, and I was beyond pissed off, using the angry adrenaline to make sure he stayed where I wanted him.

"Just the guy I wanted to talk to."

"Are you fucking crazy?" Outrage flared behind the fear in his eyes, and Jaden shoved himself out of the chair back onto his feet, attempting to push his way past me.

That so isn't gonna happen. I grabbed him by his shirt front. "Are you going to tell me what the *hell* is going on, or do I have to beat it out of you?" I'd never actually done that before, but I was more than willing to give it a shot.

"Get off me," he yelled.

Oh, well. I raised my fist and punched him in the jaw. Not as hard as I could have either. I can punch damn hard, but I didn't want to knock him out or break a knuckle.

"Ow!" He grabbed his face and glared at me. "What the hell did you do that for?"

Hauling him close, I tried not to wince at the sour smell of his breath. Did this guy ever brush his teeth?

"Either you tell me what's going on or they're gonna have

to wire your jaw shut. I swear, you'll be drinking through a straw for a month." The line was straight out of some cheesy movie or TV show and sounded pretty stupid coming out of my mouth, but it seemed to work.

Probably because I meant every word.

I raised my fist again. Jaden flinched back.

"Okay! Okay, but you're never going to believe me."

I snorted. "Yeah, because everything that's happening is *sooo* believable. Now stop bullshitting me and talk." For emphasis I shook him as hard as I could. I thought I heard his teeth rattle.

"Fuck! Okay, fine. Just… just let go of me."

I unclenched my fingers, but leaned in close.

"Fine. Talk."

He sat down and exhaled, his shoulders sagging as the air of defiance seemed to deflate with that breath.

"I wanted to do something different—something no one has seen before. I wanted it to be special. Extreme. Balls to the wall badass. Not just some cheesy CGI bullshit like you see in every other low-budget production. So I did some research, found a ritual to call up these shadow demons— Davea. They're like the pit bulls of the demon world. You point and they attack. Or do whatever you want them to do. They were perfect."

I stared at him in disgust.

"You thought calling up demons was a good way to make your mark? What kind of sociopathic *idiot* are you? And that's not, by the way, a rhetorical question."

He shot me a resentful glare. "It's not like I haven't done rituals before. I know what I'm doing."

"Great. So this isn't your first demon summoning rodeo. Is this the first time you've lost control of them? Or are you just chalking up the deaths to collateral damage?"

"Okay, now *that* wasn't supposed to happen," he protested. "The first time I figured I'd done something wrong. Used the wrong type of blood or herbs. Maybe not fresh enough."

I felt anger rising inside me, like lava about to burst through the earth's crust. "Let me get this straight. Someone died the first time you performed this fucked-up experiment, and you *tried it again?*"

He shrugged, looking for all the world like a sullen kid.

"Things happen. There's always a risk to conjuring, especially when you're dealing with demons. Even the lesser ones."

I counted to three. I didn't have the patience for ten.

"So you've got the right to decide if your career is worth another person's life." Wisely, he didn't reply. If he had, I might have done something I couldn't take back. I focused on breathing for a few minutes. Deep, calming breaths. Trying to let all homicidal thoughts go until I trusted myself to speak again.

"So what happened, then?"

"I tried the ritual again, and it went the way it was supposed to."

"Oh, you mean no one died this time?"

He shrugged as if the question was irrelevant.

"As far as I know."

The lava bubbled up a little higher. I managed to keep a cap on it.

"Then what?"

"Herman wanted to move things up, so I tried another trial run. It seemed to go really well." He paused, and added, "Then you found Portia's body."

I stared at him in disbelief. "And yet you did the spell *again*, with the entire cast and crew gathered around as a handy lunch buffet, in case your pet demons got hungry." It was beyond vile. "I… I…"

My words trailed off. My hands clenched and unclenched. I wanted to kill him. No, I wanted to feed him to his own shadow critters.

"It should have been okay," Jaden insisted. "They were just hungry, and Portia was… I think she drew them to her. Strong emotions can do that, especially negative ones. But tonight? Everything was perfect. It should've worked, and no one should have been hurt!"

"And yet Effie, Angel, Jack, and Joan are all dead," I said between clenched teeth.

"That's not my fault."

"If you say 'it wasn't part of the deal' I swear you will be shitting out your own teeth."

"You saw it! The Davea did what I wanted them to do, right up until I yelled *cut*. I got it on film. I got *them* on film—and it looks fantastic!" He sounded genuinely euphoric. It was for the good of the film, so it was *all* good, right?

I will not kill him.

It took every ounce of self-control I had.

"Why are those creatures still here?"

"I… I don't know. As soon as you and Connor left the ritual room, I went back to perform the closing ritual that sends them back and shuts the gate—" He wiped his forehead, looking uncertain for the first time. He peered up at me and swallowed heavily. "The circle had been destroyed and the gate was gone. Closed—and they're still here."

"So redraw your circle and open the gate again."

"It doesn't work that way."

"Why not?"

"When the original gate was destroyed, I lost control of the Davea. I *can't* get them back."

I took a few more deep breaths.

"So you're telling me these… these Davea are roaming wild and free, and can come out of any shadow they want?" I looked down at the floor. "They could just pop out of my shadow right now and rip me to shreds?"

"No, they can't use shadows cast by anything organic." He seemed irritated at my ignorance.

"So how the hell can we get rid of them?"

The uncertainty returned.

"I don't know. I think… I think someone else has taken control."

"Who?"

"I… I don't know." His gaze flickered to the side.

Definitely lying.

"How is that even possible?" I leaned in. "You *have* to have some idea, and you'd better tell me, because I'm back to the whole 'shitting out teeth and eating out of a straw' if you don't."

"I can't—"

Directly behind him, the bulb in the mirror went out.

Before either of us had a chance to move, oily black limbs reached out of the mirror, grabbed Jaden's head, and twisted it off. Blood spurted out of his neck, splattering me before I had the wherewithal to leap backward. The rotted sewage stench of the Davea filled the room, and Jaden's headless corpse slumped down in the chair.

A second Davea followed on the heels of the first, ripping into the corpse's chest to extract the still-dripping heart. It immediately vanished back into the mirror, carrying its bloody prize.

The other bulbs above the mirror begin to flicker, making little buzzing sounds as, one by one, they also went out. Soon the only light left came from the bulb in the ceiling. Hissing and gurgling noises emanated from the dark corners of the mirror. I could see shadows moving, taking shape. Ice began to form on the mirrors and walls.

Wiping yet more blood from my eyes, I looked around for some sort of weapon. No crowbars, no handy chunks of wood, nothing except Kyra's makeup kit. Unless the threat of a badly executed makeover frightened the Davea, I was shit out of luck.

The first demon roiled in the shadows, oozing toward me slowly, almost as if it was toying with me. My hand fell to my hip, where Jeanette's knife rested in its sheath. I didn't waste time breathing a sigh of relief. I pulled the knife out, happy to have seven inches of steel in my hand, instead of rubber.

The Davea dove for my head, going for another decapitation.

Sorry, no second take for you.

I dropped out of the way and lunged to the side, slicing across its torso and releasing more of the noxious fluid that served as its blood. The thing gave a squeal of pain and melted back into the darkness.

Leaving Jaden's corpse where it lay, I got the hell out of Makeup.

CHAPTER THIRTY

I slammed the door shut behind me. I knew it wouldn't stop those things if they decided to come after me, but I'd take even the illusion of safety right about now.

Hesitating briefly, I shoved open the door leading to the front offices and the lobby. I wanted to check the outside view from the lobby on the off-chance the Davea's influence had a cut-off point and there might be a safe way to escape.

The fluorescent strip lighting on the ceiling still illuminated the hallway, but the lobby area was dark ahead of me. Keeping my knife at the ready, I reached the lobby and twisted my hand around the doorframe to flip the switches. When the lights came on, I was careful to stay away from any furniture that could cast a shadow.

I ran to the door, locked from the inside with a simple deadbolt. There was a rolling metal security gate drawn shut in front of it, and iron bars protected the windows.

My heart fell. The view of the parking lot was the same ebony nothingness I'd seen through the elephant doors. No traffic, no buildings, no people.

Just death.

A hissing sound from Herman's office made me whirl around. The door was ajar cracked about a foot. A soft light glowed from inside. Approaching slowly, I took a cautious sniff for the telltale putrescence of the Davea. The only thing apparent was the scent of freshly ground coffee beans.

I stuck my head inside. Herman leaned up against the table that held his Breville espresso machine, looking as if he could barely stand on his own. Even so, he made a cappuccino, humming softly as he did.

"Herman?"

I spoke gently, not wanting to startle him.

He jumped anyway, spilling frothed milk over the side of his cup. Then he saw me and gave a bright smile that was more of a death's head grimace.

"Lee," he said with genuine warmth. "Did you need something? May I offer you an espresso or cappuccino?"

Oh, man. Despite what he had seen, Herman seemed totally unaware of what was going on in his studio—living in his own little world where a perfectly brewed coffee made everything better. *He must be worse than we thought.*

"I'll take a raincheck on the coffee," I said as calmly as possible given the fact I had blood splashed all over me and he didn't appear to notice. "We need to call the police and our cell phones aren't getting any signal. Can I use your phone?"

"Normally that'd be fine, but—" He pointed across the room, where the landline phone lay in pieces. "I can't remember how it happened, but I don't think it's going to work too well."

My heart sank.

"You're probably right about that," I said evenly, even though I wanted to scream in frustration. "How about we join the rest of the cast and crew in the soundstage, then? We should probably all stick together."

The two of us made our way back to the big hallway,

Herman calmly sipping his cappuccino. He didn't seem to notice the smell or the mess as we passed by Makeup, nor did he comment on the fact I had my knife out and kept swiveling my head back and forth as I kept an eye out for more Davea.

We made it to the soundstage unmolested, though, to find everyone huddled around the two tables. Breanna and Dan immediately hurried to Herman's side. He smiled at them, unconcerned. Breanna looked at me and I gave a little shrug as if to say, *"Hell if I know."*

Eden and Kyra ran over to me, followed by Connor. "Don't you do that again!" Eden exclaimed, giving me a fierce hug.

"I had to try my phone," I said. "And I got ahold of Sean and managed to tell him a little of what was going on before the line went dead. He's not dumb. He'll call the police."

"That's something," Connor said.

"I also checked the lobby exit."

"And?" Kyra looked at me hopefully.

I shook my head. "It's a no go. We can't go outside until the sun comes up or until the police arrive."

Of course, we couldn't be sure that the unnatural darkness would recede when the sun rose. And if the police arrived before then, they might be slaughtered as soon as they stepped foot on the parking lot.

A whiff of dead flesh and old sewage wafted through the air. I looked up into the rafters above and saw *things* forming in the gloom. Pulsing in and out like jellyfish before slowly coalescing.

Heading our way, they avoided the pools of light cast by the few bulbs burning above, skirting the edges of illumination like pedestrians avoiding mud puddles. There was light where we huddled, yes, but there were also too many shadows.

Shit shit shit.

Involuntarily I backed into a C-stand. It held one of Connor's 1K lights, a hefty thing that looked like a miniature turquoise garbage can. The stand wobbled precariously. Connor and I grabbed it just before it toppled over.

We looked at each other. He immediately hit the switch. Nothing happened. He stooped to find the power cord, and swore.

"What?"

"We were using this to light the front of the *Bootes*," he growled. "It had an extension cord."

"So move it to a wall outlet!"

"The nearest one's over there." Connor pointed to the wall about twenty feet away. I could barely see the outlet through the gloom.

"Where the hell is the cord?"

"I used it this morning," Kat spoke up, her tone timid. She pointed to the beverage table. "I've got the urn and the hot water kettle plugged into it."

"We can go without coffee," I said for the first time in history. "We need that cord now!"

Half a dozen Davea slithered out of the shadows as I spoke, looking for a dark passage through the light. One melded with the darkness under the craft service table, reaching for Peter.

"Peter, move!" I shouted.

He looked over at me, terrified, frozen in place.

Really? The *only* time the kid didn't immediately jump at an order. I ran over even as the shadows grabbed his leg. As I watched, slices appeared in the fabric of his pants, blood spurting out of each one. Peter screamed.

The shadows hissed and *chortled*. The sound snakes would make if they could laugh. Ribbons of blackness wrapped around his uninjured leg and pulled. Peter's scream cut off as something jerked him partway under the table, his head hitting the ground with an ominous *crack*. I leapt forward, wrapping one arm around his back, looping my hand under his arm just as his body was jerked into the blackness. My hand went with it.

Icy cold seeped into the tips of my fingers, into my hand and moving up my arm, but I didn't let go. I didn't dare, because whatever had a grip on him would surely kill him if I lost this grim game of tug-o-war.

The thing yanked on Peter's legs again, nearly pulling him from my grasp.

"Help me!" I shouted.

"Lee, here!"

Someone slapped a Maglite into my free hand, the switch already on. Struggling to keep my hold on Peter's limp body, I aimed the beam under the table. Something hissed. Cold breath wafted out along with a whiff of putrescence. I choked on the stench. But where the Maglite beam hit, the shadows retreated, then coiled their way around out of reach of the light. The Davea did not want to let go of its prey.

It hissed again, jerking hard on Peter's legs.

I wrapped my fingers in the fabric of his T-shirt and threw myself across his torso, trying to keep the beam aimed under the table while keeping my limbs and body out in the open.

Despite my best efforts, I was losing the battle.

Another hard tug, and he went nearly all the way underneath. Something popped inside his arm—probably a bone dislocating. I was glad he wasn't conscious. Someone grabbed hold of me around the waist, adding their strength to mine.

"I've got you, Lee."

Ben.

Even with his help, though, when the Davea gave another yank my fingers slipped, nearly losing their grip on Peter's shirt. I had no choice. I dropped the Maglite, letting it clatter to the floor, and grabbed him under both arms. White-hot pain raked along my arms and I screamed, fighting the primal instinct of self-preservation.

A sudden strip of bright light illuminated the unconscious PA's face and body, and the entire underside of the table. Connor had the 1K plugged in and turned on. Steam rose from the Davea's body. It gave an unearthly shriek, wriggling like an insect pinned to a board, and let go of Peter's legs as it searched for a way to escape the light. Finally it slithered behind a box of plastic forks, vanishing into the thin strip of darkness behind it.

Ben and I pulled Peter out into the open. His pants were in ribbons, his legs badly clawed, but it looked like the demon that grabbed him had been too busy playing tug-o-war to kill him. If we could get him to a hospital, he stood a chance.

Connor swiftly knocked open the flaps of the 1K, turning the strip into a full-on flood of bright light, shining straight at the elephant doors, illuminating both tables and the people huddled nearby.

"I think I've sadly underestimated the importance of good lighting," I said to him.

Connor managed a strained version of his superior smirk. "Perhaps next time you'll listen."

Ben tapped me on the shoulder. "I don't want to be a

killjoy here," he said, "but those damn things are still up there."

Connor and I looked up. Ben was right. The Davea floated above us in the shadows, circling over our heads like sharks, taking turns swooping downward to see how close they could get to their prey without touching the light. The temperature dropped noticeably whenever one of them dipped near.

Well, hell.

"Where are the rest of the lights?" I asked in a low urgent voice.

"I have a couple of handheld spots and Maglites over there—" Connor jerked his head toward the wall near one of the tables. Too many shadows. "The 2K and the fill spots are still in the ritual chamber."

I groaned. "Are there any more stashed someplace else?" *Someplace we won't be instant demon chow?*

"The 5K!" Connor exclaimed. "It was finally delivered yesterday. That beauty can deliver a beam of light twenty-six feet in diameter, from twenty feet away at full flood."

This was good.

"Where is it?"

"I'm not sure. Most likely in the equipment room."

Which was in the back of the soundstage near Jaden's FX area. In the dark.

Not so good.

"Are you sure?"

"No."

I turned to Herman. He was contemplating the dregs of his cappuccino.

"Herman."

Nothing.

"Herman!" I smacked my hands together in front of his

nose. He jumped, finally looking at me.

"Lee." He shook his head as if to clear it. "What is it? What do you need? I can make you some coffee if—"

"No coffee!" A hurt, almost confused look came over his face. I softened my voice and continued. "Herman, we need to know where you put Connor's 5K spotlight when it was delivered."

"His 5K…" Herman opened his eyes wide, then shut them again. "It's—" He rubbed his temples. "It's in my office. I meant to have it brought out but I've… I've been distracted."

I turned to Connor. "I can get it."

"Are you crazy? It weighs over thirty pounds and—"

I snorted. "Oh, please. I bench-press ninety on a bad day."

He rolled his eyes. "That's all well and good, but—"

"Lee." Ben pointed over to the beverage table, where Kat puttered around on autopilot, picking up stray cups and napkins and tossing them into one of the trash bins.

"Kat! Get away from there!"

She looked up, but didn't budge.

"*Kat!* Move *now!*" My voice cut through the air like the crack of a whip.

She wasn't fast enough. A shadowy claw raked her back, slicing through the leather of her bomber jacket with frightening ease. She screamed and stumbled, giving the demon time to grip one of her arms.

I jumped over a fallen folding chair, then picked it up so I could smash it down on the black and oily claws now wrapped around Kat's wrist. The Davea emitted an earsplitting shriek—pain and rage combined in the unholy sound.

Another one swooped down to try and claim the prize. Michael ran over clutching a crowbar, swinging it hard and fast at the Davea's bulbous head. No effect. The demon turned mid-air and swiped at Michael's face. He jerked back just in time. Dropping the crowbar, he scuttled back into the safety of the light.

Snatching up the crowbar I slammed it against the Davea that was holding Kat until it finally let go, black liquid dribbling onto the floor from its injuries. She was groaning loudly, but at least she'd stopped screaming. Looping an arm around her waist, I half dragged, half threw her into the safety of the light, her blood splashing onto my forearm.

Ben and Joe took her from me, easing her to the floor as she gasped in pain.

"I'm going to go get the 5K," I said.

"You can't get it by yourself," Ben said even as he took off his T-shirt and used it to staunch the flow of blood from Kat's wounds.

"Look," I said, "for whatever reason, it appears I've won some crazy fucked-up lotto here 'cause I'm the only one who can actually hurt those things. I can fight them and win. They might even be afraid of me. So out of all of us, I'd say I have the best chance of getting the light and making it back here alive."

"Yeah, okay fine, so you're the chosen one," Ben shot back. "But how the hell do you plan on lugging thirty pounds of 5K and defending yourself at the same time? I go with you, you grab one of those handhelds, keep it on me as best you can, and I'll carry the light while you keep those fucked-up creepy-crawlies off us."

I started to argue, but he was right. If we were going to get the 5K, I needed help.

"Okay, you're right. There's only one problem with your plan." I looked him up and down. "You're too damn tall for me to even begin to cover you with a handheld."

Ben opened his mouth to argue, but it was his turn to let it go.

"I'm the smallest one here," Kyra said. "I should go with you."

I looked at her tiny frame. "Can you carry thirty pounds and run?"

"I think so." She sounded uncertain.

I shook my head. "If you're wrong, it's your life we're talking about. I'm not taking that chance."

"I—"

"I will go with you." Darius pushed his way to the front of the huddle. He patted Kyra on one arm. "It is brave of you, but I can easily carry the light. And while I am not as small as you, I *am* smaller than the giant here."

I nodded. It might work. I smacked the crowbar into the meat of my palm.

"Okay. Let's do this."

CHAPTER THIRTY-ONE

I hefted the crowbar in one hand and the Maglite in the other, giving silent thanks that I was used to using both hands for handling weapons and fighting. If not quite ambidextrous, I was damn close.

Darius had a smaller Maglite and an impromptu weapon of a C-stand arm with a gobo head assembly attached. A solid chunk of metal, the gobo head made a wicked mace, so even if he couldn't kill a Davea, it might slow it down long enough for me to take it out.

I looked around at the surviving cast and crew, all of them standing close together in the safe zone of light. I wanted to give some kind of rousing speech to keep their spirits up. Lacking inspiration and speech writers, however, I had to make do.

"Everyone, be sure you stay in the light. Those things can't get you if they don't have a shadow to use as a gateway."

"What about this?" Michael gestured to the shadow cast by his arm. "What's stopping them from coming through any of our shadows?"

"According to Jaden, they can't use shadows cast by organic matter. Nothing living."

"What does Jaden know about this shit?"

"He summoned them in the first place. He lost control of them, and they killed him." That elicited some panicky chatter, which I headed off. "So all of you should be okay if you stay where you are. But if you try to make a run for it…" I let my voice trail off. They'd seen how fast the Davea could manifest and take down prey.

Eden stepped forward, clutching one of the handheld spots. "I'll cover you with this as long as I can," she said, turning it on. I gave her a grateful smile.

"Stay safe," Connor called to me, still keeping all of his attention on the 1K.

Darius went first. I stayed back about ten feet so I could keep him covered with the flashlight's beam. The problem was, the further back I stayed, the longer it would take me to get to him if anything attacked. I'd have to trust my reflexes and speed.

The light dipped in sync with my movement. I kept it as steady as I could. Sibilant chuckles and guttural noises whispered and gurgled from the darkened soundstage the further we got from the catering tables. They seem to be everywhere, so I did my best to ignore them. Instead I focused on the man in front of me, staying alert for any movement around him.

Darius went through the double doors and I followed. One lone fluorescent tube at the far end of the hall was still lit. The other tubes were cracked. Melting icicles on the ceiling dripped water onto the linoleum. The creatures had been busy.

I saw things out of the corner of my eyes, shadows elongating and then retreating as if playing with us. They kept their distance at first, and the chuckling and hissing became white noise in the background. Then one of them lunged at me as I passed the door to the darkened Makeup department. I dodged, smashing it on the side with the crowbar. It fell to the floor and I hammered on its head until it stopped moving. The light bobbed wildly, but stayed on Darius.

Steam rose up as the fallen demon did its impersonation of the Wicked Witch of the West, dissolving into the floor even as another one soared down from a darkened corner of the ceiling. I dodged out of the way of its claws with scant inches to spare and yet another Davea attacked, leaving me no time to do anything but fall onto my back, thrusting up with the crowbar as it landed on top of me. The crowbar gutted it and I got showered with yet more noxious black goo.

"Look out!"

I looked up just in time to see Darius with the gobo head raised to bring it smashing down on the demon. Just as he did it dissolved, splattering me with its fluids. I threw myself to one side and the crowbar smashed into the linoleum where my head had been.

It's all in the reflexes, I thought.

"Guess you killed it," Darius said casually, as if he hadn't just nearly brained me. He held out a hand. I took it and he pulled me to my feet. I scooped up my flashlight where it had fallen.

We made it to the front without any further attacks. The light in Herman's office was thankfully still on and the temperature normal. I didn't turn my flashlight off, but I felt safe enough for the immediate moment to lower it. Darius lowered his, as well, but we both kept our weapons ready.

We did a quick scan of the room, looking for the 5K. Darius checked along the walls, digging into a pile of boxes in one corner while I looked behind Herman's desk. I didn't see anything that looked like a big light. Just a couple of books, one of them lying open on the floor.

It looked old, with parchment pages instead of paper and hand-inked lettering instead of print. Simple illustrations. There were several of the same kinds of circles and symbols that Jaden had drawn for the so-called ritual effects.

I was so focused on it that I almost missed the movement in the periphery of my vision. Only this time it wasn't a Davea. It was the sharp point of a knife aimed at my chest with a speed that almost took me by fatal surprise.

Reacting purely on instinct, I fell backward, grabbing the bottom of Herman's expensive ergonomic chair and shoving it at my assailant as the momentum of his thrust carried him forward. He gave a grunt as the back of the chair caught him in his midsection.

"Darius, what the fuck?"

I scrambled back like a crab on my elbows and feet, never taking my eyes off of the man I'd thought was my coworker and ally.

"I am sorry for this, Lee, but you kill too many of them. Things must go as planned."

"What things? What plans? What the fuck!"

If I'd hoped Darius would go into a long-winded monologue and give me time to figure out some strategy, I was sorely disappointed. He kicked the chair back at me as I rounded the corner of the desk. It caught me on one hip and sent me sprawling on the carpeted floor in the middle of the office.

The crowbar flew out of one hand, the Maglite out of the other.

Shit.

Tossing his flashlight aside, Darius leapt over the desk, using one hand to propel himself, the other clutching the same knife he'd used in our fight. Not the rubber prop either, but the stainless steel version.

I lunged for the crowbar, but Darius grabbed one of my legs and yanked, pulling me back toward him before my fingers did more than graze it. I rolled onto my back before he could bring the knife down between my shoulder blades, slamming the palm of one hand against the edge of his wrist so the thrust went off to one side. The point of the knife buried itself in the plush carpeting an inch away from my shoulder.

Unfazed, he pulled the knife out, throwing his body on top of mine to keep me in place, and aimed for the center of my throat this time. I grabbed his hand, holding the knife at bay. I was strong, but he was stronger and whatever mojo had kicked in when I fought Axel and the Davea failed completely with Darius.

A very small part of me wished that someone was filming this fight, because I bet it looked pretty epic. And it looked like it would be the last one I ever fought.

"Why are you doing this?"

He didn't answer, just continued to press down on the knife, the point less than an inch away from my throat.

My arms trembled, threatening to give out against his superior upper body strength and leverage. I tried to throw him off of me, but his balance was too good and he knew how to center his weight, effectively holding me in place. The knife descended another half an inch. I strained against it, knowing I couldn't hold out any longer.

So I stopped resisting and redirected my energies into jerking his hands and the knife as far to the right as possible, while pulling my head and neck in the opposite direction. It was a risky move and I'd probably need a chiropractor if I survived, but it was all I had.

The point skimmed the edge of my neck, scoring a line down the side but missing the flesh and—more importantly— my jugular. Losing his balance, Darius fell forward, and I shoved as hard as I could, throwing him off me.

He swore in Romanian, lashing out at me as I went for the crowbar again, catching the back of my right calf. I felt the sting as the steel sliced through denim and flesh. As he went for another cut, I kicked out like a donkey, smashing the side of his hand with my heel hard enough to make him drop the knife.

I scrambled to my feet, panting.

He winced, shaking his wrist and hand.

"You are very good stuntwoman, Lee," he said. "I would have worked with you again." He reached for his knife without taking his eyes off me. I could swear I saw real regret in them. "It is too bad you must die."

As a professional reference, it left something to be desired.

Darius reset, and I backed up, hitting one of the standing bookshelves and then the wall. Nowhere left to go.

He came in for the killing blow.

But the knife never reached me.

Obsidian claws flashed out of a shadow under one of the books on the stand, closing in on Darius's wrist. He screamed as both knife and hand fell to the floor, blood gouting out of the stump where his hand had been. Before he could do more than stare at the tattered remains of his wrist, the same Davea ripped a hole in his chest.

I snatched my Maglite off the ground, but the Davea had already gone, taking Darius's heart with it before his corpse slid to the floor. Standing in shock for a moment, I shone the beam around the office, looking for shadows. Waiting for it to be my turn. After a long stretch, however, it became obvious—for whatever reason—they were leaving me alone.

Stumbling over Darius's corpse, I retrieved my crowbar, tucking it under one arm, then turned to the pile of boxes along one wall. I found the one holding the 5K and picked it up, grunting with the effort. Then I slowly made my way out of Herman's office, down the hall and back toward the soundstage, trailing blood and limping the entire way.

CHAPTER THIRTY-TWO

I staggered out onto the soundstage, knees buckling beneath the weight of the 5K. It felt more like sixty pounds than thirty by this time.

"Lee!"

Ben saw me limping toward them and immediately turned a handheld spot on me until I'd reached the safe zone.

The remaining cast and crew kept as close to the center of the light as possible, some standing and a few sitting with arms wrapped around their knees. Eden held the other spotlight connected to the extension cord. Kyra sat next to Kat and Peter, who both lay curled up, eyes closed. Peter looked really bad.

Herman was on his feet, swaying back and forth ever so slightly, looking entirely unaware of his surroundings. The Tymons stood nearby, keeping a close eye on him. I dumped the box at Connor's feet. He scooped it up with the possessive care of a mother for her newborn baby.

"Paul," he barked, "Grab a C-stand."

"Girl, you're bleeding," Ben said with concern.

Connor looked up sharply. "Are you hurt?"

I waved it off. "It's just a cut," I said. "I'll be fine."

Ben rolled his eyes. "Sure. Now sit down and let me take a look at it."

"As soon as Connor gets that light turned on," I said, eying the small shadow cast by the box. Most likely there was too much light from the 1K, but I was still on high alert for opportunistic Davea.

Connor removed the 5K and I immediately kicked the box outside of the circle. Just in case. He plugged the cord into the same extension cord that powered the 1K, and our end of the soundstage was awash in enough light to let everyone spread out and sit down.

I would never again make fun of Connor's 5K obsession.

"I think we're okay for now," I said. "If we stay in the light until morning, we can get out of here." It didn't look as if Peter had that long, though. If we didn't get him medical help soon, he wasn't going to make it.

"Fine." Ben gestured to my leg. "Now let's take care of this." I plopped down on the floor without another word, but gave a hiss of pain as Ben pulled blood-sodden denim away from the wound.

"Sorry, kid," he apologized. "It's sticking a little bit."

No shit.

"Try this." Joe held out a water bottle stripped of its label. Guess he'd taken my warning about shadows seriously.

Ben twisted the lid off and gently poured some of the liquid onto my wound, giving me the rest to drink. I polished it off in two swallows, tossing the bottle out into the darkness.

"It's not too deep," Ben said. "Looks pretty clean, too. What happened?"

I hesitated. Should I tell them the truth?

"Where's Darius?" Breanna asked with impeccable timing.

I shook my head. "One of those things got him," I said truthfully. I didn't need to feign the regret that crept into my voice. I'd liked Darius. We'd worked well together. Too bad he'd tried to kill me.

Breanna gave a little cry and buried her head against Dan's shoulder. He looked stunned. Joe looked down at the floor, and then back at me.

"What the fuck?" he growled, anger flaring in his eyes. "How many people have these motherfuckers killed?"

"Ten."

We all turned to look at Herman, standing near the 5K as if sunning himself in its rays.

"But only seven of them count," he added. "Seven lives and seven hearts. Seven—" Then he collapsed, his limp body smashing into Connor and the C-stand that held the 5K. Connor stumbled backward. The stand and light wobbled briefly—

—and toppled to the ground with a crash. The beam of the 5K flickered and went out.

People screamed, scrambling to get back into the small circle left by the 1K. Except Herman. He sprawled on his back, unconscious, just outside of the light, one foot entangled in the extension cord that was plugged into the wall.

Even as I charged toward him, knife in hand, the Davea swarmed out of the shadows and into his open mouth. His body jerked, pulling the extension cord out of the wall.

The 1K went out as well.

Someone yelled, but surprisingly that was it. The terror in the air was palpable. I think most people just froze, hoping that if they didn't move, the monsters couldn't find them.

The Davea could see in the dark.

We needed to plug that extension cord back into the outlet.

"Eden," I said, "do you still have the handheld?"

"Yes," she replied, voice shaky.

"Shine it on the outlet." A soft click and I could see the end of the cord, lying right below the outlet. "Paul, hold onto the 1K!" I didn't waste any time. I sprinted over to the wall, snatching up the cord with a yank to disentangle it from Herman's foot, and plugged it back in.

The light immediately came back on.

I did a quick head count. No one else was missing. No one else was hurt.

Something was definitely different, however.

Herman still lay on the ground where he'd collapsed, but he was no longer alone. Lying next to him was a naked woman, wasted and fragile, bones close to the surface of her flesh. Despite this, she was still beautiful, with a long, luxuriant mane of hair the color of moonlight.

Herman stirred, eyelids fluttering as a low moan escaped him. The woman next to him mirrored both the movement and the noise. A chill ran up my spine.

My first instinct was to run over and see if I could help, but something held me back. A small voice inside urged me to be cautious.

The Tymons, on the other hand, ran to the producer's side, helping him sit up. The girl stirred as well. Dan reached down as if intending to assist her, but Herman held up a hand.

"No."

Dan pulled his hand away.

The girl sat up slowly, looking around her in confusion. She looked so frail—as frail as Herman, as if the two shared the same wasting disease. In fact, they could have been twins. Same high cheekbones, same finely painted features, and the same startlingly ice-blue eyes.

Her gaze fell on Herman and she smiled widely, pure happiness lighting up those gaunt features.

"Hahriman." A world of love filled that one word.

"Sala…" Herman looked as though he would weep.

She looked down at her own body. "We are separate. We are ourselves again. How is this?"

"Magic," he whispered.

She reached out and caressed his face. He brought his hand up to cover hers, rubbing his cheek against her palm.

"You are so thin, my brother. Why have you not fed? I am so very hungry." She looked around then, seeing Breanna and Dan standing close by, and all the rest of us in the light. She smiled again.

"You have brought me a feast, my brother."

Now *that* was creepy.

"Sala," Herman said again, taking her in his arms and stroking the hair back from her forehead. "I haven't eaten because if I did, you would be too strong."

"Too strong?" Sala laughed, a lilting sound that had more than a hint of madness in it. "Too strong for what?"

Herman smiled sadly. Then he pulled a knife out from his waistband and drove it into her heart. Her eyes widened in shock.

"Hahriman…"

"Know that I love you now and always, my Sala," he whispered. He held her close as she let out a shuddering breath before going limp in his arms. He then lowered her gently to the floor, collapsing onto his knees next to her as if someone had cut his strings.

Holy shit. Several people gasped. I was one of them.

Then the room was silent except for the sound of Herman weeping. Great hitching sobs of pure grief.

"It worked, Herman," Breanna said uncomfortably. "You're finally free."

Dan nodded.

Herman looked up at them, his face a portrait of pain and loss. He started to speak.

"I—" Whatever he planned on saying was cut off by a coughing fit.

"Someone help," Breanna cried. "He needs water!"

No one moved. I didn't blame them.

Herman continued to cough, hard enough to rack his entire body as though his chest was being ripped apart from the inside.

Oh, hell. I snatched up a bottle of water and took it over, unscrewing the lid and putting it into Herman's hand. He took a sip, then another.

"Lee," he said simply. "I wanted to wait until the film was finished. Wanted to make sure everyone I'd hired would have one last project they could be proud of before—" He started coughing again, harder this time, doubling over with the strength of the spasms. Flecks of blood spotted his lips.

"It's as I feared," he whispered. "I can't survive without her."

"Herman," I said. "What the hell is going on?"

The coughing continued. The flecks turned to spots of blood, all the color in his face draining away. He crumpled, falling from his knees onto his side, curling up into a fetal ball.

I leaned closer and put a hand on his cheek. The flesh below my palm was cool as mortician's wax.

"Lee... help me." He looked up, and his voice was barely audible. I bit my lip and fought to keep eye contact, resisting the urge to look away.

"What do you need? I'm right here."

"I need you…" he whispered.

I took his hand, cradled his head with the other. He reached for my face almost blindly and gently ran his fingers along my cheekbone, soft as a baby touching his mother. He slipped them around my neck—and then his grip tightened.

"I need you."

CHAPTER THIRTY-THREE

Fast as a striking snake, he pulled me in and kissed me, open mouthed and hard. There was no lust in it—only a raw hunger. His strength was unreal. He had a death grip on my neck and one of my hands was pinned against his chest. I couldn't pull away or twist out of his grasp.

Then it began.

His touch created a creepy warm sensation, radiating out from his lips and hands, soaking into my body. The rising heat permeated my flesh, organs, and bones, turning everything to putty as it oozed through me. I felt like a spider's victim, injected with some horrific venom that was slowly liquefying me from the inside.

Our eyes locked onto each other from only an inch away, Herman's gleaming with excitement. I struggled to pull my mouth away from his kiss, but my lips seemed *bonded* to his. His probing tongue licked mine and I realized our tongues had joined together, as well. I tried to scream, but only a muffled sound of terror escaped.

Why isn't anyone helping me? But it was all happening too fast. I felt his fingers on the nape of my neck, merging into my skin. His other hand had already welded itself onto mine, our arms now connected by a thick knob of flesh that had been our fists.

He continued to draw me closer into his embrace, pulling me down, not just onto him, but into him. Our legs and torsos merged together in an almost sickeningly sexual way. We were literally becoming one flesh.

I felt my face and head sliding down into his. The last thing I saw were his eyes before they merged into mine.

I gave one last silent scream and blacked out.

†

Nothingness. I could feel nothing, sense nothing—no body, no me. Only my bare thoughts suspended in a perfect sea of black void.

Am I dead? Where am I?

You're with me, came an answer from somewhere else in the darkness. *Come. See.*

I awoke.

Or at least the blackness was gone.

I found myself—whatever that meant now—somewhere very different. Golden sand. Turquoise water. Two naked children, a boy and a girl, playing at the water's edge. Darkness descending, flashes of lightning. The smell of ozone permeating the air. When the darkness dissipated, only one child was left lying stricken on the sand.

The scenery changed.

Ibises flew overhead. The sky was bright and the air hot, thick with the fragrance of incense and the music of lyres.

I stood atop a ziggurat, overlooking a sunbaked metropolis. A honeycomb of whitewashed buildings, porticoes, dusty unpaved streets, canals, and date palms, all surrounded by high stone walls. Alongside ran a great glittering river, trailing off to the horizon in either direction. The view took my breath away.

I turned—or was it me?—and strode past rows of towering columns through the forecourt to the sanctuary within. I was a passenger in someone else's flesh, with no control of my body.

Am I dreaming?

No, this is our memory.

Our?

Hers and mine. My sister Sala. When we were one.

Harpists and vestal virgins silently bowed to me as I entered the temple sanctum, traversing with great solemnity a sacred carpet woven in an interlocking red and blue design. It led to a throne of iron worked with silver and gold, and patterned with a thousand tiny bars of alabaster and ivory, seashell, carnelian, and lapis lazuli. Beams of light from ingeniously placed windows high overhead caused it to shimmer with divine radiance.

I took my seat.

This was the mighty city of Uruk, six thousand years ago, along the banks of the Euphrates. Where she and I first became gods. Behold. Mirrors of polished silver lined the chamber, ringed by votive lights. My gaze turned to one of them.

There Herman sat enthroned, bare-chested except for a pectoral of cobalt stones, wearing a kilt of the finest blue linen. His plaited beard magnificent and immaculately groomed with oils and resins. Sala was also bare-chested save for a beautiful beaded collar of blood-red carnelian, which matched her skirts of brilliant crimson. Eyes lined with kohl and lips as red as roses.

The two of them were a single individual. Herman was the right half of the body. Sala the left. Divided down the middle with perfect precision, their flesh, clothing, and jewelry blended seamlessly. This wasn't a cheesy circus sideshow act. This was the real thing.

A shaven-headed priest in a white woolen kilt came forward and offered his obeisance.

"Divine Hahriman and Salamakhis, our sacred Mother-Father. Accept our offering and so bring fertility to our land, our herds, and our children." A double line, twelve pairs of boys and girls, approached along the sacred carpet. The first couple knelt before the throne.

"We accept your love and sacrifice, and grant you life abundant in return." The voice emanating from our mouth was doubled. Herman and Sala speaking as one. We stretched out both hands to bless the youths kneeling before us. Sinuous white tendrils writhed from our palms and fingertips.

The victims were devout and well prepared for their fate. Some shuddered at our touch, but none wept or screamed even though they knew what was to come. Even as their blood streamed agonizingly out of them through a thousand tiny filaments and their flesh turned to crumpled parchment. The pathetic handful of remains was swiftly removed to make room for the next young couple… and then the next and the next, one pair after another.

I couldn't look away and didn't have eyes to close as the horrific show continued. Herman's grasp on me wasn't just a physical absorption, but a psychic one as well.

I was trapped in him.

Body, mind, and soul.

He had more to show me. His—no, *their* memories continued to fill my thoughts. We walked through a forest of tall dark pines, stepped out into a glade, where moonlight glistened on an artesian spring. A ring of light surrounded the waters and a chorus of androgynous figures held lit candles and sang a hymn in Greek.

Halicarnassus in Asia Minor, Herman told me. This was our shrine. Here we were the demigod Hermaphroditus and the nymph Salmacis, whose bodies came together at the sacred fountain...

†

The sound of trumpets, cymbals, and raucous laughter echoed off gleaming white marble floors and Corinthian columns. We reclined on a silken couch, surrounded by crowds of fellow revelers and a small army of slave attendants. All around us, an orgy was in full swing. I was—we were—rolling and moaning, locked in an embrace. We couldn't quite tell if our partner was male or female, or who was doing the penetrating.

They loved us in Rome...

I could sense the nostalgia in Herman's thoughts.

We bathed in rose petals. We were consort to sweet and terrible young Elagabalus, the lovely mad god-emperor...

†

The years and memories spun on, as Herman and Sala's fortunes rose and fell through the ages. They hid from the forces of the Church, attended to by covens of hedge-witches in the woods of Romania and Russia...

Were marvels of the Sun King's court at the Palace of Versailles...

Traveling with Roma clans in multicolored wagons...

Performing for disreputable theater troupes in the seedy underbelly of Victorian London...

But the world was becoming more modern, and they could no longer keep it at bay. They could no longer move through life as half man–half woman. Sala had to hide. To go below, sunken into her brother's very flesh except for the ever increasing occasions when she needed to feed. That was the shape they took as they came at last to the new world, to Gilded Age New York, to the Wild West, to San Francisco, to Hollywood…

Where Herman knew what he had to do.

Sala had become insane. Weak. We were dying. But you have strength, Lee. So much strength. You are going to help make me a god again. Do you understand what I am offering you?

You want to play with me forever and ever? I responded. *No thanks.*

You will be immortal. We both will.

Will you send the Davea back to whatever hell they came from and spare these people?

The Davea are already gone. Their work is finished. These people will feed us. Sustain us.

No, I thought. But this time I shielded my thoughts from him by sheer force of will, blocking his access to my mind. I sensed his surprise—and his rising displeasure.

Lee? Don't shut me out. Open yourself to me. I could feel his thoughts probing into my mind and his frustration that I could keep him out.

My only chance seemed to be to keep him off balance. I could sense his rising fear as he tried fruitlessly to penetrate, like a frustrated madman beating his fists against the walls of my mind.

What are you?

Suddenly his emotions shifted. Rage became disbelief, then shock, which melded into fear.

You… you are Blood of the Blood… Sweet Mother of Demons… you are of the Blood!

His hold on me loosened, then slipped completely away.

†

My eye—*eye?*—opened.

The concrete was cold where I lay on the studio floor, Sala's

356

pitiful corpse crumpled beside me. Herman had lost his grip on my mind and body, but how long would this freedom last?

I tried to stand, but could only move half my body.

Was I paralyzed?

I looked up to see Connor standing by the 5K, staring at me in horror. I shifted my gaze to my legs and feet. Only one of them was mine, wearing my ankle boot and torn jeans. The other wore half of Herman's expensive pants and loafer.

We were co-joined, just as he and his sister had been for thousands of years.

Finally we rose. Herman's fear gave way to exultation. He—*we*—took in a deep breath, reveling in the raw strength that circulated through our body.

The Blood of the Blood.

We are one again.

We turned to face the Tymons, who knelt and stared up at us with rapt adoration. Herman reached out with his hand, touching Breanna on the face.

"You will be my first," we said with affection.

No! I screamed even as the filaments emerged from his fingers, penetrating her skin to extract her life essence. Unlike the supplicants in the vision, Breanna screamed in agony.

The tiny ever shrinking part of me that was still *just Lee* acted without thought or hesitation. Twisting away, dragging Breanna with me, I reached down and snatched the dagger from Sala's body. Before Herman could respond, I plunged it into his—*our* heart with all my might. He let go of Breanna and made a grab for my wrist, but wasn't fast enough. Our scream echoed through the soundstage, ripping our throat raw. Until suddenly…

I was screaming all by myself.

The world faded to black again.

CHAPTER THIRTY-FOUR

The next time I opened my eyes, Sean's concerned face was the first thing I saw. I was back in the hospital.

Talk about *déjà vu*.

"Hey, hon," he said, his face breaking into a relieved smile. The difference this time around was that Seth stood right behind his father, looking as though he hadn't slept in days. When he saw me spot him, he practically pushed Sean out of the way so he could give me a fierce hug. It hurt, but I didn't complain.

"The crew send their love," Sean said. He pointed at a little table, swimming in floral arrangements, get-well cards, and several six packs of my favorite beers, bows stuck on top of each bottle. There was even an adorable wolf-cub plush toy. Sean handed it to me.

"Randy sends his best," Sean said. Seth scowled. Sean ignored him and continued. "He wanted to be here when you woke up, but we thought it was a good idea to just have family for now."

I rubbed my face against the soft fur. It smelled like Randy, all citrus and chai spices. Then I looked into its eyes and shuddered. Ice blue, like Herman and his sister.

My chest hurt.

A lot.

It seemed as if there should be something to show for the pain—something along the lines of a triple bypass scar, but the skin on my chest? Smooth. Unbroken. I guess it wasn't weirder than anything else that had happened.

The knife cut on my calf, on the other hand, left an ugly puckered seam that might or might not fade with time and applications of Vitamin D oil.

At least it wasn't on my face.

†

This stay in the hospital was relatively short. Three days total, during which I talked to Detective Fitzgerald, corroborating what the rest of the survivors had told her. I guess they'd talked me up pretty big, so while I had a lot of questions to answer about Herman Dobell's death, she never mentioned bringing charges against me.

Since the knife buried in Herman's chest was clutched in his own hand, the final ruling was suicide.

Eden and Kyra visited me in the hospital, bearing a two-pound box of See's chocolates. We made plans for a visit to Ocean's End as soon as I was up to it. Ben and Joe stopped by, bringing a combination get well and thank you card signed by most of the remaining cast and crew. The Tymons were conspicuously absent. They'd disappeared from the studio before the Kolchak Division had arrived.

Connor was also a no-show, which kind of hurt. I suspected the things he'd seen had been more than he could handle. He did, however, send a huge bouquet of flowers with a mini Maglite sticking out of the center of the arrangement and a note that said, "Remember, lighting is important."

I wasn't sure whether to laugh or cry, so I did both.

†

The evening after I came home from the hospital, Sean, Seth, and I sat in our usual places at the kitchen table. We were drinking RuinTen, a triple IPA from Stone. Sean had brought home a dozen bombers as "a special treat."

Something was up. He'd done the same thing when I was fourteen, and it was time for the facts-of-life discussion. Back then it had been hot fudge sundaes instead of beer. Sean's uncomfortable demeanor seemed pretty much the same, though.

"So," I said. "How come I'm not dead?" My tone was deceptively light. Inside I was thrumming with nervous energy, my heart pounding at twice its normal speed.

Sean took a deep breath, tapping a finger on the side of his glass.

"Well, hon, you know how you've always thought you were a hundred percent human?"

"Uh, yeah."

"Well, that's not entirely true."

"Ooookay." I took a swig of very good beer, trying to absorb his words. I found myself slowly detaching from my emotions—possibly because this meant Sean had kept something from me all these years. I couldn't deal with that right now, so I shoved it into the back of my mental closet.

"Let's set that aside for a moment," I said carefully. "And deal with things one at a time, beginning with Herman and his sister. He showed me things when—" I stopped, unable to suppress a shudder as I remembered the feeling of melding with him. "What was he? What were *they*?"

"Dobell and his sister were a Janus demon," Seth answered. "The *first* Janus demon. Two souls trapped together in one shared body."

Sean nodded. "The screenwriters were helping him," he said. "They wrote the ritual that would enable Dobell to finally separate his soul and body from his sister's."

"He couldn't do it himself?"

"No. He needed someone else to enact the spells, summon the Davea to collect the sacrifices—"

"Seven deaths, seven hearts," I murmured.

"Exactly."

"So he fooled Jaden into summoning the Davea by playing on Jaden's ego. As for the Tymons..." I shook my head. "They were writers. Herman was probably the first person in Hollywood to treat them like they mattered," I said. "No wonder they worshipped him." He really *had* been too good to be true.

Time to get to the heart of it all.

"Herman told me I was 'of the Blood.' He called it 'Blood of the Blood,' and I'm pretty sure he was using a capital B there. What the hell does that mean?"

Sean and Seth exchanged glances.

Seth nodded.

Sean heaved another sigh and drained his bomber. He cracked open another bottle and settled back in his chair.

"The earth is old," Sean said. "It was born out of the same chaos that created the universe, billions of years ago. The same chaos that gave birth to the Elder Gods. These old ones spawned other deities that eventually rose up, either killing or imprisoning their parents."

His voice deepened, taking on the formal cadence of a storyteller, or a prophet, and his expression became stony. The room seemed to grow darker—though that might have been my imagination.

"One of these younger gods, El, created the first people.

Adamu and Lilitu. Now known as Adam and Lilith. However, Lilitu wasn't content with her mate. As history records, she left, finding happiness with Ashmedai, one of the lesser gods, and bore him children. When El, at Adamu's behest, sent three seraphs after Lilitu, she refused to return.

"So El cursed Lilitu, turning the children she'd borne to Ashmedai into the monsters that walk in the shadows. Pandora's Box had been opened and could not be closed. These creatures have haunted humankind's nightmares ever since."

A shiver ran up my spine. If Sean ever got tired of stunt work, he had a future of narrating spooky opening monologues in horror films.

"Only Lilitu's human descendants have a hope of putting the monsters back in Pandora's Box and shutting the lid forever." Sean stared at me. "Your mother was a direct descendent, Lee. And so are you."

I stared at him. Drank some more beer.

"So you're telling me all the stuff in the Bible, about Adam being the first man on earth, is true." I stared, not sure what to think.

Sean rubbed his forehead as if massaging away a headache.

"It's not as simple as that. The Bible is one religion's simplistic version of a complex history that spans millennia."

"What about evolution? Are you saying that's all bullshit?"

"No. Ashmedai went to war against El and lost. He and Lilitu were imprisoned. Several of their children, however, escaped El's curse. It is from those children that Lilith's human line is descended. A second line came from Adamu and his second mate, Eva. These humans were Blood of the Blood. First Blood."

I opened my mouth to make a Rambo joke, but thought better of it.

Sean continued. "Most of the First Humans were wiped out in one of the many cataclysms that have swept over this planet, surviving only with the help and interference of their Creator. The earth, in the meantime, continued to evolve on its own. Another line of humans eventually emerged from the sea of chaos known as the primordial soup.

"While most of the First Humans died, Lilith's demonic offspring continued to flourish and procreate. Her descendants have been charged with hunting down these monsters, to pay off the debt their ancestress incurred against humanity, and eventually free her from her prison. They were given an amulet inscribed with ancient sigils that would bestow anything—even a simple stick—with the power to kill the demonspawn."

My hand went to the amulet around my neck. Sean nodded.

I opened my mouth to speak and ended up taking a swig of beer instead. I tried to savor the richness and flavor, but ended up chugging it instead. I didn't know what to say, so I opened another one.

"I know it's hard to swallow, hon, but—"

"Actually this goes down really easily," I said, holding up the bottle. "A lot easier than the crock of shit fairytale you just told me."

Seth bristled, but before he could open his mouth to slam me, his father held up a hand.

"Give her some time to process this, Seth."

I made a sound that was part laugh, part sob.

"How the hell am I supposed to *process* this? You're telling me I'm a direct descendant of Lilith, the 'Mother of Demons'—" I couldn't resist using finger quotes there. "—and that it's my job to kill her nasty offspring in order to pay off an ancestral debt and free her from some hell dimension. I mean, what the *fuck*, Sean?"

He winced. I drank more beer, trying to calm the pounding of my heart and the raw fury running through my veins.

Why would they lie to me like this?

They have *to be lying, right?*

"You guys are having some sort of joke here, right? You're bored, Seth hasn't caught any flies lately, no wings to pull off, so let's screw with the girl who got dropped on her head. Is that it?"

"How could you ever think we'd do that to you?" Sean stared at me with a combination of anger and hurt that made me feel both defensive and shitty at the same time.

"I... I don't know."

I put my head on the table for a minute, trying to shove the headache—and heartache—back inside.

Seth shook his head in disgust.

"Haven't you learned *anything* over the years?"

"Seth." Sean gave him a warning glance.

"No, let me finish." Seth glared at me. "After all Sean has done for you, how can you possibly think he'd lie to you about this?"

I returned his glare without backing down.

"Then why didn't he tell me any of this years ago?" I shot back.

"Stop it, Lee!" Seth slammed a hand down, rattling the bottles. "Stop trying to make this Sean's fault!"

"I'm not!" I shouted. Then I took a deep breath and continued. "I just... I just don't understand why he didn't tell me sooner."

"You weren't ready. Sean knew it would be hard for you to absorb this."

"I'm not a goddamn sponge," I snarled. "Why not tell me when I was a kid? Back when I believed in dragons and shit?" I gave a little laugh. "Hell, I *still* believe in all that stuff, and a hell of a lot more. Now you're telling me I have to *fight* them?"

"Not all of them." Sean drained his second bomber. He pulled another out of the six-pack and popped the top.

"So if I'm getting this right, you're telling me I should have killed Axel because he's a demon and therefore a child of Lilith."

"It's not that simple."

"Of course it's not," I said, trying to keep my voice level. "Look, it's not fair for you to expect me to just accept this. It's a lot to swallow."

Sean reached out, putting one hand over mine. It took all of my willpower not to snatch it away. But I didn't. I left it there, telling myself this was the man who raised me. Who loved me. Who wouldn't play crazy games with my head, just for the sake of being cruel.

"So this is something I've inherited from my mother, like some really fucked-up recessive gene, one that's been passed down along one *very* small family line for millennia." I frowned at a new thought. "Then why do *you* know about it?"

"Our family has been tied to yours for a long time," Sean said quietly. "It wasn't an accident that I was your father's best friend." ·

"The car crash. Was it—"

He shook his head. "Your mother was tired of the fight."

"Where does that put people like Randy? Or Drift and Tater? Hell, by this logic I *should* have killed Axel. I'm not gonna get much work in the industry if I go around killing every half-demon, cave troll, or shifter I run into."

"It's more complicated than that," Seth growled.

"So you've said," I muttered.

"Just as a third line of humans evolved," Sean said, "so did the supernaturals. Lilith's children mated with other gods and demons, some with creatures from other worlds. Some of those mated with mankind. Not all of them are evil. The longer this has gone on, the more diluted the bloodlines have become—but there's still only one line of First Humans descended from Lilith."

"Why not tell me sooner?" I asked. "Why wait until I'm in my twenties?"

"El deemed it fair that each of Lilith's descendants have ample time to train in whatever arts of war were deemed necessary. You had to be ready."

We sat in silence for a few minutes.

"How many kills pay off the debt?" I finally asked.

"I don't know," Sean answered.

"Well, I may suck at math," I continued, "but if Lilith's demonic rug rats have been doing the nasty and making little monsters for all these centuries…" I stopped. It was an overwhelming thought.

Sean and Seth didn't say anything.

"This isn't *fair*!" I burst out. "How come some ancient, out-of-fashion god gets to screw with my life?"

"El has worn many names," Seth said. "Including Yahweh. He currently just goes by God."

Well, hell.

"And if I say no?" I finally asked. "Decide I don't want the job?"

"Now that you've come into your heritage, Lilith's children will always be drawn to you. You'll know it when they're near… at least those who want to kill you. You'll have no choice but to kill them first. If you don't—"

He reached out and gently touched the amulet around my neck.

"Your mother tried to say no. It cost her and your father their lives."

I thought about that. Finished my beer.

"Is the demon that killed my parents still alive?" I asked.

Sean hesitated, then answered, "Yes."

"Good," I said coldly.

EPILOGUE

"No PBR tonight, huh?"

Marge raised her eyebrow as I set down my usual load of beer and chips on the counter. It'd been a week since I'd had my "Come to Yahweh" talk with Sean and Seth. I was dealing with it by throwing myself into familiar routines, such as making beer runs for the gang.

"Drift brought a buttload of Stella over," I said. "I think we have enough cheap beer to last for the night."

"You gonna be done ringing this little girl up any time today?" A deep voice spoke right behind me. I nearly dropped the salsa in surprise, then turned to see who the hell had managed to get that close without either Marge or myself noticing.

At first glance he looked like your typical over-confident urban cowboy type. You know, with the too clean designer jeans, a crisp white shirt, and Frye boots straight off the assembly line. Trying hard to make an impression.

I wasn't impressed.

Little girl, my ass.

And yet, something about him made me take a second glance. If I ignored the "trying too hard" wardrobe and unfortunate choice of words, he was kind of tasty. Mid-thirties or so. Shaggy mane of reddish hair, almost auburn. Pale-blue eyes set in improbably tan skin. Big, lots of muscles under those clothes.

He had three bottles of red wine, some cheese, salami, and a box of crackers cradled in strong arms and large hands. Probably just bought himself a few acres after a good film deal.

"Do I know you?" I asked.

He looked me up and down with frank appreciation, not bothering to hide his interest.

"Do you want to?" His voice hit all the right notes, sending a ripple of unwanted interest up my spine. I ignored it.

"Doubtful."

He grinned at me, looking like he was in on some secret joke that I probably wouldn't find funny. Something unsavory danced in the back of those cold blue eyes. I stared at him, head cocked slightly to one side. Sean would call it my "looking at a bug" expression.

Hunky or not, this guy set off my creep-o-meter.

"You're new here, aren't you?"

He raised an eyebrow, grin widening. "Just bought the property at the end of Harris Road. Up in the hills, all the way at the end of the line."

"I know the one," I said, I kept my voice neutral, not wanting to sound impressed. This dude had money to burn if he could afford to buy the DuShane place.

"Figured you might." His gaze burned into mine.

"Well, hopefully you'll get used to the pace out here." I smiled, channeling my best Daisy Duke imitation. "We country mice do things a mite slower than you city folks."

With that, I turned back to Marge. "Y'know I think I will take a case of the PBR, too. If they don't drink it tonight, it'll be one less trip I need to take tomorrow, right?"

I gave her a wink and sauntered back to the fridge, well aware of how tight my yoga pants were as I bent down and took my sweet time pulling out the beer. I felt the man's gaze on me the entire time. Part of me wanted to take a hot shower, scrub myself really hard… but part of me liked it.

I sauntered back up to the counter, putting the PBR next to the rest of the beer.

"Pabst Blue Ribbon? Oh, sweetheart…" The man shook his head. "Whoever you're shopping for sure as shit has no taste."

I gave him a smile with no warmth behind it. "I am but the messenger."

"Well, they need to pay the messenger a little better. Or at least teach you the difference between good beer and piss water."

Well, color me pissed-off.

"Let's take a look at your wine," I said. "Granted, the selection here isn't huge, but while Apothic is okay for the price point, it's not holy water. If you're going for more bang for your buck, the Sin Zin is much better. And if you can afford the DuShane place, your budget could go for Sterling. So how about you get off your fucking high horse, okay?"

My new neighbor grinned again. "You know where I live if you get bored with the PBR crowd."

I gave the jerk a cold stare. "Cold day in hell, thanks." I picked up the rest of the beer, turned to leave, then stopped. "And for the record, I'm drinking the Dogfish Head."

With that, I stomped outside, brushing past an obscenely expensive silver Porsche 911 Turbo parked in front of the porch.

"Asshole," I muttered.

As I loaded the beer into the back of the Xterra, the

hunky asshole exited the store and sauntered over to the Porsche. He got inside and started the car. Then he grinned at me, gave a little salute, and roared out of the parking lot and up the road.

There goes the neighborhood, I thought.

APPENDIX

Lilith Sumerian Incantation Notes—Don't try this at home!

Amelatu Abanaskuppatu Tiamatu, ati me peta babka
> Gatekeeper of the threshold of the abyss,
> open your gate for Me

Annitu, dalkhu sa ina etuti asbu
> Behold, ye demons who dwell in darkness

Bu'idu salmu la minam Kurnugi, Erset la tari, La'atzu
> Black Ghosts Without Number from the
> Netherworld, the Land of No Return, the
> Spirit World

Nisme annu nusku! Nisme annu sisitu! Elu ma semu annu kishpu!
> Hear this incantation! Hear this summons!
> Raise up and obey this spell!

Uzna sakanu. Pana sakanu. Kima parsi labiruti
>   Set the Ear. Set the Face. Treat her in
>   accordance with the ancient rites.

Lequ annu libbu!
>   Take this heart!

ACKNOWLEDGMENTS

2016—the year I wrote *The Spawn of Lilith*—was a rough one. My mom lost her fight against cancer in January and I spent the next few months in a haze. I meant to keep a list of everyone who helped me with this book, but I'm pretty sure there are gonna be some gaps here. So… to everyone who helped me get through what was arguably the worst year of my life and to those who shared their knowledge, experience, and time to help me write this book… thank you. If I forgot to mention you here, forgive me. It's not from lack of gratitude or appreciation. And I know I'll kick myself when I remember who I forgot.

First, family and friends who helped keep me sane. Be it from regular infusions of chocolate; care for our animals when we needed to travel; advice and sanity checks when I thought I was losing it; or sharing their grief to help me make sense of my own: Maureen "Dude" Anderson, Jane Thorne Gutierrez, Anne Stevenson, Aldyth & Brad Beltane, Jim Motch & Maureen Zogg, Rebecca Babcock, Owen Hodgson, Charly Kayle, James Robinson, Gail Ferris, Sue Thomas, Ocho, Jessica Bateman, "Trainer Tim", Chris Martindale, Martha Allard, Chris & Merrilyn Galante, Ben Smith, Julie Lynn, Nikki Guerlain, Lisa Lane, Aimee Hix, Jess

Lourey, Casey Fleischer, Jill Brackmann, Jennifer Paynter, and my second dad, Bill Galante.

Special thanks to my sister Lisa, who helped keep me on track when I thought I couldn't finish; to Loren Rhoads and Cynthia Badiey for life-saving writing dates; to Janna and Aimee, who sent me socks when I was sad; and to Sara Jo and Jonathan for inspiration, opportunities, and one of the best jobs ever.

Much gratitude and appreciation to Jonathan Maberry, Charlaine Harris, and Seanan McGuire. You exemplify the meaning of "paying it forward."

There's always a lot of research involved with my books and this time around was no exception. Huge thanks to stuntman Jayson Dumenigo, stuntwoman Alina Andrei, and actress/writer Amber Benson. Each of these three very busy professionals was gracious enough to spend an hour or so each answering many questions by yours truly. Also thanks to Steve Chaloner, Marcy Meyer, Elizabeth Buxton, and Joe McGuinan for research and inspiration for this and other projects.

Thanks and much affection to Dan'n'Jan'n'Kim, Scott Dawson, and Richard Moore for so many fun years training at the Academy of Theatrical Combat. Hugs to Christopher Villa who started it all with a knife fight at that Ren Faire so many years ago. So many good memories spent with the Duellists (you know who you are) and the Rapier half of *Rose & Rapier* (lookin' at you, Brian). Thank you, Jack West, for letting Brian and me join your stunt team on Ninja Nymphs in the 23rd (or 22nd? I can't remember) Century. And huge hats off to every stunt player over the years who's risked—and some lost—their lives creating some spectacular stunts.

Many thanks to Jill Marsal, who is officially my dream

agent. I wonder how I ever got by without her and am just so grateful that I don't have to anymore!

Continuing appreciation for the amazing people at Titan Books: Nick Landau and Vivian Cheung, Laura Price, Paul Gill, Gary Budden, Lydia Gittins, Katharine Carrol, Hannah Scudamore, and most importantly, Steve "DEO" Saffel, who continues to help me grow as a writer and remains a joy to work with.

Finally, much love and gratitude for my husband David, who is always willing to brainstorm on the beach and knows just what to bring me home from the library when my inspiration runs dry.

ABOUT THE AUTHOR

Dana Fredsti is an ex B-movie actress with a background in theatrical combat (a skill she utilized in *Army of Darkness* as a sword-fighting Deadite and fight captain). Through seven plus years of volunteering at EFBC/FCC, Dana's been kissed by tigers and had her thumb sucked by an ocelot with nursing issues. She's addicted to bad movies and any book or film, good or bad, which includes zombies. She's the author of the *Ashley Parker* series, touted as Buffy meets *The Walking Dead*, the zombie noir novella, *A Man's Gotta Eat What a Man's Gotta Eat,* and the cozy noir mystery *Murder for Hire: The Peruvian Pigeon*. With David Fitzgerald she is the co-author of *Time Shards*, a new trilogy of time-travel adventures, and she has stories in the *V-Wars: Shockwaves* and *Joe Ledger: Unstoppable* anthologies.

TIME SHARDS
DANA FREDSTI & DAVID FITZGERALD

IT'S CALLED "THE EVENT," AN UNIMAGINABLE CATACLYSM THAT SHATTERS 600 MILLION YEARS OF THE EARTH'S TIMELINE.

Our world is replaced by one made of scattered remnants of the past, present, and future, dropped alongside one another in a patchwork of "shards." Monsters from Jurassic prehistory, ancient armies, and high-tech robots all coexist in this deadly post-apocalyptic landscape.

A desperate group of survivors sets out to locate the source of the disaster. They include twenty-first century Californian Amber Richardson, Cam, a young Celtic warrior from Roman Britannia, Alex Brice, a policewoman from 1985, and Blake, a British soldier from World War II. With other refugees from across time, they must learn the truth behind the Event, if they are to survive.

SPLIT FEATHER
DEBORAH A. WOLF

Siggy Aleksov sees demons and talks with creatures she knows aren't really there. Taken from her family as a child, she is dogged by memories of abandonment, abuse, and mental health issues. Siggy suffers from a hot temper, cluster headaches, caffeine addiction, and terminal foul language.

She complicates her life even more when she saves the life of a talented assassin sent to kill her. Deciding to get the hell out of Dodge, Siggy travels to the Alaska bush to find out who she really is. The answer is more fantastic that she could have imagined—and she can imagine a lot.

"Fun, entertaining urban fantasy."
SFF World

For more fantastic fiction, author events, exclusive
excerpts, competitions, limited editions and more

VISIT OUR WEBSITE

titanbooks.com

LIKE US ON FACEBOOK

facebook.com/titanbooks

FOLLOW US ON TWITTER

@TitanBooks

EMAIL US

readerfeedback@titanemail.com